The Historic
Christmas Tree Ship

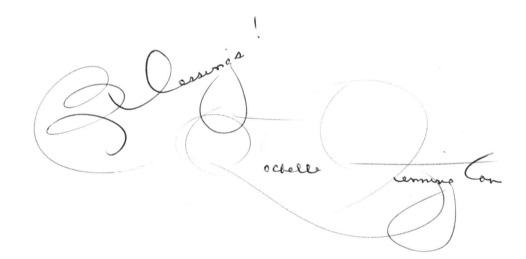

The Historic
Christmas Tree Ship

A True Story of Faith, Hope and Love

Published by Pathways Press

Rochelle Pennington

The cover art is taken from the original painting Port City of Chicago, by American Folk Artist Carol Dyer, Copyright 2004 Mystic Seaport. Mystic Seaport commissioned the painting to be a part of its American Port Cities Collection.

Mystic Seaport - The Museum of America and the Sea - is the nation's leading museum. Located along the banks of the historic Mystic River in Mystic, Connecticut, the Museum houses extensive collections representing the material culture of maritime America and offers educational programs from preschool to post-graduate. For more information, call 1-888-973-2767 or visit www.mysticseaport.org.

Manufactured in the United States of America

Published by:

Pathways Press
1-800-503-5507

ISBN: 0-9740810-1-9

Dedication

This book is dedicated to Captain and Mrs. Schuenemann's surviving family:

Grandchildren

William Edward Ehling, M.D.

Great Grandchildren

Barbara Jean Ehling

Patricia Ann Bensmiller

Lynn Ellen Bedeker

Great, Great Grandchildren

Rory Edward Bedeker

Brady Edward Bedeker

William Edward Lee Bensmiller

Jennifer Lee Ann Bensmiller

Jeffery Lloyd Lee Bensmiller

Table of Contents

Introduction

Captain Herman Schuenemann became affectionately known as "Captain Santa" for his yearly voyage from Michigan's Upper Peninsula to Chicago with a load of freshly cut Christmas trees. Families would wait anxiously at the docks for their choice of the best trees.

Captain Schuenemann's voyage of 1912 was to be his last. Fully loaded and ready to sail, the *Rouse Simmons* set out for its final destination on the southern end of Lake Michigan. Despite the crew's best efforts, the ship was unable to withstand the gales of the Great Lakes and went down off the coast of Two Rivers, Wisconsin.

Today, the Christmas Tree Ship is remembered as one of the most "storied shipwrecks" of the Great Lakes, and it has held its place in history for nearly a century already.

Through vintage photographs, newspaper clippings, and interviews with persons directly connected to the story, *The Historic Christmas Tree Ship* details the extraordinary events surrounding this loved legend.

1909 photo of Captain Herman Schuenemann (center), Mr. Colberg (right), and W. L. Vanaman (left) standing among Christmas trees.
(Courtesy of the Chicago Historical Society)

Chapter One

The Schuenemann Family

"More than a century ago, when Chicagoans brought a Christmas tree home, they knew it came from one of the many ships that sailed north to small towns in Michigan and Wisconsin to bring back trees and greens for the holiday season. Although many small merchants plied the tree trade, the Schuenemann brothers became tragically famous throughout the city."

Just the Arti-Facts – A Winter Tale
http://www.chicagons.org
(Chicago Historical Society Internet Site)
December 1998

The Schuenemann Family

At the center of the Christmas Tree Ship legend beats the heart of Captain Herman Schuenemann, the "gallant skipper" who delivered evergreens to Chicago in the late 1800's and early 1900's.

Born in 1865 to German immigrants, Herman lived in a little house beside the water. His eyes were blue, like the sea he loved, and they witnessed many hardships in those early years. Yet despite a childhood lived amid poverty and disease, the trials of his early life became the tool by which his adulthood would be shaped into one of compassion, generosity, and courage.

Perhaps it was destiny that Herman was born to a family surnamed "Schuenemann" – a German word meaning "wonderful man" – for more than a name, these words became Herman Schuenemann's legacy.

Each Christmas, Captain Schuenemann sailed from Chicago to northern Michigan where he picked up a load of freshly cut evergreens. He loved Christmas, and loved sailing his Yuletide cargo back to Chicago where the city was waiting. There, he would dock his old schooner near the Clark Street Bridge and, once anchored, crowds would come aboard to find the perfect tree for Christmas. Year after year, the people of Chicago crowded in await of the captain's arrival.

Vincent Starrett, a Chicago newspaper journalist who personally knew Captain Schuenemann in the early 1900's, reported that "the Christmas season didn't really arrive until the Christmas Tree Ship tied up at Clark Street." And according to the *Chicago Tribune* of December 22, 1974, Captain Herman and his boat became "as much a part of Chicago's Christmas as Santa Claus."

Although the Schuenemann legacy rests primarily on Captain Herman and his family, the tradition actually began with two men, not one.

Captain August Schuenemann, Herman's oldest brother, was the first Schuenemann to ship Christmas cargos, beginning in 1876. He continued the tradition until November of 1898 when his ship went down in a terrible November storm. All on board were lost. Captain August, nicknamed "Christmas Tree Schuenemann", was bringing a load of trees to Chicago when the gale hit.

It was a heartbreaking loss for Herman who stared across the waters, waiting. But the brother he loved so much was not coming home.

The Rouse Simmons *in her declining years carried what Chicagoans saw as cargoes of joy and delight - Christmas trees that became the stuff of dreams for a generation. And Captain Schuenemann loved to guide his tree-laden ship into the Chicago River and up to the Clark Street Bridge...*

Docked at Clark Street, the captain and his crew would welcome the crowds that came to pick over 300 to 400 tons of Yule trees on the decks. The sounds of joyous laughter mingled with screams of discovery as eager buyers found their "ideal" Christmas growths. The clip-clop of horse hooves echoed under the bridge as wagon wheels thundered accompaniment...

With decks covered with Christmas trees, she filled her hold with boughs that could be used for wreaths and nativity scenes.

Great Lakes Boating
December 1990
Bill Keefe

"Neither white-haired, rotund, nor bearded, but reputedly a jovial man, Herman Schuenemann was the closest thing to Santa Claus that Chicago's children could ever hope to meet."

Chicago History
"The Magazine of the Chicago Historical Society"
December 1992, Volume XXI, Number 3
Frederick Neuschel

TRADITION TURNS TO GRIEF
Chicago Tribune
Chicago, IL
December 22, 1974

With the massive influx of Germans during the latter half of the 19th century, the demand for Christmas trees boomed. Land transportation from the north was poor and the Schuenemanns' venture was an immediate success. Not only could customers get trees, they could have the fun of selecting them on shipboard.

The ship's arrival became an annual social event. Whole families came to meet it. Those whose tree-shopping time coincided with the crew's dinner hour were customarily invited to dine on board as well...

A family could take home a six or seven foot tree for 75 cents or so. Some trees, 20 feet and higher, were never sold; they were given away – to Chicago churches and orphanages.

Business was brisk and in a few years other lake captains were also into the Christmas tree business at cities and towns along the lakeshore...

Capt. Herman and his boat became as much a part of Chicago's Christmas as Santa Claus.

"Many families made a trip by sleigh to the harbor to select a tree which they would later trim with candles and strings of cranberries and popcorn."

The Ship's Log
Vol. 4, #3 and #4
Dec. 1980/Jan. 1981

As fate would have it, Herman was not on board his brother's ship when it sunk because he was home caring for his wife and newly born twin daughters. The joyous news of birth was accompanied by the tragic news of death in 1898.

Herman now needed to make a decision whether to continue the Schuenemann tradition, or to call it quits.

Remarkably, despite his brother's death, and despite the ever present danger of sailing November's storm-tossed waters, Captain Herman summoned the courage to load another cargo of evergreens that very same year and sail it to Chicago so the city would have their trees by Christmas. Although his partnership with August had been severed by the fury of Lake Michigan, the Lake could not destroy the determination of this family to carry on despite its punishing blows.

In December of 1898, the year of Captain August's tragedy, a church newsletter in Chicago announced Captain Herman's arrival: "We want to draw our readers' attention to the largest and best store of Christmas trees, garlands, wreaths, and similar items that is to be found in Chicago. It is at the southwest corner of the Clark Street Bridge where Captain Herman Schuenmann has docked two big ships which together contain more than 11,000 trees… You should visit Captain Schuenemann and give him kind regards from St. Pauls."

St. Pauls United Church of Christ, one of the oldest churches in Chicago, was founded in 1843 by German immigrants. (The church's original name was the German Evangelical Lutheran St. Pauls Congregation.) Three generations of Schuenemann family members worshipped there. They felt a sense of belonging among others who shared both their heritage and beliefs. St. Pauls is still a thriving congregation today, and it houses an absolute treasure trove of information surrounding the history of the Schuenemann family. Old newsletters in the church's historical archives contain many personal stories about the family, making it quite clear that the people of this congregation loved the Schuenemanns, and the Schuenemanns loved them back.

Reverend Rudolph A. John, pastor of St. Pauls in the late 1800's and early 1900's, recorded an entry in 1897 that reads: "Our old sea dog, Captain Schuenemann, is back again safe and sound from his long voyage to the northern woods of Michigan. This summer he bought one of the most beautiful and best ships, a vessel he is properly very proud of. After a long trip he is back in the local harbor with a cargo load of the most beautiful

Christmas trees. The *Mary Collins* is docked at the southwest corner of the Clark Street Bridge and is visited by thousands every day, who buy their trees and garlands from the always friendly captain. The giant Christmas tree, which shone during the bazaar in the [church] gymnasium, was brought to Chicago by Captain Schuenemann especially for the ladies, and is undoubtedly the largest and most beautiful tree which has ever been brought to Chicago for Christmas."

The language chosen to announce Captain Herman's arrival in 1897 was "safe and sound." The risk the Schuenemann Brothers faced was well understood. Captain August's ship, the *S. Thal,* would succumb to the waves only one short year after this article was written, and then two years later, Captain Herman's vessel, the *Mary Collins,* would also be lost when it crashed into a shoreline in Upper Michigan. (Since the vessel sunk in shallower waters, all on board were rescued.)

According to testimony given by Ernest Williams, as published in the *Manistique Pioneer Tribune,* Manistique, MI, on October 12, 1978, the

IN THE TREE BUSINESS FOR YEARS
Chicago American
Chicago, IL
December 5, 1912

For more than twenty-five years Capt. Schuenemann had operated boats in the tree trade on the lake…

The average load for the schooner was between three hundred and four hundred tons of trees. The big trees were loaded on deck while the wreath material and small trees were put into the hold.

Schuenemann lost the schooner, *Mary Collins,* in a lake storm some years ago. The crew was rescued.

The Schuenemanns have sailed Christmas voyages in the *Maggie Dall,* the *Ida,* the *Jessie Phillips,* the *Truman Moss,* the *George L. Wrenn,* the *Rouse Simmons,* and the *Thal.*

wrecking of the *Mary Collins* happened as follows: "The first I ever knew of Captain Herman Schuenemann was when he sailed the *Mary Collins* high and dry on the limestone shore, one-half mile east of Little Harbor, Michigan. How this all came about was like this: At Thompson, Michigan, they always had a light on the South Dock to guide navigation. The pilot on the *Mary Collins* said, 'There's Thompson,' and steered directly for it. But this light happened to be a kerosene lamp lit in an upstairs window in a log cabin one-half mile east of Little Harbor."

Always, sailors were leery of the "angry storms" and "screaming blizzards" November unleashed in a moment. Very few ships sailed in vicious November for this reason. Grave danger was ever present for the Schuenemann family, but the brothers kept their fears at bay. Some wondered how they could keep delivering their cargos up against such a challenge, but the Schuenemanns only questioned: How could they not? They were the Christmas tree people. It was as simple as that. They believed in what they were doing, and they believed what they did mattered.

Fourteen years after Captain August perished, the Schuenemann family faced yet another tragedy when Captain Herman's ship, the *Rouse Simmons,* went down on November 23, 1912. Everyone on board drowned.

The Sheboygan Press of Sheboygan, WI, reported the tremendous loss on December 6, 1912, acknowledging the danger that had always played a part in the Schuenemanns' lives: "Captain Schuenemann sailed the waters of Lake Michigan since a boy and had carried many a boat to safety through the heavy gales." But the stormy lake had, once more, caught up to the Schuenemann family. The survivors needed to decide, again, if the tradition would die also.

> *"It is indeed a hard and heartbreaking task to write of Captain Schuenemann, our good faithful brother, who for so many years has been with us in our work and faith. For almost thirty years this good man, sturdy, honest, faithful, has sailed the waters of the Great Lakes, in summertime in the lumber trade, and in November, braving many an angry storm and rough sea to bring great cargoes of trees and branches and red berries to make the children's holidays brighter and happier. And this time he has not returned."*
>
> Pastor Rudolph A. John
> December 1912

Personal Remembrances of Captain Schuenemann

Every time I cross the bridge over the Chicago River at Clark Street I think of the Christmas Tree Ship I used to visit as a young reporter, more than fifty years ago. It had been coming to Chicago since 1887, deep-laden with a fragrant cargo of green, snow-powdered evergreens from northern Michigan for the holiday trade. It used to dock behind the old redbrick commission houses near the bridge, where hordes of citizens and their families visited it a week or two before Christmas. They were captivated by the idea of picking out a personal tree from the heaps aboard the schooner... When snow fell on Chicago's streets in December, we may imagine, fathers used to say, "Guess I'll have to go down to the Clark Street Bridge to see if the Captain is in, and get us a tree." The Christmas season didn't really arrive until the Christmas Tree Ship tied up at Clark Street...

It is here, with the loss of Captain Herman, that the story takes a curious turn. With both brothers now gone, only women remained.

Captain August's wife, Rose, was yet living, as was Captain Herman's wife, Barbara. Rose Schuenemann stood steadfastly beside her sister-in-law in the dark hours of 1912 (along with another sister-in-law, Bertha), caring for her in her grief, waiting with her during the painful hours when details of the tragedy drifted in slowly. If there was anyone who understood the ache in Barbara's heart, it was Rose. She assisted Barbara in many ways, including writing letters, seeking any information on the ship's demise that could be learned.

One of the letters written by Mrs. Rose Schuenemann was addressed to Captain A. E. Dow, master of the schooner *Augustus* of Manitowoc, Wisconsin. His response to Rose, dated December 15, 1912, is on file at the Wisconsin Maritime Museum in Manitowoc, Wisconsin. It reads, in part: "I think that the *Simmons* went down somewhere north of here. If you see Herman's wife, tell her that if I can do anything to help her that I am anxious to do so. I am awful sorry for her."

These were difficult days for Captain Herman's wife, Barbara, and their three daughters, Elsie, Pearl, and Hazel, the apples of Captain Herman's eye.

That was the ship I came to know. Covering its arrival was my favorite Christmas assignment; probably I started to report the event as early as 1908. Usually I began my visit with a glass of Christmas cheer with Captain Herman in his cabin, and we discussed the perils of the deep as if Lake Michigan were the Atlantic Ocean.

The scene on deck was picturesque and is still memorable. A brisk trade in evergreens went forward all day and sometimes at night, as householders and dealers came and went; and prices were not excessive. For seventy-five cents one could buy a full-sized tree, and for a dollar have his choice of the best. They all went quickly for the Christmas Tree Ship was a Chicago institution.

Gourmet
December 1966
Vincent Starrett

Yet Barbara Schuenemann was determined to see her husband's purpose through to the end – not only his end, but hers. Nothing would block her path from making sure everything her husband believed in would yet live – not fear, and not despair. In her hands Captain Herman's memory was in safe keeping.

The *Chicago Daily News* of November 28, 1913, interviewed Barbara Schuenemann just prior to her schooner being loaded with Christmas trees one year after her husband's death. She had this to say: "We'll load the trees on it and tie up at the old dock, and our customers will come to us as they have in former years. They know where to find us. The *Rouse* is gone, and her captain is gone, and the crew is gone – but Christmas will find the survivors still on deck, and Chicago will have her Christmas trees as long as the Schuenemanns last."

True to her word, the captain's bride continued in her loving task until she breathed her last. Prior to her passing, Pastor Jacob Pister wrote the following acknowledgment of Barbara Schuenemann's very last Christmas in 1932, her final goodbye to Chicago: "She is here to help bring joy this year like never before. She dispenses Christmas trees. You all know her. It is good Mother Schuenemann, the widow of ill-fated Captain Schuenemann, the Christmas ship man, who never returned to the shores, but with his great cargo of Christmas trees went down into the deep in that terrible night of storm. And since then Mother Schunemann has felt the urge to carry on. The *Chicago Tribune* never fails to pay her a tribute of respect and honor."

Mother Schuenemann was a hearty soul who not only stayed the course in carrying on her husband's Christmas tree business, but who stayed the course in continuing on in her husband's commitment to the poor. Although Captain Schuenemann was a Christmas tree merchant who sold thousands of trees to Chicago families each year, he also gave generously from his heart to churches, orphanages, and poor families, as did his wife and daughters after he was gone.

Barbara Schuenemann's death notice, published in June of 1933, memorialized her by saying she was a "remarkable woman whom the people of Chicago loved because of her devotion to the children at Christmastime." And her obituary read, in part: "Mother Schuenemann was known and loved by thousands, and hundred of thousands, throughout our great metropolis."

The Schuenemann family had served the citizens of Chicago well, from the least to the greatest, during approximately fifty dedicated years, and the friendships forged lasted generations. Chicago's Mayor Harrison was a regular patron of the Schuenemanns, as were many persons of poverty, known to few.

Harry Hansen, a reporter for the *Chicago Daily News* in the early 1900's, wrote that Captain Herman Schuenemann was "a jovial man, with a very ruddy complexion and laughing wrinkles around his blue eyes, and everybody liked him." "Everyone" included the rich, the poor, the young, the old.

From one end of Lake Michigan to the other, Captain Schuenemann was surrounded by life's greatest asset: friends. The *Manistique Pioneer-Tribune,* published in the Upper Peninsula of Michigan (near where Captain Schuenemann loaded his Christmas trees), reported on December 6, 1912:

> *"The records of the Schuenemann family show both the lights and the shadows of human life. Joy and sorrow have come into the houses, and tears of happiness and pain have dimmed the eyes of men and women."*
>
> St. Pauls Church Newsletter, 1913

Photo of Mrs. Barbara Schuenemann giving a free tree away to two small boys.
The caption read: "Widow Gives Away 1,200 Christmas Trees."
(Courtesy of the *Chicago Tribune*)

SCHOONER LOST
The *Rouse Simmons*
With Entire Crew,
Including
Captain Schuenemann,
Believed to be Lost
Manistique
Pioneer-Tribune
Manistique, MI
December 6, 1912

The boat in question left this port on November 22 with a cargo of Christmas trees for the Chicago market...

Shortly after leaving port severe gales swept over the lakes...

Captain Schuenemann has been making annual trips to this port for many years in quest of Christmas trees and ground pine for the Chicago market. The Captain had many friends here who regret the disaster that has befallen him.

"The Captain had many friends here who regret the disaster that has befallen him." If there is one word that reveals itself more than any other in the Schuenemann story, it is the word "friend".

In 1912, the year Captain Herman's ship went missing, the *Chicago Inter Ocean* newspaper interviewed the captain's oldest daughter, Elsie, on December 11, 1912. She was on board the schooner, *Oneida,* where she was selling Christmas trees while news of her papa's disappearance was still coming in. Elsie was quoted as saying, "Our friends have been very, very kind to us. It is not exaggerating to say that 500 persons have called here and at our home to offer aid."

W. C. Holmes, of the W. C. Holmes Shipping Company in Chicago, was a friend of the Schuenemann family and donated the schooner, *Oneida,* for Barbara and her daughters to sell their trees from in 1912 when the *Simmons* went missing. Captain Herman had "commanded a ship for years" for Mr. Holmes. The *Chicago Inter Ocean* also reported that "scores of seamen, friends of Captain Schuenemann, offered their services on the craft." Sailors

> *"Chicagoans had come to regard the ship's appearance on their waterfront as a sure harbinger of good cheer, and the captain always had a kind word or friendly wave to spare."*
>
> *Upper Peninsula Sunday Times*
> Escanaba, MI
> December 24, 1978
> Roger LeLievre

sent their wives and daughters to aid the Schuenemann survivors as needed, giving "any aid they could to relieve the stricken family."

A relief fund was also established to benefit the families of the lost crew "in response to an appeal from sailors, shippers, and merchants for whom Captain Schunemann worked, and friends," according to the *Chicago Inter Ocean* of December 10, 1912.

The Schuenemann legacy lived on for many reasons, not the least of which is that the story exemplifies the best of humanity: faith, hope, love, devotion, courage. The Schuenemann lives were those of giving – and living – the message of "Goodwill Toward Men" - despite emotional and financial difficulties.

Although the Schuenemanns experienced the financial ebbs and flows of life as all families do, they were basically people of modest means. Yet despite their comfort level - some years meager and other years more - their generosity towards those in need never wavered. They understood poverty, and they understood the pain that came with it.

In 1912, the year of Captain Herman's demise, the Schuenemann family suffered a particularly difficult year financially. (Many lean years followed the more prosperous years the family experienced in the late 1800's.)

Every penny the family owned in 1912 was invested in the cargo of evergreens Captain Herman had harvested that season, and, thus, every penny went to the bottom of Lake Michigan with the captain's ship. It was an unspeakable loss.

Despite this, Barbara Schuenemann, faced with certain financial ruin, made a point to deliver a Christmas tree to St. Pauls in 1912 during the peak of her grief. Recorded in the church records is written: "We must not send out this review of our great Sunday School work without adding a word about

> "*Herman Schuenemann was an experienced sailor and was respected as a veteran captain, an honest trader, and a good family man.*"
>
> A Most Superior Land
> Volume IV of the *Michigan Heritage Series*
> Dated 1983
> Published by Two Peninsula Press
> Michigan Natural Resources Magazine

our Christmas celebrations. They were occasions so successful and so rich in blessings that we shall long remember them with a glow of satisfaction and gratitude. The big tree for the church was kindly donated by Mrs. Herman Schuenemann, who in the kindness of her heart positively refused pay for it."

Captain Schuenemann, every Christmas, gifted evergreens to churches, including St. Pauls. In 1906, six short years before the captain's death, St. Pauls recorded the following entry: "Captain Schuenemann, the old mariner, who gets within an ace of being shipwrecked every year when he sails away to Santa Claus' Land to get a big ship full of Christmas trees, what did he do? Well, he sent a wagon load of trees, and wreaths, and festoons to the church, the parsonage, and the Orphan Asylum. And when a meek little man went down and asked for the bill, Captain Schuenemann roared down Clark Street like a foghorn: 'Blow the bill!' So that's what became of that bill. It's blowed!"

If the captain had been alive in 1912 he would have made sure a tree stood tall and proud in the cathedral of St. Pauls, and his wife knew this. So, she did as he would have. The captain may have gone down with his ship, but everything he believed in was yet alive on the shores. Other hands became his hands, and they carried his memory forward.

Christmas came again to Chicago in 1913 and the city found the Schuenemanns as they had in Christmases past - on the docks - greeting their customers, selling their trees, weaving their wreaths, united in purpose, working shoulder-to-shoulder, together. Barbara had chopped trees alongside her husband, and now she would chop trees alongside her daughters.

The Schuenemann legacy is one of courage coupled with faith, a story of commitment to those we love, as well as to others. The very idea of the Christmas message and the Christmas tree being at its center – the symbol of everlasting life and everlasting hope – encompasses who the Schuenemanns were, and what they believed. This is their legacy, and it has lived on from one generation to the next, kept alive by poets and painters, by songwriters and by storytellers. They are the Guardians who continue to breathe life into these lives long gone.

Also keeping the memory green are the many persons entrusted with the care of files located in museums and other historical organizations. Colleen Henry, church historian of St. Pauls, is one such person. She oversees the Schuenemann family records at her church with love enough to lead you

CHRISTMAS TREES FOR KIDDIES.

By a staff photographer of The Daily News.]
CAPT. ELSIE SCHUENEMANN AND HER SISTER ON BOARD THEIR SANTA CLAUS SHIP IN THE CHICAGO RIVER.

Captain Schuenemann's daughters carry on the family tradition with their "Santa Claus Ship".
(Newspaper clipping dated December 7, 1917, *Chicago Daily News*)

to believe this family is her own. Her kindly assistance throughout the research process of this book was a blessing without measure.

Mrs. Henry contacted me out of the blue when she learned I was working on a documentary concerning the family. Her first letter read, in part: "The Schuenemanns were obviously highly thought of in the St. Pauls congregation. If we can be a small part of perpetuating his (and his family's) memory, then we would be very pleased to do so."

More correspondence followed. "Get a cup of tea and check out the latest installment of the Schuenemann saga!" wrote Mrs. Henry in one letter.

Soon others from St. Pauls joined in. A retired church secretary, Ruth Klinke Baur, age 95, and life-long member, was instrumental in connecting me with descendants. William Rossberger, age 73, another life-long member, took time to share lovely memories with me. He graduated from the same high school as one of the Schuenemann grandchildren, and was also confirmed in the same class. He was a paperboy in the late 1930's and delivered newspapers to "the sisters" on his route (Captain and Mrs. Barbara Schuenemann's three daughters).

Mr. Rossberger's grandparents purchased Christmas trees from Captain Schuenemann, and he remembered his grandmother saying that it "just wasn't Christmas" the year Captain Herman's ship went down.

Christmas pageants from Mr. Rossberger's childhood were themed after the Christmas Tree Ship, and he still carries vivid memories of being costumed one year as a tree, and another year as a candle. "I am a candle shining bright," laughed Mr. Rossberger, remembering his rehearsed lines from a lifetime ago.

He told me how Elsie Schuenemann, the oldest of the Schuenemann daughters, taught his Sunday School class. (According to Mrs. Henry, the

> *"Herman Schuenemann was a local celebrity in the early 1900's. He wasn't a rich man, just a working family man. The schooner owners weren't wealthy."*
>
> Barton Updike, Director
> Chicago Maritime Museum
> As quoted in the *Chicago Tribune*
> December 21, 1990

GIRL CAPTAIN TO BRAVE LAKE THAT KILLED FATHER

Sea-reared Elsie Schuenemann will command another Christmas tree craft in place of vessel lost in recent storm causing havoc on Lake Michigan. Young woman who as a child played with boats, not dolls, feels no fear of tempestuous waters in which her parent lost his life in voyage bringing a cargo of holiday greens to the citizens of Chicago.

Miss Elsie Schuenemann sailed vessels with her mother after Captain Schuenemann's tragedy.
(Newspaper clipping dated December 9, 1912, *Chicago Daily Journal*)

daughters were as active in the church as their parents were.)

Elsie Schuenemann was still teaching Sunday School in the 1930's when Mr. Rossberger was one of her pupils. She was also a teacher in 1912, at age 20, the year her father's ship went missing.

The *Chicago Record-Herald* interviewed Barbara and her three daughters in 1912 on Christmas Day after they closed down the ship they had sold their trees from. It was reported: "Mrs. Schuenemann's daughters, of whom there are three, came to the boat late in the evening, and the sad mother closed up shop to go home with her children for a cheerless Christmas night. The oldest of the girls, Elsie, was then carrying in her arms a bundle of Christmas tokens which represented the nearest the family came to holiday festivities. She had not forgotten a little group of children, who looked to her expectantly. The inexpensive presents were for members of her Sunday School class. 'They are the only presents I bought,' said the fair-haired miss. 'They are just remembrances for the little boys and girls in the Sunday School class I have taught.'"

Miss Elsie Schuenemann continued to support her mother in the family business until the mid-1930's. She became the backbone of the operation and would, too, acquire a nickname Chicago would come to know her by. (Mrs. Barbara Schuenemann had been lovingly referred to as "Mother Schuenemann" and her husband as "Captain Santa" because of his generosity in giving free Christmas trees away to any family who otherwise wouldn't have been able to afford one.) Miss Elsie was known as "The Queen of Christmas Trees" according the following article acknowledging her 1917 wedding: "This is not the end of the 'Tale of Christmas Trees' – no. There's another chapter and it has to do with The Queen of Christmas Trees herself, the daughter of the doughty captain who went down in the awful storm with the ship, laden to the guards with trees for Chicago's children. Yes – you've guessed it – I knew you would, because you've read in the papers of the girl who brings a ship down from the wilds of Northern Michigan laden to the last inch of space with trees for the children's Christmas. And, you will agree, that when Captain Elsie Schuenemann was married, it could only be near a big Christmas tree. Well, so it was. She came to church in the early dusk of the evening to the giant tree which she had brought out of the Northern woods. You saw it, did you? Top reached away up to the organ loft. It was not quite dark in the great, still church, but we turned the lights on so that the tree would shine and glitter and glow in all its beauty for the girl who had brought it. The man who came with her was Arthur E. Roberts… There came a few others with them – the nearest and dearest on earth to them – and there in the glory of the Christmas tree they were married. And their new ship sailed out upon the wide sea, laden as heavily with hopes and plans and prayers as the other one was with trees."

The Schuenemanns. Theirs was a story of tragedy and triumph, of helplessness and of hope.

In Two Rivers, Wisconsin, at the Rogers Street Fishing Village Museum, a display sign commemorating the Schuenemann Brothers reads: "Born in Ahnapee, Wisconsin (present day Algoma) to parents who immigrated from Mecklenburg, Germany, August and his younger brother Herman grew up along the shores of Lake Michigan. It was on the lake that the brothers were to make their living, and it was on the lake where each would meet their death as a master of a Christmas tree ship."

The Schuenemann boys were born into this world beside the waters, and they left it within. Each had perished, it is true. Yet it is Life, not Death, that has the final word on this family. Every time their memory is recalled, the Captains live on in the breaths that speak their name. Their ships may lie at the bottom of The Lake, but the essence of who they were is alive, alive, alive yet on shore.

"Few people had ever given so much joy to so many others simply by doing their jobs as did the Christmas tree captains of Lake Michigan."

Chicago History
"The Magazine of the Chicago Historical Society"
December 1992, Volume XXI, Number 3
Frederick Neuschel

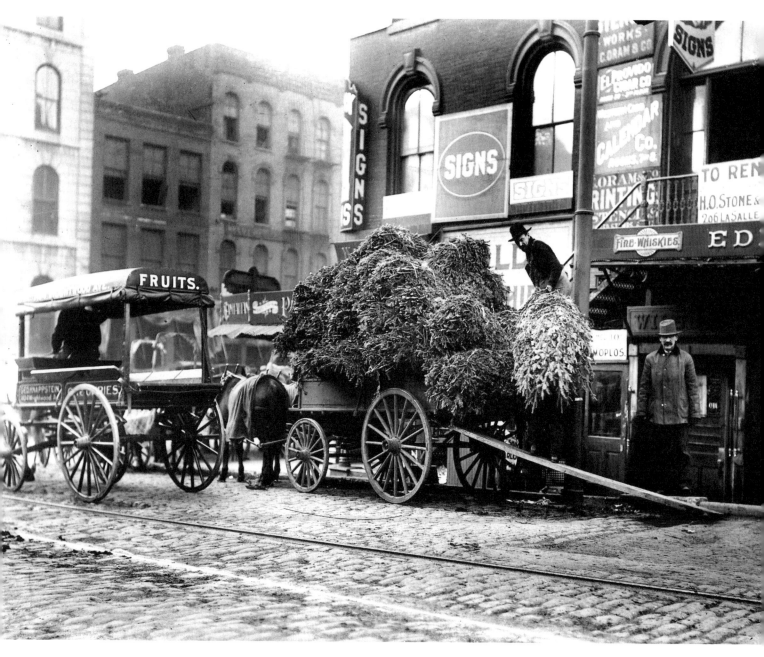

Wagonload of Christmas trees being hauled downtown Chicago in 1904.
(Courtesy of the Chicago Historical Society)

Chapter Two

Christmastime in Chicago

"When the first snowflakes of December fall and shoreline residents scrape the frost from their windows to catch a glimpse of the whitecapped Lake, memories still surface of the Christmas Tree Ship *and the tradition she represented to the people of the Windy City. Her story is as much a part of the holiday tradition as is holly and tinsel."*

The Porthole
December 24, 1981
Roger LeLievre

Christmastime in Chicago

Chicago's first municipal Christmas tree was erected in December of 1913. A tree dealer gifted the evergreen to the city as a memorial to commemorate two men who had been an integral part of Chicago's Christmas celebrations for a quarter of a century prior: Captain Herman and Captain August Schuenemann.

According to the book *Chicago Christmas: One Hundred Years of Christmas Memories*, written by Jim Benes: "The huge tree was a gift to the city from Milwaukee Avenue tree dealer F. J. Jordan. He was a former partner of schooner captain Herman Schuenemann, who, with his brother August, in 1887 began making yearly voyages from Manistique, Michigan, bringing a shipload of Christmas trees to Chicago. When their ship arrived, Chicagoans knew that the Christmas season had really begun. It became a tradition for countless families to purchase their trees from the Schuenemanns, taking the evergreen right off the ship docked near a bridge at Clark Street. August Schuenemann and his ship, the *S. Thal*, were lost in a Lake Michigan storm while bringing trees to town in 1898. Brother Herman met a similar fate with his schooner, the *Rouse Simmons*, in 1912, one year before Jordan decided to commemorate the brothers with his gift."

Author Jim Benes included the following summary of the spectacular event in his book:

Imagine this: a cold, foggy, and rainy Christmas Eve afternoon, and Michigan Avenue, between Monroe and Washington, is a sea of humanity. The crowd spills out into Grant Park. The mood is festive and expectant.

It happened in 1913, when Chicago erected its first municipal Christmas tree. It stood thirty-five feet high and was festooned in a myriad of electric lights that according to the Chicago Tribune, *"the newsboy, the bootblack, the poor of the city can gaze upon and claim it as their own."*

The program started with the Chicago Band performing for more than an hour and a half. The music began with "Onward, Christian Soldiers" and included selections from Rossini's "Stabat Mater" and the "Hallelujah Chorus" from Handel's Messiah.

Near the Art Institute a huge screen had been erected, and at five o'clock a series

---

> ### "Captain Schuenemann supplied an average of one tree for every fifty of the city's population."
>
> *Chicago Inter Ocean*
> Chicago, IL
> December 5, 1912

The Christmas Ship

It was the Christmas Ship
    that brought joy to us here,
Those trees were grown up in Manistique
    and brought on down each year.
The *Simmons* was her name
    three-masted schooner was her frame,
And the winter-wild waters of the lake
    she always overcame.
The set of her captain's face
    and the smile within his eye
Electrified that Chicago dock
    and all its passers by.
But especially us kids
    with excitement that was there,
We'd bring home a tree from the Christmas Ship
    with holiday in the air.

Excerpted from the song "*The Christmas Ship*"
Lee Murdock, Singer/Songwriter

"It was a happy day in the city when the Christmas Tree Ship was sighted. People, laughing and joking, scrambled aboard as soon as the ship docked. Selecting a tree from the deck was as popular as cutting your own tree is now."

December 20, 1975
Source of Article Unknown
On file at:
Great Lakes Historical Society

of safety-first films were shown. At just before six o'clock, Mayor Carter Harrison II mounted the platform that stood before the great tree. He was accompanied by trumpeters from the First Illinois Calvary and by mounted police.

The mayor gave a short address and concluded by saying, "Let us hope the lights on this tree will so shine out as to be an inspiration to Christian charity and to inject new courage and new hope into the hearts of those not so fortunate as we are." Then he pushed a button.

Hundreds of multicolored lights went on. So did a Star of Bethlehem at the top of the tree. The lights reflected and played off clouds of steam from half a dozen idling Illinois Central locomotives specially stationed behind the tree, creating a kaleidoscopic effect.

The crowd cheered. The band struck up a "Salute to the Nations" and a medley of national anthems that concluded with "America." Then, from the third-story balcony of the Chicago Athletic Association, came a fanfare of trumpets from members of the Chicago Grand Opera Company, who were dressed in costumes from the period when Christ was born.

The chorus of the Grand Opera Company from their perch on the north portico of the Art Institute followed with another song. Then there was more fanfare of trumpets, more solo performances, and it all wrapped up around seven o'clock when the crowd joined the band and the ensemble in singing "The Star Spangled Banner."

One official noted the huge size of the dissipating crowd and remarked, "There must have been over 100,000. This leads us to believe that we ought to continue the affair."

The towering evergreen at the center of the festivities on Christmas Eve afternoon 1913, was a fitting memorial to the Schuenemann brothers who had supplied many families in the city, gathered in crowd that day, with Christmas trees year after year, and decade after decade. Even Mayor Harrison had been a regular patron of the Schuenemanns who came to recognize the familiar faces of two, and even three, generations of the same

In an article titled "A Look at Chicago in Christmases Past," the *Chicago Tribune* published the following on December 23, 1979: *"According to research material in the Chicago Public Library's archives, families loved the idea of boarding the ship for this important purchase of the season. The captain, Herman Schuenemann, and his brother, August, made many friends."*

Photo of Captain Schuenemann's daughters selling trees, wreaths and garlands in 1917, as published by the *Chicago Daily News*. Captain Schuenemann perished in 1912, but his family carried on in the Christmas tree business until the 1930's. *(Courtesy of the Chicago Historical Society)*

> *"The Schuenemann family's activity was more than a business. It was a seasonal tradition that deserved remembrance."*
>
> *Milwaukee Sentinel*
> Milwaukee, WI
> November 21, 1987
> Jay Joslyn

Personal Memories of the Christmas Tree Ship

Chicago's Yuletide season began when the Christmas Tree Ship arrived with evergreens lashed to her masts and rigging. Her hold held thousands of young pines and balsams from northern Michigan. Residents would travel out of their way to see the ship in the Chicago River. Children, especially, were anxious to see the ship that brought Christmas trees from the far north.

Her skipper would welcome throngs of Chicagoans aboard almost as soon as the ship's moorings were secure. The choicest trees were the first to be sold. Whole families would hurry to the dock to get the pick of the crop. Many wandered on deck to watch the Captain's daughter, Elsie, weave pine branches into wreaths, which were also for sale.

My personal memories of the Christmas Tree Ship go back to December 1911 when my father operated a small grocery store in Chicago. Just before the Christmas season, he took me to the Clark Street Bridge to see the schooner and to order trees to sell during the holidays.

I still recall the old three-master with its rigging and trees lashed to the masts, and the wintry smell of pine from the Michigan woods. My father greeted the Captain in German and we were given a tour of the upper deck and living quarters. Some 50,000 trees were stacked on the ship and dock. It was a novelty for eager customers to buy trees directly from the ship's berth.

After my father placed his order for trees, the Captain invited our family and another German family, by the name of Luehrs, for a Christmas dinner. As I remember there was lots of conversation in German and stories by the Captain relating to his sailing experiences. The main dinner course was venison and a bear roast. My sister, Ella, who was then one year old, attracted the attention of Elsie [Captain Schuenemann's eldest daughter], who wanted to be the babysitter. The gathering at Yuletide was a joyful, old-fashioned family get-together and a Christmas I will always remember.

Phil Sander
Kenosha Ramblings
Copyright 1991

family.

Chicago's population in the late 1800's (when the Schuenemann brothers started selling their evergreens) included many German families who brought their beloved custom of decorating the "tannenbaum" with them. Christmas trees were a remembrance to them of the Old Country and a tradition held dear.

Captain Herman Schuenemann and his family lived in the heart of Chicago's German community at 1638 N. Clark Street. The Germania Club of Chicago still stands today in the same location on Germania Place - only blocks from the Schuenemann's home address in 1912. (Captain Schuenemann supplied Christmas trees to the Germania Club every holiday.)

According to Don Hermanson, a life-long resident of Chicago and a scholar of the city's history, meeting halls were important to the Germans because the language barrier was very strong between the different ethnic groups. Pubs, clubs and social places were an important piece of everyday life during this period of time. (The larger German gathering places were also used for dances.)

Although Captain Schuenemann's home was torn down and is now a parking lot for the Moody Bible Institute church on Clark Street, visitors to the former address are still able to get a feel for the surroundings as they may have been in 1912. The Schuenemann home was in view of Lake Michigan, and it faced the water. Also, the home was only a short walk to the Clark Street Bridge where Captain Schuenemann docked his schooner just off of Michigan Avenue. If you were to walk from the Schuenemann's Clark Street address to the bridge today, you would pass many of the same buildings Captain Schuenemann walked past time-and-time again on cobblestone streets and red, paved-brick walkways during his lifetime that are still standing.

It was a privilege for me to join Don Hermanson for a private tour of "Schuenemann's Chicago" and listen to the wealth of knowledge he shared in regards to the city as Captain Herman Schuenemann would have experienced

> *"The city of Chicago was full of Germans, and without doubt many of them clung to the old and cherished customs of their fatherland. Surely they would be happy to buy Christmas trees, and the Schuenemanns would be happy to supply them."*
>
> The Christmas Tree Ship
> Elisabeth P. Myers
> Date Unknown
> On file at: Door County Maritime Museum

it in the late 1800's and early 1900's. According to Mr. Hermanson, horse-drawn streetcars were used during the earlier years until electric streetcars later replaced the "horse cars." The "row houses" between Clark Street and Michigan Avenue were "typical of the architecture" used a century ago. Although many original buildings yet stand, maintaining some of the flavor of Chicago at the turn of the 19th century, many have been torn down, a point to which Mr. Hermanson adds: "More than the buildings were torn down; memories went with them."

Not only was the Schuenemann home located in the heart of the German community (an area where the German work ethic was very obvious with its immaculate and spotless streets), it was also located in an area that housed the heart of the marine community. Hiring halls were located here, near the water, where captains could employ sailors looking for work. Many shipping outfitters were here as well, supplying every need for the repair and upkeep of vessels. It was a "perfect" area for a captain to take residence.

"The Germans and the Scandinavians were the primary mariners," said Mr. Hermanson. "These men were 3rd and even 4th generation marine men."

During Captain Schuenemann's days, many of the old, wooden bridges were "swing bridges" – bridges that pivoted open so ships could pass through, according to Mr. Hermanson. However, these bridges were later replaced by metal bridges.

Chicago saw many changes during the nearly fifty years the Schuenemanns supplied Christmas trees to the city. The Christmas tree business also evolved through the years. During Captain Herman's lifetime, the trees were sold directly from a schooner, but the family's evergreen trade ended with the Schuenemann daughters selling trees in the 1930's from a little store on LaSalle Street. Also, the trees sold in later years were transported by railway instead of being shipped by boat as they had been

> *"I guess the kids are gladdest of anybody to see us come pulling into the river every December,"* said Captain Schuenemann. *"There's generally a little crowd of them on the rail of the bridge when it swings open for us, and they wave their hands and cheer, and we cheer back. Some of them think we are actually coming from the North Pole."*
>
> Chicago Inter-Ocean
> December 7, 1909

during Captain Herman's life.

After Captain Herman died in 1912, his wife, Barbara, and their daughters continued on in the business until Barbara's death in 1933. Then, following Barbara Schuenemann's death in the summer of 1933, her daughters continued on for a few more years. The *Chicago Tribune* reported the following on December 13, 1934, under the headline "Daughters Carry on for Schuenemann": "Old timers of the near north side who noted a sign '*Captain and Mrs. H. Schuenemann's Daughters* above a tiny store almost obscured by Christmas trees at 1641 North LaSalle Street yesterday, recalled the tragedy of 22 years ago when Captain Schuenemann, a pioneer in Chicago's Christmas trees business, and his crew of 17 men went down in Lake Michigan while bringing home a cargo of trees on the captain's boat, the *Rouse Simmons.* They were reminded, too, of the heroic effort of Mother Schuenemann in carrying on her husband's business. But Mother Schuenemann died two years ago, and now their three daughters, Mrs. Elsie Roberts, Mrs. Pearl Ehling, and Mrs. Hazel Gronemann, all of 158 Eugenie Street, carry on in the Christmas tree business. They find, as did Mother Schuenemann, plenty of trees left over for the destitute homes west of Clark Street. Yesterday Mrs. Ehling, bundled in heavy clothing, sat in the office of the Christmas tree shop making wreaths of balsam with her sister, Elsie. The third sister is a teacher at the Graham Stewart School. Helping the customers was 'Big Bill' Sullivan, the only member of Captain Schuenemann's crew alive after the fateful trip. Had he not had 'a hunch,' he would have drowned with the rest, he revealed yesterday. 'I went up with the crew,' said Sullivan, 'but when it came time to come back with the cargo of 15,000 trees, the lake was stormy. I simply had a hunch, that's all. It looked bad, so I told the captain I would come back on the train. I did. Three days later the *Butcher Boy*, another boat, came in with the news that the *Rouse Simmons* had gone down with all on board. I was afraid almost to tell Mrs. Schuenemann, but I got courage to go around – they lived just back of this store on Clark Street. When Elsie, who was a little girl then, saw me, she backed away in fright, as if I were a ghost. They had heard the news that I was reported drowned with the rest. I helped as best I could, because the Christmas tree business had to go on. We got more trees. The captain's wife was plucky. She went after the trees herself. Every year, until during the war, when the government bought her boat, she brought the trees down in the vessel. She loved those trees.' Mrs. Roberts, since her mother's death, has gone to northern Michigan woods to superintend the cutting of the trees, selecting the fullest and prettiest ones in the forests."

Captain and Mrs. Barbara Schuenemann's grandson, Dr. William Ehling, is still alive today, and he remembers the Christmas tree lot located at 1641 N. LaSalle Street mentioned in the above article where his mother (Captain Schuenemann's daughter, Pearl) sold trees from in the 1930's with her sisters, Elsie and Hazel.

Dr. Ehling shared many memories with me when we gathered at his eldest daughter's home south of Chicago where I was invited as their guest for a wonderful meal – served on "Aunt Hazel's antique dishes" - and an overnight stay.

Dr. Ehling told me stories of playing hide-and-seek among the Christmas trees when he was a small boy in the early 1930's. He also remembered hearing about the "12 foot ceilings" at the 1638 N. Clark Street address where his Grandpa and Grandma Schuenemann had once lived before the building was razed. Interestingly, the 1641 N. LaSalle Street address is directly behind the 1638 N. Clark Street address. (The Schuenemann daughters chose a building in the backyard of their parent's old address to sell their trees from and to hang their sign: *Captain and Mrs. H. Schuenemann's Daughters*. It was a curious name for their business, and it showed that the Schuenemann name continued to be held dear by the city of Chicago.

All three sisters lived on separate flats of the 158 Eugenie Street address in 1934 - only a short walk across the street and down the block from the LaSalle Street lot. (Mrs. Barbara Schuenemann also lived at this address prior to her death.)

When I asked Dr. Ehling if he remembered a man named "Big Bill Sullivan" who was mentioned in the *Chicago Tribune* article, his memories came to life within him with incredible vigor, as if awakening from a long sleep. First, he wanted me to know that "Big Bill Sullivan" was a nickname for the man - "after the famous fighter." The man's actual name, according to Dr. Ehling, was William F. Tietz. This man was not only a friend of the family's, but he was a "big protector" to "Little Billy" (as Dr. Ehling was called in his childhood) and was also a handyman who felt an allegiance to look after Captain Schuenemann's loved ones. Dr. Ehling told me, "I think 'Sully' felt bad for getting off Grandpa's boat." (Although the article names "Big Bill Sullivan" as "the only member of Captain Schuenemann's crew alive after the fateful trip," another crew member by the name of Hogan Hoganson also got off the ship in the Upper Peninsula of Michigan prior to the ship setting sail – and some reports say there were others.)

"Big Bill Sullivan" was not alone in offering Mrs. Schuenemann and her daughters assistance when Captain Schuenemann went missing. There were many, many friends who looked after the family. One of these was a man by

Captain Schuenemann's daughter, Hazel.
(Courtesy of the Schuenemann Family descendants.)

EVERGREENS HERE FOR CITY'S YULETIDE

Photo of Captain Schuenemann's daughters weaving wreaths.
Pearl Schuenemann, left; Elsie Schuenemann, right.
(Newspaper clipping dated December 6, 1913, *Chicago Daily News*)

the name of Captain J. O. Colberg. When I showed Dr. Ehling a photograph of his grandfather standing between two men on the deck of his Christmas tree ship, Dr. Ehling was overjoyed to see the photo. He recognized the man standing to his grandfather's left immediately. "By God, it's Jack Colberg!" shouted the doctor.

"You knew this man?" I asked.

"Absolutely!" answered Dr. Ehling. "He was a great, great friend of our family's, as well as being a great friend of Grandpa's. I remember him coming over often to share meals with us."

Although twenty years had passed since Captain Schuenemann had perished, his friends in Chicago were still regularly looking after his wife, daughters, and grandchildren out of loyalty for the beloved captain. The Schuenemanns not only *had* many friends, theirs was also a reputation for *being* a friend.

Dr. Ehling shared a vivid childhood memory with me that illustrated how the Schuenemann family honored their friendships with others. He remembered his family "driving and driving" during one summer trip with his mother and father by car around Lake Michigan. At last, they came to a great evergreen forest at the northernmost tip of the lake where a winding road led them deep into the woods. A cabin was in the center of the forest where "a little, old couple who used to sell Christmas trees to Grandpa" lived. Dr. Ehling's mother, Pearl, had come to visit these "old friends" of her father, Captain Schuenemann.

According to Dr. Ehling, "The cabin was a very humble place, and these people had little because it was the depression years. But they shared generously with us what they had."

Time had passed on, but the friendship had not. The cabin Dr. Ehling visited in the middle of the forest was in the Upper Peninsula of Michigan near the towns of Manistique and Thompson. Only a handful of miles separated these neighboring communities, and residents from each shared friendships with the Schuenemann family.

I interviewed several persons in Upper Michigan whose families personally knew the Schuenemanns, and who gave residence to Captain and Barbara Schuenemann in their homes during the Schuenemann's extended stays in Thompson and Manistique when trees were harvested. (These interviews are included in other chapters of this book.)

The Upper Peninsula of Michigan – where winters are long and Mother Nature's temper is short - was directly connected to Chicago's Christmases.

Evergreens supplied to the city came from the great wooded north near these port communities. It was advantageous for vessel captains to ship trees by boat since railways could become snowbound, as well as roadways. Heavy snowfalls affected both of these means of transportation, while waterways gave vessel captains an edge. Transporting trees by ship was, at times, the fastest means to get cargos through under snowbound conditions in November (or temporarily the *only* means). Waterways did, however, pose their own unique problems, especially concerning storms on the open waters.

Although Captain Schuenemann owned 240 acres of land in the Upper Peninsula of Michigan in 1912, and harvested trees on property he owned, he purchased trees from the locals in the earlier years of his Christmas tree business. The "locals" included both the residents of neighboring communities, as well as Chippewa Indians living along Lake Michigan and Lake Superior.

By 1912, Captain Schuenemann was one of the last Christmas tree merchants left who still shipped evergreens by schooner. According to the *Toronto Evening Telegram*, Toronto, Canada, of December 22, 1945, the Christmas tree fleet "had melted down like a snowman" when Captain Schuenemann and his ship went missing in 1912. Railroads were regularly used by this time to transport trees.

Captain Schuenemann was not unfamiliar with the benefits of railroads. He used railways to haul his trees from the forests to the shoreline where the

Logging operations in Thompson, Michigan.
(As published in the book A History of Thompson, Michigan, and the People Who Lived It*)*

CITY'S CHRISTMAS TREE SHIP BECAME LEGEND 65 YEARS AGO

Chicago Tribune
Chicago, IL
December 8, 1977

In October of 1912, Herman Schuenemann and the *Rouse Simmons* set sail into history, heading north for the 300-mile trip to Thompson's Landing, near Manistique, in Schoolcraft County on Michigan's Upper Peninsula.

With Schuenemann sailed Captain Charles Nelson, his partner in several tree farms in the area…

Schoolcraft County welcomed the arrival of the Christmas Tree Ship because harvesting the trees gave late-season employment to area lumberjacks.

The county boomed during the Civil War when iron ore from the Mesabi range was smelted and turned into cannon balls in charcoal furnaces which dotted the Upper Peninsula. But by 1912, lumbering had fallen on hard times, and the Christmas tree business provided by Schuenemann was welcomed…

Thompson [Michigan] *"had gained a permanent place in Great Lakes marine history as the point of departure for the* Rouse Simmons, *the 'Christmas Tree Ship,' on her fatal voyage in 1912."*

Schooner Days in Door County
Walter M. and Mary K. Hirthe
Copyright 1986

evergreen trees were then loaded on ships. According to the *Manistique Pioneer Tribune*, Manistique, MI, of October 12, 1978, Ernest Williams gave a firsthand story of Captain Schuenemann's final harvest of trees in 1912. The article about "Cap" (a nickname the locals used for Captain Schuenemann) read: "I worked in the woods northeast of Thompson [Michigan] on what we called the ridges, cutting trees and carrying out to a road, where John Fregale with one horse hauled them out to the railroad. I worked with two sailors, John Dall and Hogan Hoganson. Hogie was a happy soul and kept singing all day but the only song was: "Ve vere sailing down de lake, De vind vas blowing free, It vas on a trip to Buffalo, From Mil-vau-kee!" Over and over, all day long, he sang. One Sunday we loaded a [railroad] flat car with trees and took them to the boat. Cap Schuenemann also had other sailors up the DSS&A (Duluth South Shore and Atlantic Railroad) who also were gathering trees and evergreens. They shipped down two carloads, to my knowledge. Cap bought lots of evergreens. They were tied into bales, firmly pressed, from 20 to 40 pounds. One young fellow brought Cap a bale that seemed too heavy so Cap shook it and out dropped some scrap iron. Cap cheerfully told the lad to bring greens but to leave the scrap iron home. A woman who gathered mud with her greens got the name of Mud Hen. Cap every year used to get the tallest tree that he could find and present it to a leading theater in Chicago. In return they gave him a season's box for his family and friends. One year he got a 35-foot balsam and my father, Leverett E. Williams, lengthened the back of his wagon and hauled the tree to the boat. Father also hauled many evergreens to the boat for people. Cap used to deck the ship over with 1 x 12 x 16 foot hemlock boards (shiplap), about 7 feet high, then when he reached Chicago he would install stoves and sewing machines and hire women to make up evergreen wreaths, etc. Simon Bouschor, a retired lake captain, had a very accurate barometer, and his son Simon Jr., who had a business in Thompson, had it. Shortly before Cap sailed for Chicago (on his ill-fated voyage) Sam told him that the barometer was 'way low and still falling, and he'd better wait.' My father also told Cap that he would never make the trip by water, but to go by rail. Cap said he wouldn't miss the trip for anything."

On November 22, 1912, the barometer was falling in Thompson, Michigan, and Captain Schuenemann was advised "he'd better wait" on sailing. But the *Rouse Simmons* departed from the harbor, and also from the Thompson people whom the Schuenemanns had come to love.

Those back on shore continued their lives in the same day-to-day activities they had once shared with Captain Schuenemann during the many years he

History and Origin of the Christmas Tree

In ancient times, trees and all of nature were held in great reverence as a symbol of rebirth. During the season of Yule, trees were brought indoors and decorated as part of pagan worship. Because of this, trees were banned in many Christian churches until the church leaders studied the words of Isaiah 60:13: "The glory of Lebanon will come to you, the pine, the fir and the cypress together, to adorn the place of my sanctuary; and I will glorify the place of my feet."

Many legends have evolved about the Christmas tree. One of the oldest is said to have happened nearly one thousand years ago when Saint Boniface, in protest to tree worshippers, cut down an oak tree, and to his amazement, a fir tree sprung from its roots. Another legend from the sixteenth century tells the story of Martin Luther, a German church reformer, who was inspired by the beauty of an evergreen tree lit by the stars on Christmas Eve. He cut down the tree, dragged it home, and lighted the limbs with candles to simulate the stars in the sky above Bethlehem.

But modern researchers believe the Christmas tree evolved from the Paradise Tree which was part of the ancient "mystery plays" banned by the church in the fifteenth century. The Paradise Tree, decorated with apples, told the story of Adam and Eve. No longer found in the church, people took the custom of the Paradise Tree into their homes. During this same time, wooden Christmas pyramids were used on Christmas Eve, decorated with candles. In the late Middle Ages, glass bulbs and the Bethlehem star were added.

Deck the Halls
An Advent "Hanging of the Greens"
Celebration
Gail Gaymer Martin

"Putting up a Christmas tree once was frowned upon in the United States. Some New England states even enacted laws against Christmas trees and Christmas revelry. Despite this, Christmas trees rose in popularity all throughout the 1860's and 1870's – especially in the Midwest where large populations of Germans had settled. The Christmas tree finally attained a measure of mainstream 'American' acceptance when the first Christmas tree was put up in the White House by President Benjamin Harrison in 1891."

The Quarterly
(A publication of the Rogers Street Fishing Village Museum)
Holiday Issue – Oct./Dec. 1995

Three photos taken prior to Captain Schuenemann's death and published in a memorial newspaper article later:

#1   Captain Herman Schuenemann
#2   Wreathmakers in *Rouse Simmons* cabin
#3   Captain Schuenemann and crew on deck of *Rouse Simmons*
(Newspaper clipping dated December 5, 1913, *Chicago Daily News*)

and his family made the journey north each fall. According to the book *A History of Thompson, Michigan, and the People Who Lived It* by Florence "Alex" Meron, life in the community of Thompson included the following activities when the snows and cold weather of November arrived: "Skiing was a popular pastime. Most of this was done on homemade skis. Sleigh ride parties were also popular. The sound of sleigh bells on the harness could be heard for miles as the horse pulled the cutter or sleigh over the snow. Heavy fur robes covered the sleigh riders, and heated stones were used to warm their feet. An inviting fire, lunch, dancing, and music waited at the end of the ride. Many of the dances were held at a large dance hall. The hall was used on other occasions for traveling medicine shows, lodge meetings, revivals or large parties such as oyster suppers. These suppers were put on free-of-charge by one of the lumber companies and usually drew large crowds. Despite the cold weather, winter activities drew nearly as many participants as did summer sports. Ice-skating on the North Millpond was one of the most popular winter activities. The pond was actually part of Lake Michigan just north of the mouth of the Thompson Creek. The pond froze over smooth, as it was mostly enclosed and protected from the waves of the lake. Many of the local people were excellent skaters. The northern lights added to the beauty

STORY OF CHRISTMAS TREE SCHOONER THAT NEVER RETURNED
Manitowoc Daily Herald
Manitowoc, WI
December 14, 1912

Christmas 1912, just a few more days and the joyful Yuletide season will again take possession of this Earth. Joys and pleasures are recalled, sorrows as well.

The loss of the Christmas Tree Ship, the schooner *Rouse Simmons*, with her crew of 16 men, near Two Rivers Point, on November 23rd, will bring a gloomy Christmas to the homes of those who braved the elements to bring to the Chicago market, and to the Chicago homes, the evergreens of good cheer.

Years, yes, for a great many years, this old veteran of Lake Michigan, each Christmas season, sailed forth from the shores of northern Wisconsin or Michigan, loaded with a cargo of trees. When the *Rouse Simmons* arrived at Chicago with its cargo of twenty or thirty thousand trees, the boys and girls in that large city felt sure that Christmas soon would arrive...

Fishermen recently have found entangled in the meshes of their nets, fragments of Christmas trees and other wreckage, and it is about conclusively decided by marine men that the *Rouse Simmons* foundered in the immediate vicinity of Two Rivers Point.

of these evenings as they streaked across the winter sky. Skaters warmed themselves by a big bonfire on the shore."

Thompson was a place of sleigh rides and lap blankets; a place where you could see your breath hanging in the frosty air by the end of September. Winters arrived early here, and summers arrived late – and they still do.

A History of Thompson, Michigan, and the People Who Lived It includes information dedicated to the telling of the Christmas Tree Ship story as it related to the locals in the communities of Thompson and Manistique, Michigan. Here, evergreens were brought out of the forests by horse-drawn bobsleds and loaded into the ship's belly by lantern light in the evening. Also included in the book are details concerning Chicago.

Although the author, Alex Meron, lived in the Upper Peninsula community of Manistique for sixty years (where she served as County Historian for forty years), she told me in a heartwarming conversation that she was also connected to the Schuenemanns through the city of Chicago where she was born and raised only blocks from the Schuenemann's Clark Street address. Ironically, she and her sisters were among the needy children who received a free Christmas tree from the Schuenemann's at the holidays during their childhoods. Alex and her sister, Jessie, who is now nearly 90 years of age, both remember Barbara Schuenemann and her daughters.

Another child who remembered receiving Christmas trees from Barbara Schuenemann - as well as from Captain Herman Schuenemann - was Jimmy O'Malley. Born in 1894 to Irish immigrants, Jimmy was the oldest of their nine children.

He remembered "carrying a dime" - clutched in his little hand – down to the ship where he and his family climbed aboard.

The arrival of Captain Schuenemann's schooner "generated so much excitement that nothing else in the world mattered when the Christmas Ship was coming in." Captain Schuenemann's schooner was greeted with such exuberance "you could hear shouts in the street" as the vessel approached. Boys and girls, waiting on tiptoe, shouted, "The Christmas Ship is here! The Christmas Ship!" Smiling, pudgy faces waved to the captain, and the captain

---

"An element of the 'old fashioned' in Chicago's Christmas had disappeared when the Rouse Simmons *sank."*

Chicago Today
December 21, 1969
George Leposky

The "Good Ship Christmas Tree"

As Christmas time approaches and children begin to think of Christmas trees, their parents recall the days of the Christmas Tree Ship.

The "Good Ship Christmas Tree," operated by Captain Herman Schuenemann from 1887 to 1912, used to herald the start of the Yule season for Chicago youngsters.

Tied to the dock at the southwest corner of the Clark Street Bridge, it stood with tree-filled decks and its Santa Claus picture of a captain, Herman Schuenemann. Chicagoans, young and old, came to marvel and stayed to buy.

People liked the good feeling of buying their Christmas tree out on the open decks of the schooner. For a dollar you could have your pick of the lot.

The Captain made it a social visit, too, with his cook whipping up a meal for as many as 40 at a time.

Old newspaper clipping on file at:
The Great Lakes Historical Society
Source and date of article unknown

"Some Christmases the captain would bring a surprise along on his ship. Once, he brought a bear to delight the youngsters, and another time, an eagle. And always, there was an extra tree for some needy family or schoolroom."

Chicago Daily Tribune
Chicago, IL
December 10, 1959

"The Christmas Tree Ship – My Prices Are The Lowest." The banner hung between the schooner's masts, stretching above the snow-covered planks and her deck cargo of thousands of evergreens. The scent of pine trees and cut wood hovered over the ship, blending in the bitter air with all the other smells of the busy waterfront.

Small boys chased through the festive streets shouting that the Schuenemanns had arrived again.

In Chicago, for more than forty years, the arrival of the "Christmas Tree" schooner from the north inaugurated the holidays.

Sea Classics
January 1977
Volume 10, No. 1
Fred Hollister

"One captain who had an extraordinary understanding of advertising hype was Herman Schuenemann. His schooner's arrival each year at the southwest corner of the Clark Street Bridge became a tradition. As soon as the mooring lines were made fast, Schuenemann could be seen stringing electric lights from foremast to mizzen and putting out his sign: 'Christmas Tree Ship. My Prices Are The Lowest.'"

Newmonth
Nov./Dec. 2000
Scottie Dayton

waved back.

Although Mr. O'Malley passed away in the 1970's, his memories live on in his granddaughter, Mrs. Jean Kopecky, who heard her grandpa talk about how important the Christmas Tree Ship was to him when she was a little girl. Nearly fifty years have now passed since she listened to her grandpa "reliving his memories and going back to find the warmth," but she remembers well the "twinkle in his eye" as he recalled the kindness Captain Schuenemann bestowed upon the O'Malley family.

"I am the carrier of my grandfather's history," Mrs. Kopecky told me, as she shared memories of her grandpa's Christmases long past, but not forgotten. "I don't remember my grandfather speaking of any other Christmas memory, or special holiday moment from his childhood, other than the Christmas Ship."

"To my grandfather, the Christmas Ship represented hope," said Mrs. Kopecky, "because his family was so extremely, extremely poor – *dirt poor*. They had nothing. And yet they received a Christmas tree, gifted to them from the Schuenemanns, during several years when the family fell on particularly hard times."

"If my grandfather's family had not received a free tree," said Mrs. Kopecky, "they would not have had any. Every penny was precious to the family. There was hardly enough money for food; and certainly no money for a tree."

She told me how her grandfather looked to the arrival of the Christmas Ship as the most "highly anticipated" moment of his holiday.

"Wearing shoes that buttoned up to his ankles – even with holes in – and faded, hand-me-down clothes, my grandfather headed to the docks with his brothers and sisters to see the Captain," said Mrs. Kopecky. "Regardless of how cold it was, or if someone only had one mitten, nothing else in the world mattered when the Christmas Ship sailed in. My grandfather wouldn't have missed it for anything."

The O'Malley family was able to purchase a tree some years, but there were other years when they were gifted a tree. Despite this charitable exchange, Captain Schuenemann always made sure the kids maintained a feeling of dignity and pride when they were empty-handed.

"Captain Schuenemann allowed the kids to sweep on the ship for a while so they would have a sense of having earned their tree," she told me. (Captain Schuenemann lived through an impoverished childhood and had a soft spot for the poor. As an adult, he also experienced financial struggles – especially

CAUSES CHRISTMAS TREE SHORTAGE
Chicago Daily Journal
Chicago, IL
December 5, 1912

The loss of the cargo is expected to result in a shortage in the holiday Christmas tree market.

In addition to the 35,000 Christmas trees, the boat carried wreaths and ferns for holiday decorations.

Chicago firms today sent orders to northern Wisconsin and Michigan for the cutting of more trees, which will be shipped to the city by rail.

New Hampshire and Vermont cutters also were wired for trees.

Chicago dealers in wreaths started the manufacture of additional supplies of paper wreaths to take the place of those which have been lost in the schooner.

CHRISTMAS TREE FISHED FROM ICY LAKE WARMS HEARTS OF LONELY TENDERS
Chicago Record-Herald
Chicago, IL
December 26, 1912

A little fir tree yesterday finished an interrupted journey and in a small room in the Carter Harrison crib, off the end of East Chicago Avenue, lived out its destiny as an important part of a Yuletide decoration.

It was picked out of the cold waters of Lake Michigan a week ago. For days it had been swirling around the end of the crib in the eddies and currents. Lawrence Nelson, keeper of the crib, gazed down on the ice-incrusted branches and ordered it brought out of the water.

CHRISTMAS TREE CHEERS

"Get out a boat hook, boys," he said, "we'll have a real Christmas tree. That's what it was intended for in the first place. Probably started for Chicago in the poor old *Rouse Simmons*. Well, we can use it on the crib. Heave it in."

So it was brought out of the water. For a week it lay on the crib, its sodden branches gradually drying out. Three men – the keeper, his one helper, and the cook – sat around it yesterday evening and spun yarns and indulged in reminiscences.

in the final years of his life. When his wallet washed ashore after the *Rouse Simmons* sunk, there was not even a single dollar inside.)

The O'Malley kids' heights "went down like steps, one right after the other," said Mrs. Kopecky, "and when the kids carried their Christmas tree home on their shoulders, it looked like a giant bug, with nine sets of legs beneath it, walking along the street."

"My grandfather was the oldest," said Mrs. Kopecky, "so he held the heaviest end of the tree where the branches were fullest, while his youngest sibling, on the opposite end of the tree, reached up high and held the tip."

A century of Christmases have gone by since the "evergreen bug" paraded along Chicago's cobblestone streets and past gaslight lanterns decorated with Schuenemann wreaths. Yet the smiles born from Captain Schuenemann's kindnesses are still lighting up the faces of grandchildren and great-grandchildren who have become the living repositories of their ancestor's oral history.

"Always, I remember my grandpa being anxious for Christmas," said Mrs. Kopecky. "But not for the Christmases of the present. He was anxious to remember the Christmases of the past – *long* past."

Grandpa O'Malley continued to hold dear the "warmth" of his childhood days when he stood on the snow-dusted decks of the Christmas Ship with holes in his shoes.

"Just as people snuggle up to watch 'It's a Wonderful Life,' signifying the start of the holiday season, the Rouse Simmons *held that same warm and nostalgic feeling for many Chicago area families."*

The Big Pond
July 15, 1999
Steve Staedler

Oldest known photograph of the *Rouse Simmons* dated 1884.
(Courtesy of the Milwaukee Public Library/Wisconsin Marine Historical Society)

Chapter Three

The Sailing of the Christmas Tree Ship

"In 1910, Herman Schuenemann bought an interest in the Rouse Simmons *and the doughty craft became 'Chicago's Christmas Tree Ship.'"*

Soundings
(A publication of the Wisconsin Marine Historical Society)
Winter 1963-1964, Vol. 4 No. 2
Theodore S. Charrney

The Sailing of the Christmas Tree Ship

On August 15, 1868, the *Milwaukee Sentinel* announced the launching of a new sailing vessel built in one of the city's local shipyards. The schooner, christened *Rouse Simmons*, made news in several states. The Milwaukee press reported: "The *Rouse Simmons*, one of two new vessels recently contracted for by Kenosha, Wisconsin, parties, will be launched this afternoon from the shipyard of Allan, McClelland & Company. Her dimensions are as follows: Length overall, 127 feet; breath of beam, 27 feet 6 inches; depth of hold, 8 feet 1 inch; measurement about 220 tons. The model of the *Simmons* combines speed with large carrying capacity, and in this respect must be considered faultless. Her entrance, though seemingly full, is nevertheless quite sharp, and her run is really beautiful. The timber used in her construction is the finest we have ever seen put into a vessel, and the manner in which it has been put together reflects the highest credit upon the builders. The cost of the new vessel, when fully completed and ready for sea, will be in the neighborhood of $17,000. She will carry three masts, fore-and-aft rigged, with square sail on foremast. Her owners are Royal B. Tousley and Captain Akerman, of Kenosha, the latter of whom will have command. The *Simmons* is designed for the lumber trade and will ply between Manistee and Chicago."

Forty-four years after the *Rouse Simmons* was launched, the ship made headlines again – but this time not in a celebratory way. On December 6, 1912, the *Milwaukee Sentinel* reported the schooner had gone missing in "the vicinity of Twin River Point" – an area that had "long been considered one of the most dangerous portions of the lake, having earned through its many wrecks and wild waters the name of 'the graveyard of the lake.'"

The same article made mention of the *Simmons'* earlier days: "The *Rouse Simmons* was a three-masted schooner and slid off the ways in 1868, having a capacity of 16,000 bushels of grain. It was then one of the largest boats on the Great Lakes and was the pride of its builder. Later, as larger and faster boats were built, the *Rouse Simmons* was used for the transportation of iron and copper ores, lumber, piling and rough stock of all descriptions. In its career it changed hands many times, the present owner being M. J. Bonner of St. James, Michigan. Two Milwaukee men have owned the schooner, John Faville and F. S. Maxon. It was a well-built boat…"

The ship was built of native timber and was designed to carry timber. It was estimated by Theodore Charrney, "the most devoted student of the ship's

NEW VESSEL
Chicago Tribune
Chicago, IL
August 17, 1868

NEW VESSEL – The ROUSE SIMMONS, one of two new vessels recently built for Kenosha parties, was to have been launched at Milwaukee Saturday afternoon. Her dimensions are as follows: Length overall, 127 feet; breadth of beam, 27 feet 6 inches; depth of hold, 8 feet 1 inch. She measures about 230 tons. The model of the SIMMONS combines speed with large carrying capacity.

FIRST TRIP
Milwaukee Sentinel
Milwaukee, WI
September 4, 1868

The new schooner *Rouse Simmons* sailed from this port at a late hour Wednesday evening on her maiden trip.

She has gone to Manistee, Michigan, for lumber.

**SCHOONER
R. SIMMONS**
Detroit Free Press
Detroit, MI
October 30, 1868

A new vessel called the R. SIMMONS passed down yesterday, grain loaded from Chicago. To all appearance she is a new vessel... She compares well with many others, and is fore and aft rigged.

storied career," that the *Rouse Simmons* piled up a veritable mountain of lumber dockside during her lifetime spent serving the Chicago market – 200 million board feet. (*Schooner Passage*, Professor Theodore J. Karamanski) The ship could carry up to 350,000 board feet of lumber at a time.

Although the majority of the ship's life was spent hauling lumber, the vessel became tragically remembered for its last cargo: Christmas trees. On November 23, 1912, Captain Herman Schuenemann was transporting a Yuletide cargo of evergreens with the *Simmons* when the ship was caught in a ferocious storm and subsequently sunk.

Two years earlier, in 1910, Captain Schuenemann purchased part ownership in the ship that was destined to become "his coffin." (*Chicago Maritime*, David M. Young)

According to the "Consolidated Certificate of Enrollment and License" for the *Rouse Simmons*, issued by the Department of Commerce and Labor/Bureau of Navigation, the owners of the ship in 1910 were listed as follows:

> Mannes J. Bonner 1/4
> Gus Kitzinger of Manistee, Michigan 1/2
> Herman Schuenemann of Chicago, Illinois 1/8
> Martin Mathison of Chicago, Illinois 1/8

The owners listed on the Consolidated Certificate of Enrollment and License in 1911 were:

> Mannes J. Bonner 1/4
> Herman Schuenemann and Charles Nelson 1/8 each
> Gus Kitzinger of Manistee, Michigan 1/2

The final licensing papers filed in 1912 listed these owners:

> Mannes J. Bonner of St. James, Michigan 3/4
> Herman Schuenemann and Charles Nelson, both of Chicago 1/8 each

---

"In 1910, he [Captain Herman Schuenemann] acquired an interest in the Rouse Simmons. *Under Captain Herman the ship was a vagabond, wandering around the lake wherever a cargo of lumber, logs, or cedar posts took her. The Captain spent most of the shipping season in this haphazard activity, but in the fall he sailed north to collect evergreens, and the* Rouse Simmons *was transformed from a tramp schooner to a Christmas tree ship."*

Kenosha County Historical Society Bulletin
Kenosha, Wisconsin
October 1971
Phil Sander

Schooners departing from a harbor in Kewaunee, Wisconsin.
(Courtesy of the Kewaunee County Historical Society)

"The passing of the Rouse Simmons *symbolized the passing of the sailing schooner from the Great Lakes. In the years following the Civil War, almost 2,000 of these white canvassed beauties carried the commerce of the Inland Seas that are the Great Lakes. The* Rouse Simmons *was one of the last."*

Theodore Charrney
Commemorative postcard dated 1962

The *Rouse Simmons* and the Port of Chicago

The *Rouse Simmons* was built in 1868 in Milwaukee for Kenosha [Wisconsin] ownership. Her keel was laid in March and by August the vessel was launched. Her cost was $14,000. After being documented by the government, her maiden voyage was made in early September. She sailed in light trim for Manistee, Michigan, to pick up a cargo of lumber destined for Chicago. This was the first of more than a thousand ship arrivals in Chicago harbor during her lifetime. The ship spent her entire career in the lumber trade carrying scantling, joist, lath, shingles, cedar posts, railroad ties, telegraph poles and tanbark…

After four years in the service of Kenosha, the *Rouse Simmons* was sold to Charles H. Hackley of Muskegon, Michigan, formerly of Kenosha. He was perhaps the wealthiest of the forty Muskegon lumber barons of that sawdust city and his company owned a fleet of as many as seven ships during the heyday of lumbering in the 1880's. Of all the floating property owned by Hackley, the *Rouse Simmons* was his workhorse for the longest period, twenty-six years. Should you go to Muskegon today you will find a park, a library, an art gallery, a high school, a church and monuments to Lincoln and McKinley, all the gifts of Hackley to his adopted town. I believe some of this philanthropy was made possible through the earnings of the *Rouse Simmons*.

During the quarter of a century spent in the Hackley fleet, the vessel saw her share of glory and frustrations. Collisions with other ships under fog bound conditions disabled the vessel on two occasions. The vessel lost her jib-boom or cathead several times in harbor accidents placing her in dry dock for repairs. On some late season voyages the vessel came into the harbor iced up at the bow and on her sides, her deck load either jettisoned or greatly reduced, with three or four feet of water in her hold and the crew thoroughly exhausted from incessant manning of the pumps.

Several deaths occurred during her Hackley period. Once, an unlucky deck hand fell from her topmast. Another time a hand fell overboard, and still another was crushed by the hull of the ship coming against the pilings. The most spectacular death occurred in

The official number assigned to the *Rouse Simmons* in 1868 for enrollment and licensing purposes was #110024. However, this number was later changed to #110087 according to the Wisconsin Marine Historical Society.

On March 18, 1913, the ship's final enrollment papers were surrendered due to the vessel's loss. The following notation was made on the Certificate: "Foundered in Lake Michigan possibly off Two Rivers, Wisconsin, about November 23, 1912."

At the time of the ship's loss, its measurements were officially recorded as: 123.5 length; 27.6 breath; 8.4 depth of hold; 205 gross tons; 195 net tons. These measurements were slightly different than those noted at its launching

1875 [when] one William Rothwell, an English born sailing master, was given command of the ship in spite of the fact he had a drinking problem. Late in the season when storms were the rule on the lakes, the ship incurred some minor damage each trip that could usually be accounted for. In a mid-November storm, however, she lost her mainsail and used a full week for the 200-mile trip from Muskegon, Michigan, and upon arrival in Chicago she ran against the pier and lost her anchor. This brought about Rothwell's discharge and after fortifying himself with strong waters, he checked into the Sherman Hotel and committed suicide by morphine.

The third owner of the ship, a Chicago sailing master, used the vessel in the lumber trade but the receding forests made necessary trips of longer distances, hence her arrivals in Chicago were substantially reduced.

In October of 1904, while loading at Torch Lake in the east arm of Grand Traverse Bay, Michigan, she was caught at her moorings by a northwest gale that kicked up a wicked sea and started the vessel pounding against the pilings. To save the ship from breaking up she was scuttled and settled to the bottom in fifteen feet of water. Sitting thus she was sold to a Beaver Island sailing master, raised, pumped out, jacketed and floated to Charlevoix, Michigan, where she wintered. The following spring she crossed Lake Michigan at the end of a towline while the men at the pumps kept her buoyant. Up on the boxes at Sturgeon Bay, Wisconsin, the vessel received a complete refit and was placed in the tanbark trade between Beaver Island and the tanneries in Milwaukee.

In the fall of 1906 the vessel was dismasted in a violent gale and was given up for lost when the Grand Haven Car Ferry picked her up and towed her into Milwaukee harbor. She was again refitted and sailed for three years without mishap.

The most romantic period in the life of the *Rouse Simmons* began in 1910 when a part ownership in the vessel was purchased by Herman Schuenemann, a member of the Chicago family associated with the Christmas tree trade.

Inland Seas
(Quarterly Journal of The Great Lakes Historical Society)
Winter 1987 – Vol. 43 No. 4
Theodore S. Charrney

in August of 1868. (The first measurement change for the vessel was recorded at the Port of Milwaukee on June 21, 1870.)

Another change made to the vessel in later years was the addition of a deckhouse on the ship. According to the *Chicago Inter Ocean* of December 5, 1912, "Captain Schuenemann constructed a deckhouse running from the foremast to the cabin, using between 15,000 and 20,000 feet of green lumber. It was eleven feet high and would offer great resistance in a gale."

The *Rouse Simmons* took approximately six months to build at a cost of $14,000 to $17,000 (reports vary) – a sizable sum of money in 1868. As previously mentioned, the ship was "the pride of its builder" and "the timber used in her construction was the finest" – reflecting "the highest credit upon

1865 and 1866 was a busy time for the Great Lakes shipyards. A terrible and bloody Civil War had just ended and most of America needed to be rebuilt. Great three-masted wooden schooners were turned out by the dozens and they were put to work hauling cargos of wheat, store goods and lumber. If you looked out on Lake Michigan in the 1870's there was a sight to behold. Next to water, the skyline was filled with the sail cloth of giant, three-masted schooners. After the others were retired one of these ships would go down in Great Lakes history as the "Christmas Tree Ship."

By the turn of the century, many of the wooden ships would be cut down for barges to be towed by the powerful and more dependable steamships that would soon replace them.

A man named Herman Schuen-emann saw the vast number of wooden schooners retired and tied to abandoned docks. With his love for Christmas, he came up with an idea to make Christmas a little brighter for the families in his favorite port, Chicago.

Allan Holden
my.net-link.net/~prostock/rouse.html

There is an old saying that sailors are not good businessmen, otherwise, they wouldn't be sailors. Captain Herman Schuenemann was an exception to the rule.

In an age when steam and propellers were rapidly relegating sailing craft to the boneyards, he managed to keep the old Rouse Simmons *on the move and always at a profit. A deckload of boxed apples from Green Bay to Chicago, fence posts from Manistique to Port Huron, or shingles from Milwaukee to Traverse Bay, it made little difference to the Captain so long as the ship earned a few honest dollars.*

Her sails were old and patched, her cordage frayed and knotted, and her galley perpetually understocked, but the valiant old three-sticker sailed on long after newer and bigger schooners were snaked into the lonely and polluted backwaters to rot away.

The Captain's Christmas tree haul was a seasonable but highly renumerative operation typical of his enterprising spirit, a choice plum to be plucked before ice and snow ended the freshwater shipping season.

Toledo Blade
Toledo, OH
January 14, 1951
Dwight Boyer

the builders." The ship's sturdy construction served it well during its forty-four years in the lumber trade on the Great Lakes until it went missing in 1912. The *Grand Haven Daily Tribune* of Grand Haven, Michigan, reported the *Simmons'* loss on December 6, 1912: "Many a middle aged Muskegon, Michigan, man will recall the days when he helped load the ill-fated old schooner *Rouse Simmons* with lumber for the then almost insatiable Chicago market. Others will recall her weekly trips made more noticeable by the peculiar name the craft bore."

The "peculiar name" belonged to both the ship and a real man. Who was he?

According to the Kenosha County Historical Society in Kenosha, Wisconsin, as reported in the Society's bulletin in October 1971, Rouse Simmons was a citizen of their community in the 1800's and helped finance the building of the ship. Their records read: "Three Kenosha citizens with a vision of the future saw the great potential in getting into the profitable shipping business and also in building up the growing Kenosha community. They decided to build a suitable schooner primarily for transporting lumber. In 1868, R. B. Towsley, with the shipping and business know-how, and Captain Ackerman, with an excellent record of seamanship and lake port knowledge, planned a three-masted lake schooner. Rouse Simmons was not a partner, but he helped finance the building of the ship."

Although Rouse Simmons did not own the vessel named in his honor, the ship was christened with his name out of gratitude for his financial support. The Simmons family was a manufacturing power in Kenosha, Wisconsin (just south of Milwaukee) and went on to found the Simmons Company – a bedding and furniture factory. (If you are sleeping on a Simmons Beauty Rest mattress, you are connected to a piece of the Christmas Tree Ship story.)

In the pages of a dusty, old Bible, the names of other Simmons family members are recorded. The 160-year-old Bible was purchased by Raymond E. Johnson, a retired teacher, in a used book store. He paid only $7.00 for the leather-covered heirloom. Mr. Johnson writes, "In an old bookstore in Kenosha, Wisconsin, I discovered a Bible – an old Bible in excellent condition whose first page bore the handwritten inscription, 'The Property of Ezra Simmons, Rome, New York, May 21, 1843.' Ezra was the patriarch of the Simmons family who, with his wife, Maria, had brought their family from New York state to Southport (as Kenosha, Wisconsin, was then known) in 1843. On the family record pages, between the Old and New Testaments, Ezra's hand had written: Ezra Simmons, April 3, 1805, Pleasant Valley, New York; Maria Gilbert Simmons, April 22, 1809, Herkimer Co.; Zalmon

1890 photo of the *Rouse Simmons* being loaded with a cargo of bark.
The ship was owned by Charles H. Hackley at this time.
(Courtesy of the Bentley Historical Library, University of Michigan,
Ivan H. Walton Collection)

"Like many other lumber schooners, the Rouse Simmons *had her share of rough sailing during her forty-four year career. Collisions with bridges, breakwaters, and other ships had all been endured, as well as waterspouts, white squalls, and gales."*

Schooner Passage
Theodore J. Karamanski
Copyright 2000

Simmons, September 10, 1828, Pleasant Valley; Burr Simmons, July 16, 1830, Pleasant Valley; Rouse Simmons, September 15, 1832, Marcy; Ezra and Esther Simmons, February 21, 1839, Marcy. On the 'Deaths' page, other hands had written that Ezra had died in 1878, Maria in 1895, Rouse in 1897, and Burr in 1900." The entries in the Bible ended in 1900.

Although the factory has long since been demolished, many reminders yet remain in Kenosha of the family's influence on the community. There is Simmons Island, Simmons Field, and the grand Gilbert M. Simmons Library, gifted to the city by Zalmon Simmons as a memorial to his deceased son, Gilbert.

Kenosha is only one city of several along Lake Michigan with memorials directly - or indirectly - connected to the *Rouse Simmons*.

The city of Muskegon, Michigan, lies across the lake from Kenosha. Here, visitors will find many memorials placed by a wealthy lumber baron named Charles H. Hackley who purchased the *Rouse Simmons* in 1873. He held the ship in his fleet for more than a quarter of a century during his most prosperous years in the lumber industry. (This was the longest period of time any one person owned the vessel during its forty-four years.)

The ship was said to be the "work horse" of Hackley's fleet and the vessel contributed significantly to the earnings of the Hackley company during this time. Hackley later sold the vessel when the lumbering industry became less profitable, and the vessel was then passed between many owners.

Charles Hackley, according to his biography, was a man who "gave freely of his wealth to the betterment of the city where he made his millions in the 1800's. Much of his belief was founded upon Andrew Carnegie's *Gospel of Wealth* written in 1889. Like other entrepreneurs of the time, Charles felt that his wealth should be used not only to correct hardship and misfortune, but also to benefit those who wished to better themselves. In an interview, Charles Hackley said: 'A rich man to a great extent owes his fortune to the public. He makes money largely through the labor of his employees...Moreover, I believe that it should be expended during the lifetime of the donor so that he can see that his benefactions do not miscarry and are according to his intent...To a certain extent, I agree with Mr. Carnegie...it is a crime to die rich.'"

Charles Hackley lived his belief and left the City of Muskegon a hospital, a library, a school, a park, an art gallery, and an athletic field. The Hackley family also established an endowment fund to benefit the poor of the city, and another for the purpose of educational benefits.

Both Muskegon, Michigan, and Kenosha, Wisconsin, are connected to the story of the Christmas Tree Ship through the *Rouse Simmons*. Other communities are connected to the story through Captain Herman Schuenenmann. Algoma, Wisconsin, is one of these.

Algoma was Captain Schuenemann's birthplace. He was born and raised in this picturesque fishing village north of Milwaukee in 1865 – within three years of the *Rouse Simmons'* birth in the Allen, McClelland & Company shipyard in 1868. Many of the same buildings that stood in Herman Schuenemann's youth are still there today. One of these buildings houses Wisconsin's oldest winery: the von Stiehl Winery. Although this building was originally erected near the end of the Civil War to serve as a brewery, the caverns beneath the building - constructed of hand-carved limestone cut from bedrock in the area - proved to be excellent for wine production in later years.

The von Stiehl Winery has been bottling a commemorative wine for the

Commemorative "Christmas Tree Ship" wine bottled by the von Stiehl Winery in Algoma, Wisconsin.

past decade honoring the city's native son, Herman Schuenemann, and his ship. A sketch of the *Rouse Simmons* appears on the label with the following notation: "Captain Herman Schuenemann of Algoma was skipper of the *Rouse Simmons*, Lake Michigan's legendary Christmas Tree Ship."

Algoma, Wisconsin, is also home to "Christmas Tree Ship Point" – an area of land within the inner harbor that leads out to Lake Michigan. The point, within the proximity of the Algoma Lighthouse, was dedicated to all of the Christmas tree vessels and captains who transported trees to Milwaukee and Chicago in the 1800's. (A lone evergreen grows at the tip of Christmas Tree Ship Point and is lit with white lights year-round as a memorial.)

Christmas Tree Ship Point located in the harbor at Algoma, Wisconsin.

It is important to note that there were other ships that carried Christmas trees besides the Schuenemann ships. However, the Schuenemann family was most remembered because they were one of the first merchants, as well as one of the last. Their involvement in the Christmas tree industry lasted nearly a half century. Captain Herman was said to be "a pioneer in Chicago's Christmas tree business" by the Chicago press.

It is also important to note that the Schuenemann family used many vessels through the years to transport their Yuletide cargos. Although they are tragically linked to the *Rouse Simmons* – the *Rouse Simmons* was only used for two short years before the vessel and crew went down during the third year. The nickname "Christmas Tree Ship" applied to more vessels than the *Rouse Simmons*.

As an example of this, the photograph on the opposite page shows the *George L. Wrenn* in 1908. Captain Schuenemann used this ship for several years prior to sailing the *Rouse Simmons*.

The *Chicago American* of December 5, 1912, published the following information concerning Schuenemann vessels when Captain Schuenemann went missing with the *Simmons*: "For more than twenty-five years Captain Schuenemann had operated boats in the tree trade on the lake... The average load for the schooner was between three hundred and four hundred tons of trees. The big trees were loaded on deck while the wreath material and small trees were put into the hold. Schuenemann lost the schooner, *Mary Collins*, in a lake storm some years ago. The crew was rescued. The Schuenemanns have sailed Christmas voyages in the *Maggie Dall*, the *Ida*, the *Jessie Phillips*, the *Truman Moss*, the *George L. Wrenn*, the *Rouse Simmons*, and the *Thal*."

There is controversy concerning exactly what vessels were used by the Schuenemanns during what years. Other ships believed by researchers to have been used by Captain Herman include the *M. Capron* and the *Mystic*.

Captain August Schuenemann, Captain Herman's older brother, went

> *"During the late 1880's a group of schooner captains had found a very profitable end-of-season cargo – Christmas trees. The six, eight and ten-foot trees left behind by the lumberjacks were cut and bundled in early November, just as now. The wind was still free back then, too, and the schooners could carry their fragrant cargoes of good cheer far more cheaply than they could be delivered by rail or steamer."*
>
> Modoc Whistle
> Winter 1995
> Bill Ballard

1908 photo of the Christmas Tree Ship at dock in Chicago.
(Courtesy of the Chicago Historical Society)

The Ballad of the *Rouse Simmons*

This is the tale of the Christmas Ship
That sailed o'er the sullen lake
And of sixteen souls that made the trip
And of death in the foaming wake.

"Northward ho!" was the word that day,
And lightly riding the wave,
The schooner drew from the wharf away
With her crew and her Captain brave.

Northward sailed the Christmas Ship,
And the lake was fair and blue
Till she came unto the forest town
Where the firs and balsams grew.

And the Captain stood at the vessel's helm
And smiled at his lusty pack,
For he knew what joy for the babes there'd be
When the Santa Claus Ship came back.

He has laden the Christmas Ship with trees,
Till a floating woods she lay.
"And now, we must haste," the Captain said,
"For fast comes the Christmas Day."

"Captain," they said, "the sky is lead,
While the waves are cold and gray.
And the wind roars forth from the frozen north.
And will you sail today?"

The Captain stood by the schooner's wheel,
And his loud laugh roared with the breeze.
"We sail," he said, "for the children wait,
For our freight of Christmas trees."

"Full thirty years we have sailed," he said,
"The storms we have made our sport.
And the Christmas Ship has never failed
To return to the southern port."

But the wind roared down with sleet and snow
And the waves lashed toward the skies,
The Captain stood at the schooner's wheel
With the blinding snow in his eyes.

The gale through the cordage shrieked and whined
And the wanton water roared.
And the spray, as it swept before the wind,
Bit deep, like a stinging sword.

The cold, black waves sweep o'er her sides,
The sails are rent and torn.
"Captain," they cry, "Does the ship go down?
Must we die before the morn?"

No gleam of light in the whirling night
Gave promise of friendly aid.
And one by one the masts went down,
But the Captain stood unafraid.

"Captain," they cry, "the seams are rent,
And the sea pours in below.
And the schooner's pumps are old and worn."
And he answered, "Be it so!"

The precious freightage of Christmas greens
Is swept o'er the vessel's side,
And spread to the south and north and west
By the fierce gale's howling tide.

Now the wild sea grasps the Christmas Ship,
While near her and far away,
The angry wind is roaring forth
Like a tiger for its prey.

Like a chip on the ocean, aflung and tossed,
Is the helpless vessel's plight;
And strong men pray for the break of day,
Or the gleam of a harbor light.

Then, the end! A rush of the headlong flood;
A crash and a cry – and then
The waters snarl o'er the nameless grave
Of a Captain and his men.

Death bellowed afar that night on the lake
Where now moans the mournful breeze.
And far and wide the waves are green
With the children's Christmas trees.

The Captain's wife may watch and weep
On the sand by the lacy foam.
But the Christmas Ship from its Christmas trip
Shall never more come home.

And the children wait in vain
For the ship from the winter seas.
For the waves have claimed the Christmas Ship
And the children's Christmas trees.

By: Charles V. E. Starrett
Chicago Daily News, December 7, 1912

> # Information on Ill-Fated Ship Is Sought By Writer
> ## *December 24, 1960*
>
> *A Chicago writer, Theodore S. Charrney of 3737 Armitage Ave., has requested aid from persons in the Sheboygan, Wisconsin, area who have any information on the ill-fated ship* Rouse Simmons, *the "Christmas Ship" that went down in Lake Michigan off Two Rivers on November 23, 1912.*
>
> *Any information about any phase of her career, her crew or persons associated with her in any way will be helpful to him, Charrney said. He is presently doing historical research on the famous maritime tragedy.*
>
> *The* Rouse Simmons *was a three-masted schooner built in Milwaukee in 1868. She spent practically her entire life in Lake Michigan, prior to 1892 in the dry lumber trade out of Manistee and Muskegon, Michigan, to the Chicago lumber market, and thereafter as a general cargo carrier.*
>
> *In 1909 Captain Gus Larson of Sheboygan bought an interest in the 123-foot schooner and took command of her. During the winter of that year the ship lay west of the Eighth Street Bridge on the north side of the river.*
>
> *In the early fall of 1912 Captain Herman Schuenemann of Chicago chartered the vessel to carry a load of Christmas trees from Manistique, Michigan, back to Chicago to sell during the Christmas season. The Captain and his men cut the trees and loaded them on the schooner, leaving port with a full load...*

down with the schooner *S. Thal* in 1898. (The *S. Thal* was one of many ships used by Captain August.) This ship was considerably smaller than the *Rouse Simmons* and was built in Oshkosh, Wisconsin, in 1867. The cargo of trees aboard the vessel came from Door County, Wisconsin.

"Wherever tales of dying ships and dying men are told you may find the haunting story of the Christmas Ship's last voyage, a winter tragedy of Lake Michigan," wrote the *Chicago Tribune* of December 24, 1944. Under the headline 'Why Chicago Missed Its Yule Trees in 1912' the article continued: "No doubt the thing that tempts so many writers to retell the tale is its contrast – the Christmas idea and the idea of terror and lonely death. Another temptation is the mystery, for the final hours of the Christmas Ship were known only to those who lived them and died them. Schuenemann, it may be believed, was not much worried by the threat of storm. He was a veteran of

The next day the ship was seen passing Kewaunee, Wisconsin, with distress signals flying and that was the last time she was seen. Coast Guard reports said "her sails were blown to tatters, her deck swept clean, her hull sheathed in ice." The most consistent date of her sinking is November 23, 1912.

A great many details of the Rouse Simmons *tragedy are still shrouded in mystery. The number of crewmen aboard her when she went down varies with different sources from 12 to 17. Reports of a drifting bottle found with a message from the Captain inside were first confirmed, then denied, then confirmed again. Even the exact route of her crossing has never been fully established.*

As late as November 29, 1929, fishermen near Two Rivers were still reporting Christmas trees from the sunken ship entangled in their fishing nets.

According to most of the reliable sources, the list of the crew read "Captain Nelson and wife," Captain Herman Schuenemann, Alex Minogue, Frank Sabata, George Watson, Ray Davis, Conrad Griffin, George Quinn, Edward Murphy, John Morwauski, Stump Morris, Greely Peterson, Frank Fall, Edward Hogan and Philip Bauswein.

Any further information, said Charrney, will be appreciated.

The Sheboygan Press
Sheboygan, WI
December 24, 1960

storms, and so was his schooner, built in 1868. Soldiers die only in the last of their battles; ships and sailors are drowned only in the last of tempests. But ships and men grow old, and men and ships in growing old grow vulnerable."

The *Rouse Simmons*, unarguably, had become vulnerable in the later years of its life. Although the vessel had once been a grand ship, decades had passed since it had seen its prime. By 1912, the *Rouse Simmons* was rickety and ramshackled, and was one of the last vessels still afloat from the Golden Age of Great Lakes sailing when majestic schooners, with their sails raised high, filled harbors. It was a sight to behold as never before or since.

There certainly is a nostalgic element to the Christmas Tree Ship story – a remembering of a time long past when the beautiful, canvassed sailing ships were the principle means of transportation on the Great Lakes.

The *Chicago Tribune* summarized the nostalgia connected to the old

Rouse Simmons in an article published by the newspaper on December 8, 1977. It read: "In an age when the Yuletide season begins earlier and more frenetically each year, it is refreshing to remember the *Rouse Simmons* and the legend she inspired…Aside from the romance of the legend, the *Simmons* is a symbol of a more peaceful, innocent time before World War I when the horse and the sailing vessel gave their slow, gentle imprint to the tempo of life…Crowds came aboard to pick over the trees. The sounds of excitement and laughter mingled with the clop-clop of horses across the bridge and the pleasant smell of evergreens. The *Simmons* and her predecessors were left over from the heyday of lumbering when forests of white pine and spruce were cut out of Michigan and Wisconsin….It was a pleasant way to end the shipping season – surrounded by happy families a short ride from the Schuenemann home…It was the children that made it so joyous. They loved the Christmas Tree Ship as much as the Schuenemanns loved having them aboard. Yes, it was a good end for a hard summer on the lake."

The article continued: "Despite the warm glow of Yuletide feelings, life for the Schuenemann brothers was for the most part hard work and danger. But hard work and danger were things sailors had been used to since they first put to sea. Besides, it was their life. The brothers would buy old lumber schooners for a song and wring the last bit of life out of them, nosing into every port along the lake, seeking cargo. It was a chancy business made even chancier by the tempestuous nature of the lake, where storms were universally feared. No one knew better than Herman Schuenemann how dangerous late-season voyages on Lake Michigan could be…Had the *Rouse Simmons* been anything other than the Christmas Tree Ship, her loss probably would never have been remembered. Half a dozen other ships were missing after the same storm that claimed the *Simmons*, and none of their names are

> *"In 1910 Captain Schuenemann acquired an interest in the schooner* Rouse Simmons, *the most famous of Chicago's Christmas tree ships. Some have written that Herman owned the entire vessel, but that is not correct. He owned only a one-eighth interest. Captain Charles C. Nelson, of Chicago, owned an eighth and Mannes J. Bonner, of St. James (Beaver Island), Lake Michigan, owned the remaining three quarters of the ship."*
>
> Sea Classics
> January 1977, Vol. 10 No. 1
> Fred Hollister

Last known photograph of the *Rouse Simmons*.
This photo was taken by Lighthouse Keeper William P. Larson
of Waukegan, Illinois, while the vessel was entering the Waukegan port in
the autumn of 1912 with a load of lumber on its deck.
(Courtesy of the Milwaukee Public Library/Wisconsin Marine Historical Society)

"Although Schuenemann was in the prime of his life, the Rouse Simmons *had begun to show her age by late autumn of 1912 when she called at Thompson, Michigan, to be loaded with Christmas trees. The canvas was old and patched, the brightwork no longer glistened, the paint was most notable by its absence than its presence. But she was sturdy enough, felt Schuenemann, and he enlisted Milwaukee sailing master Charles Nelson as a partner in this Yuletide voyage."*

A Most Superior Land
Volume IV of the *Michigan Heritage Series*
Dated 1983
Published by Two Peninsula Press
Michigan Natural Resources Magazine

remembered. But because the *Simmons* was something special to the people of Chicago, the Christmas Tree Ship earned her place in legend and history…For the sentimental, there is the thought that men were willing to risk – and lose – their lives to make Christmas brighter. To historians, the Christmas Tree Ship symbolizes the end of an era – the death of commercial sailing on the Great Lakes. World War I was about to begin, and steam alone could keep pace with the demands of a nation preparing for war…Perhaps it was best that Captain Schuenemann, his crew, and the *Rouse Simmons* died the way they did. In a few short years the world would know that there are worse ways for men and ships to die."

The world was changing. Although schooners had dominated the waters for a time, that time had passed. By 1912 few remained, and those that did were looked upon as insignificant ships hauling insignificant cargos.

One of the cargos hauled by the last schooners afloat on the waters were Christmas trees - a cargo that couldn't be damaged if hauled in a leaking, old vessel. Moreover, it was believed the trees would literally help keep the ship afloat with their buoyancy.

Nearly one month after the *Simmons* was taken to the bottom of the lake, there were still those who believed that the ship might possibly be afloat somewhere. The *Manistique Pioneer-Tribune*, Manistique, Michigan, reported on December 20, 1912: "Owing to the nature of the cargo, the boat would not sink, and the government fears that members of the crew may still be aboard the vessel and that the wreck has drifted among islands that have no communication with the main land."

The boat should not have sunk, according to some.

Not only were Christmas trees buoyant, so was lumber as a whole, so schooners hauling any type of lumber were often overloaded. Professor Theodore J. Karamanski, in his book *Schooner Passage*, wrote: "The short hauls and buoyant cargos of the lumber trade encouraged captains to overload vessels and delay long-term maintenance."

There were concerns expressed regarding the condition of the *Rouse Simmons* when it set sail in 1912. The *Chicago American* published the following headline on December 4, 1912: "Santa Claus Schooner, Laden With Christmas Trees, Goes Down in Lake". The article beneath read: "'The *Rouse Simmons* was full of soft planks and in bad condition,' said DeWitt Cregler, a yachtsman, familiar with the famous, old schooner. 'If heavily

Final Voyage of the *Rouse Simmons*

August Schuenemann and his younger brother Herman began hauling Christmas trees from northern Michigan and Wisconsin to Chicago for the holidays in 1884. It was a most profitable venture for the Schuenemann brothers. This voyage marked the end of the shipping season because of the stormy nature of the Great Lakes. Insurance on marine bottoms ran out at noon on the last day of November, and the Coast Guard gathered up buoys and aids to navigation for the winter. November storms made travel on the Lakes hazardous...

In the latter part of September or early October, Captain Schuenemann would sail to Thompson, Michigan, and pick up a load of sapling pine and balsam trees from nearby Manistique. With a Christmas tree lashed to the mast, he would set sail for Chicago where families would go down to the dock and pick up a Christmas tree. For a quarter or fifty cents, a family could pick the tree of their choice from the deck of the Simmons.

The Christmas tree venture was one in which the entire Schuenemann family participated. Schuenemann's wife and daughters would make Christmas wreaths from the bales of lycopodeum that were also part of the Christmas cargo. Nothing was wasted or went unsold.

By the 1890's, the [Christmas tree] trip was so profitable that Captain Schuenemann and his partner, Captain Nelson, were operating as many as three different schooners each season.

November 1912 was a violent month for the Great Lakes. But on the 22nd of November, Captain Schuenemann sailed for Chicago in time to arrive there by Thanksgiving, when he would get the best press notice. Schuenemann made a difficult decision. The Simmons *would make only one Christmas tree run this year. After filling the hold of his ship to capacity, he deckloaded his ship with even more trees.*

Sea History
Winter 1987-88
Joseph A. Nowak, Jr.

"The Rouse Simmons *became a symbol of a vanishing era."*

State Journal-Register
December 20, 1987

The period between the close of the Civil War and the 1870's and early 1880's saw the greatest activity in the many shipyards located on both shores of Lake Michigan and the other Great Lakes as well. Nearly every port had one or more shipyards and the greater part of the old fleet of wind jammers slid down the ways during those years.

In 1868 the three-masted schooner Rouse Simmons *joined the rapidly growing fleet when she was launched at Milwaukee...*

During her later years she had several bad experiences, having been badly battered when caught at Torch Lake pier on Big Traverse Bay in a strong northwester while being loaded with lumber. Many of those piers jutted out into the lake and when a vessel without motor power was caught there by wind off the lake, it could not get away and many of the old sailing ships were lost in that way.

The Simmons *was raised and repaired, but a few years later was completely dismantled together with several other schooners in an easterly gale. Refitted with new spars and rigging, she again took her place in the lumber trade. But misfortune continued to follow the old vessel and in the early fall of 1909 she was involved in a collision with the schooner* Minnie Mueller *of Racine, both ships sustaining considerable damage to their head gear.*

The Sheboygan Press
Sheboygan, WI
December 8, 1941
John Kane

laden when she met a hard blow, probably every seam opened. She probably was taking water when sighted off Kewaunee, Wisconsin.'"

It was only one man's opinion, but more opinions followed. The very next day, on December 5, 1912, the *Chicago American* published an interview they had conducted with one of the crew members who had been aboard the *Simmons*. The article read: "Hogan Hoganson, a member of the crew of the lost vessel, who left the ship in fear because of her weakened condition, today told a story that added to the fears for the missing. He arrived in Chicago by land from Manistique, Michigan... Hoganson, who left the ship when it put in at a northern Michigan port, fearing the perils of a storm in a ship which even the rats had deserted, was at his home, 413 Milwaukee Avenue, Chicago, today. Hoganson made two significant charges: First, that the ship carried no lifeboats. Second, that the vessel was improperly loaded and overloaded. Miss Elsie Schuenemann, daughter of the owner of the boat, denied today that the craft did not carry lifeboats. 'We haven't given up hope,' she said. 'The *Rouse Simmons* was a brave old boat and she may have weathered out the storm. We won't give up yet.'"

The *Chicago Inter Ocean* also reported on December 5, 1912: "The *Simmons* was built in 1868 in Milwaukee and has been in the lumber traffic since. Her condition was said yesterday to be such that insurance could not be obtained other than such class insurance as would protect the owner of the cargo."

Even as the calendar turned from 1912 to 1913, discussions continued as to what led to the demise of the *Simmons*. Opinions, as one would expect, varied. Some believed the vessel was not safe, while others thought the tough, old ship should have been able to handle the voyage without difficulty.

The loss of the *Simmons* resulted in an increased discussion of safety observances relative to distress flags, lifeboats and maintenance.

The *Kewaunee Enterprise*, Kewaunee, Wisconsin, published the following on January 10, 1913: "A movement among vessel owners and the shipmasters for the enactment by Congress this winter of amendments governing the inspection and certification of lake vessels which shall pass under jurisdiction of the steamboat inspectors the barges which are now exempt. The purpose is to include the barges in the boats which must be inspected and must receive from the federal authorities certificates permitting these vessels to run. Barges are now exempted because they do not fall within the law which provides only for inspection of vessels which exceed 700 tons in size."

OLD SHIP IS LUCKY
Grand Haven
Daily Tribune
Grand Haven, MI
December 3, 1912

The old schooner *Rouse Simmons*, for which fears were felt, is the same craft which a few years ago was picked up in mid-lake one late fall day in a badly waterlogged condition by the carferry *Grand Haven*. The ferry was bound from Grand Haven to Milwaukee in a heavy sea when a craft was sighted ahead with a distress signal flying from her lone spar. She was low in the water and seemed in instant danger of sinking. Huddled together on the deckhouse, just out of reach of the sea, and drenched with the flying spray, was the crew of the ship.

Recognizing their plight, Captain Lyman, who then commanded the *Grand Haven*, headed the big ship directly for the waterlogged craft. After several attempts he succeeded in getting a line to the schooner and towing her into Milwaukee.

CRAFT WAS
UNSEAWORTHY
Chicago Daily Tribune
Chicago, IL
December 5, 1912

There were repeated rumors along the river front that the *Rouse Simmons* was unseaworthy...

No definite information as to the craft's condition was obtainable yesterday.

It was said, however, it had made similar voyages for years and had shown itself tough enough to withstand the worst of the fall storms. It was built in 1868.

Divers to the *Simmons* shipwreck site at the bottom of Lake Michigan are amazed at the "remarkable" condition the vessel is in. They will tell you that the sturdiness of the ship is still evident after nearly a hundred years underwater – even though the ship withstood more than its fair share of mishaps before it went missing in 1912. Once, in 1904, the vessel completely sank, and was later raised and refitted for sailing. (The ship's owner at that time felt the *Simmons* was worth the costs involved in raising it even though by this time the ship was already thirty-six years old.)

Jim Brotz, a diver who has been to the *Simmons* site nearly sixty times in the past twenty years is impressed with the "beautiful, beautiful schooner" – as are others. "To go through what this ship did," said Mr. Brotz, "and still be in the condition the vessel is in, is really something."

The *Simmons* had, indeed, "lived beyond her time and was very old for a wooden schooner" when tragedy took her, according to Frederick Stonehouse. His book, *Went Missing II*, tells that the ship was a well-found vessel and had survived the storm that sank the *S. Thal* – a blow that had de-masted every schooner on the lake, except the *Simmons*.

The *Simmons'* days were proud, yet numbered.

Captain August Schuenemann met his fate while hauling a cargo of Christmas trees on the *S. Thal*, and Captain Herman would meet his fate with the *Simmons*.

Yet the time-honored tradition the Captains represented lived on long after they did – especially in the hearts and minds of those who waited at the docks in Chicago for the sight of sails and the smell of pine come November.

So, too, does the memory of the *Rouse Simmons* live on as one of "the most storied shipwrecks in Lake Michigan history."

"The tale is one of many that, no matter how many times they are told, and how many victims the icy, stormy waters may claim, inspire fear, fascination and sadness in the hearts of their listeners. This is especially true of those who live along the Great Lakes shores and have seen them at their worst."

Evening News
December 23-25, 1995
Deidre S. Tomaszewski

"Historians have viewed the Rouse Simmons *as a symbol. She was neither the first nor the last sailing vessel on Lake Michigan, but her 44-year career spanned parts of two eras: the heyday of lake schooners and the period of decline. These valiant little ships had carried the commerce of the Great Lakes for more than half a century, but a changing world retired them into obsolescence. The familiar sight of The Christmas Tree Ship in the Chicago harbor, with fir trees lashed to her mast, has passed into history, but the legend of the* Rouse Simmons *will be retold each year during the Christmas season."*

Wisconsin's Underwater Heritage
(A publication of:
Wisconsin Underwater
Archeology Assn.)
December 1998, Vol. 8 No. 4
Phil Sander

Photo of Captain Sogge, commander of initial rescue attempts for the *Rouse Simmons*. (Courtesy of the Rogers Street Fishing Village Museum, Two Rivers, WI)

Chapter Four

The Storm of 1912

"*A great storm had just swept across the top of Lake Michigan and another one was brewing when the* Simmons *headed out of Manistique, MI, on the three-hundred-mile haul to Chicago. The wind screamed louder with every gust, and ice had begun to form on her rigging, but the gallant schooner started down below because Santa Claus could not wait.*"

Great Lakes Shipwrecks & Survivals
William Ratigan
Copyright 1960

The Storm of 1912

The year was 1912. The month, November. Autumn had fallen asleep in Northern Michigan, and Winter was rising. It would rise first on land, and then move to the waters, freezing them solid.

There was still time for Captain Herman Schuenemann to make his last sail of the season, but he needed to hurry if he didn't want to meet Old Man Winter, face-to-face, in the worst possible place – on the open lake.

A storm was poised and ready to strike. Ominous clouds hung low on the horizon. Yet Captain Schuenemann believed that if he hurried, he could get his ship ahead of the storm.

On November 22, 1912, he gave the order to sail. It was a fatal decision, and the lives of everyone on board were hinged to it.

Old Man Winter was challenging Captain Schuenemann to a race down the lake. One of them would reach Chicago by the following day, and the other not at all.

Captain Schuenemann knew the dangers of sailing in November - the most treacherous month of the year - as well as anyone could have. After all, he had been delivering his trees across these stormy waters for nearly a quarter of a century by this time. Most captains refused to sail in this feared month, and saw to it that their vessels were off the Great Lakes by the end of October. However, this was not an option a Christmas tree merchant had the luxury of exercising.

Late afternoon on November 22, 1912, the aging schooner *Rouse Simmons*, fully loaded with evergreens, departed Thompson, Michigan, for its final voyage. The barometer was falling and the winds were rising - a deadly combination. If Captain Schuenemann had any question about his ability to navigate his vessel safely to Chicago, his question would be answered before the sun set on a single day more.

The "Big Storm" of 1912 hit in full force sometime during the late evening hours of November 22nd and the very early morning hours of November 23, 1912. Temperatures plummeted. Heavy rains turned to swirling snow. Winds intensified. The heartbeat of the storm pounded faster and louder.

It wasn't long before the hypnotic rhythm of the waves was broken, and the convulsing waters were heaving like an earthquake. Great walls of water

Weather Forecast

The official forecast which the National Weather Service issued that Friday [November 22, 1912] gave no particular cause for alarm.

"Washington, D.C., November 22, 1912 – The weather forecast is as follows:

For Wisconsin: Local rains or snow Saturday; colder at night; variable winds becoming northwest and brisk; Sunday fair.

For Upper Michigan: Local snow or rains Saturday, variable winds, becoming northwest and west and brisk; Sunday fair."

This would not be the kind of weather which a recreational yachtsman would relish, but it was hardly cause to stop the merchantmen.

Some, benefiting from the perfect vision that comes with hindsight, would look back and say they had seen it coming. But none could have known that on the upper lakes the hard-fisted blow of winter's first punishing gale was about to be felt.

As Friday night approached, the wind built ominously out of the northwest over the upper peninsula of Michigan and Lakes Superior and Michigan. Temperatures dropped slowly from a "balmy" forty degree range. Rain began to fall.

When Saturday morning dawned, rain had turned to wet snow…

Captains around the Lakes were forced to make judgment calls. In the fall, when unexpected weather was the norm on the Great Lakes, most operated under a policy of sail when you can, and run for shelter when you must.

Anchor News
Publication of the Wisconsin Maritime Museum
January/February 1990
Fred Neuschel

"The open lake could become an unwelcoming host as mountainous waves tried to crush hapless vessels under their watery masses. Freezing temperatures would sheet rigging, sails, and spars with heavy coats of ice. The accumulating weight of ice on the ship could ominously drag her deeper into the water, changing the center of gravity and making her prone to a sudden roll, from which she would never recover. Running any cargo on the old schooners was especially dangerous in the late season."

Went Missing II
Frederick Stonehouse
Copyright 1984

"The holiday season wasn't always a time of cheer for Chicago families. In the late 1800's and early 1900's, the arduous journey attempted each year by a fleet of Christmas tree ships made Santa's trip seem like a breeze. Unlike Santa's mythical journey, if the breeze turned into a blizzard real lives were lost."

Chicago Tribune
Chicago, IL
December 21, 1990
Steve Dale

"October and November account for an inordinate number of the shipwrecks on Lake Michigan. Captains who sailed in the stormy season knew they might come back rich – or not at all. They were a unique breed, these captains, entrepreneurs who had come up the hard way, rising from seaman to skipper."

Wisconsin Trails
Nov/Dec 2003
Benjamin J. Shelak

"It was generally agreed that Schuenemann was an experienced, capable skipper. He'd survived too many storms to be otherwise. But there was also general agreement that he had shown bad judgment by setting sail that November day."

A Most Superior Land
Volume IV of the Michigan Heritage Series
Dated 1983
Published by Two Peninsula Press
Michigan Natural Resources Magazine

were being thrown at the *Simmons*. The storm seemed to be closing in on Captain Schuenemann from every direction of the compass, and he and his crew were in serious trouble.

Captain Schuenemann was no stranger to bad weather. He had fought his way through more than one severe storm in his day. According to the *Milwaukee Journal* of December 8, 1992, Schuenemann was "an experienced sailor who had come through a fierce season of gales unscathed" during one particularly rough autumn "when dozens of other vessels had been destroyed."

Captain Schuenemann knew the risks of being in the middle of the lake when the mood of the waters turned ugly. But did he know he would soon suffer the same fate as the brother he once loved?

Captain August Schuenemann, Captain Herman's oldest brother, had lost both his ship and his life during a violent November storm in 1898, fourteen years earlier. Ironically, August, too, was hauling a load of Christmas trees to Chicago when his ship, the *S. Thal*, went down just north of the city on November 9, 1898. Everyone on board perished.

The January 1935 issue of *The Chicagoan* included an article regarding the tragedy of the *S. Thal*. It was written by an eyewitness journalist who was on the scene shortly after the *S. Thal* was lost. The journalist referred to the sinking as "the pitiful tale of a little schooner laden with Christmas trees from the north woods, foundering with all on board when fairly within sight of its holiday market." The article continued: "The lake gave up its dead, tardily, but for many days the tragedy of the skipper and his little ship left its impress upon the Chicago public. Chests, doors, pieces of rail,

"*Capt. Schuenemann was a skilled seaman and he might yet have saved his ship and completed his voyage. But the pattern of storm fronts on the Great Lakes decreed a sudden wind shift to the east accompanied by snow and a lethal drop in temperature. The drenched ship, her decks, her sails, her rigging, were soon covered with a slippery sheen. Ice — the dread of every Great Lakes seaman — relentlessly thickened its suffocating mantle with every roll and passing hour. One roll too far and top heavy frozen masts would drag her to the bottom.*"

Great Lakes Travel & Living
December 1986
Marjorie Cahn Brazer

How severe was the storm that sunk the *Rouse Simmons*?

FIERCE STORM IN UPPER PENINSULA – Report from Menominee, MI, November 23, 1912 (As recorded in the *Saginaw Courier Herald*, Saginaw, MI, November 26, 1912) - "The worst snow storm this city has experienced at this time of year in many seasons is raging here tonight, and as a result, communication with the outside world is practically cut off. Telegraph and telephone wires are down… Nearly eight inches of snow has fallen. The storm is accompanied by a strong northwest wind. Great fear is felt for lake boats."

NEVER SAW WAVES LARGER (*The Sheboygan Press*, Sheboygan, WI, November 25, 1912) - "Saturday night's storm [November 23] was one of the worst on Lake Michigan in three years, according to reports made by marine men, and caused considerable damage at various ports. Large boats in the local harbor parted their mooring lines and several small fishing crafts were tossed about like corks. Captain Dionne of the Life Saving Station says that he never saw waves larger at the pier entrance than they were yesterday morning. At times the water splashed as high as forty feet onto the pier. A number of large steamers went by and as they sunk into the trough only the masts and funnel could be seen."

LAKE LASHED TO FURY (*Manitowoc Daily Herald*, Manitowoc, WI, November 25, 1912) - "The lake was lashed into fury by the high wind of Friday night and all Saturday, and till Sunday afternoon the vessels had a hard time of it [November 22-24]."

TERRIFIC GALE (*The Sheboygan Press*, Sheboygan, WI, November 25, 1912) - "The schooner, *City of Grand Haven*, owned by Captain Martin Kjelson, 2212 South Eighth Street, Sheboygan, WI, was caught out in the terrific gale which blew over Lake Michigan yesterday and was disabled off Sturgeon Bay, WI, having its jibboom, jibs, and foresail carried away, but was fortunate enough to make Sturgeon Bay harbor, although leaking badly. This trip is probably the worst ever experienced by Captain Kjelson and crew."

ONE OF THE SEVEREST STORMS OF RECENT YEARS (*The Racine Daily Times,* Racine, WI, November 25, 1912) - "Blowing at the rate of sixty miles an hour, a severe gale struck Racine, WI, Saturday evening [November 23] and continued without abating until this morning, doing great damage along the lake shore. The storm region extended all along both shores of Lake Michigan… Captain Lofesberg of the Life Saving Station said this morning that the storm was the worst experienced in this section for the last two years. The high waves kicked up by the wind broke completely over the lighthouse and the reef

broken timbers showing rot where bolts had gone through, and the sternpiece bearing 'S. Thal of Sturgeon Bay,' with the young evergreens ashore, indicated the utter breaking up of the craft."

The deadly storm of 1898 in which Captain August lost his life was, in

at times. Sweeping onto the land on the north beach, the waves carried away a large quantity of lumber which had been stored by the Greiling Construction Company near the lighthouse and scattered it along the lake shore. The waves also carried away part of the dirt which had been placed on the beach at the Sixth Street Park for 'filling up' purposes. Probably the worst damage in this section done by the storm was at North Point, where the pier built by John O'Loughlin was almost completely wrecked. Owing to the rocky bottom at this point, piles could not be driven into the lake bottom and it was necessary to build the large pier of caissons. The heavy battering of the waves caused these caissons to give way and they were carried onto the beach and greatly damaged. Hundreds of people were gathered at the lakefront here all day watching the effect of the storm."

IN PORT AFTER THRILLING TRIP – Report from Muskegon, MI, November 26, 1912 (As recorded in the *Saginaw Courier Herald*, Saginaw, MI, November 28, 1912) - "After battling for three days and nights against a sea that threatened at any time to swamp their small craft, Captain Hans Hermanson and the crew of the tug *Markham*, towing the barge *Lyman M. Davis*, reached this harbor this morning… Captain Hans Hermanson says it was the worst storm he has experienced in twenty years of service on the Great Lakes and that for the first time in his life he put on a life preserver."

STORM STRUCK (*Ludington Chronicle*, Ludington, MI, November 27, 1912) - "The storm that struck this shore Saturday afternoon [November 23] proved one of the nastiest on the lake that boatmen have experienced in a long time. It came up almost without warning and lashed the lake into fury before small crafts had time to get to safe harbor."

ONE OF THE WORST STORMS EXPERIENCED (*Sturgeon Bay Advocate*, Sturgeon Bay, WI, November 28, 1912) - "A storm of unusual violence swept over this region Saturday [November 23], accompanied by rain and snow. It continued throughout the night and the following day with unabated fury. Vessels were driven to shelter in friendly harbors, this port being no exception… the norther on Saturday and Sunday caused an abnormal rise of the water in this bay… one of the worst storms experienced on Green Bay in years. The body of water was simply a white foam."

EYE-WITNESS TESTIMONY OF CAPTAIN AUGUST HANSEN REGARDING THE WEATHER CONDITIONS WHEN THE *ROUSE SIMMONS* LEFT UPPER MICHIGAN (*The Sheboygan Press*, Sheboygan, WI, December 19, 1912) - "The *Rouse Simmons* beat out on Friday [November 22]. There was a heavy head sea running in. There was sudden nasty weather, about the most sudden I remember."

many respects, as severe as the storm of 1912 that claimed the life of August's younger brother, Herman. According to *The Chicagoan*, the 1898 storm was "general over the Great Lakes, many ships being reported in distress. Along Lake Shore Drive [in Chicago], the wind was 'the wildest in several years,' and retaining walls suffered. The water supply was 'unfit for drinking

FIRST STORM DOWNS WIRES
Old Winter Comes into Menominee in a Snowy, Blustering Fashion
The Menominee Herald Leader
Menominee, MI
November 23, 1912

Predictions to the contrary notwithstanding, Old Winter in his usual garb of white, wet snow of slushy propensities, blew into Menominee, MI, shortly after midnight this morning.

When the storm first began it was rain, but the accompanying cold weather converted it into snow in a brief time. The snowfall continued throughout the day, growing heavier toward evening.

The wind, which approached the proportions of a gale at certain times, made the first wintry day in Menominee a genuine one. The telegraph and telephone companies experienced some wire trouble...

WIND BLEW WIRES DOWN
The Menominee Herald Leader
Menominee, MI
November 25, 1912

Friday night's storm [November 22] caused much trouble on telephone, light, and telegraph wires on Grand Avenue at the Chicago & Northwestern crossing. Snow lay heavily on the wires and with the fierce north winds blowing caused about fifteen city wires to fall across Grand Avenue and also played havoc with the Chicago & Northwestern telegraph lines. The freight trains were held up from three to four hours south of Oconto on account of wire troubles.

"Danger was always a part of the voyage, because if the winter storms did catch up with them, the blowing ice and snow could swiftly turn the ship and her soft absorbent cargo into a huge top-heavy iceberg."

Sheboygan Press
Sheboygan, WI
November 22, 1974
Bob Joslyn

purposes,' rain having raised the river level, and sewage was flowing out."

Captain Herman Schuenemann was not aboard his brother's vessel when it went down in 1898 because he was needed at home. Although his life had been spared the tragedy of November 1898, there were more Novembers coming.

"Where does the love of God go when the gales of November blow?" asked old sailors. It was a question mariners on the Great Lakes had been asking for as long as anyone could remember. The Schuenemann Brothers probably heard the words countless times during their own lives, and may have asked the question themselves.

The losses suffered on the Great Lakes in the 1800's and early 1900's during November were hard to swallow. It was a month that claimed more lives than its fair share, despite the fact that there were so few ships left on the open waters.

The Great Lakes are often referred to as "The 8th Sea" or the "Inland Sea" because their characteristics are closer to those of the Seven Seas than they are to a lake. Their sheer size and depths could subject early sailors to many dangers. However, with the advance of modern technology – especially radar devices used to predict weather - losses were greatly minimized. Prior to this, though, the "closest thing these captains had to radar was dead reckoning – navigating with their eyes." (According to Barton Updike, Director of the Chicago Maritime Museum, as quoted in the *Chicago Tribune*, December 21, 1990.)

During the heyday of schooners, November's waters could at times be violent, and at times be as smooth as glass – luring sailors from the shore, leading them to believe all was well. But this could be deceiving, and sailors knew it. Storms of unusual violence could literally strike at any time, and without warning.

Because of this, worry was ever present during these deadly days. Wives worried. Children worried. Captain Schuenemann's own daughters made their father promise he would send them word of his safe arrival when he reached ports while sailing during the autumn months.

According to an article published in the *Sturgeon Bay Advocate* on October 12, 1911, it was reported: "Captain Schuenemann said that Friday was the birthday anniversary of his twin daughters – Misses Pearl and Hazel – and as they had informed their sire that they would only celebrate the event if they knew that he and his ship had reached some port in safety, which

Great Lakes Weather

The men and women who work the Great Lakes do so with the knowledge that disaster can strike with little warning. Weather, fire, collisions, and other accidents have contributed to the destruction of hundreds of strong and proud boats. Nature's angry gales and foaming water have destroyed many of the vessels that have braved these waters.

The Great Lakes are a vast theater in which the weather, strong currents, collisions, and circumstance have played a role in the destruction of countless vessels.

Weather-related events have been the cause of the most widespread destruction on the Lakes. The Lakes are constantly battered by storm action, but there are a few storms that stand out in history due to their wide-ranging impact, the large loss of shipping and crews, and extensive inland damage.

Any time of the year, the waters of the Great Lakes can be whipped to a savage fury. As winds pick up, rolling swells become pronounced. If the wind continues to strengthen, the waves become peaked; a phenomenon referred to as "Christmas trees," and most visible on the horizon. As conditions worsen, the peaks may actually be blown from the waves and visibility reduced to zero by the blinding spray.

The pattern of seasonal changes in the Great Lakes Basin has its origins in two air masses that sweep across the region. From the south, warm, humid air pushes up from the Gulf of Mexico, while at the same time cold, dry air sweeps down from the Arctic.

During the lazy days of summer, the cooler air blowing in from the Canadian northwest influences the weather in the northern lakes. As this occurs, warm air arriving from the Gulf of Mexico affects the southern reaches of the Great Lakes. This peaceful co-existence of air masses allows for calm water and pleasant days.

By fall, rapid movement of air masses from both north and south vie for dominance. This clash of fronts produces high winds and severe weather.

In winter, the lakes are influenced by three air masses. These weather features are the occasional warm front blowing up from the Gulf of Mexico, the freezing tendrils of

information they made him promise to furnish, the gallant skipper on his arrival here sent a wire to his family that he was O.K., and to let joy in the household be unconfined."

Worry was a constant companion, and understandably so. The dangers of shipping were well understood. Whole families living along shorelines were involved in trades linked to the waters. Shipping was the backbone of life during this time, and, thus, every father, husband or son who plied the waters could be the next victim claimed. For this reason, the marine community was as close knit as any other. Persons living along the shores of the Great Lakes looked at any loss as everyone's loss, a warning of the dangers, a reminder of life's fragileness.

Arctic air reaching their long fingers south, and an additional air mass, known as an Alberta Clipper, driven in from Canada's Pacific coast.

The Arctic air, known as an "Arctic blast" by those living in the Great Lakes region, arrives over the lakes as a dry air mass. Upon reaching water, this air picks up moisture. As a consequence, the leeward shores of the lakes may receive relatively little precipitation, while the windward sides may be buried under a heavy layer of snow. This phenomenon is referred to by meteorologists as "lake effect snow."

Spring, like fall in the Great Lakes, is a time of overcast days and severe thunderstorms. As in autumn, this is brought about by rapidly contending air masses. The warm Gulf air is the hammer to the Arctic's anvil. In between are the lakes, which can be subjected to fierce beatings as these forces converge.

As recently as the early twentieth century, some captains would sail in the treacherous months in hopes of getting their cargo to market and reaping a profit. This was certainly the case with the *Rouse Simmons*, famous as the "Christmas Tree Ship," which sank off Sheboygan, WI, with a load of fir trees in November 1912. Even today, ice-jammed harbors and severe weather force a mariner to pay heed to the seasonal variability in weather.

Such weather can produce waves of 30 feet or more. One can easily imagine the thoughts and fears of the early sailors as their schooners or tugs slipped into a deep trough while mountains of rolling water loomed off port and starboard. Early sailors and passengers could not rely on radar, satellite imagery, or marine weather forecasts. Theirs was an uncertain world. It was, and still is, common for vessels to leave port during the morning hours and in fine weather, only to be subjected to gale-force winds by mid-afternoon. Even with today's technological advances, it is possible for a vessel to succumb to the fury of a lake storm.

Gradually, with the advent of shipbuilding technology and improved weather forecasting techniques, wrecks have declined in number.

Shipwrecks of Lake Michigan
Benjamin J. Shelak
Copyright 2003

On November 23, 1912, another reminder was on its way. The *Rouse Simmons* was fighting to free itself from the grip of a terrible storm. It was a struggle the doomed ship was destined to lose.

Winds were howling. Gale force gusts hit 60-80 m.p.h. Ice was freezing to beards and brows, numbing sailors to the bone. And towering seas were now climbing aboard the *Simmons*, invading it, penetrating every nook and cranny.

All around the lake, similar battles were being fought by other vessels

> *"It was one of those vicious November storms that periodically rip out of the north to attack the Great Lakes with howling winds and heavy water-laden snow. Sailing craft still reigned supreme, but a skipper would have to be foolhardy, as well as bold, to venture forth on those seas on that blustery night. The captain of the U.S. Life Saving Station in Sheboygan, WI, reported breakers 40 feet high crashing over the sea wall... About thirty miles north of the city, however, one ship was trying to weather the storm – and her time was running out."*
>
> *Sheboygan Press*
> Sheboygan, WI
> November 22, 1974
> Bob Joslyn

trying to stay afloat in the brutal storm. Directly across the lake from the *Simmons*, near Pentwater, Michigan, the ship *Two Brothers* sunk, and its entire crew was drowned.

To the north of the *Simmons'* struggle, the men aboard the *Three Sisters* were taking their final breaths. By the following morning, their ship, too, would succumb to the waters, and three more men would lay dead.

Lake Superior did not escape the fury unleashed on Lake Michigan that dreadful day, nor the crippling effects the storm left in its wake. The passenger ferry, *South Shore*, was taken to Superior's bottom during the same storm of November 22-24, 1912.

On November 25, 1912, the *Muskegon News Chronicle*, Muskegon, Michigan, released the following report concerning the ferociousness of the storm that struck Lake Superior: "Harrowing stories of the fury of the gale which swept the eastern end of Lake Superior Saturday night [November 23] were told this morning by Captain Massay of the steamer *Sullivan*.... 'When we left Duluth,' he said, 'the wind was northeast, but in the worst part of the lake it shifted to northwest. The vessel became almost unmanageable as the sea came from all directions. Several of the hatch covers were carried away and heavy plate glass windows in the pilot house were smashed by mountains of sea.'"

Other reports began to surface almost immediately of damage done and lives lost. Terrifying details made headlines. The *Ludington Chronicle* said the storm was "one of the nastiest on the lake that boatmen have experienced in a long time," and the *Saginaw Courier Herald*, another

Michigan newspaper, reported the storm as "the worst snow storm this city has experienced at this time of year in many seasons." *The Sheboygan Press* in Wisconsin reported the storm to be "one of the worst on Lake Michigan in three years."

Captains also weighed in with comments. Captain Lofesberg of Racine, Wisconsin, was quoted as saying the storm was "the worst experienced in this section for the last two years," while Captain Hans Hermanson said the storm was the worst he experienced in twenty years of service on the Great Lakes. Captain Martin Kjelson from Sheboygan, Wisconsin, reported that he and his crew thought it was probably the worst storm they had *ever* experienced.

Although several ships were lost in the same storm responsible for the *Simmons'* tragedy, only the *Rouse Simmons* went to the bottom without an eye-witness to its demise. Both the *South Shore* shipwreck, as well as the *Two Brothers* shipwreck, occurred within sight of Life Saving Crews. And although the *Three Sisters* tragedy took place before a Life Saving Crew arrived, civilians were gathered on shore, attempting to give whatever aid they could to the drowning sailors.

According to the *Kewaunee Enterprise* of November 29, 1912, the *Three Sisters* "was sighted at daylight" around 7:00 a.m. on Sunday, November 24, 1912, and the shore was "soon alive with men, women and children."

The article continued: "Several boats were procured, but every effort the men made to reach the unfortunate sailors was resisted by the

"Although a more sentimental cargo than most, Christmas trees were a business, just as lumber or wheat, corn or pork. And a romantic Christmas cargo ran as many risks as any other commerce; the perils of navigation are no respecter of holidays. The tradition of lake-carried trees was continued with an occasional heavy price. By the very nature of the trade it had to be transported south in November, close to Christmas, and with freshly-cut trees. And 'gale strewn' November has always been a deadly month for vessels sailing on the Great Lakes."

Sea Classics
Jan. 1977, Vol. 10 No. 1
Fred Hollister

Another vessel met tragedy:

**THREE LIVES LOST
IN GALE
ON GREEN BAY
Men Washed
From Deck
of Waterlogged
Schooner
*Kewaunee Enterprise***
Kewaunee, WI
November 29, 1912

During the terrific gale that swept this section Sunday morning [November 24], the schooner *Three Sisters* was waterlogged in Green Bay at a point off Red River, WI, and her crew consisting of Captain Plum, an unknown, and Andrew Hanson were washed off the deck and drowned. The wrecked schooner was sighted at daylight Sunday morning.

The schooner got into trouble during the blow Saturday night, it is believed, and her plight and that of her crew, was first discovered at about 7 o'clock Sunday morning, when Mr. Gould Potier of Red River, WI, saw two men in the distressed ship wildly calling and waving frantically for help. The bayshore was soon alive with men, women and children, and several boats were procured, but every effort the men made to reach the unfortunate sailors was resisted by the heavy sea, and they were forced to turn back to shore…

All hope to save the unfortunate sailors was about given up, when Rev. Father Melchoir descended to the shore from his church, determined to rescue his drowning fellow men. He procured a small boat and assisted by Gould Potier and George DeBaker, set out for the distressed ship. They successfully negotiated part of the distance, and on seeing them approach, one of the men on the schooner jumped into the water and came slowly drifting toward the yawl on a spar. Suddenly he was seen to disappear beneath the waves and Rev. Melchoir lost no time in diving into the icy waters and rescuing him at the risk of losing his own life. The man was quickly brought to shore, but he never regained consciousness.

Meanwhile Mr. Ed Delfosse succeeded in reaching the wreck where he found two men

heavy sea, and they were forced to turn back to shore. All hope to save the unfortunate sailors was about given up, when Reverend Father Melchoir descended to the shore from his church, determined to rescue his drowning fellow men."

Unfortunately, Reverend Father Melchoir's brave attempts could not bring life to these dying men, despite a remarkable display of heroism and self-sacrifice which included diving into the icy waters toward one of the sailors who had jumped from the ship.

Reverend Melchoir was not alone in his courageous willingness to risk his own life to save another. He was joined by several men on shore who also

Another vessel met tragedy:

men, one dead, and the other so utterly exhausted that his only reply to Mr. Delfosse's entreaties and efforts to revive him was, "Please leave me alone."

Delfosse carried him into his boat and had rowed about half the distance to shore when the yawl capsized throwing both men into the bay. Delfosse escaped with a little ducking, but the sailor was held under the boat, and he was later brought to shore by Delfosse and Mr. Oliver Renier. Medical aid was secured but all efforts to revive the victim proved futile, and he died a few hours later.

FISHERMEN LOSE THEIR LIVES
Grand Haven Daily Tribune
Grand Haven, MI
November 26, 1912

Three fishermen lost their lives at Pentwater, MI, in Saturday's storm [November 23] when the 35-foot gasoline boat *Two Brothers* struck the end of the south pier and sank. According to the report of Keeper Ewald of the Pentwater Life Saving Crew, the ill-fated little craft started for harbor during the gale at 2:30 Saturday afternoon. Just ahead of her was the little fishing boat *Silver Spray,* and the life savers, anticipating an accident, were out and ready to answer any emergency. The *Silver Spray* made the harbor in safety, but when nearing the mouth, the *Two Brothers* was caught by a comber and broached into the jaws of the piers. The next roller hurled her head on the revetment, splitting her from end to end. The battered craft was carried to the top of the crib, but slid off immediately in the back wash and sank at once. During all of the time the three men on board were in the cabin of the little craft, and were not seen at all by the life savers, who hurried to the place where the wrecked craft had disappeared beneath the surface. No trace of the bodies of the men could be found, however, and at last reports none had come ashore.

displayed admirable valor. Each was later nominated for a Carnegie Heroism Medal, as was reported by the *Kewaunee Enterprise* of December 13, 1912. The article stated that these men saw the schooner "pounding to pieces and the sailors helpless." The men then took boats and "in the face of almost certain death endeavored to reach the drowning men. The seas were rolling high, the weather was biting cold, and still these men ventured in open yawls, at the risk of their lives, to extend a helping hand to the drowning sailors. The fact that several lives were lost was not due to a lack of heroism on the part of Reverend Melchoir, George Debaker, Gould Poutier and F. Delfosse."

Testimony of severe weather:

**CRAFT TOSSED
LIKE CORK,
THEN BURIED
IN WATER**
Chicago Daily News
Chicago, IL
December 7, 1912

From the lips of Capt. James Ellingson, whose home is in Milwaukee, and who has sailed the Great Lakes for more than thirty years, came the story of the fight with the raging, wind lashed waters. His trip took nineteen days and he reported ten days overdue.

"It was our last trip of the season, and when we set out for Manistee, MI, for a cargo of lumber, we expected to en-counter little rough weather," began the captain, as he watched his crew of six, among them his two sons, furl the sails. "We made the trip north in five days, loaded the boat with 167,000 feet of lumber, and prepared to depart. That was November 23, 1912.

"A strong wind sprang up that night from the southwest and increased in violence the next day. I would not venture into the teeth of such a gale, and lay at anchor until Thanksgiving Day, when the gale subsided some-what, and I thought I could cross to the west shore. The sails were unfurled and the anchor was lifted. As we pulled out to sea we saw that the water was running high and the voyage would be rough."

**WATER SWEEPS
HER DECK**

"The spray lashed our bow and hurled water high in the air. We faced the gale and a few miles farther we met it when it was at its worst. The boat was tossed about as though it were a cork, the waves pounded heavily against the bow and as we entered a trough the water swept over the deck. The craft rolled and dug her nose deep into the waves. The water was bitter cold and as the temperature was below freezing it froze upon the deck, making trips about the deck hazardous.

"The masts creaked and groaned as they strained with the heavy canvas. It seemed as though they would be torn away. There was no time for the crew to remain in the cabin, and they had to stay on deck while the waves hurled broadsides of water against her bow and sides. The foreboom, holding hundreds of feet of canvas, gave way

The details surrounding the sinking of the *Three Sisters* were well recorded. However, the details surrounding the sinking of The Christmas Tree Ship were virtually non-existent, at least for a while. The ship seemingly vanished into thin air after being sighted briefly by the Kewaunee Life Saving Service late in the afternoon on November 23, 1912. A lookout at the Kewaunee, Wisconsin, station reported seeing a schooner flying distress flags. It was later learned this ship was the *Simmons*.

Several clues emerged in the weeks following the storm to support the theory that the *Simmons* was in dire need of help in its final hours, as

under the strain and snapped. While the other boys worked at the wheel and bow, we – myself and two boys – fastened the pounding boom. To keep the boat from getting too heavy from the water and ice, barrels of salt were poured all along the deck."

sized craft and, imagining the pounding the others got, as one or two are smaller, I consider myself lucky. I am going home to my family now."

CREW STICKS TO TASKS

"The crew stuck nobly to their places and although the boat, which carries 215 tons, quivered under the shocks of the hammering waves, we managed to reach Sturgeon Bay, WI, that night, where we put into the harbor. We did not dare venture out until the weather permitted.

"It was a terrible voyage and I would not have taken it had I known it would be so rough. My boat is a good

Captain Schuenemann and his twin daughters. (Newspaper clipping dated December 5, 1912, from the *Chicago American*)

Master of Lost Christmas Ship and His Orphaned Children

Her Sails Were Torn by the Weight of Ice

In the face of a rising gale that sent every other vessel on the Lakes beating frantically for shelter, the Rouse Simmons *spread her patchwork canvas to the hungry winds and swung on an east southeast track into the surging seas of Lake Michigan...*

If none aboard the Rouse Simmons *were aware of the folly of defying the elements in a badly overloaded and aged schooner, there were others, afloat and ashore, who stared incredulously at the sight and ominously predicted disaster...*

Awe-struck by the sight of the gray-sailed old schooner butting into the rising seas, they shook their heads...each confident that whatever Captain Schuenemann's reputation as a seaman was, this was to be his last trip...

The gale blowing west southwest whistled over Wisconsin, gathered new strength over the tossing wastes of Green Bay and thundered on over Lake Michigan...

Caught now in the stunning force of winds that screeched onward at 60 miles per hour, the schooner heeled far over to port as the storm-taut canvas bent her topmasts like willow wands. Protestingly, her ribs and deadwood groaned as the weight of the seas dropped on her weathered deck planking and tore at her bulwarks. White water covered her port rail almost continuously while the seas boarding her over the bow hammered uncessingly at her lashed deck cargo.

Huddled in the small stern cabin and the lower deck bunks while Captain Schuenemann fought the wheel, the 17 crewmen listened to the wild, discordant shrieking of the gale as it played an agonizing symphony in the time-worn top hamper of the venerable ship.

Above the gurgling rush of the seas they heard the brash strumming of the gale laboring at the big sticks. Wildly, the wind discarded the masts and

indicated by its distress flags. First, bundles of Christmas trees floated ashore. This meant one of two things: Either the relentless pounding of the waves had washed the trees off the deck, or the trees were intentionally thrown off the ship by the crew when the vessel started taking on water from the waves.

The *Milwaukee Sentinel* of December 4, 1912, reported: "It is believed that the captain threw the trees overboard to lighten the vessel."

One week after this statement was published, a bottle was found with a note inside written by Captain Schuenemann. The note, in part, stated:

howled through the maze of shrouds, stays, and lifting blocks converging near the trestle trees. Blocks, stays, wire, rope, and chain, each gave out its own peculiar snarling chant audible above the anvil chorus of the mast hoops, each clanking and chattering a different eerie dirge against the masts and booms...

Below them they heard the tortured moaning of the mizzen mast laboring in her white pine steps. Forward in the hull, the fragrant beds of pine and balsam trees packed solidly from keelson to stringers, deadened the sound of her joints working and whining in a nagging chorus.

Sometime during the night, as some of the men were checking the lashings, a tremendous sea swept over the ship. With a sodden, scraping rush the bundled trees went over the port side taking two seamen and the small boat for good measure.

Freed of some of her burden, the Rouse Simmons *shook her jib stays like a punched drunk fighter...*

Lashed together near the wheel, whose violent thrashings now claimed their combined efforts, were Captain Schuenemann and first mate Nelson...

The seas still swept over the gallant old schooner, but when they rolled onward they left a thin white coating of ice, a coating that thickened with each succeeding sea. By 8 o'clock the Rouse Simmons *was helpless. Her rigging was a rigid formation of ice with her white-sheathed masts jutting up like frosted church spires. Huge knobs of ice grew alarmingly on each tackle block, cleat, lanyard, and chock.*

Held down by the mounting tons of ice that built up on her bobstay chains and martingale rigging, her bow sloughed into the surging green seas with a beaten, almost subservient spirit. The water cascading into her hold through the battered hatch covers fell upon the bundled trees, and soon water and cargo were turned, as one, into ice.

Toledo Blade
Toledo, OH
January 14, 1951
Dwight Boyer

"leaking bad." This statement would support the theory that the trees were thrown overboard by the crew in an urgent effort to lighten the load. The *Simmons* was an old ship. If the sea was pounding on it, there is every reason to suppose it was leaking, as the captain said, sinking it lower into the waters.

But the note also included the sentence, "Sea washed over our deckload Thursday." If this was the case, then the trees on deck may have gone

Lake Michigan and the other Great Lakes have a reputation for devouring ships. And Lake Michigan has taken more than its share.

Why have these tragedies occurred? According to Mark Gumbinger, a student of Great Lakes' shipwrecks, the difference in temperatures between wind and water gives birth to great storms over the lake, especially in October and November when most shipwrecks occur.

"The lake water is 40 or 50 degrees; cold Arctic air masses come down from Canada," he explained. "That creates small water hurricanes over the lake."

Such a combination of wind and waves can blenderize a ship in minutes.

Another factor is the degree of chop on Lake Michigan. Oceans, because they are so large, produce huge, slow-rolling waves. But inland lakes with their smaller acreage are filled with sharp, choppy waves. "They can really batter you," Gumbinger said.

Exclusively Yours
May 1998
Kathleen Winkler

"Forty-four years old in 1912, the Simmons *undoubtedly creaked and yawed under her load. Captain Schuenemann believed the old tub had one more trip in her, but there were those who thought differently when the* Simmons *left Thompson's Landing under a lead-hued sky on November 22, 1912, bound for Chicago. Schuenemann thought he could sail before a lakes gale if he could only put water between his ship and land."*

Great Lakes Boating
December 1990
Bill Keefe

overboard with the waves. Although we cannot know precisely what happened, what can be known for sure is this: The storm was wreaking havoc on the ship.

In addition to trees going overboard, the Schuenemann note further stated a small boat had been "washed over" along with two crew members. If two men, indeed, were washed over, they would have fallen to an almost certain death.

A second note, found approximately six months later on a beach north of the *Simmons'* sinking, seemed to support the idea that one or more of the men aboard the ship may have been lost in raging seas. The note, signed by Captain Charles Nelson, Captain Schuenemann's partner, was dated November 23, 1912. Captain Nelson wrote: "Schooner *Rouse Simmons* ready to go down…all hands lashed to one line." If the accuracy of this letter is relied upon, Captain Nelson tells us an important detail regarding the storm's severity.

"All hands lashed to one line" meant that every man on board was tied to the other men with a rope linked around each sailor's waist. The end of the rope would then have been tied to the ship's mast to prevent the waves from washing crew members overboard. Sailors "lashed" themselves together only in the most severe storms when the danger of someone being washed overboard was close at hand. If two crew members had already been washed off the ship, as indicated by the Schuenemann note, the remaining men were attempting to make sure this didn't happen again.

"God help us," were the words Captain Schuenemann chose to end his note. He was a man of deep faith, and was praying a final, desperate prayer before the end came. Perhaps the others on board were asking God for help also, or perhaps they were simply asking a question that had never been answered: "Where does the love of God go when the gales of November

> *"The crew of the tug* Burger, *which was also battling the gale and towing the schooner* Dutch Boy, *sighted the Christmas tree laden craft. To their astonishment, they saw the* Simmons *head into the open lake while they were doing their utmost to reach port and safety. Evidently Captain Schuenemann wanted to be a safe distance from shore, preferring the open lake to being blown against the land."*
>
> Lore of the Lakes
> Dana Thomas Bowen
> Copyright 1940

How severe was the weather on the Great Lakes during search efforts?

REVENUE CUTTER LOOKS FOR TRACES OF SCHOONER (*Milwaukee Daily News*, Milwaukee, WI, December 5, 1912) - "At 10:30 o'clock this morning the Marconi wireless station in this city picked up a message from Captain Berry of the *Tuscarora* saying the cutter was pursuing the search for the missing [*Rouse Simmons*] under great difficulties. The message reported that the fog over the lake was so dense that a vessel 200 feet distant could not be seen. Captain Berry said, however, that the search would be prosecuted regardless of the weather conditions. Captain Berry said before leaving Milwaukee that if the vessel were still afloat he would find her, and if she had been lost in one of the recent gales, as there is every reason to suppose, he will find wreckage that will establish the fate of the vessel and crew. Vessel men think the *Simmons* was dismasted and dashed to pieces in the gale two weeks ago tomorrow… The actual fate of the *Rouse Simmons* may never be known – beyond that she has been lost. It may prove another mystery of the lakes…"

FOG DELAYS HUNT FOR SHIP (*Chicago American*, Chicago, IL, December 5, 1912) - "The United States revenue cutter *Tuscarora*, fog bound while searching the lake for trace of the lost schooner *Rouse Simmons*, was driven into port at Waukegan, IL, late today to await clearer weather."

HUNT CHRISTMAS SHIP IN STORM (*Chicago American*, Chicago, IL, December 6, 1912) - "Despite the gale which would destroy hope in any landsman, search by the Seaman's Union and the United States revenue cutter *Tuscarora* continued today for the Christmas tree ship *Rouse Simmons*… The gale, one of the highest of the year, did one thing for the searching parties. It blew all the fog off Lake Michigan."

FIFTY MILE GALE STOPS SEARCH FOR THE LOST *ROUSE SIMMONS* - ANXIETY FELT FOR OTHER VESSELS (*Chicago American*, Chicago, IL, December 6, 1912) - "A fifty-mile gale lashing the Great Lakes into a fury of tossing seas today swept away any hope of the rescue of the missing schooner *Rouse Simmons*… Shipping was imperiled by the blustering nor'wester. Anxiety was felt in the port of Chicago for half a score of vessels known to be beating their way through the storm. The wind was rising at break of day. There was prospect of snow, with perhaps lower temperatures. The crest of the storm was to pass Chicago today. Beach patrols on the east coast about Pentwater, MI, were warned to a re-doubled vigilance today in the expectation that the driving gale would cast up more wreckage of the lost *Rouse Simmons*…"

MARINE NEWS (*Milwaukee Daily News*, Milwaukee, WI, December 6, 1912) - "On the lake last night a gale prevailed that made navigation extremely perilous. The wind blew at times at a velocity of sixty miles an hour… The storm on Lake Superior reached the violence of a hurricane."

GALE SINKS ONE SHIP, DRIVES TWO AGROUND AND THREE ARE MISSING (*Chicago American*, Chicago, IL, December 6, 1912) - "The *Rouse Simmons* with all on board was given up as lost, two ships are on the rocks, another has sunk, and three are missing in a fifty mile gale which is sweeping the Great Lakes. The storm today grew in fury, with no promise of abating for many hours. No hope for the *Rouse Simmons*, the old three-masted schooner, known as Chicago's Christmas ship, was held today... The storm made it apparently impossible that she could have remained afloat, even if she had outridden the storms of the previous week."

50 FACE DEATH IN LAKE WRECK - Report from Duluth, MN (As recorded in the *Chicago American*, Chicago, IL, December 6, 1912) - "Terrific winds, the highest in many years, and blinding snow today put the fifty souls on the wrecked steamer *Easton* in peril of death. All efforts to take off the passengers and crew were abandoned during the night as the wind increased in fury. The steamer is on the rocks of Iroquois Reef, thirty miles west of Port Arthur, exposed to the full sweep of the gale."

STORM MAKES PASSAGE OF BIG VESSELS DANGEROUS (*Sault Ste. Marie Evening News*, Sault Ste. Marie, MI, December 6, 1912) - "All last night at Thunder Bay...a stiff northwest gale raised mountainous waves while snow fell heavily. All the way between the Soo and the American head of the lakes are ships of various cargoes making their way through the rough seas. They are mostly coal laden. Vesselmen here today are apprehensive about those of heavy draft. In the fleet are some of the best known craft on the Great Lakes."

BLIZZARD GRIPS THE CITY (*Chicago American*, Chicago, IL, December 6, 1912) - "Hundreds of sailors on ships on Lake Michigan and the other Great Lakes were put in peril today by the most severe windstorm of the year... In Chicago the high wind caused heavy damage. Lives were periled. Many windows were blown in and roofs damaged. A Lincoln Avenue street car came near being wrecked when a fifty-foot sign was blown into the street from a building at Fullerton Avenue. The passengers in panic leaped off the car. The gale will increase in violence during the day, according to the weather observer."

ENTIRE LAKE REGION IS SWEPT BY STORM (*Milwaukee Sentinel*, Milwaukee, WI, December 7, 1912) - "All day Friday there was a lingering ray of hope in local marine circles that good tidings might drift in from the missing schooner, *Rouse Simmons*, and that after all, the boat possibly might have been saved. But up to an early hour Saturday morning, no such tidings had been received. In fact, while there is an absence of direct confirmation of the wrecking of the vessel, all indications denote that there is no longer even a remote possibility that the *Rouse Simmons* was saved..."

OTHER BOATS HAVE TROUBLE (*Chicago Daily Tribune*, Chicago, IL, December 7, 1912) - "The east wind which sprang at night is expected to cause bodies from the *Rouse Simmons* and more wreckage to come ashore. The hope that some of those on board had escaped in the life boat was abandoned following the fierce gale... The lifeboat carried by the *Rouse Simmons* would not carry five men in an ordinary rough sea, according to

(Continued from previous page)

experienced sailors. In case of heavy wind and high seas they thought it not capable of carrying enough men to manage it."

SAILORS HAVE ROUGH EXPERIENCES IN STORM (*Sault Ste. Marie Evening News*, Sault Ste. Marie, MI, December 7, 1912) - "From reports received from members of the crews of boats passing through the locks this morning, the storm on Lake Superior yesterday was the worst this year. The steamer *William S. Mack* which locked down this morning was completely covered with ice, having a coating six inches deep on the weather side and about two inches on the shelter side. The decks were also covered and the boat looked like a huge ice tower. The captain of the *Mack* reported that at times while crossing the lake he did not think that he would be able to make port, so heavy was the wind and sea. The *Mack* was loaded with flaxseed at Fort William, Ontario, and is bound for Erie, PA, to unload. The steamer *Auna C. Minch* had an experience while in the storm yesterday which happens very seldom. While bound for the Soo, the *Minch*, which was bound from Superior, WI, to Buffalo, NY, loaded with flaxseed, was riding the sea fairly well until the steamer reached a place 35 miles above Whitefish Point, MI, where the seas were heavier. One exceptionally large wave struck the pilot house of the boat and crumpled it in as though it were made of paper, throwing Captain Stewart and the wheelsman to the floor."

GREAT LAKES SHIPS BATTERED BY STORM (*Chicago Record-Herald*, Chicago, IL, December 7, 1912) - "Wind and wave set at naught the arts of man on the Great Lakes yesterday in a storm that drove every boat to haven at the imminent risk of wreck and the loss of life. Every craft that could make a harbor limped into safety. Most of those that did not suffered damage… All over the Great Lakes the gale claimed tribute... Ten boats are sheltered behind Whitefish Point, MI, at the Soo. An entire fleet of coal boats is staggering under the heavy seas and in a blinding snowstorm between the Soo and the head of the lakes. A barge sank near Put-in-Bay, OH."

STORM RAGES ON LAKES - SHIPS SEEKING SHELTER (*The Detroit News*, Detroit, MI, December 7, 1912) - "High winds and rough seas were reported over all the Great Lakes excepting Ontario Thursday. On Lake Erie the storm was the worst of the season… Many vessels, after terrific battle with treacherous squalls and heavy seas, seek shelter of harbors… Three steel freighters are torn from their moorings at Buffalo, NY, and damaged to the extent of thousands of dollars. Thirteen vessels which passed Detroit, MI, Thursday bound for Buffalo, NY, have not been heard from."

SCHOONERS WITH SAILS TORN REACH CHICAGO AFTER STORM (*Chicago Daily Tribune*, Chicago, IL, December 9, 1912) - "Ice coated and with masts broken and sails torn, the schooners *George Marsh* and *Hossack* arrived in Chicago yesterday. The captains of both ships reported the roughest voyage in fifteen years. The ships were reported missing in the storm which is supposed to have sunk the *Rouse Simmons*. The *George Marsh* arrived at 3 o'clock. It had been out nineteen days. During the storm Friday morning the foretopsail was carried away and the jibboom was snapped off. Unable to weather the storm, Captain

Herman Olsen was forced to put in at Egg Harbor, WI. During the trip the *Rouse Simmons* was not sighted. The *Hossack* arrived in a partly disabled condition. Captain Peter Peterson said the *Hossack* was caught in the fierce gale Friday morning and the topsail was torn away. The ship could not make headway and was carried for several hours with the storm. After much difficulty it reached Bailey's Harbor, WI. When it was sighted from Chicago yesterday the tug *Waukegan* started out to tow it in to dock. The lake was too rough, and the tug was forced to turn back. After waiting three hours the tug was able to reach the ship and tow it in."

blow?"

Although the bottled notes have been a point of much debate, there is no debate regarding the intensity of the storm that hit November 22-24, 1912. It was remembered as "one of the most terrific storms that ever thrashed Lake Michigan (*Manistique Pioneer-Tribune*, Manistique, MI, April 17, 1924)." Old Man Winter came calling in November of 1912, but instead of knocking, he kicked in the door.

His fury continued throughout the next couple of weeks, bringing additional treacherous weather to the Great Lakes while search efforts were underway for the missing *Rouse Simmons*. Despite diligent search through storm-tossed waters, all hope for the ship was finally abandoned shortly before Christmas of 1912.

The *Rouse Simmons* ended its once proud days in a hard fought battle against wind and wave, but eventually it became powerless against the storm. Finally, the moment of surrender arrived, and the sea prevailed.

> *"The gale of November 23rd proved itself to be the most deadly storm of 1912."*
>
> Anchor News
> Publication of the Wisconsin
> Maritime Museum
> January/February 1990
> Fred Neuschel

Photo of the Kewaunee Life Saving Station in 1911.
(*Courtesy of the Kewaunee County Historical Society*)

Chapter Five

Search & Rescue Efforts

"The story has become a legend based in fact, told and retold by old timers, especially to little ones at the fireside at Christmas. It will undoubtedly be remembered as long as silent winter stars shine down on Lake Michigan and ships continue to brave the waters of the sullen lake."

Great Lakes Sailor
Nov./Dec. 1988
Dorothy Warner Trebilcock

Search & Rescue Efforts

On November 28, 1912, the *Sturgeon Bay Advocate* of Sturgeon Bay, Wisconsin, reported the following: "The schooner *Rouse Simmons*, Captain Schuenemann, recently arrived in Chicago with a cargo of Christmas trees."

Despite the newspaper's best efforts to report marine news of local interest, the *Simmons* had, in fact, not arrived in Chicago. Rather, the ship was approximately 130 miles north of city – *at the bottom of the lake*. The *Simmons* had "gone missing" five days earlier.

Also gone missing with the ship were many facts pertaining to its loss. Communications were not what they are today. Thus, initial reports were both varied and confused, complicating the story, making it particularly difficult to follow right from the start. Search efforts included a search for the ship, as well as a search for factual information.

Because early errors were reported by newspapers in several states surrounding the Great Lakes during the initial days after the *Simmons* vanished, incorrect details were carried forward during the century that followed. Some of these included:

Captain Herman Schuenemann was referred to as Henry, Harry, Homan, Frank, "R." and Gus. He was also referred to as August, his brother who perished fourteen years before him in 1898. (Captain August Schuenemann, referenced in many of the news articles which reported on Captain Herman's loss, was said to have perished in 1893, 1898, 1908 and 1912.)

Captain Schuenemann's partner, Captain Charles Nelson, was referred to as Christian, Carl, Oscar, and "H." His last name was also reported with various incorrect spellings, as was Captain Schuenemann's.

The *Rouse Simmons* was reported in error to be the "Evelyn" *Simmons* as well as the "Rose" *Simmons*. Sometimes the word *Simmons* was spelled with one "m" and other times with two. Also, the ship was incorrectly said to be a fishing schooner instead of a lumber schooner.

The *Simmons*, a particularly old schooner on its last leg of life, was incorrectly reported through the years to be "a dashing new three-masted schooner" and "in very good condition".

Concerning ownership of the vessel, newspapers erroneously reported that the *Simmons* "was owned by Schuenemann in 1887". Other reports said the ship was owned by Schuenemann back into the early 1880's, although Captain Schuenemann did not purchase an interest in the ship until 1910.

The Christmas Ship

Christmas Ship, set your sails.
Christmas Ship, we'll tell your tales.
But remember, oh remember,
Those November gales.

A northwest wind was starting to blow.
The captain said, "We gotta go!
Don't hesitate, 'cause we're running late.
Unlash those trees out across the deck
We gotta go."

He was ready to sail out of Manistique,
He'd be back home in a couple of weeks.
Then he kissed his wife and his kids goodbye,
Then he said, with a tear in his eye, "Goodbye."

Excerpted from the song *"The Christmas Ship"*
Carl Behrend, Singer/Songwriter

"The three-masted schooner Rouse Simmons, *better known as the Christmas Tree Ship, entered the 'port of missing ships' during a mighty storm and blizzard on November 23, 1912, somewhere off Twin River Point, Wisconsin...to be numbered among the unexplained mysteries that Lake Michigan guards so well."*

Lake Michigan Disasters
Unpublished manuscript dated 1925
Discovered at the Rahr-West Museum
   and Civic Center
Reproduced by the Manitowoc Maritime Museum
Herbert Pitz

"Watch for Lost Schooner"

"Watch for Lost Schooner," reported the *Chicago Tribune* on November 29, 1912. "The life saving crew asked last evening to keep watch for the lumber schooner *Evelyn Simons*, supposed to have arrived here yesterday morning. No word has been received from the schooner since it left northern Michigan with a cargo." Later, the newspaper correctly identified the vessel as the *Rouse Simmons*.

There was no word from the ship or her crew, and in Chicago the heartbreaking vigil continued. It was not, of course, unusual for wind-powered schooners to be delayed, even to arrive several days or a week late, particularly after a heavy gale. This was also before the day of ship-to-shore radio and other navigation advances. Winter communications were slow and uncertain, and a vessel might wait

Perhaps the most interesting (although incorrect) link between Captain Herman and the *Simmons* was the statement that Herman Schuenemann had watched the ship being built. This, too, proved to be false since Captain Schuenemann was barely born when the *Simmons* made its maiden voyage. (The captain's age at the time of his death varies with the telling.)

Examining erroneous details concerning less important aspects of the story can offer an explanation why many of the more critical details concerning sightings of the vessel, and also debris washing ashore, were dizzying.

Another point of much controversy concerned the number of men on board the ship when it went down, as well as who they were. In addition to the crew, it was said there were as many as a dozen lumberjacks who asked Captain Schuenemann if they could "hitch a ride" on the *Simmons* to Chicago in order to spend Christmas with their family.

Then, there were reports of crew members leaving the *Simmons* in the Upper Peninsula of Michigan when they saw rats deserting the ship, a very bad mariner's omen. They refused to sail back to Chicago and returned on the railroad instead.

Some men got off the ship, and others got on. But who?

while aground or in a snug harbor for days without news of it reaching the maritime centers. The newspapers began to recount the storm's damage and name the vessels, lost and safe, as the days went by after the gale. And, as always, first news often had to be corrected later...

For those waiting for word, even more heart-racking than no news must have been encouraging reports that later proved to be false...

In time the family's hope for Captain Schuenemann's rescue faded (and one can be sure that the Schuenemanns held out longer than anyone else), and their life went on.

Sea Classics
January 1977, Vol. 10, No. 1
Fred Hollister

The *Chicago Daily Journal* of December 4, 1912, reported the following list of missing men:

> Capt. Herman Schuenemann, 1638 North Clark Street; owner of the boat.
> Capt. Charles Nelson and Mrs. Nelson, 1634 Humboldt Avenue.
> Stephen Nelson, mate; Chicago.
> Charles Nelson, sailor; Chicago.
> Albert Lykstad, cook; 420 North Desplaines Street.
> Gilbert Swensen, tree cutter, Chicago; home was near Humboldt Park.
> Frank Carlson, tree cutter; Austin.
> Two lumber shovers, names not known;
> Two or more lumber shovers believed to have been taken aboard on Michigan shores.

According to the above information, Captain Nelson's wife was aboard the schooner when it went down. Other accounts said Captain Schuenemann's wife was also on the vessel. The *Milwaukee Sentinel* of December 4, 1912, published the following statement: "Captain Herman Schuleman, with his wife, and fourteen hands, are lost."

Despite these initial reports, neither woman was on board. Captain Nelson's wife was no longer alive. (She had died years earlier.) And Captain Schuenemann's wife was waiting in Chicago for her husband's return, straining her eyes as she looked to the horizon for his ship during these days that were long on questions and short on answers.

The *Chicago Daily Tribune* of December 5, 1912, also reported a woman was on the ship when it sunk: "The lone woman aboard the *Rouse Simmons*," reported the newspaper, "was the wife of the captain, Oscar Nelson, who was in command."

Not only was there confusion in regards to how many persons from the Nelson family were on board, there was also confusion as to the reason they were sailing on the *Simmons*. Some reports indicated the vessel sailed "with Captain Christian Nelson and his wife as guests" while other reports indicated Captain Nelson was at the wheel of the ship instead of Captain Schuenemann. Most researchers agree that Captain Nelson was not along as "a visitor" but was a critical member of the ship. "Among the crew," reported the *Sault Ste. Marie Evening News* of December 4, 1912, "was Charles Nelson, a former sea captain who joined the crew to assist Captain Schuenemann in weathering the heavy gales that were expected."

On December 5, 1912, the *Chicago Daily Journal* published a revised list of crew members that were believed to have "perished in the lake." The list read:

> Capt. Charles Nelson, North Avenue and Robey Street; skipper and part owner.
> Capt. Herman Schuenemann, 1638 North Clark Street, charterer of vessel and owner of cargo.
> Steve E. Nelson, mate; Chicago.
> Gilbert Svenson, sailor; Humboldt Park, Chicago.
> Frank Carlson, sailor; Austin.
> Albert Lykstad, cook; 420 North Desplaines Street.
> Ingvald Nyhous, sailor; 420 North Desplaines Street.
> William Oberg, lumber shover.
> Sven Inglehart, lumber shover.
> Jacob Johnson, tree cutter.
> Andrew Danielson, tree cutter.

Five additional names appear on the *Chicago Daily Journal*'s revised list on December 5, 1912, than appeared the day before. (Also, Mrs. Nelson's name was removed on the corrected list along with the second "Charles Nelson" name listed as "sailor".)

Although it would seem progress was being made, this was not necessarily the case. On the same day as the *Chicago Daily Journal*'s revised list ran, another list was published by the *Chicago Daily Tribune*. This list read:

"There are several lists of who exactly was on board. All to a greater or lesser degree, disagree."

Frederick Stonehouse
Went Missing II
Copyright 1984

Captain [Herman] Schuenemann, Captain Nelson's partner in the Christmas tree venture.
Alex Johnson, first mate.
Edward Minogue, sailor.
Frank Sobata, sailor.
George Watson, sailor.
Ray Davis, sailor.
Conrad Griffin, sailor.
George Quinn, sailor.
Edward Murphy, sailor.
John Morwauski, sailor.
"Stump" Morris, sailor.
Greely Peterson, sailor.
Frank Faul, sailor.
Edward Hogan, sailor.
Philip Bauswein, sailor.

The name "Edward Murphy" sparked additional press coverage in Manitowoc, Wisconsin. The *Manitowoc Daily Herald* ran the following article on December 6, 1912, after receiving word of the crew list circulated in Chicago: "One Manitowoc man may have been lost with the Christmas ship *Rouse Simmons* when the boat went down, it is believed off Two Rivers Point, north of this city. The name of Edward Murphy appears in the crew of the *Simmons* and it is feared that its owner was a Manitowoc man of that name, a son of the late Maurice Murphy, who had not been heard from by relatives for some time. Inquiry is being made in all effort to establish whether Murphy was on the *Simmons*, and relatives are anxiously awaiting the result."

Although Edward Murphy's name appeared on the list published by the *Chicago Daily Tribune*, it was not included on the list published by the *Chicago American* on December 13, 1912:

Captain Herman Schuenemann, whose home was at 1638 North Clark Street.
Captain Charles C. Nelson, part owner of the vessel, 1624 Humboldt Avenue.
Andrew Danielson, of 6044 North Paulina Street.
Gilbert Svenson.
Engwald Newhouse (probably the Engwald referred to in the message), who lived at 420 North Desplaines Street.
Philip Larson.
John Pitt, of 1144 Chatham Court.
Andrew Danielson, of Haddon Avenue and Rockwell Street.
Philip Bauswein, of 3624 S. La Salle Street.
Jack Johnson, who lived at 1629 North Artesian Avenue.
Stephen Nelson (the Steve referred to in the note in the bottle).
Albert Lykstad, of 420 North Desplaines Street.
Frank Carlson, of Austin.

The *Chicago Inter Ocean*, as well as the *Chicago Record Herald*, also published crew lists which varied from others. Again, communications were not what they are today. It was a completely different world with regard to accessibility of immediate and accurate information. Thus, it was a long, slow process for relatives on their quest for answers.

Information was also unclear due to the fact that many sailors, particularly unmarried men, joined crews at the last minute, signing themselves on board a vessel at one of the many hiring halls along the waters.

The *Chicago Record Herald* of December 6, 1912, reported: "The rooms of the Lake Seamen's Union at North Jefferson and South Lake Streets was besieged during the day by friends and relatives of the sailors on the *Rouse Simmons*. On board the vessel were two close companions, Albert Luxtad and Engwald Newhouse, who had been brought up together and had sailed on the same vessels for nearly forty years. When Newhouse learned that his 'mate' had signed as cook on the *Simmons*, he went aboard as a foremast hand. Luxtad's sister, Mrs. Lena Dahl, who lives at 3319 South Oakley Avenue, stood about the office of the union yesterday waiting for tidings from the *Simmons*. Thomas A. Hanson, who is in charge of the office, said all hope of the schooner being heard from definitely had been practically abandoned by sailors who are well acquainted with the dangers of the lakes. In the crew of eleven men were three lumber shovers, John Johnson, known as 'Pink Jack', whose sister, Mrs. Benjamin Knudon, lives at 4577 Elston Avenue; Frank Carlson, known as 'Ananias', and Andrew Anderson, known as 'Big Andy'. The three lived at 418 Desplaines Street, a sailors' rooming house."

Although the above article makes reference to eleven men on board the *Simmons*, it was only a guess. On the same day, the *Milwaukee Daily News* stated: "The *Rouse Simmons* carried a crew of from fifteen to seventeen persons, according to the best advices." These numbers, too, were only guesses, and may not have adjusted for the lumberjacks who hitched a ride into their graves.

Exactly who was on board is a question that has never been adequately answered.

> *"The grim days of November 1912 are still legend."*
>
> The Plain Dealer Sunday Magazine
> Cleveland, Ohio
> December 16, 1973

Photo of the *Rouse Simmons* beside a pier.
(*Courtesy of the Historical Collections of the Great Lakes,
Jerome Library, Bowling Green State University, Bowling Green, Ohio*)

*"The list of ships lost in November grows ever longer, but
of all of them the questions of why and how are most intriguing
with the* Rouse Simmons, *the Christmas Tree Ship."*

> *Green Bay Press-Gazette*
> Green Bay, WI
> November 23, 1975
> Bob Woessner

Approximately six months after the ill-fated *Simmons* was lost, a trunk washed ashore bearing the inscription: "ROUSE SIMMONS - J. E. LATHROP". This discovery was another point of mystery since the name "Lathrop" never appeared on any of the crew lists.

It is important to note that crew lists included only those names of persons believed to have perished – *not* names of survivors. Two survivors from the original crew who sailed from Chicago with Captain Schuenemann on October 3, 1912, included Hogan Hoganson and Big Bill Sullivan. Each of these men deserted the ship in the Upper Peninsula after sighting the rats. (In addition to these sailors, there may have been others. Some reports indicate three men left, and other reports indicate four.)

A definite, final count of exactly how many men went to the bottom on that dreadful day was never conclusively determined since the log book from the ship was never recovered.

On December 7, 1912, the *Chicago Daily Tribune* reported "wives of several sailors visited headquarters of the Lake Sailors Union and gave a description of their husbands to Secretary T. A. Hanson, so if a body was found identity could be established without delay."

The gathering at the Lake Sailors headquarters was the result of an article published by the *Chicago American* the previous day. It read: "An unidentified body, believed to be that of one of the eighteen men on the lost schooner, *Rouse Simmons*, was cast up by the waves near Pentwater, Michigan, late today. The body was that of a man six feet tall and about fifty years old."

Needless to say, relatives, at their wits end with worry, feared the worst when they learned of the victim. As it turned out, the body was not from the *Simmons* but was, rather, from another vessel destroyed in the same storm. This "good news" restored hope, however brief, to the hearts of those awaiting word on the Christmas Ship.

Family members were hurled, again and again, from hope to despair as the *Simmons* was reported "lost" and then "safe", and then "lost" again. The roller coaster of these day-by-day, and sometimes even hour-by-hour, reports were difficult to bear up against. Family members wept in relief, and they wept in anguish. It was an emotional tug-of-war that tore at their hearts.

The first of many hopeful reports was published on November 30, 1912, in the *Chicago Record Herald* under the headline "Christmas Tree Boat Safe". This news seemed too good to be true, and all too soon it would be learned that it was. The article read, "Fears aroused for the safety of the Christmas tree boat, the *Rouse Simmons*, captained by Herman Schuenemann, were quieted yesterday when it was learned that the craft had been sighted off Bailey's Harbor, 175 miles from Chicago. The ship is five days overdue, but is expected to arrive in Chicago sometime today."

When the ship failed to dock in Chicago, the *Grand Haven Daily Tribune* of Grand Haven, Michigan, reported on December 3, 1912: "The old schooner *Rouse Simmons*, loaded with Christmas trees and greens…has not as yet arrived in Chicago, and fears are again felt for her safety."

On December 4, 1912, the *Chicago American* reported another sighting: "A ship captain said he thought he had seen the *Simmons* Monday [December 2, 1912] making fair progress toward Chicago." On December 5, 1912, the same paper ran the headline "Christmas Tree Schooner Sighted/Santa Claus Ship May be Safe". This article detailed another possible sighting: "The missing schooner, *Rouse Simmons*, was sighted in Lake Michigan, three miles off shore south of Racine [Wisconsin] twenty-four hours ago. This report was received today by Captain Berry of the United States revenue cutter… If in fact it was the schooner *Rouse Simmons* which the *George W. Orr* sighted, it seemed probable that the ship had been deserted or swept of its crew."

The key words in the above article are "if in fact it was". It was later learned it wasn't. The officers aboard the *George W. Orr* had been mistaken.

The tug-of-war between news of Life and news of Death continued, although Death had already proved itself victor, unbeknownst to the world the crew left behind.

On December 6, 1912, hope was restored, once again, when the *Chicago Daily Tribune* reported: "Several reports were current that the boat had put up at a harbor from which there were no telegraphic connections, and that it was waiting there for favorable winds to bring it to Chicago."

The *Milwaukee Daily News*, on the same day, reported a sighting of the ship's yawl [a type of small boat carried aboard ships] seen floating empty in the middle of Lake Michigan. It was identified as belonging to the *Simmons*. "The ship's yawl has been seen in midlake," reported the *Milwaukee Daily News*, "indicating that a part, at least, of the fifteen persons on the schooner attempted to make their escape from the wreck in the small boat, but perished."

Moment-by-moment, the story unfolded. Reports during a single 24-hour period could vary greatly due to the fact some newspapers published multiple editions of their papers each day, and details that developed in the morning could be entirely different by nightfall.

The final word on the lives lost continued to be lived out in headlines. "Ship of Christmas Now Overdue", reported the *Sault Ste. Marie Evening News* of Sault Ste. Marie, Michigan, on December 3, 1912. "Find Wreckage from Schooner" reported the *Duluth Herald* of Duluth, Minnesota, on December 4, 1912. "No Hope for Boat and her Crew of Sixteen", reported *The Detroit News* the same day. And from the *Toledo Blade* in Toledo, Ohio, readers learned on December 4, 1912: "Ship Carrying Christmas Trees Goes Down in Lake". Eight dreadful words summarized the belief of many; the lives of those on board were reduced to headlines.

"Tree Tops Point to Doom of Santa Ship" was printed in bold typeset in the *Chicago Daily News* on December 5, 1912. This was the same day the *Chicago American* ran a headline that read: "Santa Claus Boat Lost".

Despite hopeful reports scattered in between these headlines, hope was not to last.

Hope was abandoned soonest by two U.S. Life Saving Station rescue crews. One crew was from Kewaunee, Wisconsin, and the other was from Two Rivers, Wisconsin. (The U.S. Life Saving Stations were predecessors to our modern day Coast Guard.)

Both the Kewaunee and Two Rivers crews were involved in the final moments the *Rouse Simmons* spent afloat, although many erroneous reports were published detailing sightings and rescue attempts by several different Life Saving crews on both sides of Lake Michigan. The facts are as follows: The Kewaunee crew sighted the stricken vessel with its distress flags flying, and then they notified the Two Rivers crew to the south who attempted an unsuccessful intercept of the vessel. (The Kewaunee crew felt they would be unable to reach the vessel because they only had row boats. The Two Rivers crew was in possession of a gas-powered surf boat.)

According to the *Kewaunee Enterprise* of November 29, 1912, it was reported: "Last Saturday afternoon [November 23, 1912], the lookout at the local Life Saving Station sighted a schooner several miles out in the lake being driven before the heavy north gale that prevailed on the lake and flying distress signals. The schooner was too far away and the sea too rough to make an attempt towards manning the life boat and putting out for the craft possible, so Captain Craite made efforts to secure the services of a tug, but none were available. Shortly after, snow began falling pretty heavily and the distressed boat was lost sight of. Captain Craite then telephoned Captain Sogge of the Two Rivers Station and the crew from that city immediately started out in the lake in their power boat in search of the craft."

The *Sturgeon Bay Advocate* of December 26, 1912, published testimony from Captain George Sogge of the Two Rivers crew: "On November 23rd, at 3:10 p.m., I received a telephone message from Captain Craite, keeper of the Kewaunee station, saying that a three-masted schooner was sighted off that

Photo of the Two Rivers U.S. Life Saving Station crew in 1907 practicing a rowing drill in their oar-powered surf boat.
(*Courtesy of the Rogers Street Fishing Village Museum, Two Rivers, WI*)

"Little do you know of the hardships,
Nor do you understand
The stormy nights we did endure
On the lake of Michigan."
Old Mariner Song

harbor, about five miles out, displaying signals of distress, with foresail and jib-top sail set and coming south. I immediately launched my power lifeboat and at 4:20 was rounding the Two River Point six miles north from the station. I then expected to see the schooner. We could see nearly to Kewaunee, but there was nothing to be seen. I kept on running north about eight miles from the point; then changed my heading out in the lake for one hour. By this time it was dark. There was nothing to be seen of the schooner, nor wreckage, nor signals. It started to snow heavy, and considering that we had been making a very thorough search for the distressed vessel, and that I had done all in my power, and all there was in my judgment to do in the case, we set our course for the station. The trip, as may well be imagined, was not a very pleasant one, but our only regrets were that we had put forth our best efforts in that direction without avail. My opinion about the schooner reported seen off Kewaunee is that the vessel was probably waterlogged, and that the crew was unable to keep her on her course and squared away before the wind and sea in order to keep the craft afloat. Being loaded with a cargo of green spruce – if this schooner was the *Rouse Simmons* – she foundered somewhere in mid-lake, as during the night of November 23rd a northwest gale was blowing and a very high sea running. It would only be by remarkable good luck and excellent handling that a vessel could have reached an east shore harbor that night."

Captain George Sogge's daughter, Louise, was interviewed on December 26, 1982, by the *Herald Times Reporter* of Manitowoc, Wisconsin, regarding her memories of the fateful night seventy years earlier when the *Rouse Simmons* went missing. The article read: "She was only nine years old at the time, but Mrs. Louise [Sogge] Jorgensen of 31 N. Eighth Street has vivid memories of that day in 1912 when the Christmas Tree Ship, the *Rouse Simmons*, with its load of Christmas trees, sank off Point Beach, north of Two Rivers, Wisconsin. There were no survivors. The ship sank at the height of a violent snow and windstorm. The day was November 23, 1912. Louise's father, Captain George Sogge, commanded the Life Saving Crew at the Two

> *"The sturdy* Rouse Simmons *had survived serious storms in the past, but not this one. It was spotted in obvious distress at various times but could not be reached with aid."*
>
> *The Goderich Signal-Star*
> Ontario, Canada
> June 14, 2000
> Skip Ghiilham

CREW SEARCHES FOR DISABLED VESSEL

The Chronicle
Two Rivers, WI
November 26, 1912

Last [Saturday] afternoon, Captain Craite of the Kewaunee Life Saving crew notified Captain Sogge of the local crew that a sail vessel, flying distress signals, passed that port headed south.

The local crew went out in search of the schooner, but could not locate it. After remaining out in the lake in a raging snow storm until 8 o'clock, the crew returned to port. There was a big sea and a high wind, and the trip was a most unpleasant one for the crew. The beach has been patrolled since Sunday and it is the opinion of many that the vessel foundered.

"For five hours guardsmen searched through mist and darkness but the Rouse Simmons, *carrying the ultimate symbol of Christmas cheer, was never found."*

Herald-Times Reporter
Manitowoc, WI
November 7, 1987

Rivers Coast Guard Station. The Sogge family lived at the station. Louise remembers the telephone call from Captain Craite from the Kewaunee Coast Guard Station. He told Captain Sogge that the Kewaunee Station had sighted the *Rouse Simmons'* distress signals off Kewaunee, but that his men couldn't possibly go out to help as they had only row boats in Kewaunee, no power boat. 'Our men got on their warm clothes and launched the boat. It was the worst blizzard and blowing storm I can ever remember,' Louise said. 'Only one of our men stayed in the lookout, as we called it, to stand watch. He was John Gagnon. And when the men were gone for many hours,' Louise said, 'my mother told him to get some rest and she stood watch.' Louise remembers going from window to window, watching for the men to come back, 'but we were able to see little of the lighthouse on the pier where we would be able to see the boat coming back. I really don't know how long they were out,' Louise said, 'but it seemed an eternity to us.' They went out the next day, too, but never found any trace of the ship. The captain of the *Rouse Simmons* was Herman Schuenemann. Louise said her sister, Esther Sogge, heard from the Schuenemann girls and 'they were so hurt because the Kewaunee men didn't try to save their father and crew.' But there was no way they could have helped, with only row boats, in that fierce storm."

It is not difficult to understand the hurt the Schuenemann girls were feeling when we consider the love we each hold dear. It was their pain speaking, and pain is companioned, many times, by anger and disappointment. Who among us would not have wondered in our rawest moments if all had been done to save those aboard if, among them, someone we loved and cared for perished too?

Even complete strangers questioned the decision-making process of the Kewaunee Life Saving Station captain. On January 9, 1913, the following Letter to the Editor appeared in the *Sturgeon Bay Advocate*: "Please give me space in the columns of the *Advocate* for a few words regarding the mishap to the schooner *Rouse Simmons*. I read in your paper of a recent issue Captain Sogge's statement of what he and his crew did after being notified by the Kewaunee Station that a schooner was in distress about five miles out, running under foresail and jibtop sail. Now, what I want to ask is why did not the Kewaunee Lifesaving crew run out and respond to the signals of distress? And if they were unable, they surely could have secured a fish tug to do the work for them. It is my candid opinion that had this been done, every one of those 14 lives would have been saved. Captain Schuenemann and his crew knew there were Stations at the canal, Kewaunee and Two Rivers Point, and that was his reason for having his signal of distress up, and it must have been awful for him and his men to pass within five miles of a Lifesaving Station in broad daylight without getting help. I ask for humanity's sake, what excuse has the captain of the Kewaunee Lifesaving Station to offer for his failure to respond? On the same afternoon a scow broke adrift at the Sturgeon Bay canal, and a current carried her out into the lake. Tugs went to her and towed the craft to Algoma. When this could be done with a scow, it is my belief the *Simmons* crew could have been saved easily. The *Rouse Simmons* yawl was also too small to accommodate 14 men. This was an unusual number for her to carry, which was on account of getting the trees from the woods. Of course, we can only guess what happened to the *Rouse Simmons*, and also where she foundered. It is my idea that she sank somewhere between Kewaunee and Two Rivers Point. The Kewaunee Lifesaving crew should be able to give us some information, and we would like to know the exact time she was last seen by them. Would also like to hear from the captain of the schooner *Resumption* where he saw the *Simmons* yawl. There are probably some of the other masters that saw the vessel after she left Manistique, and passed wreckage from her. With the above information, I believe we will be able to guess pretty close to where the schooner sunk. Milwaukee, Wisconsin. January 4, 1913. Signed, G. C."

The letter was a scathing accusation by "G.C." of Milwaukee who directed an attack on the Kewaunee Life Saving Station captain. The "candid opinion" of G.C. was that "every one of those 14 lives would have been saved" if the services of a tug had been secured and "the *Simmons* crew could have been saved easily."

It is less difficult, by far, to be on the outside looking in, questioning the professional judgment made by another, than it is to stand in the place of the same person who was called to make a fateful decision in a life-or-death moment.

The rescue crews who manned the U.S. Life Saving Stations surrounding

---

"The winter of 1912 proved to be a rugged season on the Great Lakes, and that November storm was one of the worst, with winds measured at 60 knots, and a blizzard following the gale."

Milwaukee Journal
Milwaukee, WI
December 8, 1992
Margaret H. Plevak

Lifesaving Service

Prior to 1877, the Lifesaving Service in Two Rivers comprised of local volunteers – many of whom were formerly commercial fisherman. Captain H. S. Scove, a shipbuilder in the city, was in charge.

On May 1, 1877, by authorization of the Congress of the United States, a United States Lifesaving Service Station was opened in Two Rivers. This was the second U.S.L.S.S. opened on Lake Michigan.

The first federally funded Life Saving Station Keeper was Oliver Pilon, a local resident from one of the city's first families. Pilon had also headed the volunteer crew and took over as Keeper when the government authorized the Station. Pilon served in this official capacity from 1877 until his death in 1892. Pilon died from pneumonia several days after performing an icy rescue.

Joseph Dionne succeeded Pilon. In 1894 Dionne was awarded the Congressional Medal of Honor for the dramatic and hazardous rescue of crew and cargo of the steamer *W. L. Wetmore*.

George E. Sogge served from 1903 until his retirement in 1920. Sogge is remembered most for answering the call to help the crew of the famous *Rouse Simmons* or "Christmas Tree Ship".

"Storm Warriors"

Keepers of stations were appointed by the district superintendent and the crew was selected by the Keeper. Both Keeper and crew were examined by a board of inspectors.

The Keeper had to be under forty-five years of age, possess good health and character, be able to read and write, and possess a mastery of boat craft and surfing. He permanently resided at the Station and had absolute authority over his men.

Surfmen had to be under forty-five years of age when entering service, be physically fit and skilled in life saving tactics. They were required to reside at the Station from mid-April to mid-December. Six to eight surfmen were assigned to a Keeper. Men were ranked according to skill, with Number 1 being the most skilled and Number 6 being the least skilled.

Keepers were paid $200.00 yearly and crews not more than $40.00 per month. Volunteers were awarded not more than ten dollars per rescue of a human life.

Plaques on display at the Roger's Street Fishing Village in Two Rivers, Wisconsin.

the Great Lakes in the late 1800's and early 1900's were *not* cowardly men. They knew a little something about what needed to be done, and when, as it concerned the demands upon them to pull back sailors from death's door as they hung in the balance there between this world and the next. These men regularly laid their lives on the line for others, and they knew the supreme value of every second.

Ironically, Captain Craite of the Kewaunee Station had done *exactly* as had been suggested by G.C. in his letter. According to the *Kewaunee Enterprise* of November 29, 1912, Captain Craite gave testimony that he had, indeed, made effort to secure the services of a tug, although unsuccessfully, and then contacted Captain Sogge of the Two Rivers Station only after his attempt failed. (It is important to note that many persons had access to only one or two newspapers and, because of this, they did not get the whole story, as was the case here.)

Despite the controversy concerning certain aspects of the *Rouse Simmons* tragedy, one significant piece of the story without dispute concerned the severity of the weather. "It was the worst blizzard and blowing storm I can remember," said Captain Sogge's daughter, Louise, later.

Lake Michigan was in a rude mood on November 23, 1912. You could feel its temper rising against you. Lighthouse keepers and rescue crews around the Great Lakes had their hands full.

The weather from the previous day had deteriorated quickly. Winds whipped wild out of the west. Waves crashed. Snow was falling steady by mid-day, decreasing visibility. The lighthouse at Two Rivers was not even visible from the Life Saving Station in close proximity, yet the rescue crew stationed there forged into the mad winds and mounting seas at 3:10 p.m. With every beat of their hearts, they knew time was ticking down for those aboard the distressed schooner.

Sunset was nearing. The last rays of daylight were fast falling as these men labored into the pounding surf and then entered the chaotic sea. Each rescue worker who left the Station that afternoon did so with the full knowledge of the price he was called to pay.

All over the lake, others were fighting similar brutal battles with the storm as it unleashed "unabated fury" on vessels.

The gale continued to grow in intensity, and the jaws of the storm closed around the Life Saving crew. Through the dusk of night the rescuers searched, plowing their way through confused waters churning at the will of the wind. Shaking and shivering, soaked through and through, they looked long and hard for the doomed schooner in the falling dusk, then into the darkness, until at last they turned their vessel homeward. It was a dangerous journey, a terrifying storm, and an unspeakable loss.

Back at the Station, others were waiting under wild skies for the crew to come back, not knowing if those who left earlier would return again after the Station door closed behind them.

Who among us can claim with certainty the next Hour's knowing? No one. Each of us is subject to the same twists in Fate. Yet for those involved in life saving services along the Great Lakes a century ago, the odds of Fate turning for the worst were significantly raised.

Photos can show us the faces of these men – men of steady shoulders and steady hands, of steady hearts and steady eyes, but they cannot show us the courage behind those eyes. They cannot show us the memories hidden away inside, memories of struggle, and memories of strain. Photos will never be able to capture their spirit, their bravery, and their willingness to risk saving others at the cost of losing themselves.

I have wondered, more times than I can count, particularly when I am safe in my home, and warm, if I would have had courage enough to answer these calls for help. The wind howls loud and long here, and I've listened to it for over forty years, very near to the shore where the *Rouse Simmons* crew members took their last breaths while almost within view of the rescuers who tried to reach them.

I drive by lighthouses along the coast and think for a while, too, on the lonely keepers who served these beacons a lifetime ago, men who stood steady in their faithfulness to others whom they knew not.

It is humbling to think upon the sacrifices of these men. The Great Lakes are full of stories of extreme heroism, and stories of its exact opposite.

Two years after the *Simmons* went missing, a lighthouse keeper by the name of Robert Carlson was watching out his window during a storm on Lake Superior's "Shipwreck Coast" (northeast of the *Simmons'* loss) when he spotted a fishing tug pounding in the waves off shore. Then, the ship suddenly flipped completely upside down, capsized in the turbulent waters. Eleven men on board were drowning.

Although lighthouse Keeper Carlson knew there wasn't a moment to spare, he needed help in rowing his large boat across the stormy waters where the men were perishing.

Workers from a nearby fishery ran to shore when they witnessed the tug go under. Keeper Carlson pleaded with these men to join him in the boat, but

Photo of the Two Rivers U.S. Life Saving Station crew standing near two rescue boats used by the Station. On the left is the "Monomoy" rowing surfboat and on the right is the motor surfboat with gas engine believed to be the boat most likely used in the search for the *Rouse Simmons*. (*Courtesy of the Rogers Street Fishing Village Museum, Two Rivers, WI*)

his pleas were met with silence.

According to the educational video "Superior Lights on the Shipwreck Coast" the men looked at the water, and then they looked at the weather. The winds were "practically knocking them down," and none would volunteer. They were afraid.

Keeper Carlson's wife had followed him out the door and was now standing alongside her husband at the shoreline.

"Do you want me to ask my wife to row?" demanded the Keeper, thinking the men would surely volunteer if they knew a woman was going to take their place. But the men, again, stood mute.

At this point, Keeper Carlson reached inside his pocket and pulled out a gun. He raised it eye level, took a deep breath, and then said five words: "Volunteer…or I start shooting." The gun clicked. He was dead serious.

Two men stepped forward and joined the Keeper in his boat. Because of this, three men left shore that day, and fourteen came back.

Keeper Carlson ended his career in 1931 after serving the lighthouse for twenty-eight years. "The life of a lighthouse keeper is that of solitude, and few people can truly say they really like it," said the Keeper at the close of his days. "Still, there is something noble about it, for every day a lightkeeper is helping someone."

Sacrifice. Nobility. Service. There was no shortage of stories on the Great Lakes that exemplified the best of humanity, including the story of the heroism displayed by the Two Rivers rescue workers who were willing to risk their own lives for the sake of saving those aboard the *Rouse Simmons*. Their efforts remain one of the supreme triumphs of the *Simmons* story, despite the controversy surrounding the decision of the Kewaunee crew.

Another point of controversy involved an incident which occurred approximately one hour prior to the *Simmons* sighting by the Kewaunee Life Saving Station. The ship, at this time, was due north laboring in heavy seas when it was spotted at 2:00 p.m. by the *Ann Arbor No. 5* car ferry.

According to an article published in the *Sturgeon Bay Advocate* on January 23, 1913, Captain T. Bernsten gave testimony regarding the specifics of the incident following a discussion he had had with the car ferry's captain: "Having had a talk with the captain of the *Ann Arbor No. 5* about the fate of the schooner *Rouse Simmons*, both he and the mate of the steamer informed me that they had seen the vessel on the afternoon of the day she met her fate. According to their story, the carferry was about five miles off Kewaunee, Wisconsin, and three miles to the north'ard when they sighted the schooner about 2 o'clock. She was flying no signals of distress as far as they could see, although she was about half a mile from them at the time. The vessel appeared to be listed badly and they thought something was wrong, but as there were no signals visible they did not deem it necessary to go to her, never thinking but what she would make harbor in safety... In response to the question as to how far he thought the *Simmons* would be off Kewaunee when she reached a point abreast of that port, the captain said on the course she was going, she would probably be about three miles out when she reached there. From the circumstance connected with the loss of the *Simmons*, it appears to me that the flag code in use on the ocean could be introduced on the Lakes to great advantage and benefit. With the use and understanding of the code, there would be no excuse for anyone not knowing the condition of a craft as far as the flags could be seen, as they would tell just what their trouble might be. The introduction of these flags could be made at a small expense, and the code learned in a short time. While our legislators are framing laws for safe-guarding mariners, let them require that the code system be installed and they will have accomplished a step in the right direction."

Captain Bernsten relayed a delicate version of the events surrounding the sighting of the *Simmons* by the steamer *Ann Arbor No. 5* to the *Sturgeon Bay Advocate*. The *Chicago American* of December 10, 1912, was more direct with their coverage. Under the headline "Steamer Vessel Reported to Have Ignored Call from 18 Doomed Men/Urge Federal Inquiry", the paper wrote: "Reports indicating that a steam vessel refused aid to the schooner *Rouse Simmons* a few hours before the old three-master was lost with eighteen men on board reached Chicago today. Sailors declared they would urge a federal inquiry."

The controversy concerning the *Ann Arbor No. 5* episode centered on the statement by its captain that the *Simmons* was not flying a distress flag when sighted and, because of this, the steamer did not offer the ship aid. To this claim, the *Chicago American* article responded: "Seamen declared there was a grave doubt as to the truth of the statement that the *Rouse Simmons* was not flying distress signals at that time. An hour later, at 3:00 p.m., she was flying signals of distress plainly visible to the Life Savers at Kewaunee."

These were serious charges waged against the *Ann Arbor No. 5*, and they sparked a heated debate. Some believed the *Simmons* was surely flying a distress flag when it was sighted by the steamer, and the *Ann Arbor No. 5* intentionally passed it by. Maybe the captain feared his own vessel would end up at the bottom of the lake if he stopped to offer aid. (Despite what the captain may or may not have been thinking, he continued to deny he ever saw a distress flag on the *Simmons* before it disappeared.)

Reports concerning the distress flag were varied and confused, complicating the story immensely. The Kewaunee crew said they saw it; the *Ann Arbor* said they didn't. An eye-witness report also surfaced on November 24, 1912, in Port Washington, Wisconsin. (Port Washington was many miles south of where the ship was believed to have sank, and the sighting there on November 24 was one day *after* the *Simmons* went to the bottom.)

The *Port Washington Star* published an article on December 14, 1912, under the headline "*Rouse Simmons* Sighted Here". The article read: "The vessel was last sighted off Port Washington, Wisconsin, on November 24th by Herbert Smith and Frank Wilson who were making lake observations. At the time she was apparently about eight miles from shore and battling with heavy seas, showing signs of being in distress, but the observers noted no distress flag and felt that the vessel would be able to make the harbor at Milwaukee. Others report noting the vessel from the hill and that she carried a distress flag, but that fact was not reported until too late to render any assistance to the vessel. It is presumed the boat sank some place between here and Waukegan, Illinois."

Two of the eye-witnesses said they didn't see a distress flag, others on a hill said they did. (And, most importantly, how could anyone have seen a ship that was already at the bottom of the lake?)

The Rouse Simmons*, once one of Lake Michigan's proudest vessels, was carrying Yule trees to Chicago when a storm and tragedy struck...*

Violent late November storms lashed the Great Lakes. Gale and even hurricane force winds whipped Lake Michigan's frigid waters into foam...

Sailing to the windward of a 60-mile gale blowing west by southwest, the schooner traveled 100 miles of raging, storm-tossed waters before dawn. By morning the wind had backed into the eastward, and the lake was hidden by a blinding blizzard.

Old newspaper clipping on file at:
The Great Lakes Historical Society
Dated December 1967
Source unknown

Reports of *Rouse Simmons* Sightings by Rescuers

"The buffeted ship was next sighted off Kewaunee, WI, still heading south, with distress signals flying. A Coast Guard power launch was dispatched from Two Rivers, WI. For five hours, the rescue boat plowed through the blizzard and the high waves before getting a glimpse of the doomed ship during a momentary lull in the storm. She was in the distance, sitting low in the water with waves washing the decks, her sails in ribbons, and ice covering the hull and rigging. Then the storm closed in again, and the ship was lost in the swirling blizzard. Though they continued searching, the rescuers never saw her again."

Wisconsin Then and Now
State Historical Society of Wisconsin Publication
December 1973

"A storm hit Lake Michigan the day of the 23rd [November 1912] and the schooner, a veteran of the lakes for 44 years, must have been hit hard. She was sighted off Kewaunee, WI, with a distress signal flying. The Two Rivers Coast Guard Station was called and guardsmen in a 34-foot power launch were sent out to help, but due to the weather they saw her only once in the snow storm that covered the lake."

Great Lakes Shipwrecks, Volume II
Kimm Stabelfeldt
Great Lakes Marine Historical Collection

"All efforts to send help to the stricken craft met with failure. Right after being sighted, she sailed back into the storm. A heavy snow cut visibility to zero. Farther, down the lake, another jagged break in the weather gave members of a courageous lifeboat crew the last tantalizing glimpse of the *Simmons,* her hull coated with ice, her sails in tatters. Then the storm closed around her for the final death struggle."

Great Lakes Shipwrecks & Survivals
William Ratigan
Copyright 1960

"The men of the United States Lifesaving Station, Two Rivers, WI (forerunner of the Coast Guard) spotted the *Rouse Simmons* with her distress flags flying as she battled the seas to stay afloat. The U.S.L.S.S. surfmen launched their powerboat to attempt a rescue. As they approached the schooner, they could see that she was completely iced over, with most of her rigging and sails tattered or gone. When they were less than an eighth of a mile from the schooner, a snow squall suddenly slammed into the surfmen, blinding them. By the time the squall blew itself out, the *Rouse Simmons* was gone, and the ship's master, whom many of Chicago's children considered to be Santa Claus, was lost to the fury of the lake. The year 1912 was a somber one in Chicago. There was no Christmas Tree Ship, no Captain Santa, and no trees for many needy families."

United States Coast Guard Magazine
December 2000

Chronological Search and Rescue Developments

LIFE SAVING CREW PATROLS LAKE IN SEARCH OF THREE-MASTED REPORTED DISTRESSED (*Manitowoc Daily Herald*, Manitowoc, WI, November 25, 1912) "Responding to a call from Kewaunee, WI, which told of a three-masted schooner in distress sighted off that port and being driven by the gale southward, Captain George Sogge and crew of men from the life saving station at Two Rivers instituted a search and for five hours Saturday night [November 23] patrolled the lake off Two Rivers Point in search of a vessel bearing the description sent out from the lookout at Kewaunee. The search was abandoned Saturday night only after it became too dark to continue, but the vessel was not seen. Early Sunday morning the crew made another effort but failed to find any trace of the schooner. The message from Kewaunee reported the vessel flying a signal of distress. The lake was lashed into fury by the high wind of Friday night and all Saturday and till Sunday afternoon the vessels had a hard time of it."

WATCH FOR LOST SCHOONER/LIFE SAVERS LOOK OUT FOR LUMBER BOAT AND CREW WHICH WERE DUE HERE YESTERDAY (*Chicago Daily Tribune*, Chicago, IL, November 29, 1912) "The life saving crew was asked last evening to keep watch for the lumber schooner *Evelyn Simons*, supposed to have arrived here yesterday morning. No word has been received from the schooner since it left northern Michigan with a cargo." (A correction was published later showing the schooner's name to be *Rouse Simmons*, not *Evelyn Simons*.)

CHRISTMAS TREE BOAT SAFE/CRAFT, FIVE DAYS OVERDUE, SIGHTED OFF BAILEY'S HARBOR (*Chicago Record-Herald*, Chicago, IL, November 30, 1912) "Fears aroused for the safety of the Christmas tree boat, the *Rouse Simmons*, captained by Herman Schuenemann, were quieted yesterday when it was learned that the craft had been sighted off Bailey's Harbor, 175 miles from Chicago. The ship is five days overdue, but is expected to arrive in Chicago some time today. It is thought that the rough weather was responsible for the delay of the boat…"

FEARS ARE AGAIN FELT (*Grand Haven Daily Tribune*, Grand Haven, MI, December 3, 1912) "The old schooner *Rouse Simmons*, loaded with Christmas trees and greens…has not as yet arrived in Chicago, and fears are again felt for her safety. When six days overdue at Chicago, the schooner was reported off Bailey's Harbor, 175 miles from Chicago, November 28. Since that time no further word has been heard from her."

STILL LOST IN LAKE (*Chicago American*, Chicago, IL, December 4, 1912) "The candlelight of hope for the safety of the sailing schooner *Rouse Simmons*, nearly two weeks overdue in Chicago with a load of Christmas trees from the Michigan woods, was flickering badly. It flamed up a little when a ship captain said he thought he had seen the *Simmons* Monday [December 2] making fair progress toward Chicago. But it died down again when the schooner failed to make port."

ROUSE SIMMONS NOT FOUND (*Chicago Record-Herald*, Chicago, IL, December 4, 1912) "No word came yesterday from the *Rouse Simmons*, the Christmas tree laden schooner now many days overdue at port here. Inquiry at countless coast towns brought forth nothing but answers: 'Nothing known of the *Rouse Simmons.*' Despite the gloomy outlook, the wife of the belated vessel's captain maintains that there is no cause for alarm. Last night at her home, 1638 North Clark Street, she gave the technical explanation of 'head winds' for her husband's delay and added that the newspapers were showing the greatest worry."

LOSS OF SCHOONER *SIMMONS* IS CONFIRMED (*Manitowoc Daily Herald*, Manitowoc, WI, December 4, 1912) "Missing for two weeks, but reported safe several times, the schooner *Rouse Simmons* of Chicago is now known to have gone down on Lake Michigan with her captain and fifteen men. Definite information of the loss of the *Simmons* has been received."

ROUSE SIMMONS WAS UNDOUBTEDLY LOST IN LAKE MICHIGAN (*Duluth Herald,* Duluth, MN, December 4, 1912) "The revenue cutter *Tuscarora* is reported to have left Milwaukee in search of the missing ship. When seen a week ago Saturday, off Kewaunee, WI, she was running under shortened sail in a gale of snow and rain and making heavy weather of it. She was flying signals of distress. Lifesavers who attempted to reach her were driven back by the storm."

SCHOONER DISAPPEARED (*Chicago Daily Journal*, Chicago, IL, December 4, 1912) "A week ago a boat answering the description of the *Rouse Simmons* was sighted off Kewaunee, WI, flying distress signals. Persons on shore could see huge piles of Christmas trees on the deck. A fierce snow storm prevailed at the time, but life savers from Two Rivers, WI, went to the rescue in a motor boat. When the storm ceased the schooner had disappeared."

SCHOONER BELIEVED LOST IN MICHIGAN (*The Detroit News*, Detroit, MI, December 4, 1912) "According to messages received by the Chicago harbor master and the life saving station officers, the *Rouse Simmons* was sighted off Pentwater, MI, more than a week ago with distress signals flying and making a weak effort to keep her course during a severe gale. The captain of the Pentwater life saving crew attempted to reach her in a motor boat. The high sea and the wind hindered him, and he lost sight of the schooner. Acting on the suggestion of the Pentwater captain, the officer in charge of the station at Two Rivers, WI, and his men started a search in the neighborhood where the boat was last seen."

BOAT PROBABLY PERISHED (*Chicago Daily Journal*, Chicago, IL, December 4, 1912) "Telegrams received by the United States Internal Revenue Cutter Department and marine men convinced them that the boat probably perished between Pentwater and Ludington, Michigan… The reports from Pentwater and Ludington discouraged marine men and others in Chicago who had hoped that the schooner had put into some port because of the fierce wind storms which swept the lake. Few of them held out any further hope for the crew."

(Continued from previous page.)

GOES DOWN IN LAKE (*Chicago American*, Chicago, IL, December 4, 1912) "Storm-tossed wreckage found on the beaches near Pentwater, MI, late today told the story of the loss of the schooner *Rouse Simmons*. The vessel, it is now practically certain, went down in midlake with seventeen persons on board... The finding of the fragments, which pointed to the tragedy of the wind-beaten three-master, was related today by Captain M. R. Ewald, officer in charge of the Pentwater life saving station. 'I have no doubt but that the *Rouse Simmons* went down in midlake, probably Sunday night [November 24] while the big nor'wester was on,' said the Captain in a telephone conversation with the *Chicago American*. 'The first wreckage of the ship came in on last Wednesday when a Christmas tree, plainly cut for that purpose, squared off at the base, floated ashore and was found by the patrol. After that an old-fashioned hatch like the type on the old vessels came in. The next of the wreckage was bits of deckhousing, with evergreen sticking to the splinters. The stuff is still being tossed up on the beaches.'"

RELATIVES ARE ALARMED (*Milwaukee Daily News*, Milwaukee, WI, December 5, 1912) "Two weeks ago relatives of the fifteen men comprising the crew and forming the tree-cutting force, became anxious for the safety of the boat and started inquiries along the east and west shores of the lake."

NO HOPE FOR THE CREW (*Chicago Daily Journal*, Chicago, IL, December 5, 1912) "Captain Sogge said that he believes the distressed boat was the *Simmons* and that the sea beat it to pieces. There is no probability that any of the crew was saved, in the opinion of Captain Sogge. In spite of the general belief among marine men that the boat with its crew and its cargo of trees, ferns and wreath branches from the northern woods has gone to a grave at the bottom of the lake, search for the boat was continued by every vessel on Lake Michigan. Wireless messages from Chicago and from the revenue cutter *Tuscarora* enlisted every lake captain and every lighthouse and life-saving station on the lake in the endeavor to trace the schooner or find wreckage which would indicate where it went down... Not since the mystifying loss of the steamer *Chicora* between Chicago and South Haven with thirty passengers has such an extensive hunt been instituted for a lost steamer or vessel. Capt. Carland of the Chicago River life saving station has been in communication with other life saving stations along the lake, and he said today that he feared that the ship is lost. 'Extra men have been stationed on all the lookouts on the east shore and between Milwaukee and Chicago in the hope of sighting the *Rouse Simmons*,' said Capt. Carland."

TREE TOPS POINT TO DOOM OF "SANTA SHIP" (*Chicago Daily News*, Chicago, IL, December 5, 1912) "Is the Christmas tree schooner *Rouse Simmons* and the seventeen persons she carried at the bottom of the lake or is she still safe and sound? The preponderance of evidence indicates she is lost. An *Associated Press* dispatch from Manitowoc, WI, says that mute evidence tending to show that the schooner is at the bottom of Lake Michigan off Two Rivers Point, twelve miles north of Manitowoc, was brought in by fishermen who in lifting their nets found entangled in the mesh several small particles of Christmas tree tops. The find was made by Two Rivers fishermen about five miles north of that city and the lifesaving crew is making an investigation in an attempt to find wreckage of the missing boat."

FISHERMEN IN PULLING UP NETS FIND BITS OF CHRISTMAS TREE TOPS (*Manitowoc Daily Herald*, Manitowoc, WI, December 5, 1912) "Mute evidence of the fate of the 'Christmas Tree Schooner' *Rouse Simmons* and the seventeen persons aboard the vessel was brought to port today by fishermen who in lifting their nets north of the city, found pieces of evergreens, the tops of Christmas trees with which the ill-fated boat was loaded, clinging to the meshes of the nets and it is believed here that the *Simmons* sunk off Two Rivers Point with her crew and passengers, numbering seventeen souls in all... Reports of the finding of bits of evergreens in their nets was made by Eugene and Moses Allie, local fishermen who have their nets about eight miles north of the city and at a point near where it is believed the missing schooner sunk."

CHRISTMAS TREE SCHOONER SIGHTED/SANTA CLAUS SHIP MAY BE SAFE (*Chicago American*, Chicago, IL, December 5, 1912) "The missing schooner, *Rouse Simmons*, was sighted in Lake Michigan, three miles off shore south of Racine, WI, twenty-four hours ago. This report was received today by Captain Berry of the United States revenue cutter *Tuscarora*, which is searching the lake for Chicago's 'Christmas Ship.' The *Chicago Evening American* received this information from Captain Berry by wireless. The report gave a hope, but only a hope. Captain Berry was of the opinion that the officers of the *George W. Orr*, who thought they had sighted the vessel, were mistaken... By wireless, the reported sighting of the boat and a general order for search for wreckage was sent along the lake shores... If in fact it was the schooner *Rouse Simmons*, which the *George W. Orr* sighted, it seemed probable that the ship had been deserted or swept of its crew. Had the *Rouse Simmons* been flying the distress signals, which it bore when sighted off Kewaunee more than a week before, the *George W. Orr* would have given aid and reported. The *George W. Orr* is an ocean going vessel of heavy tonnage and deep keel... Messages by wireless to the *George W. Orr* were at once dispatched from Chicago sending stations, and an effort made to intercept it if at dock in Milwaukee."

FAINT HOPE IN WIRELESS (*Chicago Daily News*, Chicago, IL, December 5, 1912) "The forlorn hope that the Santa Claus Schooner might still be afloat was revived for a time when a wireless telegram was received from Captain Berry, commander of the revenue cutter *Tuscarora*, that the steamer *George W. Orr* had spoken to the Christmas tree laden vessel yesterday morning three miles southward of Racine, WI... Captain Berry's belief that the skipper of the steamer *Orr* was mistaken when he reported having seen the missing schooner near Racine, WI, was borne out in a long distance telephone conversation this afternoon with the *Orr*'s captain, Herman Jaenke. 'I did not actually see the vessel,' said Capt. Jaenke to a reporter for *The Daily News*, 'but I heard the ringing of a bell, and knowing that the schooner *Rouse Simmons* had a bell I thought at first that the fog signal was that of Capt. Nelson's boat. The vessel was about three miles off shore. Now that I have learned that the government lightship is anchored about three miles off one of the piers at Milwaukee, and also possesses a bell, in addition to a fog whistle, I am

(Continued from previous page.)

quite positive that I was mistaken in thinking the boat the *Rouse Simmons*. The lake was so foggy. I couldn't see the boat, and that accounts for my error.'"

RELATIVES STILL HAVE HOPE (*Chicago Daily News*, Chicago, IL, December 5, 1912) "Wives, sisters, and a sweetheart of the crew believed to have found a watery grave still clung today to fragments of hope that the seamen may have been saved, even though their boat foundered or went to pieces."

MORE WRECKAGE FROM THE CHRISTMAS SCHOONER *ROUSE SIMMONS* WASHES ASHORE (*Chicago American*, Chicago, IL, December 5, 1912) "The search for the ship gave way to a search for the wreckage, which was expected to tell the tale of death on the storm-beaten lake. Fishermen brought in bits of evergreens believed to be part of the Christmas tree cargo of the *Rouse Simmons* from the waters off Two Rivers Point, WI. This is not far from the point of Kewaunee, WI, where the *Rouse Simmons* was last seen with distress signals flying."

SIGHT BOAT'S EMPTY YAWL (*Chicago Daily News*, Chicago, IL, December 5, 1912) "A yawl, tossing empty on heavy seas off Kewaunee, WI, and identical in all discernible respects with the single boat carried by the *Rouse Simmons*, added its own silent testimony to other clues of the tragedy believed to have been enacted. The crew of the tow barge *Resumption* came into port here today and reported that they sighted the yawl last Friday and although they were unable to signal the vessel towing them in time to put about and secure the boat, they passed close enough for one of their number who had been on the *Rouse Simmons* to feel almost certain it belonged to that vessel. The seamen believe the yawl either was torn from fastenings as the *Rouse Simmons* sank or capsized as the crew was trying to escape in the smaller boat."

SCHOONER WENT DOWN IN NORTHWEST BLOW (*Sturgeon Bay Advocate*, Sturgeon Bay, WI, December 5, 1912) "It is now quite certain that the schooner went down in the big northwest blow…though no survivor lives to tell the awful story."

SCHOONER *ROUSE SIMMONS* BELIEVED TO BE AT THE BOTTOM OF LAKE MICHIGAN (*Menominee Herald Leader*, Menominee, MI, December 5, 1912) "Grief frenzied relatives of those on board the vessel have been striving day and night since Thanksgiving Day to find trace of the missing ones."

CHRISTMAS SHIP SAFE, SAY MARINERS (*Milwaukee Sentinel*, Milwaukee, WI, December 5, 1912) "That the Christmas Ship, *Rouse Simmons,* did not go to the bottom of the lake with eleven souls aboard but has sought shelter from the recent southern winds in some out-of-the-way island and that all are safe, is the opinion of Captain William Baxter of the *Kersarge*… 'I firmly believe that the *Simmons* is safe,' said Captain Baxter. 'In 1906 when I was on the *Sophia J. Luff* we were reported as lost after we had not been heard from for ten days. The bad winds made us seek safety in a lonely island where we could not get into telegraphic connection with the rest of the world. The weather during the last week has been such that a small schooner like the *Simmons* could have made safe shores. There have been strong southerly winds and my impression is that the boat has put in at one of the Gull or Green Bay islands. I feel sure that the boat will be heard from in a few days."

NO SIGNS ARE FOUND (*Milwaukee Sentinel*, Milwaukee, WI, December 5, 1912) "The revenue cutter *Tuscarora* has been searching the lake for two days but not a trace of the missing vessel or its cargo has been found. This fact is taken as a good sign that the 'Christmas Ship' has put in at some island in order to wait for more favorable weather and a clearing of the dense fog which has been hanging over the lake for three days."

SCHOONER *ROUSE SIMMONS* WHICH ANNUALLY TIED UP AT CLARK STREET MISSING (*Chicago Daily Tribune*, Chicago, IL, December 5, 1912) "It was reported that the hatches of a ship and a large quantity of Christmas greens had been washed ashore near Two Rivers, WI, and Pentwater, MI. Still another report reached Chicago that the schooner had put in at a little out-of-the-way port seventy-five miles from the city. This could not be verified…"

SEAMEN STILL CLING TO HOPE (*Menominee Herald Leader*, Menominee, MI, December 5, 1912) "Chicago seamen still cling to the hope that the vessel may be afloat somewhere far from shore. They point out that navigation is closed and there are so few craft on the lake that a ship, if disabled, might drift about for weeks without being sighted. Faith in this theory yesterday led to the Treasurer of the Chicago Seamen's Union to telegraph to Captain Berry of the Tuscarora a request to steam out into the lake immediately in search of the *Rouse Simmons*. The Tuscarora started on receipt of the message and is now covering the course the *Rouse Simmons* is supposed to have taken. Seamen admit, however, that if the three-masted schooner sighted in distress off Kewaunee, WI, was the Christmas Ship it almost certainly has gone to the bottom. No craft could have continued long in that part of the lake without being seen by passing vessels."

DID NOT SEE SCHOONER (*Chicago American*, Chicago, IL, December 5, 1912) "The *Saranac* of Buffalo, NY, a freighter of the Lehigh Valley Line, docked in Chicago late in the day after a cautious voyage down the lake. 'We had messages of the loss of the *Rouse Simmons* and kept a sharp lookout all the way down the lake,' said the officer in charge. 'We saw nothing.' The vigilance of life savers and harbor patrols along the lake coast was redoubled today."

LIFE SAVERS BATTLE IN VAIN (*Menominee Herald Leader*, Menominee, MI, December 5, 1912) "At dawn, life savers wallowing through the heavy swell that the storm had left in its wake reached the place where the stricken Christmas Ship had been last seen. No sign of a sail was in sight. The tossing waters were as inscrutably silent as to the fate of the schooner as the dull gray clouds that lowered overhead."

FLOATING YAWL SEEN IN MIDLAKE TWO DAYS AGO (*Milwaukee Daily News*, Milwaukee, WI, December 6, 1912) "The ship's yawl, empty and adrift, has been seen in

(Continued from previous page.)

midlake, indicating that a part, at least, of the fifteen persons on the schooner attempted to make their escape from the wreck in the small boat, but perished… The floating yawl was sighted two days ago in midlake by the lumber laden schooner, *Resumption*, which made port yesterday. Her captain says the boat was waterlogged, was drifting before the gale, and bore no evidence of occupants – dead or alive. His description of the yawl agrees in detail with the boat that swung at the stern of the missing Christmas Ship when she left Manistique, MI, loaded with 25,000 or 30,000 trees for the Chicago holiday trade."

MANY BOATS EXPOSED TO LAKE STORM/MARINE CIRCLES IN A FLURRY OVER BOATS THAT ARE MISSING (*Manitowoc Daily Herald*, Manitowoc, WI, December 6, 1912) "Consternation seized marine circles today when reports showed several large lake craft missing and overdue on schedules of arrival at ports on the lake and the wires are being kept hot in an effort to locate the boats, some of which may have met the fate of the schooner *Simmons* for whose safety all hope has been abandoned."

SEARCH FOR BOAT IN OUT-OF-WAY HARBORS WILL BE CONTINUED (*Chicago Daily Tribune*, Chicago, IL, December 6, 1912) "Several reports were current that the boat had put up at a harbor from which there were no telegraphic connections and that it was waiting there for favorable winds to bring it to Chicago. One of these reports was that the boat is either in Mud Bay or North Bay…. The Seamen's Union has been asked to have a boat sent there to see if the *Rouse Simmons* can be found… Search for the missing ship will be resumed today. It is planned to explore out-of-the-way harbors into which the ship may have been driven either by unfavorable winds or by accident."

GOVERNMENT CONTINUES SEARCH (*Chicago Daily Journal*, Chicago, IL, December 6, 1912) "The federal authorities redoubled their efforts to locate the lost boat or its wreckage, despite the apparent hopelessness of the task. The United States revenue cutter *Tuscarora*, Captain Berry commanding, put out from the harbor at Waukegan, IL, to push the search vigorously. Encouraged by the clearing of the atmosphere, Captain Berry said he expected to be able within a short time to settle definitely the fate of the boat and crew. 'If they are alive we will find them providing the weather remains clear,' said Captain Berry. 'We intend to push the search to a finish.' It was the intention of local shipping men to send a chartered vessel in search of the missing *Rouse Simmons*, but the wind veered to the southwest and increased until its velocity reached forty miles an hour. Captain Carland at the life saving station said that he believed the missing schooner, if not sunk, would be found ashore in the vicinity of Sturgeon Bay, WI. 'There is a chance that she was dismasted in the storm and is drifting about a helpless mass,' he said, 'but I doubt very much if she will ever be found. The time of her absence has convinced marine men she has gone down.' The search today extended to the most northern parts of the lake, and into out-of-the-way harbors and rivers of Wisconsin and Michigan."

LAKE GIVES UP DEAD/MAY BE CHRISTMAS SHIP VICTIM (*Chicago American*, Chicago, IL, December 6, 1912) "An unidentified body, believed to be that of one of the eighteen men on the lost schooner, *Rouse Simmons*, was cast up by the waves near Pentwater, MI, late today. The body was that of a man six feet tall and about fifty years old."

MISSING SHIP IS FOUND (*Chicago American*, Chicago, IL, December 6, 1912) "Hope of possible safety for the missing Christmas Ship, the *Rouse Simmons*, came from two sources late this evening. First was flashed from Manitowoc, WI, the news that the lumber barge *Arizona*, two days overdue in Chicago, and feared lost in the lake, had reached there in safety, though badly leaking from the fierce buffeting she had received during the gale. This gave rise to the belief that the *Rouse Simmons* might be heard from in an equally miraculous manner. Then came the identification of the body of a man washed ashore at Pentwater, MI, as that of Tony Johnson, a fisherman. It had been reported that the body was that of one of the eighteen men on the *Rouse Simmons*. Johnson was drowned off Pentwater November 23. When assured that the victim was not from the missing Christmas tree laden ship, watchers in Chicago took heart despite the hourly reports of wreckage being washed ashore at numerous points along the lake."

BODY OF FISHERMAN FOUND AT PENTWATER/ONE OF TRIO LOST ON THE *TWO BROTHERS* DISCOVERED ON BEACH (*Muskegon News Chronicle*, Muskegon, MI, December 6, 1912) "A dispatch to the *Evening Press* from Pentwater, MI, this afternoon establishes the identity of a body found on the beach there this morning as that of Tony Johnson, one of the three men drowned two weeks ago tomorrow when the fishing vessel *Two Brothers* went down. It was at first thought the body was from the missing schooner *Rouse Simmons*."

SEARCH COAST FOR DAYS (*Milwaukee Sentinel*, Milwaukee, WI, December 7, 1912) "The last hope for the safety of the Christmas Ship, the *Rouse Simmons,* went glimmering on Saturday when the *Tuscarora* arrived in Milwaukee without having seen nor heard any trace of the missing boat or passengers. 'For three days and nights we have searched the lake but there was nothing to tell the tale of the ill-fated boat and her passengers. Day and night we coasted from Milwaukee as far as Two Rivers, but our constant vigilance was not rewarded,' said Captain J. G. Berry. The government boat left Milwaukee on Wednesday and when four miles out got a wireless that a boat had been seen foundering near Waukegan, IL. All haste possible was made to this point, but it proved to be a false alarm… 'There is no doubt in my mind but that the boat is at the bottom of the lake,' said Captain Olsen of the local lifesaving station. 'I had hopes for a time that the little craft had put in at some island, but I now think that the boat is under the sea. The heavy storms and dense fogs of the last week have been about all that a big boat could stand much less a small schooner.'"

CHICAGOANS GIVE UP HOPE (*Chicago Daily Tribune*, Chicago, IL, December 7, 1912) "Wives of several sailors visited headquarters of the Lake Sailors Union and gave a description of their husbands to Secretary T. A. Hanson, so if a body was found identity could be established without delay. That any of the crew survived is improbable,

(Continued from previous page.)

according to Captain Garland of the life saving station. Ships more seaworthy than the *Rouse Simmons* weathered the fierce storm with difficulty."

BELIEVE *ROUSE SIMMONS* LOST (*Chicago Daily News*, Chicago, IL, December 7, 1912) "When asked if he had seen anything of the *Rouse Simmons*, Capt. Ellingson said: 'No, she has gone to the bottom. There is no question in my mind about that. I have sailed the west shore, the same course as the *Simmons*, and saw nothing of her. Her captain, Carl Nelson, was a man who knew no fear, and I am afraid this is one time when it would have been better to put to port than brave the awful sea. I think the boat sprang a leak, as her deck was pretty rotten, and went to the bottom with all hands. The Christmas trees and perhaps a few bodies are all they will ever find of her.' "

LAKE TRAGEDY (*Manitowoc Daily Herald*, Manitowoc, WI, December 7, 1912) "The fate of Chicago's Christmas ship has been settled definitely in the eyes of all lake sailors. Hundreds of tangled Christmas trees and evergreen wreaths were strewn along the beach for miles."

MANY VESSELS IN PERIL (*Milwaukee Sentinel*, Milwaukee, WI, December 7, 1912) "The *George Marsh*, laden with potatoes for Milwaukee and Chicago from Washington Island has not been heard from for more than twenty-four hours. The *Arizona*, bound from Canada to Chicago, due on December 4, is still unreported. The *Minerva*, en route from Green Bay, WI, to Chicago, is thought to be the schooner sighted by the *George Orr* and mistaken for the *Rouse Simmons*, but it has not been heard from. Lifesaving stations here fear that none of the schooners have survived Thursday night's storm. The entire lake region, with the exception of Ontario, is storm swept. At Sandusky, OH, the barge *F. N. Knapp*, in tow of the steamer *William A. Hazzard*, bound up the lakes with a cargo of coal, sank to the bottom of Lake Erie. The crew was saved by a passing ship."

LAST TIDINGS ON RECORD (*Milwaukee Sentinel*, Milwaukee, WI, December 8, 1912) "The last definite tidings concerning the schooner *Rouse Simmons* comes from Port Washington, WI, where on November 24, the now missing schooner was sighted. The boat was seen and recognized by Captain Herbert Smith and F. Wilson who were making lake observations from the top of a high lumber pile on the shore at Port Washington. A storm was raging at the time and the *Rouse Simmons* was battling its way through the waves..."

REACHED CHICAGO (*Milwaukee Sentinel*, Milwaukee, WI, December 8, 1912) "Covered with ice, her canvas frozen and with several broken booms, the schooner *Minerva*, with a cargo of lumber from Manistique, MI, reached Chicago Saturday, ten days overdue, after a thrilling battle with the wind and waves. Captain James Ellingston of Milwaukee gave a graphic description of the turbulent trip of the *Minerva*. Several hours later Captain M. J. Starkey brought the schooner *Arizona,* laden with lumber from Midland, Ontario, into Chicago port...."

VAIN SEARCH OF TWO DAYS (*Chicago Inter Ocean*, Chicago, IL, December 9, 1912) "Whatever doubt remained that the three-masted schooner *Rouse Simmons* has foundered with all on board was dispelled yesterday when the schooners *George Marsh* and *William Hossak, Jr.* reached Chicago. The *Marsh* left Washington Island two days ago, picking up the *Hossak* at Sturgeon Bay, WI. Both vessels made careful search during the trip for evidence of the fate of the *Simmons*. A few pieces of water soaked pine trees, believed to be part of the *Simmons'* cargo, were seen south of Waukegan, IL, but no wreckage or bodies were found. The vessels traveled a few miles apart, covering effectively the course the *Simmons* must have taken after passing Kewaunee, WI."

SHIPS SURVIVE – ALL BUT ONE (*Chicago Daily News*, Chicago, IL, December 9, 1912) "Lake navigators, from the stern-faced captain to the deckhand, on four three-masted schooners, breathed sighs of relief today when their vessels limped slowly into Chicago's harbor. Decks and bows of each were crusted with ice while torn sails and splintered spars bore evidence of the hazardous voyages of the sailing barks in heavy gales and storm lashed sea. Their arrival dispelled all fear regarding their safety and bore out the belief of marine agencies that all sailing craft had weathered the storms with the exception of the *Rouse Simmons*, which is believed to have gone to the bottom... The boats that arrived today are: *J. B. Taylor*, left Alpena, MI, November 23 with a cargo of lumber; *Edward E. Skeele*, left Charlevoix, MI, two weeks ago with lumber, bound for Chicago; *Cora S.*, left Washington Island, WI, two weeks ago with cargo of potatoes for Chicago... In speaking of his trip, Captain A. J. Anderson of the *J. B. Taylor* said: 'We had to anchor seven times in the teeth of a gale. There was a high sea most of the time. It was the worst trip I ever experienced on Lake Michigan. We had plenty of provisions and none of my men suffered any hardship.' Captain Thomas Bernston of the *Skeele* said he was forced to anchor four times. 'At times it was hopeless to try to make headway against the wind and high sea and several times we were carried far out of our course in the gale,' he said. 'We were all glad to get into harbor this morning.'"

MADE PORT IN CHICAGO (*Chicago American*, Chicago, IL, December 10, 1912) "Three ice-shrouded, storm-beaten schooners, out on the pitching wastes of the lake since Thanksgiving, made port in Chicago today. The old three-masters, *Cora A.*, *Butcher Boy*, and *Taylor*, had weathered the worst storm in the last two decades on the Great Lakes. The schooners are of the same type as the *Rouse Simmons*, which since 1868 had defied the terrors of Great Lakes shipping..."

SCHOONER THOUGHT TO HAVE SUNK IN MID-LAKE (*The Chronicle*, Two Rivers, WI, December 10, 1912) "The three-masted schooner *Rouse Simmons*, loaded with Christmas trees which was seen passing Kewaunee, WI, on November 23 has been given up as lost. Portions of the cargo have been found strewn along the lakeshore for many miles..."

STEAM VESSEL REPORTED TO HAVE IGNORED CALL FROM 18 DOOMED MEN/URGE FEDERAL INQUIRY (*Chicago American*, Chicago, IL, December 10, 1912) "Reports indicating that a steam vessel refused aid to the schooner *Rouse Simmons*, a few hours before the old three-master was lost with eighteen men on board, reached

(Continued from previous page.)

Chicago today. Sailors declared they would urge a federal inquiry. A railroad-owned steam vessel, plying the upper lake, is said to have sighted the *Rouse Simmons* at 2 p.m. on the last day that she was seen afloat. The captain of this vessel told his story of the vessel to Captain Thomas Bernston of the *Edward S. Skeele*, a schooner which made port here, along with three others. The story of the captain of the steam vessel indicated that he had seen the *Rouse Simmons* one hour before she was seen flying signals of distress off Kewaunee, WI. 'I talked to this captain in harbor at Manitowoc, WI,' said Captain Bernston. 'He said that at 2 o'clock in the afternoon of that day the *Rouse Simmons* was seen, and probably the day she went down, he had sighted her five miles off shore. This is what he told me: 'We were doing our best against the gale when the *Rouse Simmons* hove in sight. She was running ahead of the wind with a storm staysail and everything reefed in. She was heaped toward the shore. Even under the rag of a sail she had up she was almost on beam ends and her cabin almost buried in the sea, she laid over so hard. She was about five miles off shore. I laid to so they wouldn't have to bring her about. I was afraid they couldn't make it. The *Rouse Simmons* didn't fly any distress signals then.' Seamen declared there was a grave doubt as to the truth of the statement that the *Rouse Simmons* was not flying distress signals at that time. An hour later, at 3 p.m., she was flying signals of distress plainly visible to the life savers at Kewaunee."

"STILL A CHANCE" PER MISS ELSIE SCHUENEMANN (*Chicago American*, Chicago, IL, December 10, 1912) "I haven't given up hope that father and the crew will be found safe on some of the islands. There is still a chance."

GIVEN UP FOR LOST (*Ludington Chronicle*, Ludington, MI, December 11, 1912) "It is now an established fact that the schooner *Rouse Simmons*, which left Manistique, MI, with a load of Christmas trees, and which has been missing since that time, is in the bottom of Lake Michigan, with all on board lost…she was not given up for lost until wreckage and part of her cargo were found at various places on both shores."

MARINE NEWS (*Milwaukee Daily News*, Milwaukee, WI, December 12, 1912) "Capt. Berry and the revenue cutter *Tuscarora* will be unable to carry out the request of friends of the crew of the missing schooner *Rouse Simmons* to make another search for the Christmas Tree Ship that is feared was lost in the gale on Lake Michigan late in November. The *Tuscarora* went out of commission on Tuesday of this week, when thirty of the crew were discharged. Twenty more will receive their discharges tomorrow, and there are not sufficient men on the cutter to carry out the instructions, should an order to make the search come from Washington. The friends of the crew of the *Simmons* have sent an appeal to Washington asking the Secretary of the Treasury to order the *Tuscarora* to make a search among the islands at the lower end of the lake, hoping that the schooner is in some safe retreat far from communication with the main land. Marine men declare the hope is vain. There are no islands at the lower end of the lake that could conceal a vessel the size of the *Simmons* for three weeks without the fact becoming known to some fishing craft or a lake vessel. The Foxes are frequented by many ships in bad weather. The Manitous are settled and are in constant communication with the main land. Beaver Island has a steamer connecting with Charlevoix. High Island is so close to Beaver Island that signaling would be possible. Hog Island and Garden Island are so close to the course of vessels passing up and down the lake that signals could be seen day or night. And the islands of Green Bay are out of the question. All sailor men agree that there can be no hope for the *Simmons* being in shelter behind any of these islands, or that any survivors of the boat are in safety there."

DAUGHTER OF SKIPPER OF MISSING *ROUSE SIMMONS* STILL HOPES FOR RETURN OF SHIP (*Chicago American*, Chicago, IL, December 12, 1912) "The eyes of Miss Elsie Schuenemann, daughter of the gallant Captain Herman Schuenemann of the ill-fated Christmas ship *Rouse Simmons*, are still turned toward the east, out over Lake Michigan. For the daughter of the skipper of the *Rouse Simmons* never has given up hope that some day in the near future she will hear the whistles blow long and loudly, and she will see the schooner turn its prow into the Chicago River. She, who has called herself 'a daughter of the lake,' cannot and will not believe that her father's ship has gone down, with all on board. With hope strong for the safety of her father, Miss Schuenemann has, in what she calls his temporary absence, endeavored to take his place."

NOTE IN BOTTLE TELLS FATE OF *ROUSE SIMMONS* (*Chicago American*, Chicago, IL, December 13, 1912) "The story of the fate of the *Rouse Simmons*, Chicago's missing Christmas Ship, was washed up out of the lake today. It came as a farewell message from the despairing crew. It was found in a bottle floating in Lake Michigan… Discovery of the fateful note came just at the time when a last desperate effort was being made to find the missing ship. The revenue cutter *Tuscarora* was awaiting orders in Milwaukee from Secretary of the Treasury MacVeagh in answer to an appeal to permit the cutter to start on a cruise of the northern lake waters in search of the *Rouse Simmons*."

TUSCARORA TO SEEK FOR LOST SCHOONER (*Milwaukee Daily News*, Milwaukee, WI, December 13, 1912) "The revenue cutter *Tuscarora* at Milwaukee was ordered by Secretary MacVeagh today to make another diligent search of the Northern islands in Lake Michigan for trace of the schooner *Rouse Simmons* and her crew of sixteen men. The *Tuscarora* is out of commission, but Capt. Berry will at once reassemble a crew and is expected to leave at once."

BUTCHER BOY SAFE IN PORT (*Menominee Herald Leader*, Menominee, MI, December 13, 1912) "The lumber schooner *Butcher Boy*, with a crew of seven, is safe at Milwaukee, according to a message to the agents here. It had been missing since last Saturday. The schooner sailed from Manistique, the Michigan port from which the ill-fated Christmas ship *Rouse Simmons* sailed a month ago."

STORY OF BOTTLE CONTAINING MESSAGE WAS FOUND OFF SHEBOYGAN IS DENIED (*Chicago Record-Herald*, Chicago, IL, December 14, 1912) "Reports received here yesterday from Sheboygan, WI, that a fisherman had picked up a bottle containing a posthumous message from Captain Schuenemann of the schooner *Rouse Simmons* is denied."

(Continued from previous page.)

ORDERED TO RENEW HUNT (*Milwaukee Sentinel*, Milwaukee, WI, December 14, 1912) "Captain J. G. Berry on Friday received a telegram from the government ordering him to start out on a search of Lake Michigan with the hope of finding some trace of the *Rouse Simmons*."

SEEK LOST CREW ON BARREN ISLE (*Chicago American*, Chicago, IL, December 14, 1912) "Notwithstanding the message supposed to have been received from the missing Christmas ship, *Rouse Simmons*, in a bottle found floating in Lake Michigan, the United States revenue cutter *Tuscarora* was to leave Milwaukee today to search the islands of northern Lake Michigan for traces of the crew. Orders directing the cutter to make the search were received from Washington. Captain Berry of the *Tuscarora* was to take his boat first to Belle Island, one of the larger islands of the lake that is not inhabited. Navigation for the cutter will be dangerous at this time of the year."

SEND THE *MACKINAC* TO SEARCH ISLANDS FOR LOST VESSEL (*Milwaukee Daily News*, Milwaukee, WI, December 14, 1912) "Messages countermanding the order for the revenue cutter *Tuscarora* to proceed to the lower end of Lake Michigan and search for the missing schooner *Rouse Simmons* were received today by Capt. Berry. The machinery of the *Tuscarora* partly has been taken apart and the crew discharged, and when the facts were made known today to the Treasury Department officials, Capt. Berry's orders were countermanded. However, the Department is determined a search shall be made for the missing boat, and today the cutter *Mackinac,* stationed at the Soo, was ordered to proceed to Lake Michigan and visit all the islands in hope that the *Simmons* has been behind one of them for shelter since she was last seen three weeks ago. Marine men today again ridiculed the theory that the *Simmons* possibly can be at one of the Lake Michigan islands."

RENEW HUNT FOR MISSING MEN (*Chicago Record-Herald*, Chicago, IL, December 15, 1912) "Running down a forlorn hope that the sixteen men who sailed aboard Chicago's missing Christmas tree schooner, the *Rouse Simmons*, may have reached some island in Lake Michigan from which they have been unable to escape, the revenue cutter *Mackinac* received orders from Washington yesterday to rush from Sault Ste. Marie, MI, to the northern islands of the lake."

CAPTAIN INGAR OLSEN BELIEVES REVENUE CUTTER ON HOPELESS SEARCH FOR LOST SCHOONER (*Milwaukee Sentinel*, Milwaukee, WI, December 16, 1912) "Captain Ingar Olsen of the Milwaukee Lifesaving Station says that he thinks that there is little chance for the revenue cutter *Mackinac*, which was ordered to leave Sault Ste. Marie, MI, on Saturday to search for the lost schooner, *Rouse Simmons*, of finding the lost boat. Captain Olsen has not much faith in the belief that the schooner went abeach on one of the many islands that are on the northern route of lake vessels. He thinks that if it was stranded on one of these that it would have been reported long before now. A number of these islands are connected by telephone, and the possibility of a vessel lying wrecked on one of them without being reported is small."

EFFORTS TO LOCATE MISSING *ROUSE SIMMONS* FINALLY ABANDONED (*Milwaukee Sentinel*, Milwaukee, WI, December 18, 1912) "The search for the long lost schooner *Rouse Simmons*, with its crew of fifteen men, which was undertaken last week by the revenue cutter *Mackinac*, under orders from the Treasury Department, was abandoned on Tuesday."

MEN ON SCHOONER *BUTCHER BOY* BRING LAST WORD OF THE *ROUSE SIMMONS* (*Chicago Record-Herald*, Chicago, IL, December 19, 1912) "The captain and crew of the schooner *Butcher Boy*, which docked in the south branch of the Chicago River yesterday afternoon, saw the *Rouse Simmons*, Chicago's Christmas tree schooner, put to sea from South Manistique, MI, in the face of a rising gale. Those aboard the *Butcher Boy*, which itself weathered the recent heavy lake gales with difficulty, say there is no possibility that the men on the *Simmons* escaped. 'When we saw the *Simmons* beating out,' said Captain August Hansen of the *Butcher Boy* last night, 'I said to the others: Captain Schuenemann must be in a terrible hurry to get those Christmas trees to market. I wouldn't go out into this storm for all the trees the *Mauretania* could carry. Those boys will be lucky if they don't go to the bottom. The *Rouse Simmons* beat out on Friday. There was a heavy head sea running in. There was sudden nasty weather, about the most sudden I remember. We lay through Saturday and part of Sunday, and when we did clear we had to run under double reefs and then lay three days in the lea of Plum Island. We didn't see anything of the *Rouse Simmons*, but if the *Butcher Boy* couldn't stand up against the weather I know the *Simmons* couldn't for it was an older schooner and the deckhouse full of Christmas trees fore and aft made it unseaworthy. When we made Milwaukee last Thursday the schooner was covered with ice and was down by the head badly. I don't remember when I've seen the lake ice up more quickly.'"

TO BROOM LAKE (*Manistique Pioneer-Tribune*, Manistique, MI, December 20, 1912) "On Saturday of last week, the crew of the revenue cutter *Mackinac*, stationed at the Soo, was given orders to proceed at once to Lake Michigan, and broom the upper portion of the lake for tidings of the schooner, *Rouse Simmons*, which is believed to be lost. It will be remembered that the boat cleared from this port with a big cargo of Christmas trees for the Chicago market late in November and has not been heard of since sailing. Owing to the nature of the cargo the boat would not sink and the government fears that members of the crew may still be aboard the vessel and that the wreck has drifted among islands that have no communication with the main land."

"The Life Savers rode the deadly rollercoaster of sweeping seas and crashing waves. Desperately, their eyes stared off at the horizon, hoping for a glimpse of the schooner. Dodging through a raging storm in an open lifeboat must have been a horrifying experience. The crewmen were well-trained and offered no complaints. They knew the passengers and crew were depending on them."

Went Missing II
Frederick Stonehouse
Copyright 1984

Although it was not uncommon for one schooner to be mistaken for another – especially during a storm when visibility was poor – there continued to be more than a fair share of questions surrounding this shipwreck. It was a case of who saw what and when.

Early reports indicated the Two Rivers Life Saving crew had also spotted the *Simmons* during its search. However, Captain Sogge's report contradicted this. The report read: "There was nothing to be seen of the schooner." Over the years, the hearsay of a sighting by the Two Rivers crew found its way into the record and, thus, many persons to this day believe this detail to be factual.

In the days and weeks following the *Simmons'* loss, beach patrols continued to be in operation all over the lake. Captains were asked to keep an eye out for the missing ship. Both sides of the shore were lined with people "watching night and day" in a "tireless patrol" to look for clues and search for answers.

The human factor of the Christmas Tree Ship story had far-reaching effects. Those who heard about the ship's loss found it difficult to grasp the timing of the tragedy as it contrasted itself against the great holiday of mankind. Compounded with this was the fact that a husbandless wife and three fatherless children were left in the storm's wake, and it was Christmas. Everyone wanted to help in some small way.

As a result of the storm's 60+ mile gales, telephone wires were down and limbs were torn from trees. It is not difficult to imagine the scene of debris, nor to ponder the speculation that followed. Evergreen branches on beaches were assumed to have come from the doomed schooner whether they had or not. Planks and boards that washed ashore were examined and thought to have originated from the *Simmons*. Although errors were made in identifying debris, people really did care, and they were doing their best to help. There was a sense of community – "come in unity" - at the heart of this tragedy.

People were passionate about wanting answers because of their love for the story. Chicago had taken ownership of the Christmas Tree Ship and the Schuenemann Family years earlier, and now the legacy was proving itself to be bigger than the *Simmons*, bigger than the Schuenemanns, and even bigger than Chicago. The story connected to people on a very human level, and although the tragedy of 1912 amplified this, the love people felt for the Christmas Tree Ship had existed long before the demise of the *Simmons*, and it continued to exist long afterwards. Still, there was a sense of sadness in articles published by the Chicago press during the initial days the *Simmons* went missing when the city realized it may be losing the great and grand tradition it had come to know.

At Kewaunee, the wind came up,
and it began to snow.
Rouse Simmons, she did not stop,
she still had far to go.
But the storm became a blizzard,
and the lake began to roar,
Rouse Simmons, she changed her course,
and headed for the shore.

Amid snow-whitened Christmas trees,
the captain took his stand.
He tried in vain to save the ship,
but never got to land.
And in the spring the fishermen,
who fished off Kewaunee,
pulled up their nets and found them to
be full of Christmas trees.

Excerpted from the song *"The Ballad of The Christmas Tree Ship"*
Pamela Yarwood, Singer/Songwriter
On file at: Great Lakes Dossin Museum
As published in the *Evening News*, Sault Ste. Marie, Michigan
October 1967

For those who lived around the Great Lakes, the Schuenemann story connected on yet another level. This family's tragedy became everyone's tragedy because it was a reminder of the danger that was ever present for each of them. Even if a family living on the waters had not experienced loss as a part of their past, the threat of it would always be a part of their future. (It was for this reason there was such a strong Code of Honor on the Lakes when it came to helping others in need. One never knew when it would be your own life hanging in the balance, or the life of someone you loved.)

For those who knew the pain of waiting for answers that never came, the *Simmons* tragedy opened wounds already suffered, and old memories crawled out of the shallow graves they were buried in.

Directly across Lake Michigan, only miles from the site of the *Rouse Simmons'* sinking, the community of Ludington, Michigan, was following developments in search efforts. This city was nicknamed "The Fatherless" because of all the lives lost in the shipping industry during the 1800's.

**BODY CAST UP
ON SHORE
Victim Found at
Pentwater Believed
from "Yule Schooner"
VESSELS HIT BY
STORM**
Chicago Daily News
Chicago, IL
December 6, 1912

The local mariners were made uneasy when the following boats, which were due here, were unsighted at the hours when they were scheduled for docking:

ALABAMA, owned by the Goodrich Transit Company, a passenger boat arriving from Grand Haven, Michigan; due at 6:30 a.m.; three hours later its captain, R. E. Redner, communicated by wireless that the vessel was in good condition, but experiencing a rough voyage; it arrived an hour later.

MINERVA, a three-masted schooner, carrying a cargo of lumber from Manistee, Michigan; buffeted about by sea until it was finally compelled to cast anchor in the harbor at Sturgeon Bay, Wisconsin.

ARIZONA, steamer, carrying a cargo of lumber from Midland, Ontario; boat is twenty hours overdue and is not expected to dock until tomorrow. W.E. Holmes & Co., 304 Sherman Street, Chicago, agents for the vessel, declare it has experienced trouble in battling head winds and has been obliged to proceed slowly; declared to be in good condition.

GEORGE MARSH, three-masted schooner, bringing a cargo of potatoes from Washington Island, Wisconsin; craft was forced to join the ship *Minerva* and anchor in Sturgeon Bay after fighting the waves.

J.B. TAYLOR, another three-masted schooner, sailing under the Holmes agency; sought refuge in Bailey's Harbor, Wisconsin, until the gale subsides.

**STEVEN NELSON'S
BODY ASHORE**

The body of an unidentified man, believed to have been a sailor on the missing [*Rouse Simmons*], was found on the beach at Pentwater, Michigan, according to an *Associated Press* dispatch received this afternoon. It had been washed ashore. Near the body was scattered wreckage which also is believed to be from the lost boat. The body was that of a man between 45 and 50 years old and 6 feet tall. The description

Heartfelt efforts to locate clues continued. Every flicker of hope was reported on, as well as every hope dashed.

Several schooners similar to the *Rouse Simmons* began to "limp" into ports. Many of these ships had been reported missing, as the *Simmons* had, and hope was elevated for the *Simmons'* safety as each arrived.

Government officials from Chicago to Washington D.C., including a Senator, as well as the Secretary of the Treasury, were involved in examining details of the *Simmons'* loss from every angle.

Old-timers at the docks speculated on possibilities. Some believed the ship might be floating helpless in the middle of the lake if its masts or sails had been damaged in the storm. The vessel would then be at the mercy of the wind, and the ship could be anywhere.

Others believed the ship and crew were possibly stranded on an island. They unfolded maps and made their case.

of the body tallies with that of Steven Nelson, one of the crew of the *Rouse Simmons*. Nelson was the tallest member of the crew, being nearly six feet tall; and was about 48 years old. Upon his left hand was tattooed an anchor.

TATTOO MARK TO IDENTIFY HIM

"The only sailor on the boat who answered that description was Nelson," said Thomas A. Hanson, Treasurer of the Lake Seamen's Union. "His identification can easily be made by glancing at his left hand, which bears the tattoo mark of a large anchor. He sometimes wore a mustache."

Miss Elsie Schuenemann, daughter of Captain Schuenemann, likewise classed the description of the body with that of Nelson.

Another concern was that many small communities did not have telephone communications, and the crew might not have access to "a wireless".

Some sailors wondered if the crew attempted to escape the vessel in its yawl. If so, did they make it to shore? No one knew.

Memories were also recalled of other ships from previous years that seemingly vanished but later presented themselves safe.

Sailors looked at every possibility from every angle, as they would hope someone would do for them.

While this was going on, search efforts were conducted during wind, fog, rain, and snow across the lake called Michigan, a name derived from the Algonquian Chippewa Indian word "meicigama" meaning "big sea water".

On December 5, 1912, the *Menominee Herald Leader* of Menominee, Michigan, reported: "The *Rouse Simmons* has now been missing for fifteen days. Its disappearance, if it remains as inexplicable as it is now, bids fair to become one of the great mysteries of the Great Lakes."

HOPE IS REVIVED FOR CHICAGO'S CHRISTMAS SHIP
Lake-Faring Men Believe the *Rouse Simmons* May Have Put Into Harbor to Evade Storms
IMMEDIATE SEARCH URGED
Chicago Inter Ocean
Chicago, IL
December 12, 1912

Belief that the schooner *Rouse Simmons* did not go down with all hands, but has run aground on one of the small islands in northern Lake Michigan has led lake seamen and friends of Capt. Herman Schuenemann's family to appeal for the organization of a searching party to seek the lost captain and crew.

A movement was started yesterday to put the facts before Senator Shelby M. Cullom, asking him to order the revenue cutter *Tuscarora* to make an exhaustive search of the small islands in the northern waters where Captain Schuenemann and crew of fifteen may be marooned.

Miss Elsie Schuenemann, daughter of the lost skipper, has volunteered to accompany the party...

The fact that no bodies have been found, despite vigilant lookout kept by all vessels plying in the waters where the Christmas schooner was believed to have sunk, adds conviction to the minds of lakefaring men that the boat must have put in disabled at some island.

Immediate search of the islands is necessary, as there was but a small supply of food aboard the schooner, and the crew already must face starvation if they are shipwrecked on an island and out of communication with the world.

URGE U.S. VESSEL LOOK FOR MISSING *ROUSE SIMMONS*
Sailors Appeal to Secretary MacVeagh to Order Cutter to Scour Northern Shore Line
Chicago Inter Ocean
Chicago, IL
December 13, 1912

An appeal was sent to Secretary of the Treasury Franklin Mac-Veagh yesterday urging him to order out the revenue cutter *Tuscarora* to search the islands of northern Lake Michigan for the missing crew of the lost Christmas ship, *Rouse Simmons*.

The necessity for immediate action was urged upon the official, and if the government deems it advisable to send out the boat, she will be under steam and at sea today. The *Tuscarora* is quartered at Milwaukee.

The hope of sixteen bereft families and the sailor friends of the captain and crew now centers upon the search of the *Tuscarora*.

It has been explained by lake-faring men, with charts and maps to substantiate their contention, that from the direction of the wind and the position of the *Rouse Simmons* when she ran into the face of the gale the chance of her being stranded on northern islands or reefs is more than probable.

SIXTEEN FAMILIES ANXIOUS
Sixteen firesides, those of the missing crew, some destitute because of the absence of a breadwinner, await with eagerness the word from Washington today.

The lengthy telegram sent to Secretary MacVeagh detailed the story of the missing ship and the strong probabilities of her being marooned and helpless on one of the bleak, wind-swept little land spots which dot the northern reaches of the lake.

These words proved to be prophetic beyond belief during the decades that followed as the *Simmons* continued to remain an unsolvable mystery, an inexplicable puzzle.

Closure to the story was sought, but no closure came until those who wished for it more than anyone in the world – Barbara and her girls – passed from this world to the next where the captain was waiting for them there.

The ship was not discovered until 1971, and the only person yet alive from the captain's family was his daughter, Pearl. Over half a century had passed before she knew for certain what had happened to her papa's ship.

Even then, the search continued – the search for answers and the search for information. It is important to note that much of what has been reported over the past century includes countless versions of numerous details. Some of the discrepancies include the date the ship left the Upper Peninsula (dates range from November 12 through November 25), the date the ship sank (dates range from November 12 through dates in December), the rescue crews who sighted the ship (various), the rescue crews who launched a vessel in search of the ship (various), the number of trees on board (numbers range from 2,000 – 50,000), and the city the ship departed from (Thompson, MI, Manistique, MI, Constance, MI, and Stephenson, MI, were all named).

These are just a handful of examples to illustrate the fact that even the most basic questions concerning the story can be difficult to answer because of the abundance of incorrect information that exists.

Many details reported on through the years were at odds with others, yet people continued to search for the truth of who Captain Schuenemann was. They were drawn to him in his death as others were drawn to him in his life.

On December 13, 1974, the *Chicago Daily News* published the following question from one of its readers:

> *"Even now when the roar of the lake surf is heard on a wintry day the fishermen and others along the shore recall the story of the Christmas Tree Ship and her gallant crew."*
>
> *Lakeland Yachting*
> December 1946
> Gerhard Miller

CUTTER TO SEARCH FOR MISSING SHIP
Mackinac is Ordered to Northern Lake Michigan in Hope of Finding Traces of the Rouse Simmons
Chicago Inter Ocean
Chicago, IL
December 15, 1912

The Revenue cutter *Mackinac* was yesterday ordered to leave Sault Ste. Marie, Michigan, immediately to search the waters and islands of northern Lake Michigan for traces of the lost schooner, *Rouse Simmons*, and her crew of thirteen men.

The *Mackinac* is well fitted for scout service at this season, being fully equipped with ice slashers and powerful engines. The *Tuscarora*, first ordered from Milwaukee for this service, is partially dismantled. The crew was discharged about ten days ago and the boat ordered into winter quarters.

The belief is still current in marine circles, and with the family and friends of Captain Herman Schuenemann, that the *Simmons* was driven from her course by heavy gales and was either beached or stranded on one of the many small islands which dot the northern route of lake vessels.

Owing to the lateness of the season and the formation of ice floes, regular lake navigation has practically been abandoned. If the vessel has been beached in distress, it is said the chance would be small of getting relief from passing vessels.

The *Mackinac* is expected to leave the Soo this morning and will remain out as long as there seems hope of finding trace of the missing *Simmons*.

REVENUE CUTTER BACK; THINK SIMMONS SUNK
Sault Ste. Marie Evening News
Sault Ste. Marie, MI
December 17, 1912

Voicing the prediction that the *Rouse Simmons*, the Christmas tree schooner bound for Chicago and long overdue, Lieutenant Wheeler, in command of the revenue cutter *Mackinac* arrived in the city today after scouring the islands in the northern part of Lake Michigan.

Members of the crew of the revenue cutter declare they searched carefully over the widely scattered islands and the sections of the lake surrounding them without avail. At one of the islands they took on board the owner of the missing vessel and he accompanied them in their search. When no trace of the boat was discovered the search was given up for good, all unqualifiedly declaring she had become waterlogged and sunk with all on board.

"What was the name of the master of the Christmas Tree Ship of Chicago legend? Signed, Mrs. D. L. Wilmette."

A heartwarming summary of Captain Schuenemann was published in answer to Mrs. Wilmette's question. The editorial began with the words "once upon a time" and told of a man who was "as merry and warm a man as Santa Claus himself."

"Every year he would bring to Chicago from the Far North, Michigan's Upper Peninsula," wrote the paper, "a shipload of bright, tangy balsams and tall, thick pines to help the city – particularly the poor – have a merry Christmas."

Fifty-two years had passed since this "merry" man had perished, yet Time had not forgotten him. Neither had the city he loved. The *Chicago Daily News* devoted a lengthy column to the re-telling of his story, as it had done in past years, and would do again in the future.

There was someone else who had not forgotten Captain Schuenemann either. Her name was Mrs. Charlotte Gennerich, a resident of Germany. As coincidence would have it, Mrs. Gennerich just so happened to be in the United States visiting family when the editorial ran, and she just so happened to read it. What followed next was "an unusual and very special reunion".

According to the *Streator Times-Press*, Streator, IL, of December 31, 1974: "Mrs. Charlotte (Grundmann) Gennerich of Germany, was driven to Streator on Monday by her daughter and son-in-law, Mr. and Mrs. Andreas (Ursula) von Koeppen of Wheaton, IL. The trio visited Mrs. Pearl Ehling, a resident of Heritage Manor nursing home. Circumstances surrounding the reunion came about as the result of a question posed to the "Beeline" of the *Chicago Daily News* in Chicago on December 13th. The question was simply, 'What was the name of the master of the Christmas Tree Ship of Chicago legend?' Joe Mann, editor of the question and answer type column responded with the entire story about Captain Herman Schuenemann and the legend of the Christmas Tree Ship. A letter from Mrs. von Koeppen was sent to Mr. Mann as her mother, Mrs. Gennerich, happened to be visiting in the United States when the article appeared. Mrs. Gennerich remembered well the legend and had known the Schuenemann family, having lived with her parents and sister in Chicago near Lincoln Park in the same home where the Schuenemann twins, Pearl and Hazel, lived. Pearl later became Mrs. William H. Ehling. Her twin sister, Hazel, died about 12 years ago. Mr. Mann's method of follow-up included pondering the 25th anniversary review of the legend which gave Captain Schuenemann's daughter's married names, including Mrs. Ehling. He called all people in the Chicago area with that last name until he found someone who knew the whereabouts of Pearl Ehling in Streator. It was a coincidence that Mrs. Gennerich, who returned to Germany in 1912 due to homesickness, was here at the time of the printing of the question and answer. Mr. Mann indicated he felt the 'whole turn of events' was amazing."

Sixty years had passed since Charlotte Grundmann had seen the Schuenemann family, yet she felt compelled to search for them after many long years.

Pearl (Schuenemann) Ehling was the last of the family to remain, and she became the recipient of an armful of gifts Charlotte came bearing.

What is it about this story, and this family, that keeps people searching for them? Even complete strangers show up at the Acacia Park Cemetery in Chicago asking for directions to the Schuenemann gravesite. (The cemetery office keeps the Schuenemann information card within easy reach because of the many inquiries they have had through the years.) People are searching. For what? I believe they are searching for the story Captain and Mrs. Schuenemann wrote on hearts. The written record, unarguably, is not perfect, and historians may be appalled by my asking, but I wonder if this really matters in the end. I truly believe, after years of research, that the most important piece of this story is exactly what has survived: The belief that this family did their best to make the world a better place. *This* is the core of the Schuenemann legacy as it has been handed down through the years by those who knew the family first hand.

"Sight of the little schooner brought joy and gladness to the hearts of hundreds and thousands. The arrival of the ship at Chicago, with its trees lashed to its masts, was a happy traditional occasion, marking the start of the Yule season... The owner of the Christmas Tree Ship was as much loved by his crew as he was by the thousands of children he made happy at about this time of year."

Manitowoc Herald
Manitowoc, WI
November 24, 1962

PERSONAL RECOLLECTIONS

REUNION BASED ON LEGEND OF CHRISTMAS TREE SHIP

STREATOR TIMES-PRESS Tuesday, December 31, 1974

An unusual and very special reunion of two women, who had not seen each in other in over 60 years occurred in this city Monday. The association of the two women involved in the reunion dates back to the early 1900s. One of the women, currently visiting her family in the United States, returned to her homeland of Germany in 1912.

REUNITED AFTER MORE THAN 60 YEARS were two women, who as children lived in the same home in Chicago and both personally know the legend of the Christmas Tree Ship. Mrs. Charlotte Gennerich (right) of Germany brought flowers, candy and other gifts to her long-time friend, Mrs. Pearl Ehling of Streator. Mrs. Ehling's late father, Captain Herman Schuenemann, was the generous man responsible for the legend of the ship.

(Times-Press Photo)

Photo of Mrs. Pearl (Schuenemann) Ehling with her childhood friend, Mrs. Charlotte (Grundmann) Gennerich (Courtesy of the *Streator Times-Press*, Streator, Illinois)

Again, the written record fails, but hearts haven't.

"The schooner *Rouse Simmons*, Captain Schuenemann, recently arrived in Chicago with a cargo of Christmas trees," reported the *Sturgeon Bay Advocate* on November 28, 1912. The newspaper missed the mark by a long shot, but one week later they got it right: "It is now quite certain that the schooner went down in the big northwest blow, though no survivor lives to tell the awful story."

The "awful story" went untold concerning the final moments aboard the *Simmons* as it sunk below, but the story above the waters remained. The Lake had succeeded in silencing the worst, but it was powerless to silence the best.

"The loss of no vessel on the Great Lakes aroused more sympathy than that of the Rouse Simmons, *known as the Christmas Tree Ship."*

Sturgeon Bay Advocate
Sturgeon Bay, WI
August 26, 1927

Photo of the *Rouse Simmons* with a shadowy figure visible on deck.
(Courtesy of the Historical Collections of the Great Lakes,
Jerome Library, Bowling Green State University, Bowling Green, Ohio)

Chapter Six

Superstitious Warnings
&
Ghost Ship Sightings

"Old-timers believe, according to the lore of the lakes, that Captain Schuenemann still sails the Christmas Tree Ship on stormy nights in December. How else, they ask, could the tossing waves be stained that deep pine-tree green in winter?"

The Elks Magazine
Dec. 2002/Jan. 2003
Jack Bellin

Superstitious Warnings & Ghost Ship Sightings

Throughout history, superstition has played a major role in shaping the beliefs and actions of people from all walks of life. These beliefs may have been held dearest by those brave enough to fair the open seas.

There are more than a handful of details concerning the sailing of the Christmas Tree Ship that sound more like a Halloween story than they do a Yuletide tale. Erie omens, superstitious warnings, and ghost ship sightings are hidden in every corner of this story like phantoms in the shadows. A person can begin to feel uncomfortable reading through the century old accounts of that fateful day in 1912 when the Christmas Tree Ship disappeared, especially if you are doing so at night, in a creaky, old house, as I was, half expecting someone from behind to whisper, *"Boo."*

The days and hours leading up to the ship's final voyage have become legend, and for good reason. It's one thing for a disaster at sea to include a bit of coincidence that would cause an old sailor shake his head, but it's quite another for a single tragedy to embody enough ominous details of things that "go bump in the night" to make the same sailor's head swim (pardon the pun).

Such was the case with the *Rouse Simmons*. There are so many superstitious warnings layered in this story that one can't help but wonder at the words "the fate of the *Rouse Simmons* was fixed before the vessel left Chicago (*Chicago Daily Journal,* December 4, 1912)." Those back in Chicago who believed the *Simmons* should not have sailed were 'dead on' in the accuracy of their prediction.

It would be easy to scoff at the superstitions held by sailors, easy to raise one's eyebrows in amusement when hearing of the omens sailors were convinced would determine their fate while sailing on the open waters, to pass each off with a laugh. But to the men who devoted their lives to shipping, who grasped with white-knuckled hands as their boat was tossed like a bathtub toy during a tumultuous storm, these beliefs were more than mere folklore. They were a matter of life and death. Superstitions were not passed off lightly, but were deeply held beliefs.

A pupil of superstition must sit up straight and take note. Blink an eye for a moment too long and chance missing an omen that could determine the fate of the vessel you are about to climb aboard. Overlooking a single sign could mean the demise of the entire crew.

For sailors of the Great Lakes, as well as sea-faring and ocean sailors, these superstitions were handed down from generation to generation, passed along by "old salts" who could read the world around them like a book, who could hear its voice, silent to most, but not to all. Taking note of the happenings on and around a ship was nearly a religious practice. Everything was watched with a trained and careful eye – the sky, the wind, the waves.

"Red sky in the morning, sailor take warning; red sky at night, sailor's delight," believed old sailors, as do sailors to this very day. It is interesting to note that even the Bible makes mention of these words, acknowledging them in the Gospel of Matthew 16:2-3. Here, we find Jesus affirming this belief with his words, "When evening comes, you say, 'It will be fair weather, for the sky is red,' and in the morning, 'Today it will be stormy, for the sky is red and overcast.'" He then adds: "You know how to interpret the appearance of the sky."

On November 22, 1912, trouble was brewing in the morning skies above Thompson, Michigan, where the *Rouse Simmons* was moored below, and everyone knew it. The mood on the docks was tense and foreboding. Tempers flared. Three sailors quit on the spot. Call it what you will – "the willies" "the jumpies" "the heebie jeebies" – but *something* had taken hold of the hearts of those gathered along the docks, both sailors and locals alike. One of the

> *"The* Rouse Simmons *sailed out of Thompson, Michigan, into a lake stirred into rage by snow and wind to become a tragedy, a mystery, and a legend. A tragedy because she went down with all hands aboard. A mystery because no one knows what really happened in those last hours and days. A legend because, in the passage of time, she has become the Christmas Tree Ship. The tale is one of the more engrossing mysteries of the Great Lakes."*
>
> *Green Bay Press-Gazette*
> Green Bay, WI
> November 23, 1975
> Bob Woessner

men who abandoned ship and rode the train back to his home in Chicago called it "lurking terror."

Even Captain Schuenemann's partner, Captain Charles Nelson, was concerned about sailing. Something just wasn't sitting right in Nelson's gut. He had been on edge since before the *Simmons* left Chicago. Captain Nelson's daughter, Alvida Verner, interviewed by the *Chicago Record-Herald* on December 6, 1912, said, "My father had a premonition that something was going to happen before he returned." Although Nelson's daughter did her best to talk her father out of sailing, he told her he had promised Schuenemann he would sail with him, adding: "A sailor's word is his bond. I can't go back on my word."

Captain Nelson was not a man to spook easily. At 68 years of age, it was said that Nelson was one of "the oldest lake captains, a man who had sailed the lakes for about fifty years." So, what was it that so unnerved him? Was it his premonition? Was it the ominous sky? Or was it the wisdom of his experience screaming to him that things were not as they should be?

Perhaps it was because November 22, 1912, just so happened to be a Friday. Legend warned against setting sail on a Friday. Saturday departures were viewed with high favor, assuring those aboard that their voyage would be both swift and secure. The only day on which a ship was never to set sail – never, ever - was Friday. Doing so was regarded as a very bad omen. If an urgent cargo was loaded on a Friday, captains would regularly delay sailing until midnight. Sometimes entire fleets were seen departing ports at the stroke of twelve in the Friday evening darkness. Beyond midnight it was safe to sail, but not a moment before.

There are those who would scoff at the "Murphy Friday" belief as it was called (based on the Murphy Law stating "Anything that can go wrong, will go wrong.") According to *The Ocean Almanac* by Robert Henrickson, the British Navy tried to dispel the Friday superstition in the 1800's when they intentionally laid the keel of a new ship on a Friday, launched it on a Friday, set it to sail on a Friday, and then went so far as to name the ship *Friday*. What happened next came as little surprise to most. Neither the ship nor her crew was ever heard from again. They vanished into thin air.

So, is the Friday superstition utter nonsense, or is it noteworthy? Many believed their very lives depended upon it. Was Captain Nelson among them? Did he try to convince Captain Schuenemann not to sail? Some say yes. But

DAUGHTER OF "CHRISTMAS TREE" CRAFT'S MASTER TELLS OF FEAR OF DISASTER
Chicago Record-Herald
Chicago, IL
December 6, 1912

Mrs. Alvida Verner of 1626 Humboldt Street, daughter of Capt. Charles C. Nelson, master of the lost vessel, told in the afternoon how she had pleaded vainly with her father to give up his last trip on the *Simmons*.

"A sailor's word is his bond. I know the *Simmons* isn't safe, but I promised to go and I can't go back on my word," was his answer, Mrs. Verner said.

"My father had a premonition that something was going to happen before he returned," she said. "He was 68 years old and we tried to persuade him to stay off the lake. He refused, saying he had promised Capt. Schuenemann last year that he would take the boat this year if he was able."

Hope that the Christmas Tree Schooner would be heard from definitely flickered faintly in the hearts of Mrs. Verner and Mrs. Herman Schuenemann and her three daughters early in the day, but as the hours dragged by and a heavy fog enveloped the lake that hope was nearly extinguished.

"Father has given fifty years of his life on the waters of Lake Michigan," said Mrs. Verner, daughter of Captain Nelson. *"He told me on the day that he left Chicago that it would be his last trip, and I fear that his prediction came true."*

Chicago Daily Journal
Chicago, IL
December 5, 1912

167

the *Rouse Simmons,* ignoring the legend, readied itself to depart on Friday, November 22, 1912. This decision proved yet another fateful mistake for the Christmas Tree Ship.

Several theories exist as to why Captain Schuenemann made his decision to sail when he did. Some believe he was trying to get ahead of the storm in order to outrun it. Others felt Schuenemann risked the possibility of becoming iced into the harbor if he delayed sailing, and he was worried about this. Some believe Schuenemann was concerned about gale force winds dashing his fully loaded ship against the docks if he stayed moored when the storm hit. Still others are of the opinion Captain Schuenemann was trying to get to Chicago as quickly as possible because his tree market would be most profitable if he arrived sooner rather than later. It is reasonable to assume any one of these theories may be correct, or all of them combined. Whatever Schuenemann's reasoning may or

Attracting Bad Luck

It is widely believed throughout the world that to sail on a Friday is to invite disaster. This old rule may have originated with the crucifixion of Christ, which occurred on a Friday, but the belief is common among sailors of other religions as well. If you have a choice, do not set sail on a Friday.

A vessel with a name that is too presumptuous has long been held to attract bad luck. By presumptuous, I mean a name that challenges the sea or wind, or boasts that it can better the elements or survive their meanest blows. To call a ship *Sea Conqueror* or *Wind Tamer* is simply to tempt the Fates. The gods like boat names to be humble. To call a ship *Titanic* is asking for trouble, too. In Greek mythology, the most important of the 12 Titans, the vengeful Kronos, cut off his father's genitals with a sickle, and threw them into the sea. I can imagine how Neptune, god of the sea, would feel about a ship named after the Titans. Of course, the *Titanic* was ill-fated from the start anyway – she was launched without a naming ceremony, thus greatly offending the gods.

Old superstition has it that it is unlucky to paint a ship in the colors of the sea. In olden times, vessels were seldom painted green or blue, since they had their own souls and could not presume to be part of the sea itself. Such presumption could be fatal.

The Practical Mariner's Book of Knowledge
John Vigor
Copyright 1994

may not have been, we can only guess at the answers to our question, for the only person who knows for sure lies at the bottom of Lake Michigan.

It is also reasonable for those familiar with the story to give additional consideration to Captain Schuenemann's dedication to the people of Chicago and to his Christmas tree voyages he loved so much. His yearly deliverance of trees had become a passion, a life's work.

Perhaps Captain Schuenemann was thinking about all the fallen faces back in Chicago if his ship didn't arrive. It could have gripped at his heart and made canceling the voyage unquestionable.

In support of this theory, testimony can be found recorded on a documentary produced in 1975 by WTMJ television in Milwaukee, Wisconsin. Several interviews of residents who lived in Thompson, Michigan, in 1912, persons who were with Captain Schuenemann in his final hours, were filmed. One woman told how her father had eaten lunch with Captain Schuenemann the day he was supposed to set sail. He warned the captain, "Herman, I don't think you should go. You're never going to make it." This man's daughter was then quoted as remembering Captain Schuenemann responding to her father with these words: "The people in Chicago *have* to have their trees for Christmas." Then she added, "That's what he felt."

Also included on the documentary is an interview with Mrs. Alvin Nelson whose father owned Hruska's Meat Market in Thompson, and who supplied the Christmas Tree Ship with provisions for its trips to Chicago. According to her, "My brother delivered the meat down to the boat. Every time we went down there, he had something to give us – some candy or something that he had brought from Chicago. Living where we did, we didn't see very much in those days, I can tell you that. It meant a lot to us. We knew Christmas was coming and we were all excited. We started getting out the *Sears and Roebuck* catalog

---

"Superstition of a certain type has always played a part in the life of men who follow the sea."

Lake Michigan
Ralph G. Plumb
Copyright 1941

Photo of the *Rouse Simmons* at dock with its nameplate visible.
(Courtesy of the Historical Collections of the Great Lakes,
Jerome Library, Bowling Green State University, Bowling Green, Ohio)

and started picking out what we wanted. Mr. Schuenemann, when he came, he used to always bring us a few things – you know, because he liked all the Thompson people. He had been with the Thompson people a lot. That was part of his life to come up here and get the Christmas trees like that."

The residents of Thompson looked after Schuenemann as if he was one of their own, and in many ways he was. They worried for him and his crew, especially on November 22, 1912. Mrs. Nelson's father voiced concern over Schuenemann's departure, sensing his friend's forthcoming doom. She remembered her dad saying, "He'll never make it. He'll never make it. He'll never be back in my market again."

One of the last things Captain Schuenemann did before setting sail that November was to give treats to the children at Thompson, Michigan. One of the last things he said was, "The people in Chicago have to have their trees for Christmas." And one of the last things he saw before departing from the harbor were rats fleeing his ship.

The significance of this event cannot be overstated. Upon boarding any vessel, sailors would take careful notice of the rats. Rats aboard a ship were considered to be a good omen. However, if rodents were sighted deserting a ship, this was considered an evil omen, the worst omen, the omen of omens, a warning that a dark and dreary fate awaited the ship…and soon. In the case of the *Rouse Simmons*, the rats were said to be leaving "in droves" just before the ship lifted its anchor in Michigan. (There were reports of rats deserting the eve before the *Simmons* sailed, as well as in Chicago before the journey began.) Rodents, believed by many to be "the wisest of mariners," foresaw the shadow cast upon the *Simmons* before its sails had even begun to blow. There could be no mistaking this sign in the minds of those who lived their lives on the seas.

> *"No further word was ever heard from the* Simmons, *and old sailors remembered the story of the hurried departure of the rats and shook their heads."*
>
> *Lake Michigan*
> Ralph G. Plumb
> Copyright 1941

SHIP LEFT BY RATS LOST IN LAKE WITH ALL HANDS ABOARD
Man Who Quit Boat Talks
Chicago Record-Herald
Chicago, IL
December 5, 1912

Eleven men, officers and crew of the "Christmas Tree Schooner" *Rouse Simmons* are believed to lie in the depths of Lake Michigan today, drowned because of their refusal to heed "the warning of the rats."

Wreckage and fir saplings washed ashore yesterday at Pentwater, Michigan, leave little doubt as to the fate of the schooner. The story of the only survivor of the last trip, a seaman who quit before his voyage was finished, indicates that the eleven sailed from their last port weighed down with superstitious forebodings of their impending doom.

Hogan Hoganson sat before a cozy fire at his home, 413 Milwaukee Avenue last night, and told how he escaped adding his own as the twelfth name to the list of probable dead.

GIVES NAMES OF CREW

According to Hoganson, the eleven who perished are:

Capt. Charles Nelson, master of the schooner, whose home was at Humboldt and North Avenues; Capt. Herman Schuenemann, owner of the cargo and former lake captain, who lived at 1638 North Clark Street; Steve Nelson, mate; Albert Luxta, cook, 418 North Desplaines Street; Charles Nelson, seaman before the mast; Frank Carlson, seaman, living in Austin; Gilbert Swanson, seaman, son of Capt. Swanson, retired, an extra hand, who lived at the corner of California Avenue and Division Street; Engwald Newhouse, extra hand, 418 North Desplaines Street; Phillip Larson, extra hand; Jack Pitt, extra hand; and Andrew (unknown last name), deck hand.

RATS GAVE SEAMAN "HUNCH"

"It was the rats that gave me my first 'hunch' that trouble was ahead for the *Rouse Simmons*," said Hoganson, telling why he left the schooner just before it cleared from Manistique, Michigan. "The rats had deserted the ship while it lay in the Chicago harbor. And all the way across the lake,

At least three terrified sailors (exact number varies) refused to set sail with Captain Schuenemann for the return trip back to Chicago when the rats were sighted. Their decision cost them dearly. Each sailor had his wage forfeited because those aboard were only entitled to their pay if they completed the voyage to Chicago as they had agreed to.

Those who chose to sail, failing to heed the rats' legitimate warnings, made a decision that cost them even more: their very lives. They were sailing into the storm-tossed waters just beyond the harbor's safety where Death was waiting for them there.

as we sailed for our cargo, the old saying had been ringing in my head – 'The rats always desert a sinking ship.'

"Our trip over was in as fair weather as one could wish to see, just like midsummer. Before we had left the harbor I had complained to Steve Nelson, the mate, that the sleeping foc'sle wasn't fit for a human being to sleep in, and he promised to have it looked after. He never did, and perhaps that had something to do with the way my forebodings stayed with me. Gloomy thoughts are easy to entertain in gloomy surroundings, you know."

DECKLOAD STRENGTHENS FEARS

"Well, when we had filled the hold with Christmas trees at Manistique, we were ordered to pile up a deckload of the saplings. The load grew and grew, and still they had us piling more and more trees on top. Finally I protested to Captain Nelson, telling him that if we struck heavy weather the boat would be too top-heavy to weather it. But the captain seemed to think he knew more about it than a seaman, and ordered us to pile more trees on deck.

"Then I quit. Captain Schuenemann, the owner of the cargo, told me I would get no money unless I stuck for the cruise, but I had some money and so I took a train for Chicago. Here I am – and the others?"

Captain Nelson was worried about the ship before he left Chicago, according to Hoganson. When the rats left the *Rouse Simmons*, the Captain told Captain George DeMar of the Chicago harbor police that he feared it was a bad omen.

MEN KEPT UP BOLD FRONT

"The men in the crew," Hoganson said, "pretended not to care because the rats had deserted. They laughed and jested over the old superstition, but it was grim jesting that served to hide the lurking terror that none like to voice to his fellows.

"The old schooner never carried such a thing as a lifeboat," continued Hoganson. "There was one boat on board which was 'sculled' back and forth to land the crew, but so far as any real lifeboats were concerned, they never had any on board. That one boat would

Miles Osbourn Stanley, a Thompson resident at the time, was down by the docks the evening of November 21, 1912, and personally witnessed the rats deserting. "I saw the rats leaving the boat myself," said Stanley. "I was down there the night before they sailed." He also testified as to the desertion of three sailors.

Although Miles Osbourn Stanley is no longer living, his children and grandchildren have heard the stories of the Christmas Tree Ship many times through the years from Stanley family members who have resided in Thompson, Michigan, for seven generations.

(Continued from previous page)

hold fifteen men in the Chicago River, but wouldn't have held one if we had ever launched it in rough weather.

"If the schooner has gone down, and there is slight hope now that it has not, those green spruce poles on deck were responsible for it. They are heavy, and if the boat ran into rough weather and was struck broadside by a couple of big waves, they would shift and the boat would capsize."

SEES NO CHANCE FOR SCHOONER

"I know enough of the lake to know that if that boat had made any port on the lake the news would be telegraphed here that it was safe. Not a word has been heard from it since it sailed, two weeks ago…"

Her master, Captain Nelson, was one of the oldest lake captains, having sailed the lake for about fifty years. Three years ago, it was stated yesterday, he lost the schooner *Ida*, laden with lumber, near Manistique, but the officers and crew were saved.

It has been persistently rumored that Mrs. Nelson, wife of the master of the ship, was aboard, but this was denied by Hoganson yesterday. He stated that Nelson's wife had died several years ago, and that he had seen no woman on board during the trip.

The *Rouse Simmons'* mystery may remain unsolved…but it will never die as a seaman's legend, and the rats will be watched closer than ever on all lake ships.

One grandson, Wayne Stanley, a lifelong resident of Thompson and now a grandfather himself, tells how his ancestors were "good friends with the Schuenemanns" and how Captain and Mrs. Schuenemann would sometimes stay with the Stanley family in their home while gathering their trees in October and November. Stanley recalls listening to his grandparents "speak of the Schuenemanns by first name, Herman and Barbara, and also speak of their children." The Schuenemanns, according to Stanley, were "widely, widely acquainted with everyone in the area." Even after Captain Schuenemann's tragic death, Barbara continued to return to Thompson where she had many friends.

Ancestors on both sides of Wayne Stanley's family, his father's side as well as his mother's, spoke fondly of the Schuenemanns. His granddad on his mother's side, Floyd Sample, harvested trees and picked evergreens for Schuenemann. "He did piece work for Schuenemann," recalls Stanley, "selling trees and evergreens to the captain."

It is clear that Thompson residents cared about the Schuenemanns, looking forward to the captain's arrival in the fall. It is also clear on

November 22, 1912, the residents believed they were saying a final farewell to their friend as they watched his ship head into the open waters.

"In the late afternoon of November 22, 1912, with the clock and the weather against him, Captain Herman Schuenemenn and the Christmas Tree Ship, under full sail, left Thompson Harbor for the last time. The fears of those on shore, and of Schuenemann's own crew, became a reality within a few hours. The captain had made a fatal error in judgment. As the ship ventured further into the lake, the full force of the storm hit."

The Christmas Tree Ship
1975 Documentary
WTMJ Television

The clock was ticking, a storm was brewing, and a horseshoe mounted to the side of the *Rouse Simmons* for good luck would soon be hanging by only one nail, swinging wildly in wicked winds, its luck "running out."

"There is a tradition among sailors that the doom of a vessel always is forecast when rats leave the ship. This is said to have happened just before the Rouse Simmons *lifted anchor from the harbor of Manistique, Michigan, from which the load of trees was to have been carried to Chicago. Hogan Hoganson, who lives at 413 Milwaukee Ave., was signed with the crew of the boat. When the cargo was put aboard at Manistique, Hoganson saw the rodents scurry for the docks. He refused to make the homebound voyage. At his home yesterday he told his story. 'The boys laughed at me,' he said. 'They laughed at me for they mostly were not old sailors. To them the rats leaving meant nothing, but to me, who have heard of this strange thing for years – well, I'm glad I got the hunch and came back by rail.'"*

Chicago Inter Ocean
Chicago, IL
December 6, 1912

Rats Leaving the Ship is a Bad Omen

"She's sure goin' to blow a nasty one tonight. I'd rather be here by the fire than in Captain Schuenemann's shoes on a night like this – him starting out for Chicago. I guess he knows what he's doin' though, he's sailed the lakes for years."

This, my father said as he shook down the coal stove, opened the draft, lifted high and put in a scuttle of coal. Then he sat down, took the poker and thoughtfully poked the ashes between the thin iron teeth that all base burners had those days. That finished, he just sat and looked through the isinglass at the blue flames breaking through the fresh coal. His face was red with cold from walking home against the wind.

"You know it's a funny thing and I can't get it out of my mind," he finally roused himself to say. "I know that it's just an old saying, that when rats leave a ship she's sure to go down, but it sticks in my crop and I can't get it out.

"Tonight when I went into the waiting room to fix the fire, there were a couple of roustabouts from Schuenemann's boat. They wanted to sleep in the depot to keep warm. They weren't drunk and I couldn't kick them out on such a bitter cold night even if it is against orders. They were about busted because they had planned on their pay from the return trip to Chicago.

"They felt kinda' stinkin', I think, because they left Schuenemann in the lurch. They said the rats were leavin' the ship in droves and they'd be damned if they were goin' to risk their necks when any fool knows it's the worst kind of a sign..."

This Capt. Schuenemann had come to Manistique, MI, for years. As long as my Dad had worked at the depot, I could remember him coming home every year sometime in late November and telling us that Capt. Schuenemann was in with his Christmas tree boat. It had come to be identified with Christmas to me as much as the fall issue of the Sears Roebuck *catalog with all its delicious pages of candy, nuts and toys, for his boat was always loaded with Christmas trees.*

Captain Schuenemann had thousands of trees cut from the swamps around Steuben. They were loaded from a siding onto flatcars whose sides were staked so that the trees could be piled as high as a boxcar. Besides trees, he took ground pine and boughs for decorating.

These cars went past our house on a railroad which was only about thirty miles long. It connected Manistique, MI, and the Soo Line Railroad on the south shore of the Upper Peninsula. This road, the M&LS, as it was properly named, but never called, was owned by the Ann Arbor Railroad Company. The road was called "The Haywire" by anyone who knew its weaknesses.

My father worked for the Haywire as freight and baggage man and naturally got to know Captain Schuenemann pretty well...

Past the depot the Haywire ran down to the carferry docks, where Captain Schuenemann loaded his Christmas trees from the flat cars to the deck of the boat. His ship, the Rouse Simmons, *was a three-masted schooner. The loading space was all on deck. This fact in itself was a hazard in strong winds, for it had a tendency to make the ship top heavy. Spruce trees can hold an amazing amount of snow, too. Doubtless, tons of it could lodge and add to the ship's weight above water. In a big roll, even in the hands of the best of captains, the ship could roll right on over.*

Men with less experience might have hesitated to sail on a night like November [22nd] of 1912. They would have "holed" in for a day or two, but the captain had been on the lakes in this business since 1887. He knew the risks for he had lost his brother, August, in 1898 by shipwreck with all on board. They had been partners...

Yes, he knew that the men were jumpy. He had quite a ruckus with a couple of the crew out on the dock that day. They were in a lather about the rats leaving the ship. Superstitious devils! He had tried to bulldoze them into staying, but they were hell-bent on leaving.

In spite of all handicaps, the ship sailed at dusk. With a signal from the captain the crew loosed her moorings and she began to float away from the dock. A gust of wind caught her flapping gray sails and she righted herself around in good shape to pass through the pier's shelter out into the open water. Silently into the night she sailed...

The saying that the rats leaving the ship is a bad omen may be just superstition but there is good reason to believe that they are pretty wise seamen. The Rouse Simmons *was an old ship. She was built in 1868. Who knows what the rats saw in their incessant scamperings here and there over the old seams where no man ever looked?*

At any rate, they were right.

Inside Michigan
November 1952
Roma Baker Daw

Sailors and horseshoes. They were inseparable in days past. Many sailors refused to sail on a vessel without a resident horseshoe nailed upright in the shape of the letter "U" (to "hold" the luck in.) A horseshoe was never to be nailed upside down or it was believed its luck would run out.

According to Great Lakes historian Bill Wangemann, sailors were even cautious about sailing in the shape of an inverted "U". One such sailing pattern was around the mitten-shaped state of Michigan. Sailors were hesitant to sail on ships making regular routes between Toledo, Ohio, and Chicago, Illinois – an exact inverted "U". (Detroit to Milwaukee was another inverted "U" sailing route.) Sailors were warned to "beware of ships that sail the Michigan Mitten too often because their luck will eventually run out," said Wangemann. Sailors did not want to be aboard when it did.

Fact or fancy? It depends upon who you ask. Divers to the wreckage site of the Christmas Tree Ship are of the opinion that the horseshoe hanging by a single nail, tipped, was significant, and they will tell you so. It is yet another mystifying detail to the intrigue of the story.

One can't help but wonder if the horseshoe's nail was loosened and lost when the waves started beating mercilessly at the ship, or if the nail was already gone before the ship set sail from Thompson, MI. If so, did this critical detail go unnoticed?

We can't know for sure, but it certainly is a possibility. Perhaps those aboard were too busy watching the rats. Perhaps they were too busy watching the skies. Or perhaps they were too busy trying to determine exactly how many men were going to be on board the ship when it set sail. Were they leery about sailing with the number 13 again?

This was said to have happened when the ship sailed from Chicago to Thompson. According to the *Chicago Inter Ocean* newspaper of December 5, 1912, it was reported: "When the *Simmons* left Chicago the attention of Captain Schuenemann was called to the fact that the boat carried thirteen." Captain Schuenemann responded: "Well, I'm not afraid."

If Captain Schuenemann wasn't afraid, there are those who believed he should have been. No one was foolish enough to sail with the dreadful number thirteen – either captain or crew. Most sailors would have refused to sail on such a ship, taking the "13 jinx" seriously, an omen important enough

"*Marine men who knew Captain Schuenemann and Captain Nelson today told stories which they declared bore out all the traditions of the sea and showed that the fate of the* Rouse Simmons *was fixed before the vessel left Chicago for its trip to the northern woods.*"

Chicago Daily Journal
Chicago, IL
December 4, 1912

"*Shipping men say the fate of the* Rouse Simmons *may be similar to that of the* Thomas Humes, *three-masted schooner, manned with thirteen men, which sailed from Chicago in 1892 and was never heard of afterwards. It was said yesterday that when the Simmons left Chicago the attention of Capt. Schuenemann was called to the fact that the boat carried thirteen. 'Well,' he said. 'I'm not afraid. I always take that number.'*"

Chicago Inter Ocean
Chicago, IL
December 5, 1912

"*To this day very little is known of the heroic struggle on the part of Captain Herman Schuenemann and his crew of thirteen – an unlucky number among marine men.*"

We Must Not Forget
The Sheboygan Press
Sheboygan, WI
Date Unknown

Photo of Mrs. Barbara Schuenemann in 1928
beside a Christmas tree.
(Courtesy of the Chicago Tribune*)*

to find its way into the newspapers of the day.

Was Captain Schuenemann on edge like his partner, Captain Nelson? Maybe. Both Schuenemann and Nelson, just prior to setting sail, had given fateful promises to their families that this would be their last voyage with Christmas trees.

The *Chicago Daily Journal* of December 5, 1912, reported Nelson's daughter saying her father "told me on the day that he left Chicago that it would be his last trip, and I fear that his prediction came true."

Captain Schuenemann's niece, Mrs. Elizabeth Barerlin, interviewed by the *Milwaukee Sentinel* in 1977 at the age of 91, and who was living in Chicago in 1912 near "Uncle Herman and Aunt Barbara" when the ship went missing, remembered: "Aunt Barbara made him promise it would be his last trip. Of course, when he told us it would be his last trip, none of us knew that it really would." Mrs. Barerlin was 27 years old when the ship went missing and remembered the events well.

Additionally, the *Milwaukee Sentinel* of May 2, 1984, reported: "Before he set sail on November 22, 1912, Schuenemann told relatives in Thompson, Michigan, near Escanaba, that his 1912 trip would be his last with Christmas trees."

Omens, omens everywhere. Premonitions and hunches. Gut feelings and eerie promises. The deeper one digs, the more one finds. There is a mind-boggling chain of events linked to this disaster.

Sailors lived by their gut and died by it. Theirs was a world intuitive and ever on guard, aware of lurking darkness. Sailors believed "coming events would cast their shadows." And in the case of the Christmas Tree Ship, the shadow cast over the ship and its crew was large enough to darken this story from one end of Lake Michigan to the other.

Old sailors paid attention to absolutely everything – going so far as to inquire about a ship's launching ceremony – even if the launching had occurred years earlier. (In the case of the *Simmons,* these records of launching,

> *"According to affidavits filed by Mrs. Schuenemann and others, thirteen men lost their lives on the voyage."*
>
> Sea History
> Winter 1987-88
> Joseph A. Nowak, Jr.

unfortunately, no longer exist, but if they did, a possible missing link to the story could be hidden there.)

Launching ceremonies were critical. Superstitious sailors believed a ship was cursed if anything went wrong during a launch. A ship could be stricken doomed before the vessel even had a chance to feel the wind in its sails. When the *Edmund Fitzgerald* was launched, Lake Superior's most famous and mysterious shipwreck, waves splashing on shore were so cold they caused one man who was hit by them to die instantly of a heart attack. Any deaths that occurred at a ship's launch were considered to be bad, bad news, a prediction of the coming death of the ship.

The year 1912 saw the demise of the *Rouse Simmons* as well as the demise of the *Titanic* earlier in the same year. Unbelievable to many, the *Titanic* was launched without a ceremony. No bottle of wine was broken over her bow, no words of blessing were offered for the ship and crew, and no fanfare surrounded the presentation of the ship's name. Did this have something to do with the *Titanic's* sinking? Again, it depends upon who you ask. Many old sailors viewed such a snubbing as simply asking for trouble. It would only be a matter of time before it caught up with you.

A ship's launching ceremony (or "christening ceremony" as it was commonly called) was compared to an infant's baptism because ships were believed to have souls. Vessels were not viewed as innate objects, but were considered "alive" in a sense. Thus, launchings were sacred events of much significance.

A ship's name was given at its birth and was to be kept until its death. According to Bill Wangemann, "a ship would not forgive you for changing its name."

Interestingly, Kent Bellrichard, the diver who discovered the *Rouse Simmons'* wreck (and who also did research for the WTMJ documentary in the 1970's), talked to many old timers prior to diving for the *Simmons* but could not find out the ship's birth name, only its nickname. "Many of the old fishermen," said Bellrichard, "never even knew what the name of the ship was. They referred to it simply as the Christmas Tree Ship. In fact, I didn't even know what the name of the Christmas Tree Ship was."

Parallel ceremonies commenced the births of humans as well as ships. Likewise, bells tolled at their ends. It was believed "phantom bells" would ring out over the waters when a ship met with death. It was further believed a vessel would literally "cry out" when its soul arose from the depths below.

Phantom bells were said to have been heard in the days following the

PHANTOM BELLS ARE HEARD
Milwaukee Sentinel
Milwaukee, WI
December 6, 1912

Capt. William Baxter of the *Kersarge*, who is now in Milwaukee, reports having heard some vessel sounding its bell just before sighting the Milwaukee light, and many lake sailors believe the sounds heard by Capt. Baxter were what is known to seagoing craft as "phantom bells" – bells which are supposed to ring out the story of disaster at sea.

Simmons' disappearance, and phantom cries were carried into the winds. Rationally, phantom cries can be explained by the fact that air makes sounds as it is released from a vessel which has been sunk into the pressured waters of the deep. The *Rouse Simmons'* cabin, as would be expected, was completely crushed in when the vessel was located. According to divers, this was not unusual. Cabins typically are "all broken up" on submerged vessels because of the pressure.

And speaking of phantoms, who among us believes in ghosts? Sailors did. They believed ghosts existed as surely as they themselves did. Just check the shelves of any marine library for yourself and you will find endless accounts of hauntings.

Even Christopher Columbus' journal includes an entry after he sighted the ghost of St. Elmo, a phenomenon of lights seen at sea during violent storms believed by veteran sailors to bring good luck (and safety) to sailors. Columbus wrote, "On Saturday, at night, the body of St. Elmo was seen, with seven lighted candles in the round top, and there followed mighty rain and frightful thunder. I mean the lights were seen which the seamen affirm to be the body of St. Elmo, and they said litanies and prayers to him looking upon it as most certain that in these storms when he appears, there can be no danger."

The eerie, shimmering lights had emerged from seemingly nowhere and then returned again from whence they had come.

In addition to Columbus, the writings of Shakespeare make mention of the bizarre lights, as do the journals of Ferdinand Magellan and even Charles Darwin.

According to Olivia A. Isil, author of the humorously titled book *When a Loose Cannon Flogs a Dead Horse There's the Devil to Pay*, St. Elmo was a "fourteenth century bishop, martyr, and patron saint of Mediterranean sailors who was rescued from drowning by a sailor. As a token of his gratitude, St. Elmo promised to send a light to warn those at sea of approaching storms. Mediterranean seafarers of the fifteenth and sixteenth centuries believed that the ghostly light emanated from the body of Christ." It is an intriguing claim.

The ghostly appearance of St. Elmo's "fire" is sometimes bluish in color, while other times it is white. The lights, influenced by electrical

---

Great Lakes Superstitions

Cats and Rats The very word "cat" has a negative connotation on board a vessel. Much of the gear involved in raising the anchor, a difficult and unpleasant task, used "cat" nomenclature. The cat head, cat fall, cat block, cat tackle, cat harping, cat back and cat davit all mean hard work. Little wonder then that cats, black or otherwise, have always been considered bad luck on lake vessels and were thought to be "breeders" of bad weather.

Considering their aversion to cats, it is a bit surprising that sailors seemed to like having rats aboard – likely because sailors believed rats would flee an unseaworthy ship. If rats were seen to be fleeing, it was considered a certain warning of impending doom. There were cases where entire crews deserted when word spread that the rats were leaving.

Coins Old sailors believed that throwing several small coins over the stern as a vessel left harbor assured a good trip. A coin, usually silver, was always placed under the step of each mast to guarantee a profitable career. The coin had to be placed face up – face down would invite disaster.

Horseshoes As is common in the general population, horseshoes were always good luck talismans to Great Lakes sailors. Practically every schooner had a horseshoe nailed to the davit post – prongs up so the good luck would not run out. Sometimes, they were nailed over cabin doors or to a mast. The practice was so widespread that Capt. James McConnell claimed that there were "enough horseshoes on the bottom of the lakes to shoe the entire British Calvary." Despite such cynicism, should a schooner not have a resident horseshoe, sailing was delayed until one was found.

Launchings Sailors all over the world considered the launching of a new vessel to be the most important action in determining her future luck. No matter how well built the ship was, how well named, how well crewed, fitted, or managed, it was how she was launched that really counted. Anything that went wrong during this defining ceremony was considered a bad omen. Consequently, yard crews made extremely careful preparations to ensure that everything went off without a hitch during a launch.

Deaths during a launching were an especially bad omen.

Christening a new ship with water, instead of the traditional bottle of spirits, was always considered a bad omen by sailors, causing old-timers to cringe.

charges in the atmosphere, can also appear in the colors of red and purple.

Spotting the ghost of St. Elmo was looked upon as a good omen, but this was not the case with other apparitions – especially with ghost ships. Seafaring men believed a phantom ship would be sighted immediately before a disaster at sea. It meant that "some poor sailors will soon lose their lives."

Sailors believed in things that would make the hairs on the back of a landlubber's neck stand on end. This included monsters.

Name Changes Changing a vessel's name was always considered bad luck by lake sailors. The sailors felt that when a vessel was named and launched, it acquired a unique personality. Renaming it injured that personality and the vessel reacted accordingly. There are many examples of vessels that met disaster, as the old sailors believed, because of a name change. Early sailors were also always nervous about shipping on a vessel named for a dead person. They considered all such boats cursed. They were equally leery of vessels with "unlucky" names. It was said that "give a schooner a good, but an unlucky, name and you might as well notify the coroner." Some sailors believed too many A's in a name was unlucky, as well as 13 letters in the name.

Sea Gulls With their wild and plaintive cries, sea gulls were supposed to contain the souls of drowned sailors, holding a special place in the hearts of lake sailors. A gull landing on a vessel underway was always a good omen.

Captain Harry Ingraham, an old lakes veteran, reported an extraordinary occurrence on Lake Superior. A larger than normal gull landed on the bow of his ship and, according to his lookout, called out to the man by his name. The man recognized the voice of a friend he had lost on the lake years before. The gull warned him of an unknown danger.

Whistling Whistling was treated seriously on a sailing vessel since sailors believed that it would bring on a gale. If a wind was blowing, whistling was forbidden. If becalmed, the whole crew whistled softly for a moderate breeze. Shrill whistling was especially thought to bring on a gale. On some vessels, whistling for a wind was restricted to the captain and mates.

Women and Priests Women aboard were always considered bad luck and were sure to bring foul weather. Old sailors also thought preachers to be dangerous company when aboard ship. One reason may be their habitual black clothing, coupled with their job of comforting the dying and burying the dead. Another reason may have been the belief that the devil was their everlasting enemy and would send storms to destroy them, imperiling the vessel and crew.

After a vessel carrying an early Lake Superior Methodist missionary, Reverend J. H. Pitzel, experienced a series of gales, one captain attributed it to having preachers and women aboard. He claimed that he "never knew it to fail, with women and preachers aboard, sailors were sure to have storms."

Haunted Lakes
Frederick Stonehouse
Copyright 1997

185

Are there really such things? Is it possible they exist? Maybe. Sea serpents, dragons and multi-headed monsters are all mentioned in the Bible. One such watery beast lurking in the darkened depths was referred to as the "leviathan":

Isaiah 27:1 KJV: "In that day the Lord with his sore and great and strong sword shall punish leviathan the piercing serpent, even leviathan that crooked serpent; and he shall slay the dragon that is in the sea."

Psalm 104:25-26 NIV: "There is the sea, vast and spacious, teeming with creatures beyond number – living things both large and small. There the ships go to and fro, and the leviathan."

Psalm 74:12-13 NIV: "But you, O God, are my king from of old; you bring salvation upon the earth. It was you who split open the sea by your power; you broke the heads of the monster in the waters."

Job 41:1-2, 7-10, 13-34 NIV: "Can you pull in the leviathan with a fishhook or tie down his tongue with a rope? Can you put a cord through his nose or pierce his jaw with a hook? Can you fill his hide with harpoons or his head with fishing spears? If you lay a hand on him, you will remember the struggle and never do it again! Any hope of subduing him is false; the mere sight of him is overpowering. No one is fierce enough to rouse him. Who can strip off his outer coat? Who would approach him with a bridle? Who dares open the doors of his mouth, ringed about with his fearsome teeth? His back has rows of shields tightly sealed together (other versions of text say "scales"); each is so close to the next that no air can pass between. They are joined fast to one another; they cling together and cannot be parted. His snorting throws out flashes of light; his eyes are like the rays of dawn. Firebrands stream from his mouth; sparks of fire shoot out. Smoke pours from his nostrils as from a boiling pot over a fire of reeds. His breath sets coals ablaze, and flames dart from his mouth. Strength resides in his neck; dismay goes before him. The folds of his flesh are tightly joined; they are firm and immovable. His chest is hard as rock, hard as a lower millstone. When he rises up, the mighty are terrified; they retreat before his thrashing. The sword that reaches him has no effect, nor does the spear or the dart or the javelin. Iron he treats like straw, and bronze like rotten wood. Arrows do not make him flee; slingstones are like chaff to him. A club seems to him but a piece of straw; he laughs at the rattling of the lance. His undersides are jagged potsherds, leaving a trail in the mud like a threshing sledge. He makes the depths churn like a boiling cauldron and stirs up the sea like a pot of ointment. Behind him he leaves a glistening wake; one would think the deep had white hair. Nothing on earth is his equal – a creature without fear. He looks down on all that are haughty; he is king over all that are proud."

I don't know about you, but I, for one, am not too anxious to find out if this leviathan creature exists – not if I have to cross paths with it to do so. (I'll just stay right here with the blankets pulled over my head.)

Study Bibles will give readers an explanation of the leviathan as being "possibly a crocodile." Well, I've seen a fair number of crocodiles in my day and have yet to see one blowing fire out of its mouth or smoke from its nostrils, much less being undaunted by swords, harps, spears and javelins. A crocodile? I'm thinking no.

Sea monsters, dragons, ghosts. Do they exist? What is a person to believe about such things when the same book that makes mention of them is a book many hold dear, as do I.

So, what's my point? My point is this: Maybe it's possible that there are simply some things in our midst that reason cannot explain. Maybe it's possible that not every question gets answered nor every mystery solved.

There is no shortage of mystery connected to the *Rouse Simmons* story. Nor is there a shortage of ghost sightings. Just ask around. There are even specific times said to be best for spotting the phantom ship. Christmas Eve and Christmas Day are both supposed to be good, as well as the anniversary date of its loss on November 23. Some say the ship appears most often on misty horizons at dusk, while others will tell you to look for the ship in the twilight mists of dawn.

But most often, it is said, the ship will return in the same way she left that fateful day nearly a hundred winters past: fighting her way through a violent

> *"The mysterious disappearance of the Christmas Tree Ship became the stuff of legends. Sightings of ice-coated ships made it the subject of popular Flying Dutchman legends and of a Great Lakes Bermuda Triangle."*
>
> United States Coast Guard Magazine
> December 2000

gale.

Recently I attended a Christmastime gathering in Sheboygan, Wisconsin, very near to the *Simmons'* watery grave. I had been invited to speak to an audience about the legendary ship. During the presentation I shared information about various ghost ship sightings and read from several old newspaper clippings.

Following the program, one of those in attendance came forward, leaned in ever so close to me, and whispered, "I've seen that ship."

Nonsense? Hardly. The program I just finished took place at a prestigious

---

A Sea Chest of Superstitions

• Never put your left foot down first when stepping on board ship – disaster will follow if you do.

• Black traveling bags bring seamen bad luck.

• Flowers are unlucky aboard ship because they could later be used to make a funeral wreath for someone (or everyone) on board.

• When the clothes of a dead sailor are worn by another sailor during the same voyage, misfortune will befall the entire ship.

• The feather of a wren will protect a sailor from death by shipwreck.

• A ship's bell will always ring when it is wrecked.

• In days past old sailors had a pair of open eyes tattooed on their eyelids to warn them of danger while they slept.

The Ocean Almanac
Robert Hendrickson
Copyright 1984

---

yacht club, and the audience in attendance was the Retired Teachers Association of Sheboygan County. This was no prankster making a claim, but rather was someone who had served her community long and well, a pillar of the city. Her name was Mrs. Joyce Phippen.

I wanted to hear more.

The following January I accepted Mrs. Phippen's invitation to join her for the day. Visitors fall in love with her stone cottage set on Lake Michigan's shoreline even before they reach the end of the driveway.

She has been here, in this place where she knows she belongs, since 1958, nearly half a century. She pointed out to me a pine tree planted shortly before her family moved in. It now reached into the forever skies, towering over her home.

She cherishes this place, and told me, "There isn't a day I am not on this beach. I don't feel right if my feet aren't on the sand."

The first thing I noticed, peering out her massive windows, was an old, wooden beach chair beside the shore. "That's mine," she said, and smiled.

She is an expressive lady who speaks in a lively way, using her hands as much as her eyes, laughing often.

We sat there, she and I, in front of those beautiful windows eating blackberries the size of golf balls for several hours, talking about her life and about mine. She told me her birthday was coming soon. Mrs. Phippen was nearly eighty years old and was proud to tell me so. She had earned her years and the wisdom that accompanied them.

There was a tree limb knocking on the house as we talked. It was windy, and the temperature fell to 35 degrees below zero, the coldest in a while. The wild winds reminded her to tell me about the powerful waves that crash along

> *"She was called the Christmas Tree Ship and for more than 50 years after her tragic disappearance in Lake Michigan waters in late November 1912 the legend persisted that about the same time each year ice-laden riggings and storm-tattered sails of the* Rouse Simmons *could be spotted in misty horizons, bravely plowing on in her unending search for a safe haven."*
>
> *Wisconsin Weekend*
> December 11, 1974
> Florence Lindemann

the shore with a force strong enough to rattle dishes in her kitchen cupboards.

"It can be challenging to be here with the weather," she told me. Then she added, "You just never know what you are going to see living here."

Mrs. Phippen is someone who has come to know the many moods of these waters as she has come to know herself. She has seen them at their best and she has seen them at their worst. "You have to respect Lake Michigan," she warned. "It is easy to enjoy these waters when everything is going all right, but the undertow of this lake is really something."

Once, a dead body washed ashore many years ago beneath those very windows. She ran for a blanket to cover the poor man. Quietly she told me, "I was thankful he was face down."

She speaks of these waters in terms of a companion, not merely as a part

---

LOOK REAL HARD
Christmas Tree Ship
Long Gone But
Still Remembered
Manitowoc Herald
Manitowoc, WI
November 24, 1962

Along about this time of year – off the shores of Kewaunee and Two Rivers – 'tis said that if you peer through the twilight mists of Lake Michigan hard enough you can see her.

"She's out there," contends a hardy, old freshwater sailor who remembers her well. "If you look hard enough you can make out her three masts," he added.

It was just 50 years ago on this date that the schooner *Rouse Simmons*, laden with Christmas trees, struck a lake squall and was lost at sea...

She would spread no more cheer, this gallant little schooner of the lakes. She went to the bottom with loss of entire crew and her cargo of Christmas trees.

There are those old seamen who claim, however, that the great spirit of the *Rouse Simmons* returns to the twilight mists of Lake Michigan about this time every year.

"She's not really dead," whispered one old timer recently, "it's pretty hard to kill the spirit that was the *Rouse Simmons*. She is out there, somewhere, with all her white sails blowing and she's still laden with Christmas trees to gladden the hearts of men, women and children everywhere."

Christmas Tree Ghost Ship

"Even now, there are those who think the Christmas Tree Ship may still reach port. They say if you watch the lake closely on Christmas Eve, you can sometimes see a handsome schooner scuddling along before the gale, a Christmas tree lashed to its mast."

December 20, 1975
Source of Article Unknown
On file at:
Great Lakes Historical Society

"The Rouse Simmons *was considered a ghost ship because she disappeared at sea. She was also a ghost ship because there were occasional sightings of her sailing the turbulent waters, as if still trying to make her way to shore."*

The Daily Times
Ottawa, IL
December 13, 2003
Jacquee Thomas

"A Lake Michigan legend speaks of a Flying Dutchman [a legendary ghost ship that sails eternally without reaching its port] seen during violent storms trying to complete one final delivery of Christmas trees to the people of Chicago."

Sea History
Winter 1987-88
Joseph A. Nowak, Jr.

of the world around her, but rather a part of her world within.

The lake was relatively quiet on the day of our visit. There were huge piles of ice forming near the shoreline, rising up like a mountain range extending for miles. "Tomorrow," she told me, "everything will look different. The view here changes all the time."

Mrs. Phippen is a woman who commands respect. She is regarded by others with honor, and the worth of her words is undeniable.

In front of her favorite window, as I sat in her favorite chair, she told me of seeing the ghost ship twice, both times many long years ago. Once, the ship appeared at "duskish" from out of nothingness. Once, it appeared in the dark. She remembered wondering to herself as she looked on each image, "What is this I am seeing?" The ship, as she told me, was "just sort of there, floating in the air." She tried to paint me a picture with her words: "Hazy, ice laden, misty, white."

Dusk fell that January afternoon and it was time for me to go, time to leave Mrs. Phippen, the very nice lady who just so happens to believe in ghosts.

It would be easy to dismiss such claims as nonsense until you've heard these stories firsthand from one of the many persons who have experienced them, until you've looked into the eyes of the person who chose to share his or her encounter, sometimes with hesitation and a bit of reluctance, and heard the truth of their words.

Yes, Mrs. Phippen believes in ghosts, and I believe in Mrs. Phippen, a woman who can explain a sunrise and a moonlit night like no one I have ever heard.

Ghosts. Is it possible they exist? Is it possible there are things in our midst that reason cannot explain? I think yes.

"It has been said that Christmas Day is the best time to see the ghost of the Rouse Simmons *rising out of the cold mist off Two Rivers, WI. Dawn and sunset are regarded as the best times to see the phantom ship, according to legend. If any ship sights the* Simmons, *the legend says, 'This is the Master Shipbuilder's way of indicating that the life span of your ship has run out and is about to be called to the sea's graveyard.'"*

Manitowoc Herald-Times Reporter
Manitowoc, WI
December 4, 1998
Marge Miley

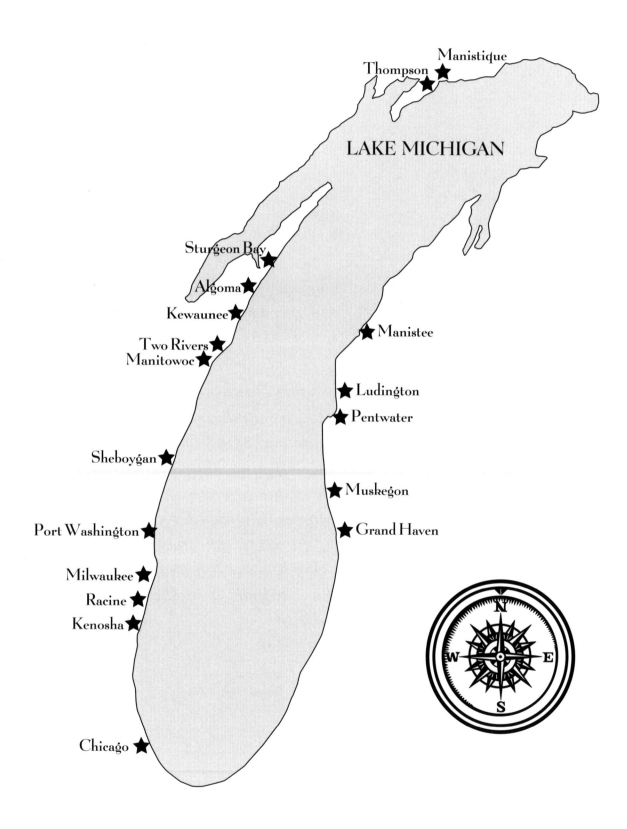

LAKE MICHIGAN

Manistique

Thompson

Sturgeon Bay

Algoma

Kewaunee

Manistee

Two Rivers

Manitowoc

Ludington

Pentwater

Sheboygan

Muskegon

Port Washington

Grand Haven

Milwaukee

Racine

Kenosha

Chicago

N
W   E
S

Chapter Seven

Clues Wash Ashore

"Somewhere off the shore of Two Rivers, WI, at the bottom of the inland sea that is Lake Michigan lay the skeleton bones of the Rouse Simmons, *ill-fated* Christmas Tree Ship *of the Great Lakes. The* Simmons *was often referred to as* The Ship of Good Cheer *for she carried Christmas trees from northern lake ports to Chicago where the Yule trees were sold and adorned thousands of city homes."*

Manitowoc Herald-Times
Manitowoc, WI
December 13, 1960

Clues Wash Ashore

One moment the *Rouse Simmons* was pummeling through tumultuous waves, whipped from side-to-side by gale force winds. The next, it had plunged to an icy grave.

When the tragic news of the *Simmons'* sinking spread, many said the legacy of the ship had come to an end. Little did they know the real story was just beginning.

It was not uncommon for fragments of a ship to be washed ashore following a wreck. A plank of wood, a tattered boot, a piece of rope. But in the case of the *Rouse Simmons*, the frigid waters of Lake Michigan carried more to shore than insignificant remains of an ordinary vessel. With every tree cast up during the decades following - *thousands* of them - came memories of the grand tradition the Christmas Ship and her captain once represented. It was as if Captain Schuenemann sent his trees one by one as a plea, "Remember me, please remember me."

Evergreens continued to find their way to sandy shorelines on both sides of the lake for a great many years, long after the Yuletide season of 1912, usually immediately after a storm that was "strong enough to stir the lake's bottom." It was also common for trees to become tangled in the nets of fishermen. When this happened, more than trees were pulled aboard the fishing vessels. Memories were pulled in as well. The story was literally being kept alive tree-by-tree.

Years passed. More evergreens surfaced. Some say Captain Schuenemann was trying to deliver his trees in death, as he had in life, throwing each up from his underwater grave by his own hand.

Eventually the trees became needleless, mere "skeletons". However, in the early years, many of the first trees washed ashore were taken home and decorated. Some of these trees looked as if they had been freshly cut, preserved by the lake's frigid waters.

Trunks from some of the skeleton trees in later years were cut up with saws, sliced up like a stick of summer sausage into small, wooden circles. These were then made into ornaments. A Christmas tree was painted in the center of each circle, and the words "*Rouse Simmons* 1868-1912" were carved below. Ironically, the trees Captain Schuenemann had hoped would be enjoyed for a single season, were now finding places of honor in homes all

**SCHOONER
ROUSE SIMMONS
AND CREW OF 17
LOST OUT IN
LAKE MICHIGAN
Cargo of 27,000
Christmas Trees**
The Sheboygan Press
Sheboygan, WI
December 6, 1912

At some point along the west shore of Lake Michigan, the crew of the *Rouse Simmons* are occupying watery graves, the schooner having gone to the bottom...

Bits of the wreckage and branches of Christmas trees, the latter a portion of the cargo, tell the story...

The schooner was loaded with 27,000 Christmas trees, and bits of evergreen wreckage picked up Thursday at Two Rivers, Wisconsin, and Pentwater, Michigan, leave little doubt but that the schooner has gone to the bottom...

The Twin River Point, where the fishermen found the wreckage and trees, has long been considered one of the most dangerous portions of the lake, having earned through the many wrecks and wild waters the name of "the graveyard of the lake."

Captain H. [Schuenemann] left Manistique, Michigan, on November 21, bound for Chicago. He sailed the waters of Lake Michigan since a boy and had carried many a boat to safety through the heavy gales.

"On November 22, 1912, the Rouse Simmons, *as usual, left Michigan with her load of Christmas trees. The next day the ship was at the bottom of Lake Michigan... She was a casualty of the autumn gales that can churn the lake into a frothy cauldron. Although the* Christmas Tree Ship *sank without a trace on November 23, she gave up clues of her resting place for decades afterward... For a quarter century local fishermen cursed after each storm as their nets brought up catches fouled by waterlogged evergreens."*

Milwaukee Journal
Milwaukee, WI
November 20, 1987
Dave Luhrssen

"The hardy captain and his crew now reposed in a cold, dark grave, but the chilled waters which had taken Schuenemann's life ironically preserved a bit of it, too. Twelve years passed, and then someone found a wallet in the lake just north of Sheboygan, Wisconsin... there were newspaper clippings still legible after years of exposure. It was Capt. Schuenemann's wallet and the clippings were newspaper accounts of his fabled Christmas tree voyages."

The Sheboygan Press
Sheboygan, WI
November 22, 1975

"[In 1924] a tug captain found a large purse in the lake belonging to Captain Schuenemann. It contained records of purchases of trees and of wages paid to crewmen, but contained no money. The writing on the paper was legible and the paper was preserved. The purse was turned over to members of the Schuenemann family."

The Evening News
Sault Ste. Marie, MI
December 18, 1971

along the lake, year after year, as ornaments on other trees. Thus, each tree's life now extended beyond a single holiday into countless more.

While some of the evergreens were carved into ornaments, others were carved into heirloom bookmarks and placed in family Bibles. Captain Schuenemann's oldest great-granddaughter, Barbara, who was named for her great-grandmother, is in possession of one of the ornaments. She proudly displays it on her tree each year. Visitors to Barbara's home in December can see the ornament, and can also see that she loves the season as much as her famous ancestors did.

Barbara's father, Dr. William Ehling, still remembers Christmases from his childhood during the 1930's. He particularly remembers ornaments that adorned his family's tree.

"There was a pickle ornament and a golden carp," shared Dr. Ehling. Then he added, "These were old German ornaments, handed down through the years."

Although Dr. Ehling was born after his grandfather's ship went missing, he told me, "I can always remember my folks talking about Grandpa."

His most vivid Christmas memory from his childhood is not of an ornament but is, rather, of his grandpa's wallet which was "brought out every year." The story behind the finding of Captain Schuenemann's pocketbook is nothing short of remarkable. A full twelve years after the *Simmons* went missing, Captain Schuenemann's wallet washed ashore in 1924 and was found by a fisherman and a lighthouse keeper near the very spot where the *Simmons* was last sighted. If finding the wallet of the Christmas Tree Ship's captain wasn't amazing enough, the fisherman's boat was, coincidentally, named the *Reindeer*.

Shortly thereafter, the wallet was turned over to family members. Dr. Ehling remembers the "burgundy colored pocketbook" that was brought out every Christmas as a cherished family heirloom. His mother would tell him, "This was grandpa's wallet."

Identification of the wallet was easily made because the pocketbook had been "wrapped in oilskin" – a type of waterproof sailor's packing – and then secured with a cord (some accounts say a rubberband). Everything inside was in excellent condition.

According to the *Manistique Pioneer-Tribune* of April 17, 1924, Schuenemann's personal card was inside the wallet as well as expense receipts and newspaper clippings.

Prior to his death, Captain Schuenemann would cut stories out of the newspaper that told of his famed Christmas voyages. He then carried them with him in his wallet.

The articles, clipped from penny newspapers, were still readable when the wallet was found. This remarkable discovery was cast forth from the bottom of the lake, and it re-opened discussion of the Christmas Tree Ship once again. The *Rouse Simmons* and its captain were refusing to remain forgotten.

The *Toronto Evening Telegram*, Toronto, Canada, ran an article about the *Simmons* tragedy on December 29, 1945: "Drowned Christmas trees, and one drowned man's wallet," wrote the paper, "must have traveled along the

WALLET FOUND IN FISHERMAN'S NET RECALLS STORY OF LOSS OF VESSEL TWELVE YEARS AGO
Pocketbook of Captain Schuenemann Contains Clippings From *The Tribune*; **Another Chapter in Sinking of Vessel Rouse Simmons**
Manistique Pioneer-Tribune
Manistique, MI
April 17, 1924

Another chapter has been inscribed upon the pages of Great Lakes history through the finding of a wallet in a fisherman's net near Kewaunee, WI, and the discovery recalls to the memory of local persons the disaster which befell the *Rouse Simmons* which at one time made Manistique, MI, a regular port.

It was back in the fall of 1912 that the *Simmons* pulled out of Manistique with a cargo of Christmas trees for Chicago. The schooner never reached her destination but bit-by-bit the telltale evidence cropped out and told the fate of the vessel. The finding of the wallet is just another episode in the revelation of facts concerning the vessel's disappearance.

Identification marks show that the wallet was the property of Captain Herman Schuenemann, well known in this city...

In the wallet, which was picked up only recently, were found newspaper clippings...

A day or two ago, the fishing tug *Reindeer*, captained by Norman Allie, came bringing in her nets to dry. The nets were strung on the reels and the weeds cast aside. Lighthouse keeper Henry Gattier who was keeper of the range lights at Bailey's Harbor, WI, at the time the *Rouse Simmons* disappeared, but now at the Two Rivers Point light, happened to kick a bunch of these weeds, and disclosed a billfold which proved to be the property of the former skipper of the *Simmons*. That it was surely his is evidenced by the fact that it contained Schuenemann's personal card, and other data which proved beyond doubt.

In it were found clippings from a Manistique, MI, newspaper which told of the departure of the *Rouse Simmons* with its load of Christmas trees bound for Chicago, memoranda of the captain's expenses, and receipted bills for oil kins, provisions, etc.

The contents of the fold were in a good state of preservation, having been pressed together firmly and tied with a cord, which kept them intact.

The place where the nets had been set in the lake is several miles out into the open waters off from Two Rivers Point, and it is believed that this is the spot where the *Simmons* went down 12 years ago with all hands.

On Friday of the same week, while lifting the nets aboard the fishing tug *Monitor* of Two Rivers, WI, Captain Manville LaFond found a human skull entangled in the nets. This is the third skull that he has picked up at this point and at one time discovered a human skeleton in the net, but while pulling the net aboard the tug the skeleton broke into pieces and fell back into the lake. It is presumed that these bones are the remains of the crew of the wrecked ship.

bottom of the lake. The undercurrent in Lake Michigan is from south to north, as the water is drawn off by the mighty pull of the St. Lawrence, a thousand miles away and five hundred feet below. The surface current is variable and may go in the opposite direction due to winds and the Chicago drainage canal."

A person never knew what would turn up on the beaches around Lake Michigan during the 1800's and early 1900's when shipwrecks were commonplace. The undercurrent of the lake was both dangerous and powerful. Anything could be thrown up from the waters below and deposited on the shore. A barrel of whiskey, a ship's rib, a piano.

According to the *Chicago Tribune* of October 21, 1880, debris from the *Alpena* (shipwrecked October 16, 1880, while en route between Grand Haven, Michigan, and Chicago, Illinois) was said to line the shore in a ragged line "which the eye followed north and south…without finding either end of it." Great piles of debris were in heaps upon the sand.

The article also stated, "Close at hand stood the piano of the *Alpena*…its keys denuded of their ivory covering…its delicate strings unprotected.…occasionally emitting weird melodies as the still lively gale swept among its cords."

It must have been an unusual sight to see a piano sitting upright on the beach, and even more unusual to hear the haunting dirge the wind was strumming into its internal strings, just as the waves had.

If the sight of the piano wasn't bizarre enough, then there were the coffins. According to the same article: "Coffins, of which, strange to say, the vessel had a large stock on board, lay around in profusion."

With such "treasures" lying around on the beach, the ill-fated cargo of the doomed ship was now up for grabs. It was an activity that delighted some, yet dismayed others.

According to the *Chicago Tribune*, the locals "gathered in the treasure cast up by the deep. Even the coffins being in some cases seized upon and taken home, in readiness for a death in the family. No attempt is being made to stop this outrage, and much indignation is felt at it being carried on so openly."

By 1924, the year Captain Schuenemann's wallet was found, Barbara Schuenemann and her daughters had continued in the captain's tradition of selling Christmas trees for twelve years. It was said of Mrs. Schuenemann and her girls in the following years by *Great Lakes Travel and Living*, "These gallant women brought their Christmas trees down the lake to grace the city of Chicago, and to sustain a living memorial to the *Rouse Simmons* and her crew."

Their faithful work began almost immediately after the ship went missing, even while search efforts were still being carried out. At the peak of grieving for their lost husband and father, Barbara and her daughters pulled together the courage to carry on in Captain Schuenemann's footsteps. They were not among the weak of heart.

Barbara and her girls not only continued on with their lives, they chose to do so among the very things ultimately responsible for the captain's death.

The trees sold that first Christmas season included evergreens shipped by rail from Upper Michigan, as well as salvaged trees recovered from shores.

> *"There are a hundred other wrecks in the vicinity of Rawley Point, seven miles north of Two Rivers, WI. The names of most of them have long since been forgotten. But the* Rouse Simmons *seemed to rest uneasily in her grave."*
>
> Milwaukee Journal
> Milwaukee, WI
> December 5, 1971
> Robert W. Wells

The Tale of the Christmas Tree

Roared the wind and rolled the wave
   That buried a helpless crew,
And a Christmas ship in a Christmas grave
   Beneath the fathoms blue.
(And marking the grave on the breaking sea
   There tossed alone a Christmas tree.)

Spinning and spinning around it sped
   Along with the sweeping lee,
Leaving behind the sunken dead
   Deep in an inland sea.
(Till dripping and sogged the waters bore
   A Christmas tree to the leeward shore.)

Dripping and green on the sands it lay
   Bright with the drying foam,
Till a fisherman came and took it away
   To his two little boys at home.
(And, my, how they laughed in childish glee
   At the sight of the beautiful Christmas tree!)

Lighted with candles and laden with toys
   Gaily and proudly it stands
On Christmas Eve, and the fisherman's boys
   Are clapping their little hands.
(And this is the tale of the Christmas tree
   That came from the grave in an inland sea.)

By: Ben Hecht
Chicago Daily Journal
December 6, 1912

BAFFLING MYSTERY STILL IS SHROUDING FATE OF SCHOONER
The Sheboygan Press
Sheboygan, WI
December 27, 1944

Baffling mystery still shrouds the fate of the schooner *Rouse Simmons*, the Christmas ship which presumably was swallowed up by the angry, frigid waves of Lake Michigan back in late November 1912, somewhere between Sheboygan and Two Rivers, WI...

What happened to the Chicago-bound ship and its 16-man crew remains an unsolved mystery. The schooner's cargo, Christmas trees hewed from the forests of the north, and being transported to Illinois to brighten the Yuletide season, were washed ashore north of Sheboygan, WI.

SCHOONER THOUGHT TO HAVE SUNK IN MID-LAKE
The Chronicle
Two Rivers, WI
December 10, 1912

The three-masted schooner *Rouse Simmons*, loaded with Christmas trees which was seen passing Kewaunee, WI, on November 23, has been given up as lost...

When the schooner, which was flying a distress signal, passed Kewaunee, Capt. Sogge of the Two Rivers Life Saving Crew was notified. The crew put out in search of the schooner in their power surf boat. The beach was patrolled as far north as Two Creeks and quite a distance out into the lake, but no trace of the schooner was found.

After it became dark the crew returned to this city, thinking that the vessel had sailed far out into the lake. There was a strong wind and a high sea at the time and it is the opinion of Capt. Sogge that the schooner was waterlogged and that in an effort to keep the boat afloat, the deck load was thrown off. Many bundles of Christmas trees were found floating in the lake and branches of evergreens were found in nets that were located in the vicinity of Twin River Point.

204

These trees, gathered from beaches, were then shipped to Chicago and sold for the benefit of all the fallen sailors' families.

A friend of Captain Schuenemann donated a schooner for Barbara and her daughters to sell their trees from. The *Chicago Daily Tribune* of December 11, 1912, reported, "The *Oneida*, a schooner similar in appearance to the *Rouse Simmons*, except for the Christmas tree cabin which Captain Schuenemann had built, has been moored at the foot of Clark Street. All day yesterday, Christmas trees, sent from the northern woods by rail, and those picked up as wreckage along the lakeshore, were transferred to the *Oneida*."

According to the *Chicago Inter Ocean* of December 10, 1912, wreaths were also weaved from wrecked trees and then sold. The article read: "In a dingy little room at South Water and Clark Streets, where a lone window overlooks Chicago river, there sat a beautiful, golden haired, sad-eyed girl. She was weaving Christmas garlands. The girl is Elsie Schuenemann, daughter of Herman Schuenemann, skipper of the *Rouse Simmons*, the lost Christmas ship which went down with all hands. The garlands she weaves are from wreckage of the cargo of the *Rouse Simmons*, picked up along shores in Wisconsin and shipped to Chicago."

Crowds came to purchase trees from Captain Schuenemann's wife and children. Some came out of pity for this family now fatherless and husbandless. Others came out of tradition, having bought a Christmas tree from the captain for as long as they could recall. They wanted to hold fast to their memories of the past.

The captain was known and loved by many, and, because of this, there were more than a handful of persons who refused to be convinced that he was now gone – despite the tell-tale evidence. Along with Barbara and her girls, others were continuing to hope and wait.

The *Simmons'* tragedy saw more washed ashore than the evergreens sold by the captain's bride. The *Sturgeon Bay Advocate* of January 16, 1913, ran the following article about an empty trunk that was discovered around the same time many trees were coming to shore. It stated: "While playing on the beach at Whitefish Bay last week, a couple of boys from this city found a bundle of Christmas trees that were tied together and had evidently been thrown up by the waves. It is supposed these came from the ill-fated vessel *Rouse Simmons*. That the trees were found so far north is nothing remarkable, as the crew probably threw the bundles overboard when they realized their boat was in distress."

LAKE LASHED TO FURY; BOATS AT ITS MERCY
Raging Seas Drive Ships to Shelter; Hope for *Rouse Simmons* Dying Out
Chicago Daily News
Chicago, IL
December 6, 1912

A raging sea, with treacherous squalls and shifting winds, imperiled a number of lake boats bound for Chicago today, and swept away probably the last vestige of hope that the three-masted schooner *Rouse Simmons* and its Yule-tide cargo of Christmas trees would sail safely into Chicago's harbor with its hardy crew of sixteen men. The roaring waters were driven by a fifty mile gale that first burst upon Lake Michigan in all its fury from the northwest, and then in suddenness veered to the southwest.

High winds and rough seas were reported over all the Great Lakes excepting Ontario today. On Erie the storm was the worst of the season and a barge sank at Put-in-Bay, OH. A gale was blowing at Sault Ste. Marie, MI, and a fleet of ten boats took shelter behind Whitefish Point. Navigation was nearly impossible.

TREE CARGO IS CAST ASHORE

When Chicago watchers peered through spyglasses for a glimpse of incoming vessels, and relatives of the crew of the missing *Rouse Simmons* kept their vigil, Lake Michigan hurled hundreds of Christmas trees on the bleak shores near Sturgeon Bay. The waves had torn them from their fastenings and they drifted in in broken heaps.

As they lay in confusion upon the shore, viewed by awe-stricken men, women and children, A. F. Putnam, a ship builder at Sturgeon Bay, sent the following telegraph message to Mrs. Herman Schuenemann, wife of the former lake captain who owned the cargo of the missing *Rouse Simmons*. It was received by her representative, R. H. Geeting, a commission merchant at 108 West S. Water St., Chicago, and read as follows:

"Trees and greens picked up here. Shall we ship them?"

WILL NOT BELIEVE DISASTER

Mr. Geeting quietly conveyed the message to Mrs. Schuenemann, who

The article went on to say: "An empty trunk with the names ROUSE SIMMONS – J. E. LATHROP painted on it was found on the beach last Friday [near Kewaunee, WI] by three boys, Gordon and Dewey Dishmaker and Art Fiala. The trunk was too heavy for the lads to carry, so the part bearing the above names was broken off and brought to the city. As this is the only wreckage that has come ashore in this vicinity that had any connection with the ill-fated craft, and which may have been washed overboard, it does not cast any light on just where the boat went down."

Christmas trees, a battered trunk, a captain's wheel. Wreckage from the

daily has refused to believe that her husband and crew have gone down with their ship, and then sent the following reply:

"Trees and greens, if enough to pay to ship, will help family much. Any bodies found? R. H. GEETING."

Mrs. Schuenemann, or her daughters, who have not permitted a tear to pass their eyes, will not admit that the ship and all are lost.

"I won't believe it! I won't!" the mother cried.

DRAMATIC STORY OVER TELEPHONE

Mr. Putnam, who is in the shipbuilding and livery business at Sturgeon Bay, WI, was reached over the long distance telephone by a reporter for *The Daily News* after the telegram had been received by Mr. Geeting. He told of the finding of the greens and of the tireless patrol of the beaches for evidence of the lost ship.

"Night and day we have watched the lake for a sight of the missing boat," he said. "The men established a beach patrol in order that they might send immediate help to the missing vessel if it appeared near our town in distress. Not only did the men take part in the search but also wives, mothers and sisters, eager to minister aid if it became necessary. Daily the waters rose and fell on the shores but nothing appeared. Late yesterday afternoon the *Sylvia*, a fishing boat, while making its way to a pier, plunged into a floating forest of Christmas trees a mile from shore. All about the fisherman lay the greens like seaweed. Then other boats reported the same experiences."

TREES PILED HIGH ON SAND

"It was getting dark then and it was dangerous to try to bring the trees ashore, as a strong wind was rising. It increased in fury, and soon the lake was roaring like a torrent. At dawn, men, women, and children braved the cold, to hurry to the lake. There, piled high upon the sand were Christmas trees, broken and torn. The water was dyed a dark green by the torn branches and trees that still lay in the waves, which even tossed their tops above the surface as they lashed each other.

"There were hundreds of them. The biting wind was forgotten and mothers and daughters

Simmons continued to surface for decades.

The wheel of the *Rouse Simmons* is a prized relic, a historical treasure, and is now on permanent display at the Roger's Street Fishing Village Museum in Two Rivers, Wisconsin.

The mystery surrounding the wheel lasted for nearly thirty years. Here's why: When the wreck of the *Simmons* was finally located in 1971, a full fifty-nine years after the ship sunk to the bottom, the navigational wheel on the vessel was missing. This was hardly insignificant because the wheel, and its attached parts, just so happened to weigh over four hundred pounds. (Some

(Continued from previous page)

mingled with fishermen in searching among the greens for timber and bodies of those we believe went down with the boat. Some even went into the icy surf to search.

"The noise of the crashing breakers and their size did not daunt some of the boldest and they even ventured to launch a boat to search the waters. The fate of those who probably succumbed with the *Rouse Simmons* might have been theirs had they been successful in getting far off shore. They realized the impossible task and decided to wait until the lumber drifted ashore."

EXPECT TO FIND BODIES

"The waves, until last night, have been running mainly off shore and I believe this has been responsible for the inability to find spars and timbers of the Christmas tree boat. We feel positive that the ship foundered near Kewaunee, WI, which is thirty-two miles from here and where it was last seen. The townsmen there also have picked up Christmas trees. We are on the watch night and day and I feel pretty sure that sooner or later bodies will appear. We are only waiting for an east wind which will bring everything to our coast, and then the mystery of the wreck will be clear."

parts were cast iron; others were steel.) Yet despite its massive weight, it had been ripped right off the ship. Many believe this "attested to the violence of the storm."

Prior to 1971, the great mystery surrounding the *Simmons* was, "Where is the wreck?" After the ship was located, the great mystery then became, "Where is its wheel?"

There have always been questions surrounding the Christmas Tree Ship tragedy. Some have remained unanswered longer than others.

It took many years to find the shipwreck site of the *Simmons* due to the depth the ship had plunged. During that time, theories were discussed and debated as to what led to the ship's demise. Many wondered about the primary cause. As would be expected, opinions varied. Some felt the ship had simply succumbed to the brutality of the storm. Others felt the trees were to blame. They believed the *Simmons* was riding too low in the water, "sagging under the weight" of its cargo.

Onlookers back in Thompson, Michigan, were quoted as saying the ship looked like "a floating forest" when it sailed from the port's safety. Some believed this was the fatal error. The excessive weight on the ship's upper deck would surely cause the vessel to become unstable when it began to ride the lake's stormy roller coaster.

Fred Hinson, a local resident of Thompson, Michigan, who saw the

Photo of the *Rouse Simmons* at dock front right in Sheboygan, WI.
(Courtesy of the Wisconsin Maritime Museum, Manitowoc, WI)

"After the terrific gale last Tuesday, when some of the fishing nets were recovered off Two Rivers, WI, many Christmas trees were found in the mesh. It was then believed that these were trees which were on the Rouse Simmons *when the vessel went down."*

The Sheboygan Press
Sheboygan, WI
October 29, 1929

James Brotz with the *Rouse Simmons'* wheel.
(On display at the Roger's Street Fishing Village Museum, Two Rivers, WI.)

Simmons depart, gave testimony in the 1970's as to the number of trees on board. He was asked, "How loaded was the ship?" His reply was, "Damn loaded."

The *Simmons* was getting heavier and heavier as more and more trees were loaded, and it was sinking deeper and deeper.

Of the opinions regarding the cause of the wreck, there were many. Some believed the vessel's sheer age was to blame. After all, its prime was long past. The ship was nearly half a century old. Most wooden schooners never saw such length of days. Did the *Simmons*, in its weariness, break apart as the waves relentlessly battered it? Was it smashed to pieces in the storm? Possibly.

Or had the *Simmons* literally "come apart at the seams" because Captain Schuenemann, it was rumored, may have failed to re-caulk the ship during the fall of 1912 due to financial strains? Maybe.

Details were examined from every angle.

Perhaps the most intriguing question of all was presented in the *Chicago Inter Ocean* newspaper of December 5, 1912, only days after the *Simmons* went missing. The article reported: "Marine circles are mystified over a vessel with all masts intact running full sail and passing a port of safety with distress signals flying. The question is why did not the vessel either tack and run into Kewaunee harbor or lay to until assistance could reach her. The theories advanced are that either the vessel was leaking badly and most of the crew was at the pumps or that some of the crew in desperation had taken to the lifeboats and the vessel was insufficiently manned."

Marine men were "mystified" – and rightfully so. They were scratching their heads, trying to make sense of a report by lifesavers at the Kewaunee, Wisconsin, station which told of a schooner, with its distress flags flying (literally screaming for help), passing a "port of safety" that was so near at hand. Why didn't the ship turn toward the shore?

Clearly, the vessel was in dire need of help, and the help it sought was within its reach. Yet it passed on by. People wondered why.

By this time it was widely believed that the ship sighted was surely the *Simmons*. It just made sense. But what didn't make sense were those final moments. What had happened?

Theories again ran wild. Some people thought the vessel was taking on water, as the *Chicago Inter Ocean* stated, and, because of this, the attention of most on board might have been drawn to the pumps. This certainly could have been the case.

Others wondered how many men from the crew were even left on the ship. Were there any? Had some been washed overboard in the ferocious gale? Had some tried to escape the doomed ship in a lifeboat? These thoughts, too, were plausible.

It was also believed by some that the wind may have taken a sudden shift just as the *Simmons* was attempting to steer toward shore, causing it to be blown back out into the open waters.

There were many "what ifs" bantered around, sometimes over mugs of beer in dockside saloons, as to why the *Simmons* didn't seek shelter in the safety of the harbor's arms, but no one knew for sure. It was all speculation. Without the ship, the truth could not be known. The only thing that could be known for sure was that one moment the ship was above the waters, and the next it was below.

The mystery lingered. Then in 1971 the ship was finally found. Questions now had answers.

Did the ship come apart at the seams? No, it did not. Was it smashed to pieces? No, it was not. In fact, the ship was in tact.

Did the wind prevent the ship from reaching shore? This answer, too, was no.

The ultimate reason why the *Simmons* went down was because the ship's wheel had been torn from its place during the violent squall.

This discovery solved a big piece of the puzzle. It was now known that the captain *didn't* turn into safety, because he *couldn't* turn into safety. Without the wheel, the decision as to what direction the ship was now headed no longer belonged to Herman Schuenemann. The decision now belonged to the storm.

The horror and utter helplessness of the crew in those final moments is hard to imagine. Did they realize they were about to face Death, or did hope yet remain? It will never be known. All that can be known is that once the wheel was gone, the *Simmons* was fighting for its life with both arms tied behind its back.

When the *Simmons* wreck was discovered with its missing captain's wheel, more questions surfaced: Where was the wheel? How was it torn from the ship?

The most reasonable conclusion agreed upon was that bundles of trees on deck had turned into huge blocks of ice as waves crashed over them. These then became deadly ramming blocks as the ship started rocking on the chaotic sea. The trees undoubtedly slid across the deck and then hit the wheel with great force, taking it overboard.

STORY OF CHRISTMAS TREE SCHOONER THAT NEVER RETURNED
Manitowoc Daily-Herald
Manitowoc, WI
December 14, 1912
Gus C. Kirst

Christmas 1912, just a few more days and the joyful Yuletide season will again take possession of this Earth. Joys and pleasures are recalled, sorrows as well.

The loss of the Christmas Tree Ship, the schooner *Rouse Simmons,* with her crew of 16 men, near Two Rivers Point, WI, on November 23rd, will bring a gloomy Christmas to the homes of those who braved the elements to bring to the Chicago market, and to the Chicago homes, the evergreens of good cheer.

Years, yes, for a great many years, this old veteran of Lake Michigan, each Christmas season, sailed forth from the shores of northern Wisconsin or Michigan, loaded with a cargo of trees. When the *Rouse Simmons* arrived at Chicago with its cargo of trees, the boys and girls in that large city felt more than Christmas soon would arrive…

Fishermen recently have found entangled in the meshes of their nets, fragments of Christmas trees and other wreckage and it is about conclusively decided by marine men that the *Rouse Simmons* foundered in the immediate vicinity of Two Rivers Point.

"With the finding of hundreds of Christmas trees and greens on the Wisconsin shore of Lake Michigan, there is no longer any doubt that the "Christmas Ship" Rouse Simmons has been lost with all hands, the number varying from 11 to 18 men. All on board were not sailors, more than half the men being tree cutters who accompanied the ship to a northern Michigan port to gather Christmas trees and greens to make the homes of Chicagoans happy during the Yuletide period."

The Detroit News
Detroit, MI
December 7, 1912

This opinion was well worth consideration, and it held for many years, at least until 1999, the year the wheel was finally washed up. It had been on the bottom for eighty-seven long years.

When the wheel surfaced, an entirely different opinion surfaced with it.

The wheel, unbelievably, was found in a fisherman's net. A tug was felt - a *significant* tug, *a four hundred pound tug* – and when the net was lifted, the wheel appeared. It was a tremendous find.

Make no mistake, the men aboard this ship knew exactly what they had just found. You see, these were fishermen from Two Rivers, Wisconsin, the area believed to be the general location of the *Simmons* wreck. The fishermen had long since heard the story of the fabled Christmas Tree Ship, and were among those who wondered about the elusive wheel.

The wheel was found "approximately a mile and a half up wind" of the location where the ship was found. This was the deadly distance the ship traveled on its collision course with certain death once the wheel went missing.

A retired gentleman by the name of Jim Brotz was awarded the great honor of restoring the ship's wheel. Mr. Brotz is well known for his restoration work on artifacts, and also for his award-winning ship models, built by hand.

Although the restoration process of the wheel took "nearly three years," he chose to volunteer his time because of his love of the story and his passion for the Great Lakes.

"I've lived on Lake Michigan my whole life," he told me, "except for four years when I served in the Marine Corps. The furthest I've ever lived from these shores is six blocks."

Although Mr. Brotz was an avid diver for more than three decades, and dove to countless wrecks, it is the *Rouse Simmons* that is nearest and dearest to his heart. He told me, "There is just something special about this ship - its history and, of course, the Schuenemann family."

Before Mr. Brotz was chosen as the man for the job, he underwent much

> *"Slowly, clues to the sinking of the* Simmons *would emerge from the lake's icy depths through the years."*
>
> *Evening News*
> December 23-25, 1995
> Deidre S. Tomaszewski

scrutiny by the State of Wisconsin. A representative from the State examined his previous work on display at the Wisconsin Maritime Museum, as well as at the American Club in Kohler, Wisconsin, before he was given custody of the wheel and permission to proceed.

It is important to note that the wheel was discovered in 1999, *after* laws were established forbidding the removal of any artifact from the waters. Because of this, the State of Wisconsin was involved with the wheel's restoration, as well as its placement in the Roger's Street Fishing Village Museum in Two Rivers. Every detail concerning the wheel was done in cooperation with the State, and under its authority.

The restoration process began with the careful removal of rust. It was tedious, tedious work because the wheel had become extremely rust-encrusted after nearly a century on the bottom of the lake. Weeks passed, and then months. The first year turned into a second year, and finally a third. The wheel was undergoing an extreme transformation under the expertise of Jim Brotz.

Also transformed during this same time were details concerning the Christmas Tree Ship's demise.

Before the wheel was discovered, it was believed the evergreens aboard had turned into a block of ice and crashed into the wheel. But the damage to the wheel did not support this theory. Rather, it was now believed the wheel had been hit by the mizzenmast driver boom – the massive support for one of the ship's main sails. In plain language, the driver boom is similar to a telephone pole (in both length and size). The rigging supporting it snapped in the storm (two separate lines), and then caused it to break loose. It was a deadly chain reaction. Once the driver boom snapped loose, it would have swung wildly until finally crashing into the wheel with tremendous force.

This opinion can be evidenced by specific damage to the wheel, particularly its handles. Several were bent at severe angles. Others were knocked completely off. The damaged handles are said to be "very strong circumstantial evidence" as to what occurred that fateful day. (The handles were replaced with 200-year-old white oak.)

Although many people were convinced the wheel positively belonged to the *Simmons*, this had not yet been proven. But proof was on its way.

The time had finally come to gently remove the last, thin layer of rust from the wheel's brass sleeve. (This is the area where the shipbuilder would have stamped the year of the ship's birth into the metal.)

Several persons were "hovering around the wheel" as they waited to see what would be found beneath the rust. This included the State Archaeologist, and also Kent Bellrichard, the diver who originally discovered the wreck in 1971.

"All of a sudden the year 1868 appeared – the year the *Simmons* was built," said Jim Brotz, "and Kent started jumping for absolute joy." The mystery of the wheel had been solved.

The three determining factors which linked the wheel to the *Simmons* were:

1. The date stamped into the sleeve.
2. The location where the wheel was found - approximately 1 1/2 miles "up wind" from the *Simmons* shipwreck site.
3. Specific damage to the wheel, as well as specific damage to the mizzen driver boom.

The prized artifact went on display in Two Rivers, Wisconsin, in 2003.

Although the Christmas Tree Ship's wheel was the last of the *Simmons'* clues to be found, additional clues from the ship came up in preceding years including several skulls, a headless corpse, and an entire skeleton.

> *"As late as 1923 trees have still been raised in the nets of Two Rivers fishermen, and on one occasion a headless corpse, believed to have been that of one of the crew of the ill-fated ship was brought to the surface. The fishermen made every effort to get the gruesome find to their boats, but it slipped back into the water and was lost, to rest undisturbed at the bottom forever."*
>
> Lake Michigan Disasters
> Unpublished manuscript dated 1925
> Discovered at the Rahr-West Museum
>   and Civic Center
> Reproduced by the Manitowoc Maritime Museum
> Herbert Pitz

NOTE TELLS CHRISTMAS SHIP'S FATE
Chicago Daily Journal
Chicago, IL
December 13, 1912

In a bottle washed ashore near Sheboygan, Wisconsin, was found the positive proof of the sinking of the *Rouse Simmons*, the Christmas ship which went to the bottom of Lake Michigan with its crew of eleven men in the heavy storm that swept over the lake two weeks ago...

All doubt as to the fate of the vessel was set at rest by the posthumous message of the doomed captain, which he wrote and sealed when he realized that all hope was gone. The bottle traveled from the north shore, where it was sent, and was found on the beach by Mike Koblibik, a fisherman.

The message was written on a page of the ship's log and was a cold statement of facts. Only one sentence was out of the ordinary, and that was the prayer of a brave man who asks his God to help him face death.

The message read: "Friday – Everybody goodbye. I guess we are all through. Sea washed over our deckload Thursday. During the night, the small boat was washed over. Leaking bad. Ingvald and Steve fell overboard Thursday. God help us. HERMAN SCHUENEMANN."

The Steve referred to was Steve E. Nelson, the mate of the *Rouse Simmons*. Ingvald Nyhous, the other sailor referred to, lived at 420 N. Desplaines Street...

While the little schooner struggled and fought its way through the gale, the merciless pounding of heavy seas opened the cracks in its side... Capt. Schuenemann, aiding in the fight, turned despairingly and wrote his obituary....

It is believed that Nyhous and Nelson, sailors, in an effort to take the wheel, were whirled off the deck as the little schooner bowed to the weight of the entering sea. Their loss was the incident which settled the fate of the Christmas ship. There were two men less to man the pumps, and the little vessel, headed to the wind, whirled in a circle and settled swiftly into its grave.

"One voice, that of the captain himself, was heard from beyond Lake Michigan's watery grave when a message in a bottle washed ashore."

Shipwrecks of Lake Michigan Video
Produced by Southport Video
Copyright 2001

Each of these body parts was found on separate occasions earlier in the 1900's, washed up very near to the vicinity where it was believed the *Simmons* had sunk.

Thus, it was assumed that these remains probably belonged to members of the ill-fated crew. But positive identification was never made.

On December 13, 1912, reports circulated that Captain Schuenemann's body had been washed ashore near Sheboygan, Wisconsin, but there was no truth to this. No human remains were ever proven to be those of the *Rouse Simmons* crew.

Each fragment washed ashore was like a bit of a jigsaw puzzle whose pieces were being revealed one-by-one, but were not always fitting into place as one would hope. When a bottled note from the Christmas Tree Ship surfaced, and then another bottled message was washed ashore, these proved to be puzzles unto themselves.

Unbelievably, the Christmas Tree Ship story contains *two* notes in a bottle, not one. The first note was supposedly written by Captain Herman Schuenemann and was washed ashore approximately three weeks after the *Simmons* went missing. The note, believed by some to be Captain Schuenemann's last words, made headlines on Friday the 13th, December of 1912. The note read: "Friday – Everybody goodbye. I guess we are all through. Sea washed over our deckload Thursday. During the night, the small boat was washed over. Leaking bad. Ingvald and Steve fell overboard Thursday. God help us. Herman Schuenemann."

The second note, allegedly written by Captain Charles Nelson, Schuenemann's partner, is said to have been washed ashore fifteen years later in 1927. This note read: "Nov. 23, 1912. These lines were written at 10:30 p.m. Schooner *Rouse Simmons* ready to go down about 20 miles southwest of Two Rivers Point, between 15 and 20 miles offshore. All hands lashed to one line. Goodbye. Capt. Charley Nelson."

If there is one aspect of the Christmas Tree Ship story that is more difficult to follow than any other, it is, in my opinion, these mysterious messages. Attempts to analyze the various details concerning the notes can be overwhelming. Here's why: Some believe the first note was authentic, but the second was a hoax. Others believe the exact opposite. Then you have those who believe both notes are legitimate, while others believe neither to be.

Bottled Message Discovered

"The fate of the gallant schooner was confirmed the following spring when fishermen in the area found their nets clogged with balsam and spruce. In addition, a corked bottle was found near Sheboygan, WI, with a note signed by Captain Schuenemann stating he had lost two crew members and their small boat, and had given up hope of survival."

> *Telescope*
> Great Lakes Dossin Museum Publication
> January 1962, Vol. 11 No. 1
> John F. Miller

"A note from Captain Schuenemann was found in a bottle later on the Wisconsin shoreline. The note stated: '*Friday – Everybody goodbye. I guess we are all thru. Sea washed over our deckload Thursday. During the night the small boat was washed over. Leaking bad. Ingvald and Steve fell overboard Thursday. God help us.*' Ingvald and Steve were crewmen on the *Rouse Simmons*. The 18 bodies were never recovered but for months after, the nets of fishermen on the Wisconsin side of the lake would become entangled with Christmas trees."

> On file at: Door County Maritime Museum
> (Written by museum staff)

"There was precious little evidence to go by. In addition to the bottled notes from Schuenemann and first mate Nelson, bundles of Christmas trees washed up on the Wisconsin shore."

> *The Christmas Tree Ship*
> WTMJ Television Documentary
> Copyright 1975

"Ten days later a corked bottle was allegedly found on the beach at Sheboygan, WI. It contained a message written on a page from the *Rouse Simmons'* log: '*Friday. Everyone goodbye. I guess we are all through. Sea washed over the deck load Thursday. During the night the small boat washed over. Ingvald and Steve fell overboard Thursday. God help us. Herman Schuenemann.*' The message never reached Barbara Schuenemann. The man who found it demanded $500 that she could not pay. Some say the message was planted by a cruel prankster, others that it was an attempt to exploit Barbara's grief."

> *The Elks Magazine*
> Dec. 2002/Jan. 2003
> Jack Bellin

BOTTLE WASHED UP ON SHORE WITH NOTE FROM UNCLE HERMAN
Milwaukee Sentinel
Milwaukee, WI
March 23, 1977
Karen Surratt

Elizabeth Barerlin doesn't like being in the limelight.

In fact, the 91-year-old resident of Luther Manor probably would prefer to blend quietly into the pastel surroundings of the immaculate nursing home where she lives.

She politely told reporters at a recent showing of "The Christmas Tree Ship" that, "I don't like all of this notoriety. I'm not used to it."

Elizabeth Barerlin is the only known living relative of Capt. Herman Schuenemann, the master of a cargo schooner that has come to be known as "The Christmas Tree Ship."

The ship, whose real name is the *Rouse Simmons*, sank with its entire crew in the icy waters of Lake Michigan in 1912. The ship was lost for 59 years until 1971, when an amateur diver, Kent Bellrichard, found it in deep water nine miles northeast of Two Rivers.

WTMJ-TV made a documentary film about the ship and its sinking. It tells the story of how the captain each year loaded the ship in Michigan with Christmas trees to sell in Chicago. It was first shown to television audiences in November, 1975.

It was known that Captain Schuenemann had a living relative in Wisconsin, but WTMJ was unable to locate her while researching the film. Like her uncle's sunken vessel that lay undiscovered in Lake Michigan for more than half a century, the pleasant Mrs. Barerlin wouldn't have minded if she, too, were not especially noticed among the other nursing home residents. But like it or not, Mrs. Barerlin was the center of attention recently as reporters converged on her.

"Is this the first time you've seen the movie, Elizabeth? Did you see it before on TV?" fellow nursing home residents inquired. A couple of the women reached over to tap her lightly, as it was announced that "the niece of the captain of the Christmas Tree Ship lives at our house." The

Frederick Stonehouse, a noted historian who is widely respected as an authority on the Great Lakes, summarized his opinion regarding the bottled notes in his book *Went Missing II* in 1984: "Whether authentic or hoax is anybody's guess, but they were purported to have come from the doomed schooner. Real or contrived? Flip a coin."

Although Mr. Stonehouse's conclusion is humorously delivered, it summarizes a serious subject well.

Another historian, Theodore Charrney, writing to the editor of *The Sheboygan Press* (as published December 24, 1960) had this to say regarding the first note in particular: "Reports of a drifting bottle found with a message

film was being shown to Luther Manor residents.

Mrs. Barerlin, dressed in a navy blue, red and white dress sprinkled with diamond flower patterns, sat with hands neatly placed in the center of her lap as the movie began.

As the film narrator's voice announced that Lake Michigan's "bottom is a graveyard" of ships wrecked in storms "that most of us never see from shore," Mrs. Barerlin sat with tiny feet in navy shoes placed neatly together under her chair.

Asked whether she remembered anything about her uncle, Mrs. Barerlin replied, "Oh yes, I was 27 years old the year he set sail, so I remember a great deal. He was my mother's brother," she continued.

"We thought an awful lot of him."

Mrs. Barerlin said her mother used to "make wreaths and evergreen ropes" from the Christmas trees, which her Uncle Herman would purchase in Thompson, Michigan, each year. Mrs. Barerlin said she had been aboard the *Rouse Simmons* "many, many times."

"I'd even eat on the ship when it was docked at the Clark Street Bridge because we used to live in Chicago."

During the showing of "The Christmas Tree Ship," Mrs. Barerlin's small hands clutched a tiny flowered pouch. She opened and closed the little purse several times as the diver talked about discovering the wreckage of the ship.

"He'll never make it,

he'll never make it, he'll never be back in my meat market again," the daughter of a Thompson, Michigan grocer depicted in the film remembered her father saying as Captain Schuenemann set sail on November 22, 1912.

Mrs. Barerlin clutched her flowered purse even tighter as the film's narrator interviewed people who remembered the Christmas Tree Ship's last voyage.

The daughter of the Michigan grocer was being interviewed again as she quoted Mrs. Barerlin's uncle replying, "The people of Chicago have to have their Christmas trees."

The *Rouse Simmons* never made it to Chicago. The ship was overloaded with evergreens, and it set sail

from the captain inside were first confirmed, then denied, then confirmed again."

It was not uncommon for those aboard a doomed vessel to write a message and send it afloat. It was also not uncommon for those living on land to participate in this activity as well. Who wasn't fascinated with a mysterious bottled message?

One of the most amazing bottled notes ever found washed ashore on a California beach in 1949. The bottle had been thrown into the Thames River (near England) by a lady named Daisy Singer Alexander on June 20, 1937. She was near death and wrote her last words on a white piece of paper. Then

(Continued from previous page)

during what was called "The Big Storm" – the worst they could remember on the Great Lakes back then.

Elizabeth Barerlin's hands began to squeeze one another... These gestures were in response to witnesses on film who recalled a captain's pocketbook, Christmas trees being washed ashore, and a bottle with a message. The bottled message read in part – "Friday... guess we're all through... God help us." It was signed "Herman Schuenemann."

The handkerchief came out of the blue flowered pouch once more. This time to wipe at moistened eyes.

Later, asked how she felt about the film, Mrs. Barerlin said, "It was interesting, but of course it was sad for me. I felt very sad because I remembered so many good things about him in our home and in his home." She said, "Aunt Barbara made him promise it would be his last trip. Of course, when he told us it would be his last trip, none of us knew that it really would."

Mrs. Barerlin remembered when the bottle with the message from her uncle washed to shore. She said, "We were all very thankful when that washed ashore."

Mrs. Barerlin then revealed a bit of family pride. "He was really my uncle," Mrs. Barerlin said. "No doubt about it. I looked up my baptismal records recently and he was listed as my godfather."

she placed the paper inside a bottle, and set it afloat. Twelve years passed. Finally, it was washed up on a California beach and found by a man named Jack Wurm. He was penniless and down on his luck. Little did he know his luck was about to change. You see, Daisy Singer Alexander just so happened to be heiress to the Singer Sewing Machine fortune, and the note inside the bottle was her last will and testament. It amounted to a single sentence naming two beneficiaries. One of the beneficiaries was a man by the name of Barry Cohen. The second beneficiary was simply referred to as "the lucky person who finds this bottle." Mr. Wurm's share of the estate amounted to six million dollars.

Notes in bottles conjure up mystery, and the mystery surrounding the Christmas Tree Ship notes remains a curious point of discussion to this very day.

Critics of the note written by Captain Schuenemann will tell you that it is surely a hoax because the note mentions "Thursday" and "Friday". They argue that the note is a prank because Captain Schuenemann didn't sail until Friday, and his ship went to the bottom on Saturday.

As reasonable as this argument seems, sailors will respond to this point by saying, "I might not know the day of the week either if a storm is raging around me and my ship is going down."

Critics of the Schuenemann note will also question the names of the two crew members in the message, arguing that neither the name Ingvald or Steve appears on the crew list. It is true that these names do not appear on *some* of the lists, but there are other lists the names do appear on. (Several lists were in circulation. They varied greatly.)

Frederick Stonehouse, in response to this argument, said, "One crew list does show a Steve Nelson aboard. Ingvald does not appear, but could have been one of four men whose names were not recorded."

Some names made one list. Other names made another list. And some names didn't appear on any of the lists, adding to the difficulty of settling this matter. (Even the number of crew members on board is not known for certain.)

Both of the names mentioned in the note had been included in some of the newspaper reports before the bottle was found. Because of this, critics believe the note was "tailored" to match previously published information about the tragedy. However, they further believe the prankster made a significant error by confusing the actual storm Captain Schuenemann was caught in during the end of November (on a Friday and a Saturday) with another storm that hit the beginning of December (on a Thursday and a Friday).

Now this may very well have been the case, but maybe not. Even those persons directly involved with the story during the critical days of 1912 could not reach common ground on the storm referred to in the note.

The *Chicago American* of December 13, 1912 reported: "The date – Friday – is believed to mean a week ago today, December 6."

The *Chicago Daily Journal* of December 13, 1912 reported: "The message evidently was written early on Friday, November 29. It was on

"The farewell notes recognized the approaching demise of the battered ship."

Milwaukee Sentinel
Milwaukee, WI
November 22, 1975

WORD FROM DEATH SHIP
Lost Ship's Story Told in Bottle
Chicago American
Chicago, IL
December 13, 1912

The story of the fate of the *Rouse Simmons* was washed up out of the lake today. It came as a farewell message from the despairing crew. It was found in a bottle floating in Lake Michigan.

The message bore the signature of Herman Schuenemann, master of the *Rouse Simmons*. It was picked up by a fisherman off Sheboygan, Wisconsin. The letter, written on a torn sheet of paper, tells in graphic language the story of the last hours of the tree-laden schooner and her crew of eighteen men.

It reads: "Friday – Everybody goodbye. I guess we are all through. Sea washed off our deck load on Thursday. During the night the small boat was washed off. Leaking badly. Engwald and Steve fell overboard Thursday. God help us. HERMAN SCHUEN-EMANN."

Michael Kovlovik, a fisherman, returning from a trip on the lake, discovered a bottle bobbing on the surface of the water off Sheboygan. He ran his smack alongside the object and picked it up.

WRITTEN IN FALTERING HAND

The black bottle was sealed with a whittled stopper, cut evidently from a limb of a Christmas tree. He uncorked the bottle and found the penciled note, written in a faltering hand on a sheet of torn writing paper.

On arrival at Sheboygan, he at once turned it over to the authorities. United States marine officials at Milwaukee, who were communicated with today, sent the news to Chicago.

The date – Friday – is believed to mean a week ago today, December 6...

"Engwald" and "Steve," referred to as having been washed overboard on Thursday, were sailors among the crew of the *Rouse Simmons*.

Discovery of the fateful note came just at the time when a last desperate effort was being made to find the missing ship.

The revenue cutter, *Tuscarora*, was awaiting orders in Milwaukee

Thursday, November 28, that a fierce storm swept Lake Michigan. Marine men have believed that the *Rouse Simmons* sank November 28 or 29."

The *Manitowoc Daily Herald* of December 13, 1912 reported: "The message was not dated, but is believed to have been written Saturday, November 23, the day a three-masted schooner in distress was sighted off Kewaunee and for which the Two Rivers Life Savers made search. This belief is strengthened by the reference to the loss of two of the crew overboard on Thursday in the message. The find of the message here clears the mystery which has surrounded the loss of the Christmas tree boat and tells a story of a heroic fight against death."

from Secretary of the Treasury MacVeagh in answer to an appeal to permit the cutter to start on a cruise of the northern lake waters in search of the *Rouse Simmons*...

Miss Elsie Schuenemann, daughter of the captain of the missing ship, up to the time of the receipt of the message had hoped that the vessel might be found among the islands in the northern part of the lake, which often afford refuge for storm-blown ships.

The Ludington Chronicle simply reported on the note by linking it to one of the storms "several weeks ago".

Many museums and credible historians will write about the bottled notes without mentioning any of the controversy. In fact, more articles written in the past century speak of the bottled notes as actual than they do with suspicion. This, of course, does not make the notes true. It only means that this is the more widely known version of the story.

As is the case with other aspects of this story, opinions regarding the notes vary depending upon whom you ask.

If you were to ask the Schuenemann family, you would find out that they believed the note written by Captain Schuenemann was true. Captain Schuenemann's niece, Mrs. Elizabeth Barerlin, interviewed by the *Milwaukee Sentinel* in 1977 at the age of 91, remembered: "We were all very thankful when that washed ashore." Mrs. Barerlin was 27 years old when the ship went missing, and was living in Chicago near her aunt and uncle. She remembered the events surrounding her uncle's tragedy very well.

Captain Schuenemann's grandson, Dr. Ehling, also recalls his family speaking of "the note from Grandpa" as being true, and also "wanting to believe the second note" written by Captain Nelson.

The most confusing aspect, in my opinion, to the note written by Captain Nelson is that it is consistently referred to as "the note from the 1920's" or "the note from 1927." Unfortunately, I have been unable to locate any newspapers that evidence a note from Captain Nelson during this period of time.

However, the following headline was published in the *Sturgeon Bay Advocate* on July 31, 1913: "Bottle Picked Up on the Beach at Whitefish Bay Containing a Farewell from Doomed Crew."

The article read: "The story of the ill-fated schooner is again revived by the finding on the beach north of the canal of a bottle containing a message from Capt. Charles Nelson, who was in command of the vessel on the night she went down with all hands. This message was found Sunday by a son of Frank Lauscher, a fisherman residing at Whitefish Bay and whose Post Office address is Sturgeon Bay, RFD No. 3. The boy was wandering along the beach while his father and uncle, Henry Lauscher, were engaged in attending to their pound net. The boy found a medicine bottle buried in the sand and was in the act of throwing it back into the water when his father noticed that it contained a piece of paper. He arrested the boy in the act by a cry to hold the bottle, which was broken open on a rock, and a piece of paper fell out on which was written the following message: *'Nov. 23, 1912. These lines were written at 10:30 p.m. Schooner Rouse Simmons ready to go down about 20 miles southwest of Two Rivers Point, between 15 and 20 miles offshore. All hands lashed to one line. Goodbye. Capt. Charley Nelson.'* The place where the bottle was picked up is about seven miles north of the canal. Frank Lauscher, who is in possession of the piece of paper, will keep it until he hears from the relatives of the captain of the lost schooner, when an effort will be made to determine whether the message is genuine. It is most reasonable to suppose that this is the only authentic message from the long-lost schooner. It would have been about the hour of night when the men realized that their doom was sealed, and securing a bottle from the medicine chest, it is likely they sent their last message to the world while waiting for the end. Washing up on the beach, the bottle was partly covered with sand until accidentally found in the manner stated."

The note written by Captain Nelson was referred to as the "only authentic message" in the above newspaper article. However, opinions about the

One observer noted that the bottled messages *"would lead one to wonder whether the crew spent their last hours writing messages instead of trying to stay alive."*

Lumberjacks and River Pearls
Jack Orr
Copyright 1979

authenticity of each note changed like the direction of the wind. The conclusion, in the end, was confusion.

A few of the conflicting reports included:

Some accounts said the Schuenemann note washed up on a beach. Others said it bobbed to the surface.

Some accounts said it was written on paper torn from the ship's logbook. Others said it was written on wrapping paper.

Some accounts said it was found by a beach watcher. Others said a fisherman found it.

Some accounts listed the fisherman's name. Others said no such man was

NO TRACE OF
ROUSE SIMMONS
Story of Bottle
Containing Message
was Found Off
Sheboygan is Denied
Chicago Record-Herald
Chicago, IL
December 14, 1912

Reports received here yesterday from Sheboygan, WI, that a fisherman had picked up a bottle containing a posthumous message from Capt. Schuenemann of the schooner *Rouse Simmons* is denied.

known.

The primary difficulty with the controversies was that most people did not get every side of the story. Most were only exposed to a single newspaper, and, thus, selected slivers of the tragedy were carried forward through oral tradition, depending upon what had been heard or read.

Even the wording of the notes changed slightly right from the start. "Steve" was also referred to as "Stede," and "Ingvald" as "Engwald" or "Endward".

Then we must consider the message from Captain Nelson found in 1913 (referred to in almost every single article written during the past seventy years as the note from the 1920's). It is another point of mystery.

The conclusion, indeed, was confusion.

Were the farewell notes from Captain Schuenemann and Captain Nelson their last words? Yes or no? Flip a coin.

"What took place on board we can only guess. The Rouse Simmons *sailed into the silence that covers all the fine ships that have fallen victim to the gales of Lake Michigan which have taken the lives of so many."*

A Fireside Book of Yuletide Tales
Edited by Edward Wagenknecht
Copyright 1948
Story by Harry Hanson

Photo of Kent Bellrichard, diver who discovered the *Rouse Simmons,*
with the ship's anchor.
(Courtesy of the *Green Bay Press-Gazette*, November 18, 1973)

"The anchor was raised by having divers hoist it from the ship's deck, and then it was towed toward shore until it grounded in about 80 feet of water. The anchor, which weighs a ton, was raised to the surface with air filled drums."

Milwaukee Journal
Milwaukee, WI
December 24, 1973

Chapter Eight

A Sunken Treasure

"In 1971, a diver, looking for another ship among the 40 or 50 wrecks that lie on the bottom off Two Rivers, stumbled on the wreck of the Rouse Simmons, *identifying it by the nameplate and the bundles of needle-stripped trees like skeletal hands in its hold. The mystery of the Christmas Tree Ship was solved."*

Exclusively Yours
May 1998
Kathleen Winkler

A Sunken Treasure

Sunken ships. Sunken treasures. Forgotten men in forgotten places. At the bottom of the Great Lakes, in darkened depths, lie the remains of countless ships that were swallowed whole when the pleasing rhythm of calm waters turned violent. The *Rouse Simmons* is only one ship of many that became a coffin for the men aboard it when they found themselves on the losing end of a deadly wrestling match with the waters.

The *Simmons'* decaying remains lie just north of Two Rivers, Wisconsin on the floor of Lake Michigan. This stretch of shoreline is nicknamed "The Graveyard of the Lake" because of the large number of wrecks claimed in the immediate vicinity. (The shipwreck site is also located just south of the Door County Peninsula, another stretch of waters known for danger and disaster. The passageway between the northernmost tip of the peninsula and Washington Island, located several miles off shore, is nicknamed "Porte des Mortes" – French for "Death's Door".

Fifty-nine years after the *Rouse Simmons* and her crew were buried in their unmarked graves, a diver from Milwaukee, Kent Bellrichard, happened upon the site on October 30, 1971, while diving alone.

Bellrichard's testimony of the fateful find was included on a WTMJ television program, The Christmas Tree Ship, recorded in 1975. "The conditions that day were very bad," said Bellrichard. "The skies were heavily overcast with light mist and fog, so I could only see maybe a half a mile, and at times, a mile. After crisscrossing the lake, and going north and south, and east and west, you kind of lose track of where you are, so I really didn't know where I was when I got the target on the Christmas Tree Ship. I knew I had a good target, and obviously from our experience with the electronic equipment I can tell if it's a bad bottom, a rocky bottom, or a shipwreck. And I was quite sure this was a shipwreck. But just *what* shipwreck, you're not really sure until you go down and look at it."

"It was a tremendous thrill the very first time I went down," said Bellrichard, "because I was 99% sure it was the *Rouse Simmons*. In fact, I came back up and got in the boat, and there wasn't anybody within six miles. It was quite rough on the lake, and there weren't any sport fishermen out, for sure. There wasn't anybody around, yet I was hollering to myself in joy that I had finally found this ship."

The sonar equipment on Bellrichard's borrowed boat indicated a shipwreck was immediately below his craft. (Metal makes a certain sound on

**SHIPWRECK
The Ghost of
Christmas Past
Rests Beneath Waters
of Lake Michigan**
Milwaukee Sentinel
Milwaukee, WI
November 23, 1989
Suzanne Kautsky Weiss

The ghost of Christmas past rests beneath the cold, murky waters of Lake Michigan, about nine miles northeast of Two Rivers.

The ghost is the hull of the *Rouse Simmons*. The Christmas past was 1912.

"It is one of 40 to 50 shipwrecks in the waters between Manitowoc and Two Rivers," said Dan Hildebrand, an amateur historian and diver from Manitowoc. He has visited the remains of the *Rouse Simmons* about 20 times in the past nine years.

"The wreck is pretty much intact. There are still bundles of Christmas trees on the bow of the vessel," Hildebrand said.

The trees, numbering in the hundreds, have been reduced to sticks with branches.

"Visiting one of Lake Michigan's legends is both exciting and eerie," Hildebrand said.

Even with powerful lights, the visibility is typically two to three feet, creating a dark, gloomy atmosphere that makes him feel as if he's visiting a tomb.

"It has a ghostlike feel to it, like someone's watching you. I think a lot of that is due to the depth," Hildebrand said. "Your mind plays tricks on you."

"You touch the railing of a sunken vessel and you know that men struggled here to save their cargo and their ship, and ultimately themselves. You can feel the drama a hundred years after the fact."

Paul Creviere, Jr., Great Lakes Diver
Author of *Wild Gales and Tattered Sails*

the sonar, as does wood. Also, a sand bottom can be identified from a rocky bottom by the particular sound each makes.)

"To an untrained ear, the sonar readings Bellrichard heard that day would have meant nothing," said James Brotz, a long-time diving partner of Bellrichard's. "But this was no untrained ear."

By the time Bellrichard, a Coast Guard trained sonar expert, had located the *Simmons* shipwreck, he had also earned himself a nickname - "The Jacques Cousteau of the Great Lakes". In an interview I conducted with him while working on this book, he told me he had been diving since the late 1950's and was happiest when he was "on the water," "in the water," and "by the water."

"Lake Michigan has always been a part of my life," said Bellrichard. "And all the Great Lakes really."

He further told me how he often wandered off when he was a boy, and his dad would always know where to find him since his childhood home was located only one block from Lake Michigan.

"I suppose my love of the water is in my blood because my ancestors came from Norway and Germany," he said.

Although Kent Bellrichard had strong feelings that he had, indeed, located the *Simmons* wreck, it took one full week for proof positive.

"When I did go down I was quite sure it was the *Rouse Simmons*," said Bellrichard. "But I had an old, rickety, handmade light that I had put together, and it broke. So, I was in complete blackness when I got down to the wreck. But I could feel it, and so I managed to tie the line that I had brought down onto the wreck. I really couldn't see too much because the light went out. I could just feel my way around in the blackness. We really went back about a week later and identified it as the *Rouse Simmons*."

"It was a little frustrating to me that I had spent so much time looking for the ship," continued Bellrichard, "and I knew when I went down the first time that it just *had* to be the wreck. But if the buoy I placed would have been gone

"The voice of my ancestors said to me, 'The shining water that moves in the streams and rivers is not simply water, but the blood of your grandfather's grandfather. Each ghostly reflection in the clear waters of the lakes tells of memories in the life of our people.'"

Chief Seattle

Rouse Simmons artifacts on display at the Rogers Street Fishing Village Museum in Two Rivers, Wisconsin. (A wooden stool, an enamel kettle, a dead eye, and a timber from the ship.)

"It is an interesting biological fact that all of us have, in our veins, the exact same percentage of salt in our blood that exists in the ocean, and therefore, we have salt in our blood, in our sweat, in our tears. We are tied to the ocean. And when we go back to the sea - whether it is to sail or to watch it - we are going back from whence we came."

President John F. Kennedy

Mystery Fate Solved

The story of the *Rouse Simmons* is continued and enriched by a surprise news feature that appeared in the *Milwaukee Journal* of December 5, 1971. The mystery fate of the schooner that sank in a November 1912 snow storm has been solved near Two Rivers Point.

On October 30, 1971, a scuba diver, Kent Bellrichard of Milwaukee, while diving for the *Vernon* (sunk in 1887), discovered another wreck. Diving down in the murky waters, he found the *Rouse Simmons*, the first man to see it since it disappeared with a crew of fifteen men that stormy day in November 1912. Bellrichard had borrowed a boat with highly sophisticated sonar from John Steele, board chairman of the First National Bank of Waukegan who has scuba diving as a hobby. Bellrichard decided to hunt for the *Vernon*. He said he placed the sonar transducer in the water. No targets showed; he drifted northwest. Suddenly he received a signal which sounded like a school of fish. After several passes in the fresh southwest wind, and two hours trying to get grappling hooks to hold, he was ready to go down.

Descending into the cold depths of the lake, he was able to identify the wreck as a schooner. Unfortunately, his light went out and considering the adverse weather and his solitary work, he decided that one dive that day was enough.

Since then, Bellrichard and John Steele have made three dives. They discovered the schooner's name on the quarterboards when their lights spelled out *Rouse Simmons*. The Christmas Tree Ship had at last been found. Still crowded in its hold were the remains of hundred of Christmas trees – the ones which never arrived at the dock at Clark Street in Chicago Harbor. The divers brought up several trees, a china bowl with letters "R.S." and a hand-cranked foghorn. One of the trees was presented to the Marine Bank of Milwaukee.

Kenosha County Historical Society Bulletin
Kenosha, Wisconsin
January 1972
Phil Sander

"Diving a shipwreck is kind of like exploring a haunted house underwater."

Michael Haynes, Great Lakes Diver

when I came back, where would I have started to look? I really didn't know. I had a depth which did help. I knew preciously how deep the wreck was, so I could have concentrated my search in that area. Eventually, I would have found the ship again. But how much time? I had already spent 2 ½ summers looking for it."

After locating the wreck in 1971, Kent Bellrichard was interviewed by Theodore Charrney. Bellrichard told him, "Nothing has ever been so exciting, and at the same time rewarding, in all my years of diving, or in all my years of doing anything for that matter."

One of the first things Bellrichard saw when he returned to the shipwreck site one week later were "hundreds of Christmas trees" – spruce and pine - in the hold.

According to John Steele, a diver who joined Kent Bellrichard on this second dive to the *Simmons* site, many of the trees were "bald" and mere skeletons. However, Steele noted that when they dug deeper into the pile of trees they found trees that "still had needles on which is rather surprising."

The Christmas trees aboard the *Simmons* had been destined for prominent locations throughout Chicago: City Hall, Illinois Bell Telephone Company, Boston Store, Marshall Fields & Company, the Central Music Hall, and also the Bush Temple of Music, to name just a few. Many theaters and churches in Chicago erected Schuenemann trees each Christmas, as did countless families.

According to Andy LaFond, a fisherman whose family has been involved in the commercial fishing industry on Lake Michigan for over 150 years,

---

When the Rouse Simmons *went down with all hands during a storm in 1912, hundreds of Chicagoans who had planned to buy their Christmas trees from its captain had to make other plans.*

Recently, after 59 years at the bottom of Lake Michigan, two of the trees arrived in Milwaukee, proof that the wreckage of the "Christmas Tree Ship" has at last been found.

The ship's name is clearly visible [on the wreck] proving that a report of several years back that the Christmas Tree Ship had washed ashore at Ludington was in error.

Detroit News
December 12, 1971

---

stepladders were used by families in 1912 in place of Christmas trees when Captain Schuenemann's ship went missing. These opened stepladders provided a similar triangular shape to a Christmas tree, and were nearly the same height. According to the memories Mr. LaFond shared with me, these "Christmas stepladders" were nicknamed "Jacob Ladders" after the Biblical text in Genesis of a ladder that reached into heaven.

Families were waiting for the Christmas Tree Ship in 1912, but the ship and crew never arrived. On board the *Rouse Simmons* was a crew member by the name of Philip Bauswein who was to be married in Chicago when the Christmas Tree Ship returned. On November 10, 1912, Bauswein wrote the following letter to his sister, Augusta, just before he left Chicago with Captain Schuenemann: "Dear Sister, Received your letter and I will see that you will get a good tree this time. We will leave here Saturday night coming, so don't write here any more, but write to Thompson, Michigan, Schooner *Rouse Simmons*. I don't know of anything else, but get ready for the wedding. Regards to all and excuse this writing because I am holding this block of paper on my knee and a little old kerosene lamp for light. Good night. With love, Brother Phil"

Philip Bauswein sent three final letters from Thompson, Michigan. One letter was addressed to his mother, and one to his fiancee. The final letter was addressed his sister. It read, in part: "This will be my last letter. I have a beautiful blue spruce tree for your baby's grave. We are all on board and will pull the ropes, and off we will be."

Philip believed the letter he wrote to Augusta would be the "last letter" he wrote from Thompson, Michigan. It was, instead, the last letter of his life. The *Simmons'* final destination was not Chicago, but was, rather, the icy waters off Two Rivers, Wisconsin.

Oscar A. Anderson, a member of the Two Rivers Life Saving Crew in 1912, recalled the deadly storm of November 23rd and shared memories before he died of the rescue efforts he and other crew members made in their

> *"Shipwrecks are to maritime studies what battle stories are to military history. They are a dramatic human-interest narrative replete with heroism and folly, individual seamanship versus the seemingly inexorable exercise of fate."*
>
> Schooner Passasge
> Theodore J. Karamanski
> Copyright 2000

Photo of Captain Schuenemann's crew.
(*Courtesy of the Chicago Maritime Society*)

search for the *Simmons*: "It was snowing so thick most of the time," said Anderson, "we could hardly see the length of our 34-foot power life boat. In fact we worried that we might get run down by the *Simmons* as she was moving before the wind, but nary a trace of her... We turned around about halfway between Two Rivers Point light and Kewaunee and returned real close along the shore. In fact, a little too close to suit me as we got into some bad breakers. There were six of us in our life boat. Had an eight man crew; one was on day off, and one was left at the station in the lookout. In my ten years in the service, 1903 to 1913, this was my most thrilling experience."

Captain Schuenemann's wife, Barbara, also received correspondence from her husband written just prior to his departure from Thompson, Michigan, according to information supplied by Theodore Charrney to the Chicago Maritime Society. "When Barbara came to her front window on Sunday morning, November 24, she did not like what she saw," wrote Charrney. "Over the trees of Lincoln Park she could see the mass of foam that was Lake Michigan. Huge waves were hitting the shoreline, sending clouds of spray almost a hundred feet into the air. The waves swept over the driveways along the lakefront, and far into the park, carrying with them rubbish and logs brought in from the water. Some of the rollers intruded all the way to the Lincoln monument, a city block and a half from the shoreline. All day long people came from different areas of the city to see the spectacle produced by angry nature. Thousands of sightseers crowded into the park and at vantage points along the lakefront to watch the waves and see them atomize into great sheets of spray. Barbara had received a postcard from Herman, late in the week, and knew that the Christmas trees were already Chicago bound. Surely, Herman would not be out on the lake on such a day. He would have the good sense to seek shelter and let the storm pass before proceeding home. Perhaps he would be a day late, maybe two, but he was surely safe in some Wisconsin harbor, impatiently waiting out the storm. How could she know that Captain Herman and Captain Nelson, and the *Rouse Simmons* with all the men and Christmas trees, were already at the bottom of the lake."

In addition to Christmas trees, the *Simmons'* cargo also consisted of thousands and thousands of evergreen branches that were to be used for wreathmaking.

In December of 1898 the *Chicago Daily News* ran the following article about Captain Schuenemann's ship, the *Mary Collins*, when it made port in Chicago: "HOW THE WREATHS ARE MADE/EVERGREENS WOVEN INTO DECORATIONS ABOARD THE SCHOONER *MARY COLLINS*. The

Answers to Possible Questions

(Informational sheet distributed to museums in the 1970's
along with a documentary video)

Depth of ship is 180 feet.

Temperature of the water at 180 feet is 39 degrees Farenheit constant.

Divers can only stay down six (6) minutes per dive due to the cold. The entire dive – going down and returning – takes 12-15 minutes. If you took more air to stay down longer, you would have to decompress as you return to the surface.

The ship is about nine (9) miles northeast of Two Rivers, Wisconsin. Kent Bellrichard, the diver/finder, has precise location.

Everything in the ship is intact, but there are no known bodies.

It would cost one million dollars to raise the ship. There are currently no plans for this.

Since it is pitch black at the depth of the ship, with a good light it is possible to see 10-15 feet maximum.

"October and November account for approximately 46% of all the shipwrecks on Lake Michigan."

Shipwrecks of Lake Michigan
Benjamin J. Shelak
Copyright 2003

Rouse Simmons artifacts
Top: Eye glasses, sun glasses, two lightbulbs.
Center: Two clay pipes, a medicine bottle, a shot glass.
Bottom: An axe, a spittoon, a jawbone from a pet dog.
(Courtesy of the Klopp Collection)

schooner *Mary Collins*, Captain Schuenemann, with 10,000 Christmas trees and ten tons of lycopodium, the pretty fine-feathered green stuff of which Christmas wreaths are made…is moored at the Clark Street Bridge. On her deck an interesting sight is witnessed. Nearly a score of girls and women are turning this green stuff into Christmas wreaths and decorations. The Captain has built over the deck of the schooner a snug board shelter, through the middle of which runs a long table. Along both sides of this sit the wreathmakers, and deftly they handle the sprigs of green. The girls on the one side – on the starboard, to be nautical – make the endless strings of green for decorations, weaving the lycopodium sprigs together with fine, soft wire… The season of work in Christmas greens lasts about four weeks, and in that time the lycopodium on the *Mary Collins* will be turned into a matter of 60,000 yards of wreaths."

The *Chicago Daily News* published an article on November 28, 1899, detailing a typical Schuenemann cargo: "Balsam and fir fresh from the Michigan woods, Norway pine, white pine, lycopodium, hemlock, spruce, fir, cat spruce, red cedar, juniper, arbor vitae and all the other evergreens that grow on the north shore of Lake Michigan are represented today in the cargo of the *Mary Collins* at Clark Street Bridge… Its coming every fall betokens the approach of the holiday season, for every year Captain Herman Schuenemann, after unloading his last cargo of lumber, takes his craft to Manistique and fills the hold and deckhouse with Christmas trees and greens."

A decade later the *Chicago Inter Ocean* of December 7, 1909, reported "half a hundred girls and women" were still weaving wreaths on Captain Schuenemann's Christmas ship, the *Bertha Barnes*. (Many different ships were used by the Schuenemanns through the years.) The article also made mention of another vessel Captain Schuenemann used prior to the *Bertha Barnes*. This ship was called the *George Wrenn*. The article read: "SCENES ABOARD THE *BERTHA BARNES*, THE CHRISTMAS TREE BOAT. 'Christmas trees are going to be high this year,' observed Captain Schuenemann as he stood on the bridge of the schooner *Bertha Barnes* yesterday and filled the bowl of his pipe with tobacco that he had been rolling in the palm of his hand… 'It is about the slimmest cargo I ever brought away… Why, I've only got about 15,000 trees on the whole ship, and you know, of course, the Chicago market depends pretty much on my supply. It's the bad weather that's to blame… Say, I'm wondering if our poor luck in getting trees this year hasn't something to do with our changing boats. We're on the *Bertha Barnes* this year. It's the first time she ever had this honor and she acts as if she's mighty proud of it. But I can't help feeling a mite sorry for the *Wrenn…*' The captain beamed his broadest smile as half a hundred girls and women came out of the cabin where they had been twining and weaving wreaths. 'Hooray for Captain Schuenemann!' shouted some of the women as they waved their handkerchiefs at the jolly old skipper who resembles Santa Claus."

The *Rouse Simmons* debuted as Chicago's Christmas Tree Ship in 1910. The *Chicago Inter Ocean* reported on November 30th of that year: "XMAS TREE SHIP SAILS INTO PORT/CAPTAIN SCHUENEMANN, WHO FOR 32 YEARS HAS SUPPLIED CHICAGO, BRINGS IN CARGO AND THREE DAUGHTERS WHO MADE SELECTION. Chicago will not suffer from a dearth in the Christmas tree market this year. Whatever may happen to beefsteaks and butter, this one necessity of life will remain within the reach of the average man's purse. Trees big and small, 10,000 of them, reached this city yesterday. Skipper Schuenemann, first aid to Santa Claus, brought in a whole ship full of them just as he had done for the last thirty-two years. With trees in the wheelhouse, trees in the hold, trees in the galley, and trees piled high on the deck amidships, she sailed into port… Captain Schuenemann is 45 years old. He was but 13 when, with his father's consent, he loaded 800 small trees on their boat and brought them to Chicago. They sold well and the next year the experiment was tried again with a larger number of trees. From that year he has never failed to make port with a holiday cargo." (There is discrepancy in the historical record regarding the exact year Captain Schuenemann made his first trip with Christmas trees.)

The cargo capacity of the *Rouse Simmons* was estimated at 300-400 tons. Captain Schuenemann would load his Christmas ships to the maximum, utilizing every free space. Also, the captain would ship as many as three cargos during a single season.

In 1912 Captain Schuenemann's load was filled to the bursting point, and when the *Simmons* shipwreck was discovered there were still "thousands" of trees on board the vessel.

One of the first Christmas trees brought to the surface was donated to the Marine Bank in Milwaukee, Wisconsin. For many years the Marine Bank used a sketch of the *Rouse Simmons* as their logo. Because of this, Kent Bellrichard felt the bank would be an appropriate place to display a salvaged "bald" Christmas tree during the holiday season of 1971.

Kent Bellrichard carried a blank check from the Marine Bank showing the *Rouse Simmons* logo in his wallet for "many, many years." (The bank has

Rouse Simmons artifacts
Top: Dinnerware and silverware.
Bottom: A barometer, a caulking mallet, a tafrail log.
(Courtesy of the Klopp Collection. The *Rouse Simmon*s artifacts in the collection number approximately 200.)

ROUSE SIMMONS

Two nameplates were recovered from the *Rouse Simmons* shipwreck site. The above photo shows a nameplate on display at the Rogers Street Fishing Village Museum in Two Rivers, Wisconsin. A second nameplate is on display at Pier Wisconsin in Milwaukee.

CHRISTMAS TREE SHIP NAMEPLATE IS RECOVERED
Herald-Times Reporter
Manitowoc, WI
July 28, 1984

A group of three divers, including one from Two Rivers, WI, recently recovered the name plate from the famous Christmas Tree Ship, the *Rouse Simmons*, which sank in Lake Michigan off Two Rivers many years ago.

Brian Barner was among the group of three divers who worked to recover the name plate...

The group is now in the process of attempting to preserve the plate. Wood artifacts which are recovered from after years in the water will deteriorate rapidly if allowed to dry, according to Barner.

However, if treated properly, the artifacts can be preserved and put on open display...

Barner said once the preservation process is completed, they may donate the item to the Rogers Street Fishing Village Museum.

Henry Willert, president of the museum association, said such an item would fit right in with other artifacts the museum has relating to similar ships on the Great Lakes.

The museum already has a mast, stone jar, and Christmas tree from the ship.

since dissolved.)

Some of the "skeleton trees" salvaged from the *Simmons* are in family attics around Lake Michigan to this very day. Each Christmas, the trees are brought down from storage and given a place of honor. Although most of these trees are simply trunks with "stubby" little branches, they are lovingly decorated nonetheless with a single star.

Visitors to the Rogers Street Fishing Village Museum in Two Rivers, Wisconsin can view a Christmas tree on display from the *Rouse Simmons*, as well as other artifacts from the *Simmons* including a 15 gallon crock, a wood stool, an enamel kettle, a dead eye, a timber, and the ship's wheel.

The Rogers Street Fishing Village Museum also houses one of the vessel's nameplates. (A second nameplate is on display at the Pier Wisconsin Museum in Milwaukee, Wisconsin. Pier Wisconsin also has a porthole from the *Rouse Simmons* in their collection.)

When Kent Bellrichard discovered the *Simmons* in 1971 the nameplates were "quite visible and still in perfect shape," said Bellrichard. Each was filmed underwater when the *Simmons* was originally located to prove the vessel had at last been found since many people believed the wreckage of the *Rouse Simmons* washed ashore in 1951 at Ludington, Michigan.

The *Sheboygan Press* of December 22, 1951, reprinted an article previously published in the Ludington newspapers. It read: "LUDINGTON, Michigan – The hulk of an old sailing vessel that washed ashore here a month ago may be the final note of the 39-year old tragedy of the Great Lakes. A veteran of the lakes, Captain Peter L. Deblake, believes the hull that washed in at Ludington State Park may be that of the *Rouse Simmons*. The *Simmons*, a three-masted schooner was lost with all hands on Lake Michigan near Kewaunee, Wisconsin, 39 years ago.

After the wreck from the *Rouse Simmons* was discovered in 1971, the ship's anchor was raised in 1973 and placed on permanent display at the Milwaukee Yacht Club. Visitors to Milwaukee can also see several artifacts from the *Rouse Simmons* displayed at the South Shore Yacht Club including

"Many original ivory white dishes with the ship's name etched on their sides are on display at South Shore Yacht Club, 2300 E. Nock Ave., Milwaukee, WI."

The Big Pond
July 15, 1999
Steve Staedler

Anchor Found
Ship's Tragedy Lingers

TWO RIVERS – The one-ton anchor from the ill-fated schooner Rouse Simmons, *better known as the "Christmas Tree Ship," which foundered off Two Rivers 61 years ago next Friday, was brought to the Coast Guard station in Two Rivers a week ago.*

When brought ashore in 43-degree weather, the anchor, with a 16-foot cross bar, 10 feet long with a four-foot fluke, was dragged into port by the 26-foot, diving-equipped boat Lake Diver.

Green Bay Press-Gazette
November 18, 1973

NAUTICAL TOUCH
Milwaukee Journal
Milwaukee, WI
June 3, 1974

Workmen erected the anchor of the Great Lakes sailing schooner *Rouse Simmons* outside the Marine Bank Monday. The historic anchor will be on display at the bank for several weeks before being permanently mounted at the Milwaukee Yacht Club. It was recovered from wreckage of the schooner in the lake near Two Rivers. The schooner is pictured on Marine Bank checks.

Fishing Village Gets Wheel of Christmas Ship

TWO RIVERS – *The Rogers Street Fishing Village recently acquired the wheel of the infamous sunken Christmas Tree Ship...*

The wheel will compliment an existing display of Rouse Simmons' *artifacts including photos, wrenches, the nameplate and a petrified timber of a once majestic Christmas tree, museum Director Sandy Zipperer said.*

Manitowoc Herald Times Reporter
February 9, 2003
Tara Meissner

dishes, a hand-cranked fog horn, and a lightbulb from a string of lights used by Captain Schuenemann to decorate his ship after he docked in Chicago.

Regarding the lightbulb, Kent Bellrichard said: "We removed some wreckage on the stern of the ship to get down into the lower cabins and into the galley. In the process of removing this wreckage, a lightbulb popped to the surface. One of the fellows aboard the boat saw it and scooped it up with a fish net. It was intact, and the filament was still good. About a month later we applied some gentle electricity to it to bring the voltage up slowly. Believe it or not, it glowed!" Amazingly, the lightbulb (which was an "early Edison" bulb) still worked after being submerged on the bottom of Lake Michigan for over a half century.

Several additional lightbulbs were later discovered by a diver named Allan (Butch) Klopp and placed on display at the Great Lakes Shipwreck Museum in St. Ignace, Michigan. The museum housed Mr. Klopp's private collection of artifacts from 1986 until the museum was dissembled in 2000. On display at the Great Lakes Shipwreck Museum were many relics including several from the *Rouse Simmons*: Axes used to cut down Christmas trees, a calking mallet used to hammer caulk into the crevices of the aging *Rouse Simmons*, dinnerware, crockery, silver spoons, eye glasses, sun glasses, kerosene lanterns, several canning jars, chisels, corked wine bottles, shot glasses, medicine bottles (including one labeled "Dr. King's New Discovery for Coughs and Colds"), several clay pipes, a ceramic spittoon, a barometer, a tafrail log (used to measure the speed and distance a ship traveled), and the jawbone from a pet dog on board the ship when it sunk.

The collection, at present, is privately conserved by the owner. The family is currently looking at the best viable options for placing the artifacts at another museum while enhancing Great Lakes history through the exhibiting of the collection.

It is important to note that all of the *Simmons* artifacts on display at

> *"Most Great Lakes wrecks are 19th and early 20th century commercial ships. Storms, fire and human error caused most wrecks. Sometimes, captains intentionally sank aging ships to collect insurance money. A shipwreck is like a crime scene. If you know how to read the clues, you have a drama right in front of you."*
>
> Paul Creviere, Jr., Great Lakes Diver
> Author of *Wild Gales and Tattered Sails*

various locations were raised in the 1970's prior to laws governing removal of artifacts from shipwreck sites being established.

The community of Port Washington, located north of Milwaukee, houses a museum in their 1860 restored lighthouse. In their collection is a Christmas tree from the *Rouse Simmons* cargo as well as a belaying pin from the ship.

The Wisconsin Maritime Museum in Manitowoc, Wisconsin is in possession of a remnant section of timber from the *Rouse Simmons* with carved letters on it, a key chain made from one of the Christmas trees from the ship, and a wooden compass box lid.

Additional displays of *Rouse Simmons* information and artwork can be seen at Dettman's Shanty in Algoma, Wisconsin, and also at the Ship's Wheel Gallery & Nautical Museum in Kewaunee, Wisconsin.

The only human remains discovered at the shipwreck site were found by Kent Bellrichard. He came upon a single skeleton while removing timbers and debris from the stern area of the ship. Bellrichard, along with two other divers, buried the unknown sailor – whom they referred to as "The Poor Soul" - in the sand near the *Rouse Simmons*. An underwater memorial vigil preceded the burial.

"The Great Lakes have time and again demanded the ultimate sacrifice from those plying their wide open waters."

The Quarterly
(A publication of the Roger Street
Fishing Village Museum)
Holiday Issue – Oct./Dec. 1995

Photo of Mrs. Barbara Schuenemann and one of her daughters selling trees and wreaths in Chicago.
The caption read: "Woman Skipper Brings in Annual Load of Christmas Trees"
(Courtesy of the *Chicago Tribune*)

Chapter Nine

Mrs. Schuenemann & Daughters Carry On

"Wives of men who sail the Lakes are a special breed. And Mrs. Schuenemann was no exception. In 1913, she went into the woods, supervised the cutting of spruce trees and prepared to make the holiday voyage to Chicago. People there must have marveled at the courage of this woman who obviously cared so much about the tradition established by her late husband. She could have sent someone else, but she herself was there."

People & Places
December 16, 1974
Dorothy Trebilcock

Mrs. Schuenemann & Daughters Carry On

The waves settled themselves in the days following the gale of November 23, 1912, but another storm was brewing back on shore in Chicago – an emotional storm that hit the hearts of loved ones who tried to beat back the darkness of fear and worry when the *Simmons* failed to arrive as expected. Hours turned into days, and days into weeks. Family members of those on board looked across the waters for sight of the *Simmons*, but they saw nothing – no ship, no sails, no husbands, no fathers, no sons.

Search efforts were limited by the season's daylight that was quickly fading into the longer hours of night. Families watched and awaited a reassuring word of their loved ones, morning until evening, evening until morn, the salt of their tears burning their bloodshot eyes.

Brave Barbara Schuenemann refused to believe the *Simmons* had gone to the bottom, at least at first. On December 4, 1912, the *Chicago Record-Herald* ran the following article: "No word came yesterday from the *Rouse Simmons*, the Christmas tree laden schooner now many days overdue at port here. Inquiry at countless coast towns brought forth nothing but these answers: 'Nothing known of the *Rouse Simmons.*'" The article continued: "Despite the gloomy outlook, the wife of the belated vessel's captain, Barbara Schuenemann, maintains that there is no cause for alarm. Last night at her home, 1638 N. Clark Street, she gave the technical explanation of 'head winds' for her husband's delay and added that the newspapers were showing the greatest worry."

Barbara was trying to hold fast, refusing to believe the worst. But fear was seeping into her heart, little by little, as reported by other news articles. Fear was also consuming the hearts of families who had crew on board, paralyzing them with grief. The silence of not knowing was a burden too heavy to bear.

According to the *Menominee Herald Leader*, Menominee, MI, of December 5, 1912, it was reported that "grief frenzied relatives of those on board the vessel have been striving day and night since Thanksgiving Day to find trace of the missing ones."

Also published on December 5, 1912, came the following report from the *Chicago Daily Tribune*: "Philip Bauswein, one of the sailors, was engaged to be married to Miss Elizabeth Martin of 2012 Peterson Street, Chicago. She and Bauswein's mother, Mrs. Frank Bauswein, of 3624 LaSalle Street, Chicago, began growing alarmed over the *Rouse Simmons'* long absence more than a week ago. On Thanksgiving Day [November 28, 1912] they set

CHILDREN HOLD HOPE
Chicago Inter Ocean
Chicago, IL
December 6, 1912

Not all of Chicago has given up hope. There are four little girls, two the daughters of Captain Herman Schuenemann, owner of the cargo, and two daughters of Captain Charles Nelson, master of the ship, that spent the whole of yesterday with their faces pressed to the windows of their homes, anxiously watching for traces of their papas' ship.

And in Captain Schuenemann's home there is a wife and an elder daughter who also refuse to believe that the boat has sunk.

"Something has happened to delay them," these women told each other during all of the day. "By tomorrow they will be sighted – by tomorrow, sure."

And the mother of Philip Bauswein, who is Mrs. Frank Bauswein, 3624 South La Salle Street, walked for three hours on the lakefront and looked and looked out to where the sea and water meet. At her side was a younger woman, Miss Elizabeth Martin, who was to have been married to Philip when the "Christmas Tree Ship" came home.

And there still was a pathetic ray of hope to be found at the Lake Seamen's Union headquarters, 570 W. Lake Street. Here more than thirty sailors gathered and talked of their comrades. They were a sober lot of men, but there was not a one but would try to smile as he recalled other overdue vessels that later had reached a port.

"Though a marine report reads: 'The Rouse Simmons *is, according to all indications, wrecked off the state coast,' the captain's wife hopes against hope."*

Chicago Daily Journal
Chicago, IL
December 5, 1912

The Happy Christmas Season
Is Drawing Near. Do you know
where to find the best

Christmas Trees

and the

Choicest Holly Wreaths

at Wholesale and Retail

Here is the place:

Mrs. (Capt.) H. Schuenemann
501 N. Clark Street, Cor. Illinois St.

Tel. Delaware 2304

Advertisement used by
Mrs. Barbara Schuenemann in 1932.

Choicest Christmas Trees and Holly Wreaths

at Wholesale and Retail

Be sure to see us this year at our new place

133 WEST CHICAGO AVENUE

MRS. CAPT. H. SCHUENEMANN

Chicago's Famous Christmas Tree Centre.

Mrs. Elsie Roberts (daughter of Mrs. B. Schuenemann)

Advertisement used by
Mrs. Barbara Schuenemann's daughters
in 1933.

out together to see if they could not learn something. A visit to the riverfront docks brought no news, and they then began calling up the Life Saving Stations along the ship's route by telephone. The women talked to the stations at Two Rivers, Ludington, Sturgeon Bay, Sheboygan, and Kewaunee. Someone of the Kewaunee station told them of the sighting of the three-masted schooner, and this confirmed their worst fears. 'We thought,' said Mrs. Bauswein, 'that the Chicago authorities ought to do something, and the next day we called on the harbor master. He laughed and assured us there was no danger, that the boat was just delayed by the wind. We weren't satisfied with that and went to County Commissioner Harris. He could do nothing for us. Then we visited a man named Smith in the Board of Local Improvements in the City Hall. He was the only person among all of those we called on who seemed to show the slightest interest in our grief. He took us to the Mayor's office. There, one of the men at the door told us to 'Come around tomorrow.' Think of telling us to 'come around tomorrow' when those men might be perishing in the lake at that moment. We never saw the Mayor. He never knew we were outside. We went away crying.'"

On Thanksgiving Day, November 28, 1912, anxiety-stricken relatives were already in contact with Life Saving Station authorities on both sides of Lake Michigan, and, according to the *Milwaukee Daily News* of December 5, 1912, it was even earlier than that. By November 29, 1912, the Mayor of Chicago had relatives at his door, and on the same day the *Chicago Daily Tribune* published the first article alerting citizens of the missing schooner. Then Chicago watched and waited, and waiting is so long.

The backbone of Barbara Schuenemann's spirit held as steady as could be expected during these initial stomach-churning days of clock watching, finger tapping, and endless pacing. She endured the slowness of time along with everyone else, helpless to change the situation at hand, forced to face off with Truth, to accept the reality that the light of hope was fading, fading, fading away.

Barbara was a person of deep faith and was undoubtedly praying for the life of her love. If she was, it was a prayer that would not be answered, a prayer that *could not* be answered because the husband she longed to step through the doorway, into this place of sweet home, was already buried at the bottom of The Lake. The time for praying had past, the life she wished spared already ended.

The winds continued to wail in the days following November 23, 1912, and the skies shed their tears. Rain, snow, sleet and fog hampered rescue efforts. Despite valiant search attempts, the *Simmons* could not be found. The only witnesses to its final demise were the silent stars, the speechless moon, and the wild wind that howled on in its strange tongue none could understand. The secret of the *Simmons* was held tight.

On December 3, 1912, the *Chicago Record-Herald* interviewed Mrs. Schuenemann who believed, at the time, that there was no cause for alarm. On December 4, 1912, a contrary article published by another newspaper, the *Chicago Daily Journal*, gave evidence of the emotional rollercoaster Barbara Schuenemann was riding between hope and despair. Under the sub-headline "Wife of Captain Schuenemann Watches and Grieves for Missing" it was reported: "Hoping against hope, Mrs. Schuenemann, wife of the captain, has sat day and night at an upper window of her home, and with powerful glasses scanned the lake in hope of getting sight of the vessel. Her home is almost opposite Lincoln Park. From her window she is able to look over the trees of the park and with the glasses can sweep the lake for miles… 'Oh, I can't believe that the ship is lost with my husband aboard,' said Mrs. Schuenemann, as she sat with a pair of glasses before her favorite window today. 'If the ship was wrecked there ought to be something to show it. If I only knew my husband and those on board were safe I would be satisfied, but the thought of them out in the cold lake suffering, perhaps starving, is more than I can stand.' The captain's wife has been made seriously ill by the strain and worry under which she has been laboring. Her sister-in-law, Mrs. Bertha Schuenemann, is her constant companion and nurse. Both women take turns looking through the powerful, marine glasses out upon the lake."

The *Chicago Record-Herald* and the *Chicago Daily Journal* were only two of many newspapers that followed the *Simmons* tragedy. The *Chicago Daily News* of December 5, 1912, published an interview they conducted with Captain Schuenemann's eldest daughter, Elsie: "A lovely girl, with hair the color of golden rod, stood at the breakwater at the foot of North Avenue and peered far out into the fog and mist. She was Miss Elsie Schuenemann, the daughter of Captain Schuenemann, the owner of the cargo. Through the sticky mist came the deep bass note of a passing freighter, but she saw nothing of the missing schooner. Each day she has gone to the water's edge to watch for her father's vessel. 'I know he will come back,' she said, although she had difficulty in keeping back the tears. 'Mother and I are not afraid. We have confidence, and I guess we are not as frightened as others.'"

Bundled up against the cold, relatives of the missing men were walking along shorelines toward nowhere, sending forth prayers over the vastness of

AT THE WHEEL OF YULE TREE SHIP

ELSIE SCHUENEMANN, DAUGHTER OF CAPT. HERMAN SCHUENEMANN, WHO PERISHED WITH THE CREW OF THE *ROUSE SIMMONS* IN 1912.

Chicago Daily News, December 6, 1915

Miss Elsie Schuenemann at the wheel of "the boat that carried Christmas trees to Chicago from Michigan." (Courtesy of the Chicago Historical Society)

GIRL CAPTAIN TO BRAVE LAKE THAT KILLED FATHER
Chicago Daily Journal
Chicago, IL
December 9, 1912

"Capt." Elsie Schuen-emann is now the way the 20-year-old daughter of Capt. Herman Schuen-emann, who perished in Lake Michigan aboard his "Christmas boat," writes her name in full. "Capt." Elsie said today she had made prepar-ations for taking up her father's work where his tragic death had stopped it. As she talked she directed in an authori-tative way the unloading of a cargo of evergreens from one of her father's boats in the Chicago River. She spoke of making a trip to northern Wisconsin for a cargo of Christmas trees and other Christmas tokens.

"It is probable that I shan't make the trip this Yuletide," she added, "but when I do make it there will be no doubt about my ability as a first-class skipper."

PLAYED WITH TOY SHIPS AS CHILD

The girl was reared in a nautical atmosphere. In her infancy she played with toy ships rather than with dolls.

"It is the life I love best of all," she said. "Though, of course, the lake will always suggest dreadful associations to my mind henceforth."

The girl captain is a slim, lithe girl with blonde hair and blue eyes, which glow with enthusiasm when she is animated.

SISTERS MAY SERVE AS MATES

She has two sisters – twins – Hazel and Pearl, 14 years old, who are attending high school. They, too, have been brought up to know the excitement and joys of life on Lake Michigan, and, notwithstanding that the lake has left them fatherless. It is possible that at some future day they may be first and second mates to "Capt." Elsie.

Then, for perhaps the first time in the history of Lake Michigan, a ship will navigate its waters officered by women.

"Miss Elsie Schuenemann knows Lake Michigan as some girls know their front yards. She has sailed across it in fair weather and foul countless times. On most of these occasions she accompanied her father, and in sou'wester and sea-going cap she would stand at the wheel and take first-hand lessons in seawomanship."

Chicago Daily Journal
Chicago, IL
December 9, 1912

the waters where their loved ones lay below. Hope and Fear co-existed simultaneously in those long hours of uncertainty as relatives navigated their way through the difficulty of those straining days, waiting for a welcomed word. Several hopeful reports filtered in, tempting relatives to wonder "Dare they believe?" Joy and sorrow, hope and fear, were layered upon each other. The hour of the crew's return was beyond knowing, and emotions teetered. One moment it seemed as if reunions were a heartbeat away, and the next moment unfolded itself in dread – in dread of what may come to pass, or what already was.

According to the *Milwaukee Sentinel* of December 6, 1912, Miss Elsie Schuenemann could be found where the sea and shore met. She was "at the lighthouse near the harbor to Chicago, to be among the first to watch her father's boat with its 27,000 evergreen trees sail into port." Elsie watched and waited, her eyes turned outward, searching for her papa whose body would not return, but whose spirit was beside her already at the water's edge, watching along with her. And only he knew they watched in vain, for he was not coming; what remained of him was already there.

On December 12, 1912, the *Chicago Inter Ocean* reported that a search party was being organized and "Miss Elsie Schuenemann, daughter of the lost skipper, has volunteered to accompany the party."

Elsie Schuenemann, age 20 in 1912, exemplified courage beyond her years. She was shouldering an experience that could have crushed her, shattered her. Instead, the fire of this trial was defining her.

The *Chicago Inter Ocean* of December 11, 1912, ran the following headline: "Skipper's Daughter Shoulders Burden". The article read: "The head of a dependent family; staggered by indebtedness; with nothing like adequate relief in sight; her mother seriously ill of grief and uncertainty; yet Elsie Schuenemann, daughter of the skipper of the lost *Rouse Simmons*, is cheerful. Misfortunes that would crush stout hearts of men do not cloud the sunshine from her life. She thanks everybody for their solicitations in her behalf. Then she asks them to forget her and her troubles and look to the

> *"Mrs. Schuenemann, wife of the captain, has been distracted with anxiety for many days... As the days and hours drag by she is slowly realizing that the chances of the* Rouse Simmons *ever docking at Chicago piers again are growing less and less."*
>
> Chicago Inter Ocean
> Chicago, IL
> December 5, 1912

fifteen other families who lost breadwinners when the *Rouse Simmons* went down. 'Look them up – they may be in need,' she said. 'I'm all right. I can fight my way out some way.' Despite the claims of the brave little skipper's daughter that the family was not destitute, it was admitted that the loss of the *Rouse Simmons* and cargo had incurred debts of over $5,000. 'But I can pay that, every dollar,' the girl continued. 'See, I have my father's Christmas tree business. That will tide us over a bit. But the families of sailors and timber cutters on the boat may be really in need. Please look them up.' People flocked from all quarters of the city to see the boat, buy trees and wreaths, and congratulate Miss Schuenemann for her spirit."

The qualities Elsie Schuenemann displayed at her young age are not the kind of qualities one is born with. They are character strengths that are taught, and principles that are learned. Elsie was indeed her father's daughter.

She became her mother's right arm in the dark days of 1912. Some of these days were bearable for Barbara, and she showed herself a pillar of strength, but others were difficult beyond imagination. Barbara Schuenemann was a woman of immense courage and she proved this, over and over, during her lifetime. Yet Grief excuses no one from the company of its presence, and Barbara Schuenemann grieved fully when she realized that nothing would ever be the same again. She wept, covering her face with her hands, trying to hold back her tears, to hold back her pain, to hold back the sadness flowing out of her eyes.

Never again would she hear the sound of her husband's footsteps on the other side of the door, or hear his laughter, hearty and rich. Never again would she lie beside him, watching the rise and fall of his chest in the early morn hours as daylight was born anew. And never again would she know the feeling of being loved as only he could love her. (She never remarried during the twenty-one years between 1912 and her death in 1933.) Never again. They were such final words, and the allness of what this meant invaded her, wearing her tired, tired heart down to nothingness. She was alone, and it was too hard to believe. She retired to her empty bed with her empty feelings.

Barbara Schuenemann's pain was still fresh, her questions still unanswered, when her eldest daughter, Elsie, began weaving Christmas wreaths and making plans to dock a borrowed ship in the Chicago harbor to sell salvaged trees picked up along the beaches of Lake Michigan. "The time spent by Miss Elsie weaving garlands and superintending preparations for the establishment of a new Christmas ship are hours stolen from the bedside of

YOUNG GIRL TO DARE LAKE'S WINTRY BLAST
Manitowoc Daily Herald
Manitowoc, WI
December 9, 1912

Lake Michigan took Capt. Herman Schuenemann's life. And Lake Michigan must make reparation to Herman Schuenemann's family – at least, such paltry reparation as can be measured in dollars and cents in the face of the bereavement that is theirs.

For when Captain Schuenemann went to the bottom of the lake with the Christmas tree ship, the *Rouse Simmons*, he took with him practically all the family's fortune, invested as it was in the spruce saplings that were to have brought a golden harvest.

Elsie Schunemenn, the captain's daughter, is the new skipper of the family, and yesterday she told of her plans to make the wintry lake and the snowbound forests of Michigan give back at least the financial part of what they lost when the *Rouse Simmons* went down in the ante-Thanksgiving gale.

HER FATHER'S DEATH WITH THE CHRISTMAS TREE SHIP DOES NOT TERRIFY HER
Chicago Record-Herald
Chicago, IL
December 9, 1912

"We are going to get another boat," said Miss Schuenemann... "I am a sailor. I have made many a voyage with my father and it may be that I shall take personal command of the new boat. Possibly I will be unable to leave my mother and the other children, but I am going after the trees myself, if I can, and if I cannot I shall be represented by an agent whom I can trust."

This was the only ray of cheer or hope that penetrated the Schuenemann home at 1638 N. Clark Street yesterday.

Across Lincoln Park could be seen the ice-covered shrouds of schooners and steamers that were limping into port as Miss Schuenemann talked of her plans to retrieve the family fortune, and as she told how she hoped for a good yield of Christmas trees her eyes continually swept the distant lake, the roar of whose surf rose now and then above the noise of the trolley cars...

"You know," the girl went on, "I cannot believe the *Rouse Simmons* is lost. There are islands in Lake Michigan; desolate tracts of land they are, it is true, but they would afford safety for the crew of any disabled ship, and I cannot help thinking that father and his men are on one of these islands."

SELLS WRECK TREES TODAY
Mother Assists Girl in Disposing of Northern Firs
Chicago Daily Tribune
Chicago, IL
December 11, 1912

The sale of Christmas trees and wreaths heretofore held on the deck of the *Rouse Simmons*, which is thought to have gone down with all its crew, will be opened today. Miss Elsie Schuenemann, daughter of Capt. Herman Schuenemann of the *Rouse Simmons* and owner of the cargo, has taken charge of the business, with her mother.

The *Oneida*, a schooner similar in appearance to the *Rouse Simmons*, except for the Christmas tree cabin which Capt. Schuenemann had built, has been moored at the foot of Clark Street. All day yesterday Christmas trees sent from the northern woods by rail, and those picked up as wreckage along the lake shore, were transferred to the *Oneida*. Miss Schuenemann had charge of several girls making wreaths.

"We will go on with the business," she said. "The sale this year will no more than pay the debts caused by the loss of the schooner. Next year, however, we expect to make as good a profit as in the past. It seems strange so few trees have been picked up, when there must have been 35,000 trees on the ship. I still feel my father must have been saved in some miraculous manner... Perhaps he is on some island, with no means of getting away."

her sick mother," reported the *Chicago Inter Ocean* of December 10, 1912. "Mrs. Schuenemann is kept in ignorance of these preparations on account of her condition."

"Captain" Elsie resumed her family's place at the Clark Street Bridge. It was where her father's customers would have expected to find the Schuenemanns, so it was there she would be found.

Although one of Captain Schuenemann's friends loaned the schooner *Oneida* for trees to be sold from in 1912, the family's original plan, according to the *Chicago Daily Tribune* of December 10, 1912, was to charter a ship. Ironically, the name of this ship was *Relief*. But *Relief* never came, physically or literally.

Along with the salvaged trees sold in 1912, two railroad cars full of evergreens were also sold. Captain Schuenemann had ordered that these trees be shipped to Chicago via rail before he set sail with the *Simmons*.

The *Escanaba Press*, Escanaba, Michigan, of November 28, 1987, reported a man named Peter Anderson was "supposed to have gone on the voyage to Chicago" with Captain Schuenemann, but he stayed back on shore, as directed by the captain, to wait for these two railroad cars of trees that had been delayed in arriving. Peter Anderson was needed to take charge of the cargo and accompany it to Chicago.

Arrival of Christmas trees by the thousands in Chicago's railroad yards.
Fort Dearborn Magazine, December 1921

With whistles blowing, the train headed south. On board was Mr. Anderson who arrived in Chicago "having heard nothing about the horrible wreck" of the *Simmons*. Captain Schuenemann's ship had met with a "rendezvous with fate," and the trees that were supposed to be delivered to the captain, would now be delivered to the captain's widow.

In 1986, at age 95, Peter Anderson's daughter, Mrs. "Bertha" Sigrid (Anderson) Harding, told the Schoolcraft County Historical Society in Michigan how her father helped Mrs. Schuenemann and her daughters sell the Christmas trees her father brought by train in 1912 from a docked ship.

Although Mrs. Harding is no longer alive, her daughter, Mrs. Lois Bryant, remembers the stories her mother told about the Christmas Tree Ship. Mrs. Bryant, age 74, told me that Captain and Barbara Schuenemann were dear friends of her grandparents, and they often stayed in her grandpa and grandma's home while harvesting their evergreens. (The Anderson Family homestead still stands in Manistique, Michigan, on the corner of Chippewa and Otter Streets.)

According to Mrs. Bryant, everyone was "one big, happy family." She told me her grandpa would help Captain Schuenemann "with whatever he needed." He liked the captain. She also remembers her mother telling her about the "Schuenemann Daughters." Mrs. Bryant's mother wore clothes the Schuenemann girls had grown out of. Captain and Barbara Schuenemann would pack up clothing for the Anderson children, of whom there were eight, and bring the clothes with them to the Upper Peninsula to aid the family. "It is fantastic when you stop and think about how these people shared," said Mrs. Bryant.

In 1912, Captain Schuenemann's family was on the receiving end of fantastic sharing. It was reported by the *Chicago Inter Ocean* of December 10, 1912: "In response to an appeal from sailors, shippers, and merchants for whom Captain Schuenemann worked, and friends, the *Inter Ocean* this morning starts a relief fund for the family. Every dollar the family possessed

> *"One never knows what they can do until they have to."*
> Elsie Schuenemann
> As quoted in the *Chicago Inter Ocean*
> December 10, 1912

TAKES FATHER'S PLACE AT CHRISTMAS STAND
Daughter of the Lake
Chicago American
Chicago, IL
December 12, 1912

From early morning until late at night they are there, this fatherless daughter and widowed mother – pathetic figures amid the ever-passing throngs with their wares…

Today and tomorrow and every day and night until Christmas Eve these two women will be there. The crowds pause, some out of idle curiosity, more to buy. Business thus far has been good; it will get better with the nearer approach of the holiday season.

The young woman has a smile on her face for every purchaser, but there are traces of grief in every line of her countenance.

"I remembered two years ago," said Miss Schuenemann today, "how just before Christmas, Fire Chief Horan came to the ship and bought his supply of greens. He did not know of the fate that was in store for him." [Fire Chief Horan was killed on December 22, 1910, along with 23 other firemen, when a wall collapsed on them during a fire.]

"Mayor Harrison has been one of our steady customers for years; so have hundreds of other persons on the North Side and the South Side. We hope they will come back this year, even if the ship and father are not with us."

Mrs. Schuenemann has little to say. Her grief is too recent.

Upon the shoulders of the girl have fallen the family burdens.

"Father will come sailing into the river safe and sound some day," Miss Schuenemann repeats to herself many times each day.

was represented in the schooner *Rouse Simmons* and its stock of Christmas trees and greens." Also reported in the article was a plan by the W. C. Holmes Shipping Company to donate a schooner for the family's use. "When news of this plan spread among the sailors on the waterfront," reported the *Inter Ocean*, "scores of seamen, friends of Captain Schuenemann, called upon Miss Elsie and offered their services on the craft. Her courage was praised by everyone. It was even suggested that the Seamen's Union charter a boat every year and send north for trees to be disposed of and the proceeds given to the stricken family."

Sailors sent their wives and daughters to assist in making wreaths. "The room in which the greens are stored, and where the women work," reported the *Inter Ocean*, "is donated by Sprague, Warner & Company."

By December 11, 1912, Barbara Schuenemann had dried her tears and was beside Elsie selling trees, greeting the many persons who came to assist the family. Barbara was trying to come to grips with her future, while coming to grips with the past. There were two very good reasons for her to recapture the courage her now dead husband had once needed years earlier when his

SAILOR'S FAMILY IS TO BE HELPED BY SUBSCRIPTIONS
***Inter Ocean* Starts Fund for Widow and Daughters of the "Christmas Tree" Vessel Captain SHIPPING COMPANY AIDS**
Chicago Inter Ocean
Chicago, IL
December 10, 1912

Subscriptions for the fund for the relief of the Schuenemann family and others left destitute by the *Rouse Simmons* disaster should be sent to the *Inter Ocean*. The Lake Seaman's Union will make up a purse today, it is understood.

"I am heartily in favor of it," said T. T. Hanson, secretary.

The employees of the Sprague & Warner Co. promised to donate to the fund.

Malcolm McNeil, of the McNeil & Higgins Company, in a letter to the *Inter Ocean*, recommending the fund says:

"I know that every good citizen who has enjoyed the Christmas trees brought here for years back by the *Rouse Simmons*, "*The Christmas Tree Ship*," will miss their Christmas tree this season.

"Now, if these good citizens will send to the *Inter Ocean* the price of their annual Christmas tree to be used for and given to the widows and orphans of the sixteen men who recently lost their lives when the schooner *Rouse Simmons* went down, and any one who would like to donate to this noble cause will also kindly send in their donations, thus making this Christmas a little brighter for those sad hearts, and bringing a reward into their own lives – a reward of self-denial, for "it is better to give than to receive," Paul said to the Centurian and to the soldiers...

A list of donors to the "*Rouse Simmons* Relief Fund" will be published in tomorrow's *Inter Ocean.*

> "*Our friends have been so good to us. I don't know what we would have done without them.*"
>
> Elsie Schuenemann
> As quoted in the *Chicago Inter Ocean*
> December 10, 1912

brother went missing, and they were looking to her for strength. Their names were Pearl and Hazel, Elsie's younger twin sisters. Their care was now her sole responsibility.

Concerned citizens in the City of Chicago were determined to relieve Barbara of some of her burden in 1912. Although the family remained hopeful of a miracle, donations were being accepted by the *Chicago Inter Ocean* to benefit all of the lost sailors' loved ones. The newspaper ran the following article on December 13, 1912: "'I still have confidence that father and his men will be found on an island, or possibly where the ship is stranded on a reef,' said Miss Elsie. 'But, oh, if they don't – then things really will look hard. Debts begin to roll up until it is most heartbreaking. But mother is determined never to go through the bankruptcy courts. She says it isn't honorable.'"

The article continued: "Thank our unknown but dear friends who have sent money to the *Inter Ocean*. They can rest assured that it is not ill-directed charity. It will not be accepted if the men are found, and every dollar sent in will be divided by us with the families of unfortunate sailors who made up my father's crew. I am asking no one to send us money, but the *Inter Ocean* can do that, and we thank them for it. I do, however, want customers for our Christmas trees… We never counted on making much out of it. But, as it is all we have this year, we do sincerely appreciate the kindness of those who find their way down this old street to buy of us. Thank everybody.'"

Much can be learned about who the Schuenemanns were as people by the direct quotations scattered throughout newspaper articles. In the above article from the *Inter Ocean* we learn Mother Schuenemann refused bankruptcy courts as a course of consideration. We also learn from Elsie that her family wished no donations to be sent to them directly, but rather, all such money be forwarded to the *Inter Ocean* where the Fund established would equally benefit all the families experiencing loss.

When the *Associated Press* learned the *Chicago Inter Ocean* established a Fund on December 10, 1912, a representative from the offices of the *Associated Press* met with Elsie on December 11th and told her they "would be willing to start a fund also." Miss Schuenemann "thanked the news agency's representative and told him that such aid would not be necessary." She graciously declined the establishment of additional assistance.

Prior to December 13, 1912, Elsie was not even open to the idea of accepting assistance. On December 11, 1912, the *Chicago Inter Ocean* quoted Elsie Schuenemann as saying, "I want to thank the *Inter Ocean* for the spirit displayed on our behalf, but as a favor to myself and mother would request that no list of donations be published. If such a list must be compiled it would be better to investigate the condition of some of the sailors and timber cutters who were on the ship. I understand that some need money badly."

The following day, on December 12, 1912, the newspaper reported Elsie saying: "If no trace of the ship is found, the money can be distributed among the families of the common sailors who are worse off than we. But if we find the ship it is my wish that all money be returned to our kind well wishers."

Elsie Schuenemann directed the representative of the *Inter Ocean* fund to hold all monies until hope was abandoned. Then, and only then, was the money to be distributed. If the ship were later located, she made it clear that every penny accepted would be returned.

"We can pay all we owe," Elsie told reporters on December 11, 1912, in her usual dignified manner, adding, "and we want to do it by giving an exchange for all values received and not through charity. We weren't brought up that way."

Elsie Schuenemann wanted customers for her Christmas trees – not charity. And customers came. "Ever since I was a little girl papa has sold his trees," said Elsie, "and lots and lots of people never think of going any place else."

Choirs were singing. Bells were ringing. And against this backdrop of "Joy to the World", the Schuenemanns were selling Christmas trees, their pain in sharp contrast to the joyfulness of the season. Because of this, many holiday shoppers did not purchase trees from Captain Schuenemann's family in 1912, and understandably so. Despite the show of bravery by Barbara and her girls, their little schooner was still a place of much sadness. And buying the family Christmas tree was supposed to be a happy event, not heavy with thoughts of death. So some people simply stayed away in 1912.

According to the *Manistique Pioneer-Tribune*, Manistique, Michigan, of December 27, 1912, "The wife and daughter of the master of the Christmas Ship attempted to fortify themselves against want by bringing a new cargo of Christmas trees to the city. They were set up for sale down on the river bank, and every day the widow and her orphans worked hard making wreaths and

Takes Father's Place at Christmas Stand
DAUGHTER OF THE LAKE

Daughter of Skipper of Missing Rouse Simmons Still Hopes for Return of Ship.

The eyes of Miss Elsie Schueneman, daughter of the gallant Captain Herman Schuenemann of the ill-fated Christmas ship Rouse Simmons, are still turned toward the east, out over Lake Michigan. For the daughter of the skipper of the Rouse Simmons never has given up hope that some day in the near future she will hear the whistles blow long and loudly and she will see the schooner turn its prow into the Chicago River. She, who has called herself "a daughter of the lake," cannot and will not believe that her father's ship has gone down, with all on board.

With hope strong for the safety of her

Miss Elsie Schueneman, selling a Christmas wreath.

Miss Elsie Schuenemann selling a Christmas wreath.
Chicago American, December 12, 1912

1928 photo of Elsie (Schuenemann) Roberts selling Christmas trees.
(Courtesy of the Chicago Historical Society)

arranging other stock… Tonight, when darkness fell, and the last hope of another sale had passed, the family found itself still in possession of considerable unsold stock. But the widow was plucky. 'I don't want charity,' she said. 'I'll fight it out. Next year we'll sell trees again and maybe business will be better then.'"

Christmas Day, 1912. Late was the hour. A reporter from the *Chicago Record-Herald* came to Barbara Schuenemann's borrowed ship to interview her. He reported on the following day: "Mrs. Schuenemann's daughters, of whom there are three, came to the boat late in the evening, and the sad mother closed up shop to go home with her children for a cheerless Christmas night… There was no attempt at celebration in the little home at 1638 N. Clark Street. In fact, the greatest concern of members of the family was how they were going to keep that same little home from being swallowed up in the financial squall which has followed the skipper's loss. They are facing bankruptcy as a result of their disheartening failure to resuscitate the Christmas tree business left so unsteady by Captain Schuenemann's losing fight with a Lake Michigan gale. Their attempt resulted in a substantial loss, adding to the already long list of obligations which they had inherited… Uncomplaining, the widow spent most of her Christmas Day on the tree ship straightening up the books which had added so many financial worries to her already abundant supply. With all she expressed determination to keep on… 'I am still in the fight. We will continue next year, for our fight is to save our home…' With the season now past, Mrs. Schuenemann is confronted with the job of disposing of the vast stock left over. She must remove it from the schooner which was loaned her for the season. Then she is facing long payrolls that have grown out of her husband's ill-fated 1912 business. In Manistique, Michigan, where Captain Schuenemann had engineered the harvest of an unusually large stock of Christmas greens, there are scores of

> *"The story of the sinking of the* Rouse Simmons, *mysterious as it is, and the loss of Captain Schuenemann and his crew, did not deter Mrs. Schuenemann and her daughters from re-engaging in this hazardous undertaking."*
>
> *We Must Not Forget*
> *The Sheboygan Press*
> Sheboygan, WI

woodsmen waiting for their pay. On every hand she is finding the same situation, and the indebtedness of the business is estimated at $8,000. 'If I can only pull through and manage to make good all the obligations contracted by my husband I will be happy,' said the widow in that connection. 'He had no doubts of his ability to make them good with the holiday business, and I know he would want me to make up every cent.'"

Barbara's resilient spirit in the face of tragedy is revealed to us in those few uttered words. "I am still in the fight," she said, expressing her "determination to keep on." Then she went about the tasks at hand "uncomplaining".

"We will continue next year," promised Barbara. It was settled in her soul.

Her husband's sacrifice had been to brave the seas so Chicago would have her trees, and Barbara's sacrifice had been to allow him. This had cost her dearly. It cost her worry, fear, and dread. In the end, it also cost her the realization that all of her fears were not for naught.

Christmas tree voyages were unpredictable journeys over unpredictable waters. Barbara Schuenemann knew the dangers, and she knew the risks. She knew all she was up against as well as anyone could have.

She had pleaded with her husband prior to his 1912 trip to give up the voyages because of the danger, and her husband had consented, promising her his 1912 trip would be his last with trees.

Yes, Barbara Schuenemann knew what she faced in no uncertain terms. Yet she also knew how important the Schuenemann tradition had become to

> *"Mrs. Schuenemann was a stalwart woman of the breed who wait and hope, but who, when hope is gone, gathers her courage and continues the task of living. She and her three daughters decided to carry on "as Father might have wished" and they made plans to sail to Chicago with Christmas trees. A schooner,* Fearless, *was chartered and Mrs. Schuenemann herself went into the woods and supervised the cutting of this special Christmas cargo."*
>
> The Christmas Tree Schooner
> Dorothy Trebilcock
> Source and date unknown
> On file at Great Lakes Historical Society

so many people. Her husband had made the decision to carry on when his brother, August, perished, and his commitment cost him no less than everything. It was a price she, too, was willing to pay.

Barbara Schuenemann could have quietly bowed out from the tradition. She could have chosen to retreat to a place as far removed from her memories as the road would take her - a place away from shores, ships, and Christmas itself lest she be reminded of those terrible days. Yet she chose to stay where she would be a companion to the details of her husband's fate. Why? Perhaps she knew there would never be a hole deep enough in the wide world over to bury her memories. Perhaps she knew her memories would be buried only when she was.

So Courage and Fear went to war against one another in Barbara's heart, and Courage won.

She understood the Lake had been her family's enemy, but it had also been their friend, having provided a source of income to the Schuenemanns for many years.

Winter melted into spring in 1913, and spring into summer. The last leaves of autumn fell, and the first snows of winter arrived, dusting the emerald hued evergreens of Northern Michigan pearly white. And Barbara Schuenemann was there to see it.

The *Chicago Daily News* interviewed Mrs. Schuenemann on November 28, 1913, when she returned to Chicago with her load of Christmas trees. She had this to say: "It was splendid up there in the big woods. I was there for eight weeks and it seemed like one long holiday for me. Perhaps it was because I felt that somehow my husband was there with me. That's where he would have been had he been alive, and I felt somehow he was there anyway. And the smell of the pines was good, and the clear, starry nights, and the sound of the chopping all day long as the sharp axes went crunching home at the feet of the young trees. I shall never miss it. Every year I shall go to the Northwoods, and after I am dead there will be others to carry on the work."

The very ground she stood on, the air she breathed, heavy with the scent

> *"The tradition carried on despite the Lake's determined attempts to quench it."*
>
> Roger Le Lievre
> *The Upper Peninsula Sunday Times*
> December 24, 1978

of pine, the stars above her, were all quiet reminders of days past when she and her husband had been together in this place. "I felt somehow that he was there," said Barbara. Her words are peaceful, her comfort certain.

This was the place her husband would have been had he not perished a whole Christmas ago. She was breathing the air he would have breathed, looking heavenward upon the stars he would have seen, and she knew she was exactly where she was supposed to be.

There is something that pulls a person back to home, wherever - or whatever - that home may be. For some it is a building - a farmhouse where four generations of your family have lived. For others, it is the people within, no matter the locale. And for still others, home can be a life's work - a feeling of contentment while doing what brings you greatest joy. For the Schuenmanns, home was not only the circle of love that united them, it was also the deep satisfaction they experienced while surrounded by their evergreens.

President John F. Kennedy once used the evergreen tree to symbolize a person's ability to withstand Life's toughest blows. He said, "Only in winter can you tell which trees are truly green. Only when the winds of adversity blow can you tell whether an individual or country has courage and steadfastness."

The President's words take on a whole new meaning for those who have lived in northernmost places where temperatures can plummet from 20 degrees above zero to 20 degrees below in a snap, and wind chill temperatures can dip even further to nearly a hundred degrees negative.

In such places the evergreen survives and thrives in a world laid bare by Winter, a world numbed into submission by the severity of the season. Submission is evident across January countrysides. Yet amid this harshness stand the evergreens, seemingly untouched by Winter's heavy hand, with a constancy strengthened from within.

Evergreens. They are symbolic of strength, courage and steadfastness. Appropriately, the Schuenemann memory will forever be linked to the trees they loved. Some evergreens have roots, trunks and branches; others have bodies, arms and legs. Barbara Schuenemann was one of them.

In 1913 the cold winds were blowing around her. She was in the Upper Peninsula gathering her first harvest of Christmas trees without her husband. A storm hit the region shortly before her ship was scheduled to head to Chicago with its load of trees. She told the *Chicago Daily News* on

November 28, 1913, after she arrived back in the city, that it was "just such a storm as that which robbed me of my husband."

Although Barbara Schuenemann had every intention of shipping her trees by boat in 1913, she actually changed her mind at the last minute and sent them by rail instead (despite many reports through the years to the contrary.)

"Mrs. Barbara Schuenemann, after ransacking the Northwoods for enough Christmas trees to go around in Chicago," reported the *Chicago Daily News,* "is back home again."

"The men wanted to sail down," Barbara told the paper, "but I refused. I thought of their wives, and then of the wives of the men who went down on the *Rouse.*"

The article went on to say: "Mrs. Schuenemannn declared that five of the trees being brought here are the largest that ever came to Chicago. The largest stands thirty-six feet, and she hopes it will be selected for the municipal Christmas tree celebration in Grant Park. Another almost as tall is being brought for the Germania Club. For years the Germania Club was supplied by Captain Schuenemann."

Barbara Schuenemann carried on her husband's legacy by doing a man's work in a man's world, a remarkable accomplishment given the fact that women didn't even have the right to vote when she and her daughters took the helm of the family operation, as well as the helm of various ships.

The *Fort Dearborn Magazine* of December 1921 reported: "In loyalty to her husband's purpose in life of providing the best of Christmas trees for Chicago, Mrs. Schuenemann took up the work after his death. Every year since, this brave sailor's wife has gone up into the forests of northern Michigan and Wisconsin, personally selected her trees, and returned with them to Chicago. Owing to the scarcity of boats occasioned by the war, Mrs. Schuenemann has for a few years been obliged to give up the Christmas ship, but has brought her trees in by rail and sold them from a little shop on Clark Street."

> *"Few realize the hardships necessary to furnish Chicago with its Christmas trees. First there were two weeks of rain, then two and a half days of steady snow. Some of the trees we brought back with snow packed in their branches."*
>
> Elsie (Schuenemann) Roberts
> As quoted in the *Chicago Daily Tribune*
> December 13, 1934

The *Chicago Tribune* of December 13, 1934, reported a family friend of the Schuenemanns also making mention to the scarcity of boats during World War I. He said, "The captain's wife was plucky. She went after the trees herself. Every year, until during the war, when the government bought her boat, she brought the trees down in the vessel. She loved those trees."

In 1921 Barbara Schuenemann did not own a vessel. Rather, she had chartered a ship to carry her trees to Chicago. The *Chicago Tribune* of December 22, 1974, reported: "Barbara Schuenemann, dubbed 'The Christmas Tree Lady,' carried on the family tradition until she was old and gray. Some years the trees arrived by rail, others by ship. In 1921 the ship she had chartered sank in Lake Superior during a storm just before she was to receive it."

The *Chicago Tribune* of June 16, 1933, reported in Barbara Schuenemann's obituary: "In 1912 Captain Schuenemann went down in a terrific lake storm as he was bringing a cargo of Christmas trees to the city on the *Rouse Simmons*. His widow continued his work, taking the helm of various craft to bring trees to the city each Yuletide for many years. Since 1925 trees have been brought by freight cars to her warehouse."

Details remain unclear as to the exact years that ships were owned, and the exact years that ships were chartered by the Schuenemann women. Also unclear are the exact years trees were shipped by rail due to severe weather, or by lack of a vessel.

St. Pauls Church of Chicago reported in December of 1917 that Elsie Schuenemann was at the helm of a Schuenemann ship. The church's newsletter reported: "And did you read the fine story of Captain Elsie Schuenemann bringing her Christmas ship, heavily laden with trees, safely into Chicago's harbor?"

The following year the church reported: "This year they had no boat, so Mrs. Schuenemann shipped the trees, thousands of them, to Chicago by rail."

"Captain Herman's widow, Barbara, and her three daughters, continued to bring evergreens into Chicago for another twenty years, first by sailing schooner, then by rail."

Soundings
(A publication of the Wisconsin Marine
Historical Society)
Winter 1963-1964, Vol. 4 No. 2
Theodore S. Charrney

Mrs. Barbara Schuenemann in the midst of the spruce and balsam trees which her little schooner, Fearless, brings every Christmas from the Northern woods to gladden the hearts of young and old at Yuletide. Left—The Fearless at its Chicago dock.

Early passersby halted on the bridge and stared down in amazement; from jib to tiny cabin aft were piled hundreds of Christmas trees—little ones for a baby's single candle, larger ones to hold a family's gifts, and big ones to fix a Sunday school's attention.

Photograph of Barbara Schuenemann's ship, *Fearless*, as published in the book: *A History of Thompson, Michigan.*
(Newspaper clippings were from the Schuenemann family scrapbook.)

Miscellaneous from St. Pauls Church Newsletters

December 1908

Buy your tree of the Captain and your wreaths and garlands from his wife. They give a smile with each and every purchase.

"They're the people you must see,
If you want a Christmas tree!"

December 1913

Mrs. Barbara Schuenemann, the widow of the captain who went down with his Christmas ship in the storms of last winter, is continuing her husband's business with commendable energy and great skill.

She made the trip to the northern woods, superintended the loading of the cargo, attended to all the numerous details, and now the Christmas Ship, bravely decorated with trees and boughs and garlands, and holding thousands of green saplings to gladden the children's hearts, lies at the accustomed place near the Clark Street Bridge.

We are quite sure that Mrs. Schuenemann will be richly rewarded by a most successful season.

December 1914

Mrs. Barbara Schuenemann is carrying on successfully the business of her husband, the captain of the Christmas Ship which went down to unfathomed depths with all on board. She has been up North superintending the loading of a great ship with Christmas greens, which now lies in the usual place at the Clark Street Bridge. With the efficient aid of her daughter, Elsie, she is disposing of the cargo and everybody hopes they will be very successful in their undertaking.

December 1917

And did you read the fine story of Captain Elsie Schuenemann bringing her Christmas ship, heavily laden with trees, safely into Chicago's harbor?

By the way, the ship lies at the old docks near the Clark Street Bridge and looks like an acre of Northern woodlands lifted up bodily and transplanted to the busy city. You will find trees there of every size, shape, and price, from the giant of the forest to the graceful sapling whose tiny branches will look well when decked in gold and silver and little colored lights.

December 1918

Chicago's Christmas would not be complete without the Schuenemann's trees. In former years the doughty Captain Herman sailed away to the North and came back with his shipload of Yuletide trees. But in the terrible storm six years ago, he and his ship went down into the depths. Then his wife and daughter, Elsie, brought the trees. This year they had no boat, so Mrs. Schuenemann shipped the trees, thousands of them, to Chicago by rail and is now selling them in a store on Clark Street, quite near the bridge. We hope they will do a thriving business to reward them for their hard work.

1920

Miss Hazel Schuenemann is at Harvard "working hard on exams" with time enough to send to her friends pictures of old Cambridge town.

October 1925

Miss Mabel Swanson, whose home in Manistique, Michigan, is in the heart of the pine tree district, was the guest of her friend, Mrs. Elsie [Schuenemann] Roberts, and was in attendance at worship with her. Mrs. Roberts will again be at her post with a large consignment of Christmas trees in a few weeks.

December 1927

Mrs. [Barbara] Schuenemann writes to us from Manistique, Michigan, that she is in the Northwoods gathering her supply of Christmas trees for the approaching season.

December 1932 (Barbara Schuenemann's Last Christmas)

As you pass down Clark Street and near the bridge, you will find a great array of Christmas trees in the improvised warehouse and on the outside of it you will be greeted with the cordial smile of a dear old mother.

A little while ago she was so deathly ill that we believed her hours on earth were counted - but here she is, a living symbol of God's eternal grace. She is again busy at her same old loving duty, feeling like a newborn child, full of enthusiasm and joy.

She is here to help bring joy this year like never before. She dispenses Christmas trees. You all know her. It is good Mother Schuenemann, the widow of ill-fated Captain Schuenemann, the Christmas Ship man, who never returned to the shores, but with his great cargo of Christmas trees went down into the deep in that terrible night of storm. And since then Mother Schuenemann has felt the urge to "carry on."

The *Chicago Tribune* never fails to pay her a tribute of respect and admiration. Her Christmas trees, which she herself sought in the Northwoods of Michigan and Wisconsin, will adorn the Christian homes of many Chicago citizens this year. There is always a desire for green trees when the long night of winter is upon us. Some of the old time folks actually brought cherry branches into their homes on Christmas Eve in the hope that they would bear blossoms for Christmas…

It is our prayerful hope that all our families in the church may be able to enjoy the happiness in their homes which the Christmas trees bring to old and young. As we place upon them the lights, let it be remembered that they are symbolic of Him Who came unto mankind at Bethlehem to be the "Light of the World."

Barbara Schuenemann was well familiar with the railway stretching from the Upper Peninsula of Michigan to the city of Chicago. She would oftentimes return to Chicago via rail after she and her husband harvested trees, saying her goodbyes to Captain Schuenemann in Thompson, Michigan, and then returning back home to await his arrival.

According to the *Chicago Tribune* of 1933, and also according to the *Algoma Record Herald* of 1925, the year 1925 may have been the final year trees were sold from a schooner docked in the harbor. The *Algoma Record Herald* article reported that Barbara Schuenemann was selling Christmas trees in 1925 from a ship, and the article also reminisced of earlier years. It stated: "In 1914 [Mrs. Schuenemann] chartered the *Fearless,* and with her eldest daughter and a crew of ten went up to the snow-packed forests. She supervised the men, and the ten lumberjacks who had worked so long for the captain, and she brought down the precious cargo. Mrs. Schuenemann has never missed a year with her Christmas Tree Ship. Gray-haired men, some of them the pillars of Chicago's business structure, now descend the rotting stairs, go aboard, and sit in the little cabin. They talk to the wrinkled woman with the calloused palms, and with Elsie, now married, of the forty years that have passed…. The woods are thinning out now, and the good trees have to be carted for miles to the water's edge. And the sharp winds slash the face and hands more bitterly than they did when the 'Mrs. Captain' was younger."

The Schuenemanns had served the City of Chicago long and well, and earned the respect of many - including "pillars" among its people.

By 1925 Barbara was aging. Her hands were calloused, her flesh, wrinkled. The "sharp winds" of life were wearing her down on the outside, but nothing could reach the inner steel of her soul. Her heart remained ever green until her very last Christmas in 1932.

"As you pass down Clark Street and near the bridge," her church reported in December of that year, "you will find a great array of Christmas trees in the improvised warehouse and on the outside of it you will be greeted with the cordial smile of a dear old mother…. She is again busy at her same old loving duty, feeling like a newborn child, full of enthusiasm and joy. She is here to help bring joy this year like never before."

Home. For some it is a building, for others, a life's work - as it was for Barbara Schuenemann when she was among her trees. Her husband had known this contentment before her, and her daughters would cherish it after she was gone.

"Every year I shall go to the Northwoods," promised Barbara Schuenemann in 1913. "It seemed like one long holiday for me. I shall never miss it."

Her promise held true until her death twenty years later. Then her promise became a prophecy: "And after I am dead there will be others to carry on the work."

In December of 1933, St. Pauls Church reported: "Mrs. Elsie Schuenemann Roberts, the eldest daughter of the departed Mother Schuenemann, is perpetuating the memory of her parents by preparing on a large scale to furnish the homes of Chicago with beautiful Christmas trees."

It was a fitting memorial, a meaningful remembrance. Captain and Mrs. Schuenemann's memory was honored with that which they loved: the evergreen.

"Christmas is a time of joy and our tale does not end on a note of tragedy. Herman Schuenemann left a wife and three young daughters. As courageous as her husband, Barbara Schuenemann picked up where he left off. The following November, a Christmas Tree Ship was again docked at Clark Street with a lady skipper and her three children. For another 22 years these gallant women brought their Christmas trees down the lake to grace the city of Chicago, and to sustain a living memorial to the Rouse Simmons *and her crew."*

Great Lakes Travel & Living
December 1986
Marjorie Cahn Brazer

Photo of Captain and Mrs. Herman Schuenemann's
gravestone.
(Acacia Park Cemetery, Chicago, IL)

Chapter Ten

A Final Resting Place

"Though Captain Schuenemann's body was never recovered, his wife is buried in Acacia Cemetery in Chicago. Strangely, the grave is said to produce the scent of fresh cut spruce and balsam."

Jim Graczyk
www.ghostguides.com

A Final Resting Place

Two names are etched into the granite of the Schuenemann headstone in Acacia Park Cemetery in Chicago, but only one body lies below: that of Barbara Schuenemann. She was laid to rest on June 19, 1933, in Grave #4, Block #21, Lot #2 of the cemetery.

Captain Herman's name is here, but he is not. He was laid to rest on the bottom of Lake Michigan nearly twenty-two years earlier.

Because no bodies were recovered from the *Simmons* shipwreck, no public obituary acknowledging the captain's death was published in the newspaper. However, a memorial obituary for Captain Schuenemann was written by his pastor, Reverend Rudolph A. John of St. Pauls Church. The obituary paid tribute to the captain whom Reverend John saw as "a good man, sturdy, honest, faithful."

Barbara Schuenemann was also memorialized by St. Pauls at her death. In June of 1933, the church newsletter announced her passing with these words: "The sudden death of Mother Schuenemann has brought much sorrow to her loved ones. More details about this remarkable woman, whom the people of Chicago loved because of her devotion to the children at Christmastime when she brought the Christmas trees to them, will be given in the next issue."

One month later, in July of 1933, Pastor Jacob Pister paid honor to Barbara's life by speaking of the "indomitable faith" she displayed in facing her greatest trial. He affectionately referred to her as "Mother Schuenemann" who "was known and loved by thousands, and hundreds of thousands, throughout our great metropolis."

Her memorial service was held June 19, 1933, at St. Pauls. Then, "from the Church she loved so well, her weary body was carried to its rest and her motherly soul consecrated to the Lord of Life."

It is not difficult to understand why the Schuenemanns felt a connection to St. Pauls. First, the congregation was primarily composed of German immigrants. Barbara (Schindel) Schuenemann had been born and raised near Frankfort, Germany, and later immigrated to America. Her husband, Herman Schuenemann, was born to German immigrants, Frederick and Louise Schuenemann, who had immigrated from Mecklenburg, Germany, and later settled in Wisconsin where Herman, their fourth child, was born.

According to Dr. William Ehling, Captain and Mrs. Schuenemann's only surviving grandson, Barbara Schuenemann was "quite an artist" and "did a lot of oil painting." He remembers one of his grandmother's favorite

**OBITUARY FOR
CAPTAIN HERMAN
SCHUENEMANN**
Written by:
Pastor Rudolph A. John
December 1912

It is indeed a hard and heart breaking task to write of Captain Schuenemann, our good faithful brother, who for so many years has been with us in our work and in faith. The papers of our city, and perhaps of all the land, have told in prose and song and picture the sad tale that has made many eyes moist and many hearts heavy.

We can add nothing to what has been published again and again. For almost thirty years this good man, sturdy, honest, faithful, has sailed the waters of the Great Lakes, in summertime in the lumber trade and in November, braving many an angry storm and rough sea to bring great cargoes of trees and branches and red berries to make the children's holidays brighter and happier.

And this time he has not returned. In former years Captain Schuenemann's arrival with his load of trees was the signal for the real Christmas activity to begin. Hundreds of thousands of little trees he brought to the great city – and this time he has not returned.

What more can we say? We do not know the secret of the waves, they have not yet given up the awful story of disaster. His good wife and three daughters, as good and faithful members of our church as the husband and father was, have heard in the sleepless hours of many a night the angry roar of the waves and have strained their eyes to find a light in the darkness. But he has not returned.

So we hold out our hand to them in silent sympathy that finds no words because it comes so deep from the heart. God comfort them! He who once stretched forth His hand to the sea and bade it hush its angry roar, walks upon the earth no more, but He who made the sea and the land and man and woman, He still lives and loves His children. And into His safe-keeping we commit the hearts that are sobbing in their loneliness and looking out into the voiceless darkness of the night.

"The dark, cold water of Lake Michigan is the shroud for these brave men who sailed forth on the Christmas Tree Ship that never returned."

Manitowoc Daily Herald
Manitowoc, WI
December 14, 1912
Gus C. Kirst

Photo of the Evangelical and Reformed St. Pauls Church of Chicago.
(Courtesy of Reverend Thomas R. Henry, Senior Pastor)

St. Pauls was one of the first six churches established in Chicago and was home to three generations of Schuenemann family members.

The 1898 building in the photo above was destroyed by fire in 1955. Two years after the fire, the church became St. Pauls United Church of Christ, the name chosen for a new denomination formed by the merger of two denominations, the Evangelical and Reformed Churches and the Congregational Christian Churches. A new sanctuary was built and dedicated on the same site.

The 1955 fire was the second fire to destroy the church. In 1871, the Great Chicago Fire also destroyed the sanctuary. The church's name at that time was the German United Evangelical Lutheran St. Pauls Congregation.

"St. Pauls" is spelled with the apostrophe omitted according to the German language.

paintings. It hung in her living room and served as a remembrance to her of days long past. On a 4 x 6 canvas, Barbara had painted a child feeding chickens in Germany.

In addition to the German connection between the Schuenemanns and St. Pauls, the peoples of this congregation had consistently exemplified a spirit of resiliency over the years, standing united through many difficult days. These were strong people, and they paralleled the Schuenemann family's courage. Twice, the Schuenemanns suffered a heart wrenching loss due to water, and twice St. Pauls suffered their own significant loss due to another element: fire. In 1871, the Great Chicago Fire destroyed much of the city including St. Pauls Church, as well as the homes of most of the congregational members, including the pastor. Despite such a devastating blow, the congregation rebuilt their church "within just over a year of its destruction."

Then, the church was reduced to ashes a second time in 1955 when a fire ravaged the sanctuary. The church record reads: "On Christmas night in 1955, St. Pauls once again suffered the horror of losing its beloved building to fire. A short in the wiring of the newly installed organ was blamed for the ferocious fire which made national news. Neighbors said the three bells in the tower rang as the tower came down. One bell survived and sits in the courtyard of the church today. The three German words inscribed on the surviving bell can still be read: Glaube, Hoffnung, Liebe (Faith, Hope, Love)."

The bells tolled for a final time on Christmas night 1955. These were the same bells that tolled for Barbara Schuenemann's passing. Fittingly, the surviving bell was inscribed with words written by the church's namesake, Saint Paul, who wrote much of the New Testament of the Christian Bible two thousand years earlier. In the First Book of Corinthians 13:13 we find St. Paul's words: "And now these three remain: faith, hope and love. But the greatest of these is love."

Fire could destroy the St. Pauls building, but it could not destroy the faith that yet remained within its people. Nor could it destroy the love that had lived within its walls, or the hope this congregation held fast to in their vision to see their church raised up once more. Within two short years, a new sanctuary had been built and dedicated. An organ was later placed and given the name "Phoenix" after the mythological bird from Greek literature that rose up from ashes and ruins with renewed youth and beauty.

OBITUARY FOR MRS. BARBARA SCHUENEMANN
Written by:
Pastor Jacob Pister
July 1933

Barbara Schuenemann, 158 Eugenie Street, nee Schindel, the widow of the departed Captain Herman Schuenemann, passed into life eternal on the 15th day of June, 1933, aged 67 years, 10 months, 13 days. Farewell services were held in her honor on June 19th at St. Pauls Church and interment followed at Acacia Park.

Mother Schuenemann was known and loved by thousands, and hundreds of thousands, throughout our great metropolis. When 20 years ago the ill fated *Christmas Ship* plying its way through the perilous tempests of the turbulent waters of the Lake finally yielded to the winds and waves and disappeared with its precious cargo of human souls and Christmas trees, a feeling of horror and sadness was evident everywhere.

The widowed mother and her three daughters gathered day after day with mingled feelings of hope and distress, trusting that by some special dispensation of Divine Grace their loved one might still make his way into some nearby port. These hopes proved in vain, the genial Captain who had sailed the waters in the decades of the past was destined not to set his foot upon the threshold of his home nor to return to his dear ones again.

As the bereaved mother and her children began to realize the extent of their loss they were fortified by the calming grace of an indomitable faith. In the power of their renewed trust in Him whose ways are always good unto those that believe in Him, she resolved then and there to carry on the work and thus every year the Christmas season brought her to the front with her large assortment of Christmas trees for all of Chicago.

Dr. Scherger, in his very appropriate words at the last rites, very feelingly referred to his visit with Mrs. Schuenemann many years ago and his urgent wish to purchase the largest tree for the little children of his Armour Mission. Reluctantly, and yet very kindly, Mother Schuenemann said to him, "I am sorry Dr. Scherger, but I cannot sell you this beautiful tree for this

The great St. Paul's Cathedral in London, England, site of many prominent occasions through the centuries, including the wedding of Prince Charles and Lady Diana Spencer, also adopted the phoenix's symbol of renewed rejuvenation and new birth after the Great London Fire of 1666 destroyed the original cathedral and four-fifths of the city with it. Visitors to the cathedral today can see a phoenix sculptured in stone with a single word inscribed beside it: Resurgam. Its meaning is "I shall rise again."

Death brings its own resurrection, but so, too, does life - the continuous resurrections we experience while we yet live: resurrections of hope, of joy, of love, and of faith. Barbara Schuenemann resurrected a reason for living in the midst of her tragedy. She rose up from the Valley of Shadows where

one is sent by me as a special gift to my dear St. Pauls Church and its children."

A few years ago the departed mother had fallen gravely ill. Humanly speaking, it appeared as though the Lord was about to call her away from us. She came to her Church once more and said farewell to us believing, as she did, that she would not be able to come again. Then the most remarkable evidence of Divine Love was made manifest as an emergency operation was decided upon. The Hand of the Lord was with the men of surgical skill and to their surprise and delight the invalid effected a miraculous recovery.

With many thanksgivings she came back to her Church and to her societies, began to give her attention to her numerous business ventures, and a week prior to her departure, decided to take over her apartments near Lincoln Park.

The last day of her earthly life was spent in strenuous household duties together with arranging her furniture and furnishings in her apartment. At the dinner table she complained to her children that she felt very weary. A few moments later she suddenly showed signs of extreme exhaustion and was gently carried to her bed. With heaving breath she responded to the urge within her soul and smilingly spoke affectionate words of farewell and a few moments later lay in the silence of death. She completed the day's work in the earthly home and hastened to the home above not made by the hand of man.

Her three daughters and their family members, including two grandchildren and an only brother and other relatives in the Fatherland, mourn deeply her unexpected departure.

From the Church she loved so well her weary body was carried to its rest and her motherly soul consecrated to the Lord of Life.

sadness could have turned her heart to stone, and she turned her eyes, instead, off her pain and toward that which remained: faith, hope, love. Death could not destroy these for it "could not kill what does not die." Tragedy could swallow the Captain, but it could not swallow the love he left behind, nor could it bring death to the faith and hope his loved ones still clung to.

St. Pauls Church acknowledged altar flowers donated in remembrance of Captain Schuenemann in their December 1915 newsletter. The article read: "On the 28th day of November beautiful flowers were sent to the altar in memory of Captain Herman Schuenemann, who went down with the Christmas Ship three years ago, by his dear wife and daughters. Thus the flowers of love are always sweet and bright, even though the snow and storms

Photo of Mrs. Barbara Schuenemann and her three daughters.
From left to right: Elsie, Pearl, Hazel, Barbara
(*Courtesy of the Schuenemann Family descendants*)

of winter make the land bleak and dreary. For Love's flowers grow in the heart and, if we but ask it, there God's sunshine is always warm."

Love. St. Pauls Church saw it as "God's sunshine" – and so did the Schuenemanns. It was Love that had sustained them in their most difficult moments. They turned to it by turning to each other and were as close knit of a family as there ever was.

At the time of Barbara's death, her address was listed as 158 Eugenie Street. This was the same address listed for each of her three daughters who lived on separate floors of a grand, turn-of-the-century home composed of four individual flats. (Although this property has since been demolished, and a newer apartment building stands in its place, several homes similar to the Schuenemann's were spared from being razed and still stand today on the same street - magnificent examples of Old Chicago architecture.)

When Elsie (Schuenemann) Roberts passed away in 1950 at Cook County Hospital in Chicago, her address was listed as 3501 Hirsch Street where she was living with her sister, Pearl, and Pearl's husband. When Elsie's son, Arthur, was born, her address was listed as 1638 N. Clark Street. She and her husband had taken residence with Barbara and were living in the same home where Captain Schuenemann had.

WOMAN SKIPPER OF CHRISTMAS TREE BOATS DIES
Chicago Tribune
Chicago, IL
June 16, 1933

Mrs. Barbara Schuenemann, "The Christmas Tree Lady," age 67, died suddenly last night in her home at 158 Eugenie Street. Death was due to heart disease.

Mrs. Schuenemann was the widow of Capt. Herman Schuenemann, who brought Chicago its first boatload of Christmas trees in 1887.

In 1912 Capt. Schuenemann went down in a terrific lake storm as he was bringing a cargo of Christmas trees to the city on the *Rouse Simmons*.

His widow continued his work, taking the helm of various craft to bring trees to the city each Yuletide for many years. Since 1925 trees have been brought by freight cars to her warehouse.

Mrs. Schuenemann is survived by three daughters, Mrs. Elsie Roberts, Mrs. Hazel Gronemann, and Mrs. Pearl Ehling, and two grandchildren. Funeral services will be held Monday morning in St. Pauls Evangelical Lutheran church.

Memorial Paintings

On Sunday morning, December 20th, 1934, we dedicated to the memory of two well known and faithful families of old St. Pauls two magnificent pictures.

On the west wall of the South Balcony, Hofman's immortal "Christ in the Garden of Gethsemane" has been reproduced by a noted artist, Max Moll, perpetuating the memory of Captain and Mrs. Herman Schuenemann. This wonderful work is a gift to the Church by the faithful daughters of these dear friends, Mrs. Hazel Gronemann, Mrs. Pearl Ehling, and Mrs. Elsie Roberts.

Hofman is perhaps the most famous of all modern religious painters. There are no religious pictures that are more popular than his "Christ in the Garden of Gethsemane" and "The Boy Christ in the Temple".

The Schuenemann memorial picture has been a great inspiration to the Pastor each Sunday morning, and we know that in the days to come it will continue to inspire and instill in the hearts of all St. Pauls worshipers the love and humility that seems to speak from the beloved face – "Not my will, but Thine be done." All who knew and remember Captain and Mrs. Herman Schuenemann will agree that just that spirit lived in their good hearts.

On the east wall of the North Balcony, Miss Minnie Groll and brothers, Philip, William and Herman Groll, have dedicated a reproduction of Holman Hant's masterpiece "Jesus, the Light of the World" to the memory of their beloved parents, Mr. and Mrs. Philip Groll. Mr. Max Moll was the artist for this beautiful picture as well as the Schuenemann memorial.

The original of this painting is in St. Paul's Cathedral in London, England, and is the only painting in the Church. Many people visit the Cathedral just to see this wonderful picture which is one of the great masterpieces of religious art. This picture, too, is an admonition to all St. Pauls worshipers to be alert, to receive the Christ that knocks at the door of our hearts.

As we look upon this work of art, we are reminded of the dear parents whose memory is revered by these good children and by St. Pauls Congregation.

We are so grateful for these visible memorials of the two families who figure so greatly in the history of St. Pauls church and her work. May God bless the children.

St. Pauls Church Newsletter
Memorial dedicated December 1934

The Schuenemann descendants shared several addresses during their lifetimes and chose to be laid to rest together at the Acacia Park Cemetery, 7800 W. Irving Park Road, Chicago. Although no gravestones were erected for Elsie and Hazel, each of these daughters was buried beside her parents. (The third daughter, Pearl, was buried in Streator, Illinois, where her only son resides.)

A modest stone, flush with the ground, marks the final resting place of the Schuenemanns on this side of eternity. Their shared gravestone lies in the "Wistaria" section of the cemetery, named for the ancient flower whose meaning is "I cling to you."

"The Rouse Simmons *and her crew were gone to the good land where it is always Christmas."*

Toronto Evening Telegram
December 29, 1945
C. H. J. Snider

Photo of Elsie Schuenemann dated approximately 1894.
(*Courtesy of the Schuenemann Family descendants*)

ELSIE ROBERTS, CHRISTMAS SHIP SKIPPER, DIES
Chicago Tribune
Chicago, IL
February 2, 1950

Mrs. Elsie Schuenemann Roberts, 58, who for years helped to carry on the Christmas ship tradition of her father, Capt. Herman Schuenemann, after he drowned in Lake Michigan nearly 40 years ago, died Tuesday, it was learned yesterday.

Captain Schuenemann had brought Christmas trees to Chicago from Michigan each year in his schooner, the *Rouse Simmons*. It sank Nov. 23, 1912, in one of Lake Michigan's worst storms. The captain's widow, Barbara, and her daughters, Elsie, Pearl, and Hazel, later took up his work with another boat.

Mrs. Roberts leaves a son, Arthur, and the sisters, now Mrs. Pearl Ehling, with whom she lived at 3501 Hirsch Street, and Mrs. Hazel Gronemann. Services will be held at 2 p.m. tomorrow in the chapel at 5525 N. Clark St. Burial will be in Acacia Cemetery.

ELSIE ROBERTS
St. Pauls Church Newsletter
Chicago, IL
February 1950

Elsie Roberts, nee Schuenemann, passed away on January 31st, after a long illness, aged 58. She was buried at Acacia Cemetery on February 3rd. Mrs. Roberts was one of our well known "Schuenemann Sisters" at St. Pauls and until a few years ago when she was stricken with illness, was very active in our congregation.

Her parents, Capt. and Mrs. Schuenemann were the famous pilots of the *Christmas Tree Ship* and for a number of years after their passing, Elsie took over this task of bringing Christmas trees to Chicago. She is survived by her son, Arthur, and two sisters, Pearl Ehling and Hazel Gronemann.

HAZEL GRONEMANN
St. Pauls Church Newsletter
Chicago, IL
Spring 1969 Issue

Hazel Gronemann, nee Schuenemann, passed away after a long illness, on January 4th. She was laid to rest at Acacia Park Cemetery on January 6th. Mrs. Gronemann was a member of St. Pauls all of her life, and had been a teacher in our Sunday School many years ago. She was always proud of her fine heritage – the daughter of the late Captain and Mrs. Herman Schuenemann of the *Christmas Tree Ship* fame.

HAZEL GRONEMANN
Chicago Tribune
Chicago, IL
January 5, 1969

Hazel Gronemann, 70, nee Schuenemann, beloved daughter of the late Captain Herman and Barbara; fond sister of Pearl Ehling and the late Elsie Roberts. Funeral Monday, January 6, at 1:30 p.m., from Rago Brothers, 5120 West Fullerton Ave. Interment Acacia Park.

Photo of Hazel Schuenemann, twin sister to Pearl.
(*Courtesy of the Schuenemann Family descendants*)

CHICAGO DAILY TRIBUNE: THURSDAY, DECEMBER 13, 1934.

CHRISTMAS TREE TRADE RECALLS A FATAL VOYAGE

Daughters Carry On for Schuenemann

Lost Captain's Daughters Carry On His Business.

Photo of Pearl (Schuenemann) Ehling, twin sister to Hazel, and Elsie (Schuenemann) Roberts. (*Courtesy of the* Chicago Tribune)

Mrs. Pearl Schuenemann Ehling (left) and Mrs. Elsie Schuenemann Roberts, daughters of captain lost in Christmas tree boat wreck in 1912, selling trees yesterday at their stand, 1641 North La Salle street.
[TRIBUNE Photo.]

PEARL C. EHLING
Bloomington Pantagraph
Bloomington, IL
July 8, 1991

Pearl C. Ehling, 92, of Streator, Illinois, a homemaker, died at 10:55 p.m. Saturday, July 6, 1991, at Heritage Manor Nursing Home, Streator.

A memorial service will be at 11:30 a.m. Wednesday at Elias Funeral Home, Streator.

Visitation will be one hour before the service.

She was born Oct. 6, 1898, in Chicago, a daughter of Capt. Herman and Barbara Schindel Schuenemann.

She married William H. Ehling June 14, 1928. He died in 1972.

Surviving are one son, Dr. William E. Ehling, Streator; three grandchildren; and four great-grandchildren.

She was preceded in death by her two sisters, one of which was her twin.

Mrs. Ehling had been a Streator resident since 1972. She was a member of Park Presbyterian Church in Streator.

Memorials may be made to St. Mary's Hospital Foundation or her church.

Genealogy of Captain Herman and Mrs. Barbara Schuenemann

Captain Herman Schuenemann and Miss Barbara Schindel were married April 9, 1891 in Chicago, Illinois. Exactly nine months later, to the very day, the Schuenemann family welcomed their firstborn, a daughter. Two more daughters, fraternal twins born in 1898, completed their family.

Children/Grandchildren:

Elsie Schuenemann

Born:	January 9, 1892
Died:	January 31, 1950; Age 58
Baptized:	March 6, 1892 – "Elsa Christine Louise"
Address at time of birth:	170 LaSalle Avenue, Chicago
Husband:	Arthur E. Roberts
Children:	One son, Arthur F. Roberts
	Born: September 10, 1920
	Baptized: January 9, 1921 – "Arthur Fred Edward"
	Address at time of birth: 1638 N. Clark Street, Chicago
	Note: This was the address of Captain Herman Schuenemann in 1912.

Pearl Schuenemann (Twin)

Born:	October 6, 1898
Died:	July 6, 1991; Age 92
Baptized:	November 27, 1898 – "Pearlie Clara"
Address at time of birth:	693 N. Clark Street, Chicago
Husband:	William H. Ehling
Children:	One son, William E. Ehling
	Born: March 4, 1930
	Baptized: September 28, 1930 – "William Edward"
	Address at time of birth: 528 Wrightwood Avenue, Chicago

Hazel Schuenemann (Twin)

Born:	October 6, 1898
Died:	January 4, 1969; Age 70
Baptized:	November 27, 1898 – "Hazel Marion"
Address at time of birth:	693 N. Clark Street, Chicago
Husband:	Clarence Gronemann
Children:	None

U.S. Coast Guard Cutter *Mackinaw* arriving in the Chicago harbor.
(Courtesy of the Chicago Christmas Ship Committee)

Chapter Eleven

Chicago's "New" Christmas Ship

"*The story of the* Rouse Simmons *refuses to end.*"

Shipwrecks of Lake Michigan
Benjamin J. Shelak
Copyright 2003

Chicago's "New" Christmas Ship

John Quincy Adams, sixth President of the United States, once said, "The influence of each human being on others in this life is a kind of immortality."

I couldn't help but think of these words on December 6, 2003, as I stood on Chicago's lakefront, my collar up, braced against a brisk breeze blowing off Lake Michigan. Others were gathered with me – *many others*. Each had come to Grand Avenue at Navy Pier to pay tribute to the lives lost nearly a century ago on the *Rouse Simmons*, Chicago's legendary Christmas Ship. Each had come, also, to see Chicago's "new" Christmas Ship, the United States Coast Guard Cutter *Mackinaw*.

The *Mackinaw* had sailed into harbor just one day prior with a load of Christmas trees, cut and bundled in Upper Michigan. For four consecutive years, more than fifty organizations, including the United States Coast Guard and its Auxiliary members, as well as the Chicago Christmas Ship Committee, a non-profit charity, have worked diligently to resurrect the spirit of the *Rouse Simmons* and its captain, Herman Schuenemann. Thousands of Christmas trees have been distributed over the past few years to needy families. The tireless dedication of countless volunteers has made this possible.

A memorial ceremony honoring the sailors lost on the *Simmons*, as well as all those lost on the Great Lakes in the merchant marine trade, is held each December. The ceremony precedes the distribution of trees.

December 2003 marked the first year I was in attendance at the solemn ceremony, a service filled with emotion and reverence, and held, appropriately, in front of the Navy Pier statue "Captain on the Helm" – an impressive bronze work of art depicting a sea captain fighting for his life in the midst of a storm. The statue pays tribute to sailors lost at sea on the Great Lakes while transporting cargo to Chicago.

The ceremony commenced when the crowd, gathered in front of the statue (and beside the *Mackinaw*), fell silent. Lake Michigan was the backdrop for the ceremony since the statue is erected at the water's edge.

Uniformed Officers were present from the Great Lakes Naval Training Center, the Chicago Marine Police, the United States Coast Guard, the International Shipmasters of the Merchant Marine, the Colin Powell Naval Cadets, the Sea Scouts, the Salvation Army, Commodores from area yachting clubs, as well as representatives from many other organizations.

After many years the "Christmas Ship" tradition has found a new beginning and is alive and well. In place of the Rouse Simmons *the U.S. Coast Guard Cutter* Mackinaw, *the largest and most powerful of the U.S. Coast Guard's domestic icebreakers, will deliver the freshly cut trees to current Chicago residents. Unlike in the 1900's, the Chicago Christmas Ship will donate the trees to the United Way and in turn the trees will be distributed to Chicago's disadvantaged.*

The reenactment of this lost Chicago tradition and its story will be held at Navy Pier.

Yachting in Chicago 2000
Barbara Thompson

"We want to thank the United States Coast Guard and the crew of the USCGC Mackinaw *for their continued support of this charitable holiday event. The 'Chicago's Christmas Ship' Committee and the United States Coast Guard want to continue to deliver thousands of Christmas trees to the less fortunate families in the Midwest every Holiday Season. 'Chicago's Christmas Ship' Committee is a volunteer group comprised of all maritime organizations throughout the Chicago land area."*

Captain Sonny Lisowski,
Executive Chairman of
Chicago's Christmas Ship

Commanding officers "offered a few words in memory of all lost mariners and, in particular, the mariners lost on the *Rouse Simmons*," said Lynn Koepke, a founding member of the Chicago Christmas Ship Committee and former Executive Officer of the Marine Safety Office in Chicago, during an interview I later conducted with her.

Also present at the service was an Honor Guard of Shipmasters, assembled near the "Captain at the Helm". The Honor Guard stood at attention before placing a memorial wreath at the statue. A second, larger wreath was then placed on "the grave" of the fallen sailors and buried at sea. The wreath had been loaded aboard a U.S. Coast Guard helicopter that approached from the distant horizon, its engines roaring. Hovering above the crowd, the helicopter pilot paused and then "dipped" the front end of his craft slightly forward in a "salute" to the statue below. Honor Guard Shipmasters, in turn, saluted the craft, and the wreath it carried, in an act of respect.

Slowly, the helicopter then flew toward the open waters, circled the lighthouse, and returned to the center of the waters where the crew paused for several moments in memory and reverence. The wreath was then released to the waters below.

While this was happening, those of us on shore stood silent as we listened to the haunting Naval hymn, Eternal Father, played by the Great Lakes Naval Brass Band, also present that day.

Eternal Father

Eternal Father, strong to save,
Whose arm hath bound the restless wave,
Who bidd'st the mighty ocean deep,
Its own appointed limits keep.
Oh hear us when we cry to Thee,
For those in peril on the sea.

"I remember the first year I volunteered to help the Chicago Christmas Ship donate trees to needy families. It was cold that year – really cold – and we had goosebumps. But they weren't on the outside. They were on the inside from all the good we were doing."

Laura Halberstadt, Volunteer

Decorating the "Chicago Christmas Ship" in 2000.
(Courtesy of the Chicago Christmas Ship Committee)

Interview with Commander Joseph McGuiness

(Commanding Officer of the United States Coast Guard Cutter *Mackinaw*)

December 6, 2003

The Chicago marine community has come together to revive the old tradition of the Christmas Tree Ship, and also to do it on a charitable basis.

Today, and this week, our mission has been to join together with charities in Northern Michigan, as well as charities in Chicago, to bring a load of Christmas trees down to Chicago on the *Mackinaw*. The Christmas trees are then distributed to various charitable organizations working in conjunction with the Chicago Christmas Ship who, in turn, distribute the trees to families who might not otherwise have the means to purchase one.

This year there are over a thousand trees being distributed, and the Coast Guard is proud to be part of such a humanitarian mission.

I think back to when I was a boy, six or seven years old, and I remember asking my parents relentlessly, "What day are we going to set up the Christmas tree? Are we going to set it up in the morning or the afternoon? When? When?"

Finally, the tree would go up, and I can remember just lying there underneath it, staring up at the lights and the ornaments. It was magic to me. It really was. These are magical, magical moments for children.

And this year, through the Chicago Christmas Ship and the Coast Guard's united efforts, over a thousand families in Michigan and Chicago will receive a Christmas tree and share in some of those moments.

The Chicago Christmas Ship is a project of goodwill. It is an all volunteer effort, and 100% of the money donated comes from private sources and is used for the purchasing of trees. No money collected is spent in any other way. Everything is donated including the lights, the trucking, and everything else that goes with the logistics of bringing the Christmas trees to town.

It is a huge, collective effort that comprises of more than 50 lake front organizations in the City of Chicago coming together in memory of Captain Schuenemann's old tradition.

As the Naval band played on momentarily, the helicopter departed, flying into the horizon until it could no longer be seen. Then, Christmas trees began to be carried, one-by-one, on the shoulders of volunteers, off the *Mackinaw*. These trees were destined for homes all around the City.

Several volunteers shared heartwarming stories with me during interviews I conducted after the event. Fred Poppe, Chairman of the Chicago Christmas Ship Committee in 2002, remembered one little girl who was given a Christmas tree and said, "I've never had a Christmas tree before." The child's mother, who was standing beside her daughter at the time, responded, "Neither have I."

Volunteer Lynn Koepke recalled another little boy who received a Christmas tree at a special presentation ceremony he attended with his mom and dad. She remembered the child holding onto the tree, standing as close as he possibly could to it. "He was so excited about that tree," she said. "And when the volunteers took it from him to tie it up so it could make the journey home, he burst into tears because he thought they were taking his Christmas tree away."

After volunteers reassured the child that the tree was only being tied with rope so it could be delivered to his house, his big smile returned.

"It was so special to see how much that little tree meant to him," said Koepke.

Although the majority of the Christmas trees donated each holiday are distributed through social services organizations, a few evergreens are presented at a symbolic presentation at Navy Pier. (Also, only a portion of the Christmas trees arrive on the *Mackinaw* when it sails to Chicago on its regular training mission for the Coast Guard in December. The balance is shipped by truck.)

According to Fred Poppe, every penny donated goes "solely for the acquisition of Christmas trees. Period."

Poppe further explained to me that the Chicago Christmas Ship Committee chooses one primary charitable organization (such as the

> *"You have not lived a perfect day, even though you have earned your money, unless you have done something for someone who will never be able to repay you."*
>
> Ruth Smeltzer

Salvation Army or the United Way) who, in turn, select recipient organizations to receive the trees. "These are community service groups, social service organizations, and also churches that work with the underprivileged," said Poppe. Ultimately, the trees are then distributed to individual needy families through these charitable groups.

During the 2003 event I was amazed at the number of trucks picking up Christmas trees at the lakeshore – many different trucks with many different business logos painted on the sides of them. Mr. Poppe explained that private companies make their vehicles available so that trees can be transported to each organization's base of operation. The trucks "go off into the neighborhoods" after being loaded at the Army Corps of Engineering parking lot located next to Navy Pier. (The parking lot is made available for the loading of trees, as well as for volunteers to park their cars during the event. Also, the Salvation Army's emergency service vehicle – filled with hot chocolate, coffee and donuts for everyone helping – is set up in this same area.)

Volunteer Don Koster, an individual who has contributed countless hours to the Committee over the past few years (and who is said to be "the hardest working fellow" by other volunteers), took time to explain many details surrounding the event with me during my time in Chicago. He currently oversees several aspects of the operation including all the electrical and decorating tasks.

Countless hands have made the "new" Christmas Ship a reality, and each volunteer has become an heir to the tradition Captain Schuenemann began so many years ago.

The Christmas Tree Ship legend is a story not simply remembered in terms of one man's life, but rather is a story that continues to be remembered for what that one life inspired in others. Those who have carried the story forward are those who have gleaned from its telling the goodness and hope

> The spirit of Christmas is found in the singing,
> in the bright Christmas trees and the bells that are ringing.
> The spirit is found in the lights everywhere,
> but the meaning is found in the love people share.
>
> *Embroidered on an Amish sampler*

"We would like to remind you how much a donation to the Chicago Christmas Ship would be appreciated. This holiday tradition of giving Christmas trees to less fortunate families with children continues for the fourth year. We want to keep this tradition alive by the support of those who enjoy the history of Lake Michigan and the great mission we continue to perform, which is giving – over the years – thousands of Christmas trees to less fortunate families with children. Remember the children who, through no choice of their own, would not have a Christmas tree that symbolizes the joys and goodwill of the Holiday Season. In many cases, these families have never had a Christmas tree. We DO make a difference in the world we live in, especially to the children that we make smile."

Captain Sonny Lisowski,
Executive Chairman of
Chicago's Christmas Ship

Please accept my donation of $_____ for Chicago's Christmas Ship.

Make checks payable to:

Chicago's Christmas Ship
Chicago Council, U.S. Navy League
c/o 403 N. County Line Road
Hinsdale, IL 60521-2404

Name _____

Organization _____

Address _____

_____

City/State/Zip _____

(All contributions are tax deductible according to IRS Regulation 501c3.)

we each have the privilege of creating in the life of another human being. We literally can "step" into this story and make it our own.

And for those who choose to share a small donation, they may know the satisfaction that somewhere a child will awake on Christmas morn to a tree where no tree would have stood before had it not been for the kindness of a stranger.

The *Mackinaw* has carried more than trees to Chicago. It has carried hope. With every tree handed off the ship, a message has come with it to its recipient: Someone cares about you. You are not alone.

The greatness of the Schuenemann story, indeed of every story, is not how it ends, but how it begins. Not how it begins at the beginning, but rather how it begins anew in the heart of each person when the story has ended, or so it seems.

Chicago's Christmas Ship was "born" into existence through the simple telling of a simple story in the summer of 2000. Coast Guard Auxiliary member Jay Crissey shared the legend of the Christmas Tree Ship with Ray Seebald, Captain of the Port of Chicago, and Jon Nickerson, Commanding Officer of the Coast Guard Cutter *Mackinaw* in 2000 while the *Mackinaw* was in port.

"Wouldn't it be great to have a Christmas Tree Ship again?" asked the gentlemen after hearing the story.

This simple question triggered an event that has captured the hearts of many in the Windy City including those involved in the maritime community, charity personnel and civilian volunteers. It is an event that has turned into a "rich maritime tradition" for Chicago.

"By the end of the day, Captain Seebald and Commander Nickerson had jumped on the idea with two feet," said Mr. Crissey. "From there the whole thing started."

"Happy Holidays to you and yours, and please support this wonderful cause. All donations go for the purchasing of Christmas trees. Not one dollar is spent in any other way.

What is brighter, a star or a child's smile? May the skies be bright that December night and the faces of children and their smiles be even brighter from your support."

Captain Sonny Lisowski,
Executive Chairman of
Chicago's Christmas Ship

(Lambert/Hulton Archives/Getty Images)

Captain Herman Schuenemann
(Courtesy of the Chicago Maritime Society)

By Christmas 2000 (the very first Christmas after their conversation), the Chicago Christmas Ship was a reality. A small question had turned into a larger vision.

Jay Crissey served as Vice Chairman for the first two years of the Chicago Christmas Ship under the leadership of Chairman Dave Truitt. Each of these gentlemen shouldered up many hours, along with Captain Seebald, who was also "extremely instrumental in the planning stages," according to Captain Truitt. "He made it a point to be present during the development of the entire vision." The overall program was formalized, and the master operational plan developed, in conjunction with Coast Guard participation.

"We needed support from the commanding Officer of the Coast Guard," said Crissey, "and Vice Admiral James Hull was the man who gave it. Admiral Hull commanded the entire 9th District of the Coast Guard at the time – which is all of the Great Lakes."

Mr. Crissey loves sharing his passion for the Chicago Christmas Ship with others. He told me: "You can't be much prouder of this event than I am. Everything we've done together in delivering trees to underprivileged children has meant a lot to all of us."

Before our interview ended, Mr. Crissey said something to me while we were discussing the "difficult places" many of the Christmas trees are destined for. "I was an orphan as a child," he shared quietly. "It may be that subconsciously this was a motivating factor for me to help other children whose families have fallen on hard times financially or emotionally." And "help" he has.

Christmas 2003 marked the 4th year anniversary of the Chicago Christmas Ship. Following the event, Mayor Richard M. Daley of Chicago, along with the City Council, presented the Chicago Christmas Ship Committee with a Resolution that recognized their efforts in "bringing the true spirit and meaning of Christmas" into the lives "of children in needy families within the City of Chicago."

"Be it resolved, that we, the Mayor and Members of the City Council of the City of Chicago, assembled in meeting this fourteenth day of January,

---

Captain Schuenemann once told a Chicago newspaper that he shipped trees every year *"because of the joy I find in the eyes of children that come aboard my ship to find the perfect tree for Christmas."*

2004," acknowledged the Resolution, "do hereby commend the Chicago Christmas Ship on its goodwill endeavors."

Captain Schuenemann changed the lives of people around him, and also changed the lives of people he would never know. These include many of the individuals who have worked diligently and collectively on the Committee over the past four years, presently under the leadership of Chairman Sonny Lisowski, a man with a heart as big as life itself.

Captain Schuenemann also left his impression on a little girl named Ruthie Erickson who never got the chance to meet him. She was five years old in 1912 and was waiting at the docks with her papa for the Christmas Ship to sail in. Captain Dave Truitt, former Chairman of the Christmas Ship Committee, shared the true story of "Little Ruthie" with me. He also told me about a play that the Chicago Underwater Archeological Society performed in 1990. The drama retold the legend of Ruthie Erickson who "waited and waited" for the Captain in 1912 at the harbor until her father finally said, "Ruthie, everybody is gone. It's cold. The wind is blowing. We should go home now."

The sea of faces along the dock that day in 1912 had dwindled to only those of the Erickson Family. Yet Ruthie wanted to wait longer, telling her papa, "But Daddy, it isn't Christmas without a Christmas tree."

Eventually, the family left that night, carrying only their heavy hearts home with them.

Captain Truitt was given the honor of playing the role of Captain Schuenemann in the 1990 drama. At the end of the play, he told the audience, "There really was a Christmas Tree Ship, and there really was a Captain Schuenemann. There also really was a Ruthie Erickson."

As fate would have it, Ruthie was present in the packed audience that night in 1990, unbeknownst to the actors and actresses. The 83-year-old had heard about the play and was in attendance with her daughter.

Then, the "sweet, wonderful, soft-spoken little lady" came forward, "supported by her daughter who helped her up onto the stage one step by one step," according to Captain Truitt.

The coincidental meeting of "Captain Schuenemann" and "Little Ruthie" turned emotional. According to Captain Truitt, he looked into the audience which was filled with "older, successful, dignified people," and everyone was crying.

Captain Truitt, acting on an impulse in his heart, reached for a Christmas tree on the stage and handed it to Ruthie, saying, "I couldn't give you a Christmas tree in 1912 when you were five because of reasons you now know, but I give this tree to you today. Merry Christmas, Ruthie!"

Ruth (Erickson) Flesvig had waited 78 long years for her Christmas tree, and over the distance of this time, she had told the story of Captain Schuenemann and his Christmas Tree Ship to her children and grandchildren each holiday. Her children later wrote a book about their mother's memories.

Captain Herman Schuenemann touched the lives of people he would never know, and the volunteers of Chicago's Christmas Ship are doing the same. They are spending their hearts each Christmas giving a charitable gift of time to others, dispelling some of the darkness in this "weary world" that there may be rejoicing in The Season of Miracles.

And somewhere, a lifetime from today, others may be telling their children and grandchildren about paste ornaments and tin foil stars that once decorated a Christmas tree they received as a child from the Chicago Christmas Ship Committee.

The strength of humanity lies herein: in the willingness for each of us to leave the walls of our own hearts, and our own lives, and connect with the hearts and lives of others. A Babe born in Bethlehem told us so. The Life born in the hay had come to say, "Feed the hungry, clothe the naked, serve one another in love, and share. And do unto others, for it is more blessed to give than it is to receive."

Serving one another is Life's supreme effort. And may others come to know these words are true because of you.

"The Christmas Tree Ship has come full circle. Let the history continue. We will make our love of the sea and our charitable tradition of 'Peace on Earth, Goodwill Toward Men' an event that will last for decades to come."

Captain Sonny Lisowski,
Executive Chairman of
Chicago's Christmas Ship

Acknowledgements

Heartfelt appreciation to the following individuals who provided critical information and personal interviews included in *The Historic Christmas Tree Ship:*

(In alphabetical order) Ruth Klinke Baur, Maggie Becker, Kent Bellrichard, James Brotz, Lois Bryant, Paul Creviere, Jay Crissey, Barbara Ehling, Jim Graczyk, Gerald Haegele, Laura Halberstadt, Don Hermanson, Virginia Johnson, Tom Kastle, Butch Klopp, Lynn Koepke, Jean Kopecky, Don Koster, Andy LaFond, Sonny Lisowski, Joseph McGuiness, Florence "Alex" Meron, Kurt Muellner, Nadine Nack, Marion Orr, Joyce Phippen, Fred Poppe, William Rossberger, Phil Sander, Brad Schmiling, Richard Smith, Wayne Stanley, Deane Tank, Dave Truitt, Jon Van Harpen, William Wangemann, Carolyn Williams and Sandy Zipperer.

Special gratitude to Colleen Henry, Church Historian of St. Pauls United Church of Christ in Chicago, for her generosity of time and spirit in assisting me throughout the project, and also to Emily Clark Victorson (a private researcher from Chicago) for her extraordinary helpfulness in locating vintage documents included in *The Historic Christmas Tree Ship.*

A very special "thank you" to Captain Schuenemann's grandson, Dr. William Ehling, for his kind assistance in sharing personal family memories.

Endless appreciation to research specialists at the following institutes who provided historical material from their archives: Wisconsin Marine Historical Society, Wisconsin Maritime Museum, Pier Wisconsin, Wisconsin Underwater Archeology Association, Chicago Historical Society, Chicago Maritime Society, The Historical Collections of the Great Lakes (Jerome Library, Bowling Green State University), Great Lakes Dossin Museum, Great Lakes Historical Society, Bentley Historical Library (University of Michigan), Kenosha County Historical Society, Kewaunee County Historical Society, Port Washington 1860 Light Station Museum, Chicago Christmas Ship Committee, Getty Images Archives, Rogers Street Fishing Village Museum, Butch Klopp Collection, Ship's Wheel Gallery & Nautical Museum, Dettman's Shanty Museum, and the Acadia Park Cemetery.

Deepest gratitude to Sarah Vollmer, Design Specialist at ep➤direct, and to her entire staff for their incredible dedication and tireless efforts on behalf of *The Historic Christmas Tree Ship!* You are all amazing!!!

Much gratitude to everyone at Network Printers for their meticulous attention to detail.

Heartfelt acknowledgement to Mystic Seaport for extending permission to use Carol Dyer's beautiful artwork on the cover, and also to the following individuals who allowed me to quote from their work:

Lee Murdock, Singer/Songwriter, for use of lyrics from his song "The Christmas Ship" (Contact info: Lee Murdock, Depot Recordings, P.O. Box 11, Kaneville, IL 60144-0011 Phone: 1-630-557-2742)

Carl Behrend, Singer/Songwriter, for use of lyrics from his song "The Christmas Ship" (Contact info: Carl Behrend, Old Country Records, HCRI, Box 123, E7099 Maple Grove Road, Munising, MI 49862 Phone: 1-906-387-2331)

Southport Video for use of quotations included in the video *Shipwrecks of Lake Michigan 1912–1958* (Contact info: Southport Video, 4609 74th Place, Kenosha, WI 53142 Phone: 1-262-552-5411 or 1-800-642-9860)

Deepest gratitude also to my mom and dad, and to all my brothers and sisters, for their steadfast encouragement!

And most importantly, I thank my children, Nicholas and Erica, and my husband, Leslie, for believing in my dreams and believing in me. Their love makes everything I do possible.

Cover Artwork

The Port City of Chicago image featuring the Christmas Tree Ship ROUSE SIMMONS is also available as a limited edition fine art. Each limited edition print is hand signed and hand numbered by Carol Dyer. A certificate of authenticity is provided with each print.

Boxed Christmas cards with this same image are also available. They come in a box of 20 cards with envelopes. The message inside reads: "May this Holiday Season and the New Year bring you Peace and Happiness."

If you would like to learn more about American Folk Artist Carol Dyer and see more of her wonderful artwork, you may order her book <u>Album of American Traditions</u>, published by Mystic Seaport (ISBN 0-939510-95-2).

To purchase any of these products, call the Mystic Seaport museum shop at 800-331-2665, send an email to wholesale@mysticseaport.org, or visit <u>www.mysticseaport.org</u>.

Your purchases directly support the education and preservation programs at Mystic Seaport – The Museum of America and the Sea.